SONGBIRD

ALSO BY SAMANTHA LEIGH

Valentine Bay Series
Ready For You
Meant For You
Perfect For You
Only For You

Aster Springs Series
Wallflower
Sunshine
Songbird

SONGBIRD

samantha leigh

Cover design by Echo Grayce at Wildheart Graphics
Editing by My Notes In The Margin
Proofreading by VB Edits

A catalogue record for this book is available from the National Library of Australia

ISBN: 978-0-6459988-9-4 (paperback)
ISBN: 978-0-6459988-8-7 (e-book)
ISBN: 978-1-7643089-0-8 (hardback)

For those who have ever felt lost in life or in love...
May you find your way, may you fulfill your dreams,
and may the journey be as beautiful as the destination.

AUTHOR'S NOTE

My books are low on angst and big on feel-good vibes, but they occasionally touch on topics that may be difficult for some readers. *Songbird* features minor suspense elements, including stalking and violence, and discussion of suicide (off-page and historical).

To see a complete list of content warnings for all my books, including *Songbird*, please visit my website at samanthaleighbooks.com or scan the QR code below.

And most importantly, take care of yourself.

xSam.

PROLOGUE

Finn

ONE YEAR EARLIER

I STALK DOWN THE VACANT hotel hallway toward the doors to the penthouse suite, parsing the commentary running through my earpiece and scanning an intersecting corridor for threats. America's reigning princess of pop, Rosalie Thorne, walks behind me while two other protection officers bring up the rear. Our goal? To deliver the global superstar to her home for the night.

After a sweep of her suite to make sure it's safe to enter, I return to the doors and let her slip inside. Her chin is dipped, her eyes on the carpeted floor, and her murmured *thank you* is barely audible under her breath.

"Stay alert," I warn the team before they take up stations in the hallway, one by the door and the other by the elevator. "Shift's not over for another six hours."

They nod without hesitation, used to taking my orders even though I've only been on the job for two months, but the looks they give me barely hide their thoughts. Linley is mildly curious, but as a skilled bodyguard with a long career behind her, she must have seen worse than a client favoring the new former SEAL over personnel with little personal protection experience. Brewer, on the other hand, is a dick. He smirks like he knows something he shouldn't, and if that *something* is the presumption that I'm doing more than guarding Rosalie's bed at night, he's smart enough to keep his mouth shut. Barely.

Whatever. I don't give a shit about his opinion, and I don't have the energy for workplace politics. Rosalie Thorne is my client, and if she prefers me to shadow her over anyone else, then so be it. I'm not here to launch a new career. I'm here as a favor to a friend and to keep a woman alive. That's it and that's all.

I double-check that the exit is secure and then take my place outside Rosalie's en suite bathroom. The door is ajar and steam billows out into the bedroom. I lean into the opening so she can hear my voice, carefully averting my eyes from the shape of her petite silhouette behind the foggy glass.

"Everything all right in there, Miss Thorne?" I call out.

"I'm fine," she responds in a dreamy tone that tells me she's enjoying the hot water.

Satisfied she's safe, I stand at ease and murmur into my earpiece. "Songbird has landed."

And then I wait.

When the water cuts off, I step outside the bedroom to give Rosalie her privacy. Ten minutes later, she reappears wrapped in one of those white terry-cloth robes she likes so much. Her damp blonde waves hang down her back, her cheeks are pink from the steam, and her mouth is stained with the remnants of her trademark coral-pink lipstick. I follow her to the kitchen, and when she orders room service—a pitcher of hot cocoa and two mugs, the same as always—I stand in the corner as she slides onto a high-backed chair at the oversized dining table. And just as she's done every night for the first eight weeks of her six-month world tour, Rosalie dips into the pocket of her robe and pulls out a ratty old deck of cards.

"Gin rummy?" she asks.

At the slight shake of my head, she drops hers to the side and pushes her lush lips into a pretty pout. "This will be the last time," she promises. "*If* you can beat me. Best out of five."

"Miss Thorne." I keep my voice flat and professional. "I'm on duty. It wouldn't be appropriate."

"That's not what you said last night." Her baby blues sparkle with mischief. Her laugh is musical and light as she shuffles the cards like my surrender is inevitable, even when I give her nothing in return.

"Oh, come on," she says with a sigh. "Just until I'm tired enough to sleep?" When I hesitate again, she rolls her eyes. "The suite is clear. Brewer and Linley are outside. I'm still coming down from the high of playing to a stadium with fifty thousand screaming fans. I need to unwind."

"With gin rummy?" I deadpan.

"Yes. And warm almond milk."

"Miss Thorne—"

"Don't make me get bossy. You know how I hate throwing my weight around." She smiles a little, like she's trying to make a joke, but then her throat bobs in a nervous swallow. "And you also know I can't sleep otherwise."

Yeah. I do know that.

I calculated the risks the first time I gave in, but I still reevaluate the variables again now. We're in the penthouse in the best hotel with the highest security standards in New Orleans. We've swept the floor as well as the suite, and any threat to Rosalie's safety needs to get through Linley and Brewer before it reaches her door. And in the unlikely event that happens, they're never getting through me.

Judging that the risk of danger is low enough to play a game of cards with the client at her request, I lower myself into the chair opposite Rosalie and wait as she deals. When I reach out to swipe up the hand that belongs to me, she stops me with a tentative brush of her fingers on mine. Her skin is unnaturally warm from her shower, and my heart rate kicks up a little.

It shouldn't matter that she's beautiful. Any other bodyguard probably wouldn't notice it. Another bodyguard wouldn't let her touch him like this either. Another bodyguard would remind himself that she has a boyfriend, and a public profile, and a life that's really fucking complicated. But I ignore all of that and keep my hand exactly where it is under hers.

"Thank you," she says, but something about the way she says it makes me wonder what she's thanking me for.

"You're welcome," I reply.

A knock sounds on the suite door, sharp and urgent, and I stand while speaking into my earpiece. "Is that room service?"

The lack of response from the team makes my hackles rise, and I drop into a mode of operation I've only ever used on duty. Focused. Lethal. "Brewer? Linley? What's the situation?"

The extended silence is louder than any kind of alarm bell.

"Go to the bedroom," I tell Rosalie. "Lock the door. Then go into the en suite bathroom and lock that door too. Don't come out until I come back for you or someone else from your security team tells you it's safe. Ask for the code word."

Rosalie gets to her feet woodenly and pins me with terrified eyes. If adrenaline wasn't flooding my veins, and if my head hadn't already dipped to that place it goes to block out distractions and emotions, her fear might have broken me.

"Miss Thorne," I say firmly. "What is the code word? Do you remember?"

She nods, too scared to speak, staring at my chest. And I'm an idiot, because of all the ways I might snap her out of her stupor, I lift a hand with the intention of cupping her cheek and tilting her face up to mine. I remember my place at the last moment and instead wave it slowly in front of her blank gaze.

"I need to hear you say it," I tell her.

The motion of my hand brings her around, and her eyes seek mine. Whatever she finds there puts a little steel into her back. "Songbird," she whispers.

"Good." The impatient rap of knuckles on the door sounds again, and I reluctantly remove my hand to point at Rosalie's bedroom. "Go. *Now.*"

I follow her, wait for the click of the turning lock, then race to the front door. More thumping greets me, and I check the peephole to see who's there, but it's covered by a hand on the outside.

Fuck.

I pull my gun from its holster, holding it low as I call out, "Who is it?"

"Room service!" calls an unfamiliar voice.

It's male and edgy and wrong. Room service shouldn't have made it past Brewer at the elevator, let alone Linley at the suite door.

"Leave it outside," I shout. "And back away."

Silence, and then...

The light on the electronic lock beeps and flashes green, the door swings open, and a wiry man barely more than half my size throws himself through it, screaming and slashing at the air with a bloodied kitchen knife.

He doesn't get any farther.

It takes me a split second to note he's wearing a hotel staff uniform, and I take a shallow slice to the forearm at the same time I spot Linley collapsed on the carpet outside and the hallway otherwise empty. Thank Christ this guy is alone—but where the fuck is Brewer?

Head clear and heart pounding, I use the butt of my gun to stun the intruder, grunting as I twist him into a fucking pretzel and disarming him before slamming him to the ground and planting a violent knee between his shoulder blades.

"You psychotic motherfucker," I growl as he fights the way I twist his arm almost out of its socket. His hair is lank and dull, and he stinks like stale sweat and bourbon. I hold my breath as I press my body weight into him.

I lean in close enough to whisper beside his ear. "Keep fighting and I'll end you now. You won't be the first man I've killed."

He sinks into stillness for a minute, then jerks into life when a gentle gasp alerts us to the fact that we're not alone.

I look up to see Rosalie hovering barely twenty paces away, one hand over her mouth and the color draining from her too-pale cheeks. In her other hand, she grips a brass candelabra tight enough that her knuckles are white. The candelabra is shaking. She's shaking.

"I was scared," Rosalie whispers. "I heard shouting. What if he hurt you? What if..."

She trails off as the guy beneath me snarls, spittle flying, and writhes to get free.

"I'm okay," I reassure her. "You're okay," I add to reassure myself. "We're both going to be okay."

Shared fear and relief pass between us before Brewer bursts down the hotel corridor, gun held low as he registers the situation with one sweeping glance.

"Was he alone?" my partner demands.

Rosalie's attacker giggles, a chilling sound that makes my stomach turn. "Yes, I'm alone," he says. "I'm not sharing my beautiful angel with anyone. Those pretty lips belong to me."

Rosalie wretches, and I throw my knee into the guy's back. "Shut—the fuck—*up*," I bark before turning to Brewer. "It looks that way," I say between clenched teeth, "but I haven't had a chance to search the floor outside the suite. Where the hell were you?"

"Taking a fucking leak—"

He glances at Rosalie and then cuts off without finishing his sentence. Instead, he kneels just outside the open doorway, presses his fingers to Linley's throat, and then runs a qualified hand over her still form.

"She's breathing," he reports before speaking into his earpiece. "Linley's down. Wound to the lower left flank. Head contusion. Blood loss. Suspect apprehended. We need backup and paramedics."

Rosalie's attacker lurches again, throwing himself against me and smashing his head into the floor hard enough to break a fucking tooth. Brewer produces a set of handcuffs, and I shift my position to give him room to snap them around the guy's wrists.

The knife lies discarded on the white carpet, staining the pristine wool with bright red blood.

I glance at Rosalie. Her breathing is shallow and her gaze is glassy. She opens and closes her free hand like she's trying to work feeling back into her fingers.

When I'm confident that Brewer has the guy in hand, I let my teammate drag him into the hall and cross the room to Rosalie. The candelabra falls from her hand as I reach her, and though my heart is racing, it manages to speed up again with worry at how hard she's trembling. I pick up her hands, knowing and not caring that I'm not supposed to touch her unless it's to protect her, but at the clammy chill of her skin, I decide touch is a kind of protection, and one I'm only too happy to provide.

She grips me like she's afraid to let go.

"I can't feel my lips," she tells me as her attention drifts toward the open doorway, then the bloody weapon, and back to her hands engulfed between mine. "They're... cold? I can't feel them. I can't feel my lips."

My gaze drops to her mouth, pale and almost purple at the tips of her plump cupid's bow, and Rosalie's lashes flutter as her tongue sweeps out a little. I lean into her, wishing I could hold her and warm her with my body, but I can't. I'm her bodyguard. She has a boyfriend. There are a hundred reasons this is wrong, including the way Rosalie leans into me too.

In the end, it doesn't matter that I do the right thing. That I put duty and honor before temptation and resist the way Rosalie's very *being* dismantles all my carefully constructed defenses. It doesn't matter that I'm always the good guy, because the next day, I get fired.

ONE

Rosalie

THE DRESS IS NICE. THE dress is fine. The dress is... Well, it's... it's kind of...

Oh, who am I kidding? This dress is *beautiful*. It's breathtaking and romantic and fits me like a song. The way I love it makes my throat close—but not in a good way.

I lay my palms flat against my middle. Tiny beads and threaded sequins stab my skin and make me press a little harder. A hundred tiny pinpricks feel a thousand times better than being strangled by this existential dread.

My personal assistant Lauren hovers at my shoulder. "*Wow*. You look gorgeous, Rosalie. And I'm not saying that because you pay me to. I say it with my whole chest and an obsession with bridal couture to back me up. This dress is going to break the Internet."

I manage a smile despite the queasy roll of my empty stomach. She's such a liar. Maybe not about the dress but about everything else.

Violet James, the designer responsible for my dream dress, drops her eyes and fusses with the lace falling off my shoulders to hide the self-conscious rise of color in her cheeks.

"It really is stunning," I tell her, because it's true, and it's not Violet's fault I'm in this mess. "Stunning and... perfect."

She replies with a shy smile before stepping back and regarding my reflection in the enormous three-way mirror. "When I saw this lace in Paris, with all the roses and the birds hidden in the detail, I had to have it, even though I had no clue how I might use it. Now I can't imagine it on anyone but you."

I force down a swallow, square my shoulders, and face the picture in the mirror. Blonde curls. Blue eyes. Small stature. It's me... and it's not me. I'm having an out-of-body experience. I pinch some of the softer fabric between my fingers, exploring the texture until it brings me back to earth.

Oh, God. I can't do this. I can't get married. Not wearing the most incredible dress I've seen in my life... to a man with the ugliest heart I've ever known.

Breathe, I remind myself. *Just breathe.*

I lift my chin and then my skirt, step off the carpeted dais onto the hardwood floor of Violet's San Francisco design studio, and instantly lose three inches. In bare feet I'm barely five foot tall. I cross to the wall covered with sketches and photographs and fabric swatches and point to a glossy page torn from a magazine. Although I've been here a dozen times, I discover something new at every fitting, and in this picture, a curvy model stares down the lens wearing a fuchsia-toned bra-and-panties set underneath a matching lace-trimmed robe.

"Is this your new lingerie line?" I ask.

Violet materializes at my side and runs her fingertips across the paper. "Yes. It's mostly mulberry silk in vibrant colorways as well as classic neutrals. Every piece is simple but sensual. Designed to make the person wearing it feel confident and comfortable in their own skin. Beautiful. Sexy."

What I wouldn't do to feel confident again. At home in my own skin. Beautiful. Sexy. Like a person and not a product. Desired for the right reasons. Someone a man wants to earn instead of just another investment he owns.

"I'll take one of everything," I say. "In white, black, and coral pink."

Violet's brows shoot up. "One of *everything*?"

I hesitate, thinking of the spending limit on my credit card. I've got more than enough funds to cover it, but Chip will see the purchase on the statement and want to know why I spent thousands of dollars on lingerie. Out of habit, I prepare my excuses.

I was thinking of him and how much he'd like to see me wearing it. I promise I won't buy anything else for another six months. It's all returnable, so no harm done, right?

I *feel* a hush come over Lauren, a gleeful silence that rolls off her in waves, and I grit my teeth. Chip will know what I did today long before he receives the credit card statement because Lauren will tell him the first chance she gets.

My muscles tense at the thought of it, and I wonder what glitch in the universe put me outside my bedroom door at the exact moment they thought they were alone and decided to screw in my bed. And what's wrong with me that it's been six weeks and I've been too afraid to confront either one of them?

It's the dress, I decide. This magnificent dress that will go to waste. It's the wedding invitations and the thousands upon thousands of flowers. It's the press releases and the contract for exclusive pictures with *Celebrity* magazine. It's the social media scrutiny and the pain that'll come with having my humiliation splashed all over the people's screens.

It's my fear of being alone.

But then Lauren makes a noise. A deep kind of hum in the back of her throat that sounds a lot like satisfaction, and I see it again. A flashback of betrayal tangled up in my two-thousand-dollar ivory silk sheets. My personal assistant naked and moaning and wearing *my* shoes.

Lauren and Chip. Chip and Lauren. *Chip. Chip. Chip.*

Better late than never, something snaps, and I'm suddenly *mad*.

Screw her. And screw *him*. Buying new underwear is a small thing, but it feels so big.

"One of everything," I confirm. "And add a few more pieces in powder blue and cherry red."

"Absolutely, Miss Thorne." Violet's brown eyes are wide and there's a breathlessness to her voice. "Thank you."

I give Violet a small smile, but at least this time it feels genuine. "You're welcome."

Wondering if my racing heart is a result of anger or anxiety, and then deciding it's probably a mix of both, I move down the wall a pace or two at a time, stopping when something catches my eye and letting myself be distracted by the diary of Violet's career. It's fascinating, and I forget myself long enough that I'm taken off guard by a trio of candid Polaroids. Each one is a picture of Violet James and Chord Davenport, her famous hockey player boyfriend, wrapped up in each other's arms. Their happiness is a stark reminder of how hopeless my own situation is in comparison, and panic hits me hard and fast enough that my head spins.

How did I get here? How could I be so weak? So dependent? So *stupid*?

"The driver will be here in twenty minutes," Lauren announces, and I glance at her as she raises an eyebrow in Violet's direction. "Unless you need more time?"

"No," she replies. "I think we're done."

Violet turns to me, beaming over hands clasped underneath her chin. I bet that's the face she gives to all her clients, but I wish she wouldn't look that way at me. I'm about six seconds from a full-blown anxiety attack but, apparently, I hide it well.

"We're finally finished, Miss Thorne," Violet says. "Your dress is ready for Saturday. I'll have it pressed and boxed and delivered to your Los Angeles address by end of day tomorrow. Is that all right?"

Is that all right? *Is that all right?* No, it's not all right. But how do I say that? How do I tell her this dress and this wedding and *my whole entire life* are all huge mistakes?

As I concentrate on breathing at a steady pace, my gaze slides to a framed photo on the wall. It's new, or at least, I haven't noticed it before, and the joy it captures practically hurls itself at me. The picture was clearly taken on a farm or a ranch somewhere. A pretty redheaded bride and her good-looking groom clasp each other mid-laugh in the foreground. Violet and her boyfriend are mid-kiss to one side. A young blonde woman grins, a bouquet of flowers in one hand and the grasp of a happy little girl in the other. A pretty brunette is on the far side, smiling down the barrel of the camera, next to a man so broad and so tall his tux can't hide his size. Neat blond hair, warm eyes the color of cognac...

I gasp, then belatedly raise a hand to cover the sound. Lauren's head whips up from her mirrored compact, an opened stick of bright coral lipstick halfway to her mouth.

"Lauren," I say, struggling to keep my voice smooth. "Run out and find me a salad. And a filtered iced water with lemon."

"*Now?* The car will be here soon. We can pick something up on the way to the airport."

It's hard to stay calm, but I need her to go before I lose it. "My blood sugar feels low," I lie. "I'll be lightheaded in half an hour."

"There's an organic delicatessen just down the street," Violet suggests. "They make great salads. Gluten-free muffins too."

"That's perfect." I shoot Lauren an exasperated look. "You should hurry."

I can tell she wants to argue, brow furrowed and mouth unhinged, but she gives in with an exasperated glance at her smartwatch. "Fine. I'll be back as soon as I can."

Violet walks Lauren out of the private studio and through the display room of her flagship store, releasing her into a throng of people shouting and holding up cameras, and at the click of the door closing behind her, a little of my anxiety disappears. One less problem to worry about.

Now for the bigger, and more stubborn, obstacle. The six-foot-five slab of animated marble standing just inside the studio door.

"Daryl?" I say. "Please step outside. I'll undress and then we'll leave."

A small crease pops up between his thick dark brows. "You want me to leave you alone in the studio? Chip won't—"

"Just while I change," I tell him, thinking on my feet. "And I need to talk to Violet about, uh... women's things... to do with fabric and my, um... bridal underwear."

At his flicker of discomfort at the mention of *women's things* and *underwear*, I press my advantage. "Ten minutes," I beg. "This is a big day for me. I need ten minutes with Violet to talk in private."

Violet gives me a curious look when she returns to find Daryl on the wrong side of the doorway and another when I indicate she should shut him out of the room, but she doesn't say anything when she joins me in front of the photograph that makes my heart skip every other beat.

I gesture at the picture. "Is that—" I stop myself just in time and rephrase the question. "Who—I mean, where— What was the occasion?"

If Violet notices my agitation, she's too polite to point it out. "Chord's brother was married last week at his ranch in Sonoma Valley." She points to the faces behind the plate glass. "That's Dylan—the groom. And that's Poppy—his wife. The little girl is Dylan's daughter, Isobel, and the woman holding her hand is Daisy. She's Dylan's younger sister and Poppy's best friend."

I point at the picture again. "And that's you?"

Violet flushes prettily. "Yes. That's me. And Chord, of course. That woman over there with dark hair is Chord's other sister, Charlie, and the man next to her is the middle Davenport brother. Finn."

Finn. Finn Davenport. It *is* him.

"And Finn," I say a little breathlessly. "He lives on this ranch?"

"Silver Leaf Ranch & Vineyard in Aster Springs," Violet clarifies. "And yes. Sort of. Finn has a bungalow. It's a cabin, really. Small, a little rundown, and nestled up against the river. It suits him. He likes to keep to himself."

I study the picture, running my eyes over the hard edges of Finn's shoulders and the square set of his smooth jaw. The barely there smile on his full mouth and the restrained twinkle in his steady gaze, like he's amused by something nobody else sees.

Finn Davenport. The last decision I made by myself, for myself.

"Do you have a car?" I ask.

"Me?" Violet looks over her shoulder like I might be talking to someone else in the otherwise empty room. "Yes. It's parked in the private lot out back."

Adrenaline makes my pulse skitter. Is it hope? Fear? Insanity? I can't tell and I don't care. "Can I borrow it?"

"Borrow it?"

"Yes. Borrow it."

"Now?"

"Immediately. I need to get out of here before Lauren comes back."

"But..." Violet's gaze sweeps down my body. "Your dress?"

I snatch up my purse from where I tossed it on a blush-colored cushioned sofa, then look down at my gown. It took ten minutes to fit and button me into it and will take as many to get me out. I can't risk changing and missing my chance to run.

"No time." I hike the skirt up at my hips to let her know I mean business. "I'll take it now."

To her credit, Violet asks no more questions before she crosses the room to collect her car key. She's clearly not sure she should hand it over. *I'm* not sure she should hand it over, but there must be a reason I stumbled across that photo today. A sign or fate or a cosmic nudge to go in another direction, and I haven't felt this sure about anything in a very long time.

This is my shot. Finn is my shot. He's how I'm going to reclaim control of my life and my career and find my way back to the woman I used to be. Before Chip Daniels set his eyes on an easy prize, sank his teeth into my soul, and sucked my spirit right out of me.

At the last minute, I remember to remove my engagement ring, dragging the six-carat oval-cut diamond off my finger and handing it to a surprised Violet.

"Can you give this to Lauren when she gets back?" I ask. "Tell her she can have it. I think she'll get the message."

Violet gapes at the giant diamond sparkling on her palm. "Are you sure that's what you want?"

"It is," I confirm. "It really, *really* is."

So, with Violet's car key in one hand, my purse in the other, wearing a fifty-thousand-dollar wedding dress, and with my hopes pinned on a man I barely know, I run.

TWO

Finn

APRIL IN SONOMA VALLEY THIS year has been wet, which means the ground in front of Mom and Dad's old place is soft and muddy, and I'm taking advantage of it by digging up the old stone path. It's got to be at least thirty years old, chipped and discolored, but it leads from the porch to the dock at the river, so it couldn't come out until I had time to replace it with a new one.

And that's all I've got these days. Time.

It's hard work, the monotonous kind that empties my mind, and it takes hours. By the time I've dug up a couple hundred chunks of flagstone, I'm covered in sweat, my boots and T-shirt are caked with mud, and every muscle in my body burns like hell.

It feels good.

When I've tossed the last piece of stone into the back of my truck, I climb the porch steps and swipe up my bottle. I pour water down my throat, then tip back my head to splash the final drops over my face and hair. I shake away the moisture, and as the droplets fly, my old Lab lifts her head to watch with unimpressed eyes.

"Sorry, girl." I give her head a rough pat, and a contented rumble sounds deep in her chest. "Didn't mean to wake you."

She yawns and resettles herself on the porch swing, blocky head resting on her paws as she looks out lazily over the yard. After a moment, she snorts and looks up with those deep brown eyes, her brow wrinkled in accusation.

"I know it doesn't look like much now, but it'll come together." I frown at the wide stretch of grass and churned-up muck as I lower myself onto the other end of the swing. "Eventually."

Positioned toward the rear of my family's hundred-acre ranch and vineyard, in the center of a clearing and surrounded by redwoods, the bungalow I call home is what renovation shows call a fixer-upper. I've been trying to fix it up for the better part of a year, but it'll never be what it used to be. The way it was when I was a kid and my parents were still alive. But that's okay. As soon as I realized I couldn't turn back time, I decided to make the place better.

Making it better gives me purpose. And I'm the kind of man who needs a purpose.

I lay a hand on Dakota's back and ruffle her coat before I stand. "Break's over," I announce just as the gentle hum of an expensive engine reaches my ears. Dakota raises her head, ears pricked and nose twitching, and when the gleam of a silver sedan comes into view, she launches from the swing with the grace of an overfed eight-year-old Labrador and parks herself at the top of the porch stairs.

I lean my elbows on the balustrade and watch the brand-new hundred-thousand-dollar Mercedes roll up my gravel drive. I've got no idea who's behind the wheel or what they want, but they're obviously lost, so I settle in to catch the moment they figure that out and try to turn their shiny little car around.

I'm not an asshole. I just have a low threshold for bullshit and stupidity, and I've got a feeling that a rich city-slicker getting stuck in the mud is going to serve up plenty of both.

It doesn't take long.

The driver doesn't even pause when the tires move off the loose gravel and onto slick ground, and everything's fine until the rear wheels hit the mud. The car instantly loses traction, but instead of stopping and trying to reverse onto solid footing, the driver floors it. The car lurches forward before it stops again, and a chuckle catches in the back of my throat as the engine roars, the wheels spin faster, and mud flies in all directions.

When the engine settles and the tires come to a stop in twin trenches of soggy dirt, I push myself off the banister with a sigh.

"Guess I should help, right?" I mutter as I step around Dakota. She whines a little in reply.

I jog in the direction of the car, but I'm less than halfway there when the engine revs again and the tires start to spin. I cringe as mud explodes in the air, shooting far enough to pelt me in the chest and head.

"Jesus Christ," I grumble, turning my head as I wait for the hits to stop.

When they do, I squint at the dark car windows to get a look at the clown responsible. I can't make out more than a shadow, so when the wheels stop spinning, I duck my head and move a little faster, hoping to get to the car before the driver steps on the gas again. I make it without taking another mud shower, but before I can rap my knuckles against the tinted glass, a woman pops up out of the open panoramic sunroof.

My heart hits my throat. Holy fuck. Rosalie Thorne.

I'm silent as she stares down at me, her soft blonde hair falling in perfect waves around her shoulders and the shade of her baby blue eyes as startling now as it ever was. I absently register tiny signals that she's nervous—the twitch of a dark-lashed eyelid and the quick pass of her tongue over coral-painted rosebud lips—before her brows pull together and she crosses her arms underneath her breasts.

"Well?" she demands. "Are you going to help me out of here or not?"

"Are you—" I push my fingers into my hair, and when they catch on a clod of dirt, I shake it off. "Are you serious? What are you doing here?"

"Can we talk about it inside?"

"Inside my *house*?"

"Yes."

"But..."

I'm annoyed by how long it takes me to recover from the shock, but when I do, my default settings switch into gear and I lean into them to recenter. I scan the car and decide it's probably not hers—Rosalie Thorne uses a driver and a town car. It's also empty, which means she's alone. And she's never supposed to be alone.

"Where's your security?"

Her jaw tenses and her elfin chin lifts a little. "I gave them the slip."

I exhale through my nose and reply through gritted teeth. "Why?"

"Because I've left Chip."

"You—"

"And he doesn't know it yet."

"He doesn't—"

I cut myself off with a quiet grunt, widen my stance, and cross my arms over my chest, reflexively assuming the posture that makes me feel most in control. I'm glad she left that jerk—he made my skin crawl—but I can read between the lines. She's here because if she hasn't already set her life on fire, it's about to go up in a white-hot blaze of fucking drama. And I'm not available for drama.

"Actually, that might be a lie," she continues. "It took me hours to find this place. He must know I'm gone by now."

"Which again raises the question: why are you here?"

"Because I need your help."

"You need *my* help?"

Rosalie sighs and raises a hand to her forehead to block the glare from the afternoon sun. "Yes, so can I please come in?"

"You fired me, Rosalie."

Using her first name feels almost illicit—as her bodyguard, I only ever referred to her as Miss Thorne—but I'm not her bodyguard anymore, and I want to be sure she knows it.

Maybe I also want her to remember why.

"I didn't fire you," she says. "Chip did."

The sound of that asshole's name on her lips again sets off a spasm in my neck. "Same difference."

She blinks like she doesn't know how to answer that, then says, "Well, now I'm rehiring you."

"I don't want the job."

"I'll pay you double what you made last year. Triple."

"I'm not for sale."

I meet her glare for glare until her shoulders drop and she releases a sad breath. She looks around like she's only now realizing she's on her own in the middle of nowhere.

"Can I use your bathroom?" she asks as the stubbornness melts from her spine. "Grab a glass of water before I drive back?"

Fuck. I *am* an asshole.

"Yeah. Of course." I open her car door, as if that one little gesture will make up for forgetting my manners, and groan.

This is the problem with money and fame and celebrities. Everything's a freaking circus.

"What are you wearing?"

Standing on the driver's seat with her head sticking out the roof of the car, Rosalie looks down at her dress. It's a strapless style, leaving the fine bones at the base of her neck bare. Folds of lace fall from the bodice around her upper arms and encase her to the wrists, and the skirt is so billowy I have to stop myself from asking how she could be irresponsible enough to drive in it. The whole thing is layered with delicate embroidery and intricate bead work, and even though I know nothing about fashion or bridal couture, I do know my brother's girlfriend designed this dress, and Violet is the best there is.

I also know that Rosalie looks beautiful. But that's beside the point.

"It's my wedding gown," Rosalie explains. "I was at my final fitting when I saw a picture of you on Violet's studio wall and I thought... It doesn't matter what I thought." She drops down into the seat with a flatness to her expression that matches the weariness in her voice. "Let's just get this over with."

She saw a photo of me and drove straight here without stopping to change out of her dress? That gives me a moment of hesitation. A flash of guilt. Or maybe obligation. But I refuse to be drawn into her world. I'll be polite. I'll pull her car out of the mud. Then I'll wish her well and get on with my life.

Maybe this time, if we say goodbye, I'll never have to think about her again. That'd be a nice change.

I stand beside the open car door and wait for Rosalie to step out, but she sits there with reams of fabric gathered in her arms, looking at me like I'm missing something. I glance over at the porch where Dakota watches us with a wagging tail. Weirdest dog ever. Doesn't like stairs.

"She won't bite," I say to Rosalie, "if that's what you're worried about."

"Ah, no." She points to the mud. "That's what I'm worried about."

I glance at the ground, then up again with a single raised eyebrow. "You're kidding."

"Absolutely not. This is a fifty-thousand-dollar dress."

"That you'll never wear again because you're no longer getting married."

"But... But..." She looks down at the fabric like it's a vortex for common sense. "It's so beautiful."

"So... what do you expect me to do?"

"You'll have to carry me."

My laugh comes out as a snort. "*Carry* you?"

"Yes. But you need to change first." She takes me in from head to toe with a fast, sweeping look. "There's no point being carried over the mud on the ground only to be covered by the filth in your hair and on your clothes."

"*Filth?*"

"You heard me." She wrinkles her nose. "And you smell."

Maybe the correct response is to be offended. Maybe the gentlemanly thing to do is to go inside, put on a clean shirt, then do as she asks and carry her into the cabin. And maybe I shouldn't be surprised at how comfortable she is with giving me orders. But I'm not offended. I'm not feeling gentlemanly. And she can be as bossy as she likes—as long as it's not in my front yard after she tore up the ground with her driving and then had the audacity to ask me for help.

Does she not realize I've been gone from her life for a year? Because I'm all too aware of that fact.

I reach around to the back of my neck and drag my dirty T-shirt up over my head. Rosalie gasps and I give her a shit-eating grin.

"What are you doing?" she demands.

I turn the shirt inside out and use it to rub the dirt and sweat from my hair and face, then wipe my hands before I throw it to the side. "Getting cleaned up for you."

I unbutton my jeans and unzip my fly, then push them down my legs. It's a tricky maneuver to get out of and back into one boot at a time as I drag my jeans past my ankles, but I manage it just fine, then toss my jeans away too. When I'm in nothing but my boxer briefs and muddy shoes, I hold out my arms.

"Are you ready?" I ask, then give her no time to answer before I scoop her up and out of the car. "Good. Let's go."

She squeaks her displeasure, but that's about all she can do. She's tiny—five foot nothing and a hundred and ten pounds soaking wet—yet the dress is enormous, which makes walking awkward. Plus she smells so damn good, which makes it hard to concentrate.

She's stiff with disapproval, her arms crossed, eyes staring off into the distance, and there's a rosiness to her cheeks, like being carried over wet ground is a hardship for *her*. All I want to do is laugh. Not because any of this is funny but because it feels so good to finally hold her. Better than all the nights I've stared into the darkness and wondered what she was doing, who she was with, whether she was safe. Worse than the two months I worked for her and spent every minute resisting the impulse to cross the line between right and wrong. Because after today, I'll always know what it feels like to have her body pressed against mine, and what am I supposed to do with that information after she's gone?

It takes less time than I might have liked to cross the yard, climb the porch stairs, and swing open the front door to the bungalow. Dakota follows with a playful bark as I carry Rosalie over the threshold.

"There." I set her carefully on her feet—bare, I notice, though now doesn't seem like a smart time to ask why—and Rosalie manages to look anywhere but directly at me as she straightens her skirt and tugs at her lace sleeves. I point to the rear of the bungalow, past the kitchen and living area, like she's actually paying attention. "The bathroom is at the back. It's small, but your dress should fit. There are bottles of water in the fridge. If you need me, I'll be outside hauling your car out of the mud."

I don't expect a response, so I head outside. Ignoring my shirt, which is basically a rag balled up in the muck, I scoop up my jeans and tug them on before I go around to my truck and pull out the largest, flattest stones I can find. I wedge them beneath the rear wheels of the Mercedes, then straighten as I clock the dirty license plate personalized with a name I recognize.

Huh. It's just like my rich hockey player brother to buy his girl a new car every other month. I wonder if Violet knows her runaway bride was headed here when Rosalie took her keys, slipped past her security, and bolted out of the city.

Scowling, I squeeze myself behind the steering wheel. Then I wait with impatience as the automatic settings whir and the chair eases back. I'm still scowling as I shift into reverse and ease the car backward, gaining traction on the stone and only stopping once all four tires are parked on gravel. And I continue scowling as I go around the side of the cabin to retrieve the garden hose, turn it on, and aim the spray at the dirty vehicle.

No security. No fucking security! What the hell is Rosalie thinking? Why is she here asking for my help? And why, after she let her asshole fiancé fire me, should I still care?

I watch the water hit the hood and the mud slide off the silver paint in satisfying rivulets, take a deep breath, and pull myself together. Rosalie's life isn't my problem. Not anymore. What happens in her relationship with Chip World's-Biggest-Douche Daniels is none of my business. How she handles her safety is a conversation she needs to have with her *actual* security team—and good luck to them. They're going to need it.

When the Mercedes no longer resembles a rally car, I pack up the hose, grab my dirty T-shirt, and head back inside to put on a new one. It's the least I can do before I carry Rosalie back to the car and send her on her way. But when I step through the front door, I find her kneeling on the kitchen floor, her arms around Dakota's neck, her face buried in golden fur, and her shoulders shaking with unmistakable sobs.

Dakota glances up at me with reproachful eyes and I can almost hear her telling me off. *Are you happy now?*

Ah, Christ.

Taking care to move the expensive dress out of my way, I drop to my knees on the hardwood beside Rosalie. When she doesn't let go of Dakota or lift her head to acknowledge me, I set a tentative hand on her back.

"Rosalie? Are you okay?"

Of course she's not okay, you dumbass.

Rosalie's cries get a little louder, her shudders a little more violent, and Dakota whines uneasily in response. Slowly, and with as much care as I'd take to disarm an explosive, I pull Rosalie's arms from Dakota's body and wrap them around my neck. I take it as a good sign that she allows it, so I pick her up, carry her to the sofa, and sit with her in my lap.

And then I let her cry.

She weeps on my bare shoulder, tears dropping from her cheeks to my chest, while I make soothing noises and stroke her hair. The tenor of her cries gives me the impression she's been waiting a long time to let them out, and it takes fifteen minutes for her to grow calm. The whole time I sit quiet as stone, giving her a safe space to release whatever pressure has been building inside her.

When she raises her head with red-rimmed eyes that aren't quite sure where we stand, I sigh and drop my head back. I'm going to regret this. I know it. The longer she's here, the harder it'll be to let her go. Again.

"Okay," I say. "Let's talk. What the hell is going on?"

THREE

Finn

I SLIDE ROSALIE OFF MY lap to fetch her the water she still doesn't have and a box of tissues she didn't ask for, then scale the ladder to the loft that is my bedroom. I'm dragging a clean T-shirt over my head when I return to the living area, but this time I seat myself at a professional distance on the smaller sofa opposite Rosalie and Dakota, who's curled up next to her leg and watching me with wary brown eyes.

So much for man's best friend. My pup has clearly shifted her loyalties, and I don't blame her. If it's a toss-up between the pretty woman with tearstained cheeks and the asshole who made her cry, I know who I'd want to sit beside.

"I never realized you had so much ink," she comments.

I glance down at the khaki-colored cotton covering the pictures on my chest, abdomen, shoulders, and upper arms.

"Nothing above the collarbones. Nothing below the elbows. Makes it easy to hide them when I need to."

"Smart," she murmurs.

"Thanks."

Rosalie's shoulders rise in a deep breath as she runs her gaze around the place. An open-concept kitchen, dining, and living space that at best could be called cozy. Mismatched rugs, both threadbare and new. A wide-screen television set on an old hand-carved entertainment unit and patched floral-print curtains at the casement windows. Vaulted ceilings with exposed timber beams and a nineties-era kitchen with a two-burner stove. The shadowy heights of the loft at the top of the rickety-looking ladder.

The kindest word to describe the place would be rustic. It's clean and tidy. It has electricity and hot water. It's private and it was built out of love, and that makes it worth more than any designer Los Angeles compound. I'm probably only one of half a dozen people who think so, but that doesn't make it less true.

"Your home is nice," Rosalie says as she toys with the screw cap on her water bottle. "Have you been here long?"

"Yes and no."

Her forehead creases with exasperation, and I shake my head.

"You talk. I listen. Let's start with why you drove all the way out here with no personal security in a car that doesn't belong to you, wearing a designer wedding dress you don't need—and no shoes."

Rosalie lifts her dress to expose her ankles and checks out her pink-polished toenails before she abruptly raises her head again. Hope shines in her eyes. "Does this mean you'll take the job?"

"No. It means I want to know why I found you crying on my kitchen floor."

She throws a troubled glance toward the spot, and her manicured hand strays to Dakota's coat.

"I don't know why it took me so long to admit that Chip is a bad guy. I mean, I've known for a while, but I couldn't find the courage to do something about it. But he is, you know? A bad guy."

She pauses for my response, and my jaw feathers. I'm not her bodyguard anymore, but it's still the dynamic that defines our relationship, and it's not a bodyguard's place to voice opinions on his client's personal life. It's definitely not his job to pass judgment on her choice in men. But Rosalie's fiancé is a world-class creep, and I could tell as much from the first and only time I met him. The day after *that* night.

Rosalie nods to herself with a contemplative tilt to her mouth. "You agree. No—don't try to deny it. I can tell. And as long as I'm not paying you to be diplomatic, you may as well say exactly what you think. It would be good to know there's at least one person in this world on my side. Someone to tell me I'm not paranoid or weak for running away."

Rosalie's lonely. She's *alone*. And it's his fault. Time to cut through the bullshit.

"The guy's a dick," I agree. "And you're better off without him."

Rosalie stares, blinking quickly, before she suddenly sits up straighter. "Exactly. And that's why I'm here. I need somewhere to hide while I figure out my next move."

"Hide? From *him*?"

What the fuck did that monster do to make Rosalie have to *hide*?

"From Chip," she agrees. "From Lauren, my personal assistant. From my security team. And from the press."

"Wait." I set my elbows on my knees and lean in as she raises red flag after red flag. "Why do you need to hide from your assistant? Or your personal security?"

Rosalie nibbles her bottom lip as her fingers tighten in Dakota's fur.

"You can trust me," I assure her, "with as much or as little as you feel comfortable sharing, but if you want my help, the more I know, the better."

"So... you'll take the job?"

I growl a little, a deep rolling protest that comes from my chest, and she bites back a tiny smile.

"Fine," she says. "But did you know that when you came on board last year, you were the only person on my entire protection team that I hired myself? The only person I'd hired for *any* team in the last three years?"

I didn't know that, but her question is rhetorical.

"I wasn't supposed to do it," she continues, "but... I

don't know. That moment is the first time I remember being aware that Chip's need for control was *out* of control. I waited until I was alone, then opened my laptop. I did an internet search, chose an executive security firm on a whim, and sent an inquiry. And they sent you."

That security firm belonged to a military buddy—someone I considered a best friend who built his own private protection business after he was medically discharged five years ago. I never had any intention of getting into the bodyguard game, but I also wasn't prepared for how lost I'd feel leaving the SEALs after ten years of service. How I'd miss having a reason to get out of bed every morning. My buddy Jack needed help and I needed focus, so stepping up when he asked was a no-brainer.

In hindsight, taking the job with Rosalie wasn't the kind of help Jack needed, but given everything that happened last spring, I don't know if I'd change anything. And that's a hard thing to admit even to myself.

"I didn't know Chip was going to fire you," Rosalie adds. Her expression is open and honest. "After what happened in New Orleans, I thought he'd want to promote you but..."

My fists curl as fear flickers in Rosalie's eyes. "We don't have to talk about it," I tell her, referring to both the attack and what happened afterward, and it occurs to me that maybe she doesn't want to talk about any of it. Certainly not a crazed man with a knife in her penthouse suite, but perhaps not even what happened afterward. That brief moment between us, if it happened at all. Being in her orbit again, I'm reminded of how exceptional she is, and it's laughable that she ever thought of me as more than just her bodyguard. It'll be easier to get through the next few hours if I believe that. So if she doesn't want to talk about that night, then neither do I.

Rosalie clasps her hands in her lap. "After New Orleans, Chip said the situation was too serious to risk inexperienced people on my team. He hand-picked everyone after that. Everyone. Everywhere."

I bristle at being labeled *inexperienced*. I wasn't the one who put Rosalie in danger, and who knows what would have happened if I hadn't been there to answer her door?

"What about Lauren?" I ask. "She was your assistant long before last year. That makes one person you can trust."

Rosalie's throaty chuckle sounds forced. "She's been sleeping with Chip for weeks, if not months. And she spies for him. Tells him where I am, what I eat, what I say, what I *don't* say. Not that he doesn't manage every facet of my life anyway, but there are some things women only share with other women, you know?"

Her hands fidget in her lap, and I wish I could reach out and settle them. Rage is rarely helpful in situations like this, but just because I know to ignore it doesn't mean my blood isn't boiling. Rosalie laughs again, a nervous sound that aims to trivialize her hurt, and I wonder if, despite the circumstances, she still loves Chip. I suppose, if I'm being charitable, I can understand why.

Chip Daniels is a music industry mogul—a record executive and producer responsible for some of the biggest acts in the business. Fifteen years Rosalie's senior, he's also her manager and has been since her first label dropped her at twenty-one. Chip and Rosalie went public with their relationship a year later and they've been together ever since.

This isn't the kind of information I usually know, but Rosalie's personal life was part of the background file I had to read when signing on as her bodyguard. I know more about her than she realizes.

"I'm sorry about Lauren," I say. "Sometimes people let you down."

Rosalie shrugs. "She was never my friend. Just another person on the payroll."

Money. Just one more thing wrong with the world. I've got no interest in it, and I'm not a man who exchanges his time for a dollar and never thinks about the cost. When Jack asked me to take the gig protecting Rosalie, I didn't say yes to collect the paycheck. I took the job as a favor to a friend, and I took it seriously because a woman's life was at stake.

And from what Rosalie is telling me now, maybe in some ways, it still is.

"So what do you need?" I ask.

Her face lights up, and beside her, Dakota lifts her head and blinks. "You'll take the job?" she asks again.

"Nope." I raise my hand when she starts to argue.

"I'm not just another person on your payroll, Rosalie, and if I take your money now, you'll never believe that."

"But—"

"What do you *need*?"

Rosalie is silent for a moment, the cast to her head speculative, but then her tight nod says she understands me.

"A couple of days to figure out my next steps?" Her request sounds like a question, her confidence still building, and I'm careful to not let any reluctance show on my face. "As soon as Chip realizes I'm not coming back, he'll want to control the narrative. Public perception is everything in this business, and he won't let it get out that I left him because he's an emotionally abusive cheater. I just can't deal with the media or the paparazzi or the rumor mill right now. I need quiet and space and a chance to think without all the noise. Maybe I'll find the strength to take back my life, because I can't give Chip more of me than I already have." Her voice drops low enough that I need to lean in to hear her. "I *can't*."

That fucker's not taking anything else from this woman. Ever.

"You won't," I tell her. "And it's a deal. A couple days on your own, which will give you time to figure out your next move. This place is yours. I'll—"

"You're not leaving, are you?"

Rosalie's eyes widen, her hand straying toward Dakota and her fingers tightening in her coat.

"This is a one-bedroom cabin," I explain. "A one-*bed* cabin. There isn't room enough for both of us."

"But..." She looks around the bungalow again, this time with a shortness to her breath. "We can make it work. I'll sleep on the sofa."

"Rosalie—"

"I don't want to be alone. Not here. Not like this."

I sigh and nod slowly. "Yeah. I know."

She sags and releases a relieved breath. "So you'll stay?"

"I'll stay—on the sofa."

"*This* sofa?"

Her snort is surprisingly indelicate and my lips twitch. "What's so funny?"

"Nothing," she says, but I like that she's trying not to smile. "Nothing at all."

"Okay. So if we're going to do this, let's do it. Where's your phone?"

It's in her purse, which is small enough to have gotten lost between the sofa cushions and the fabric of her dress. When she pulls it out to show me, I'm pleased to see her phone's switched off.

"I didn't want to deal with Chip," she explains. "If he'd called me on the way here, I might have turned around."

"You did the right thing. I assume he has some kind of tracking app on this thing?"

"Just the one installed with the phone."

I nod even though there's a good chance she's wrong.

"This cabin is a black spot for cellular networks. It's safe to turn on your phone again, but switch it to airplane mode to be safe, and then wait until I remove any tracking software before you connect to my Wi-Fi."

"Okay."

She tucks away her phone again as I get to my feet. "I'll get your luggage from the car and then make you something to eat while you change. I'll keep it simple. You might not feel hungry now, but you're running on adrenaline and your system needs fuel before you crash. No gluten. No dairy. No meat. No processed sugars. Did I get that right?"

No idea what'll be left in my kitchen after I subtract my favorite food groups, but I've been in tougher binds than this.

Rosalie hops up so fast I hesitate.

"What's wrong?" I ask.

"My luggage?"

"Yeah. What about it?"

She responds with a shamefaced wince. "I... don't have any."

"You don't *have* any?"

She throws up her hands like I'm the unreasonable one. "I didn't know I was running away when I left the house this morning! It was spur of the moment. I didn't even have my own car. All I have is my purse and this dress."

"Okay." I nod with equilibrium I don't feel. Nothing's ever simple. Not with Rosalie. "You can wear something from my closet tonight, and tomorrow... tomorrow, I'll find you some clothes."

She waits below while I climb the ladder to the loft and rummage around for something appropriate. The best I can find is an old button-up flannel.

"Here." I offer the shirt to Rosalie, then stand there like an idiot as she holds it up to get a better look. "I don't suppose you can make it up the ladder in that dress."

She glances at it and then shakes her head with a light laugh. "Ah, no."

"I'll wait outside while you change."

I'm halfway to the door before she stops me. "Um… Finn?"

"Yeah?"

"I need to ask another favor."

"All right. What is it?"

Her graceful throat works as she tosses her head, and wearing that dress while she does it, she's a princess commanding her subject. This ought to be good.

"I can't take this gown off by myself. It has too many buttons and they're all in the back."

She can't be serious. "So… what do you expect me to do?"

There's that chin lift she loves so much, followed by an order I can't possibly obey. "I need you to stay and undress me."

FOUR

Rosalie

IT'S FUNNY THE THINGS THAT make you afraid and the things that don't.

I was afraid the night my grandmother died. I was eighteen, so it's not as though I needed her to take care of me, but she was all the family I had.

I was scared the morning my label dropped me because they didn't approve of the tracks on my sophomore album. I thought if they didn't like my music, nobody would.

I've had stalkers and deranged fans and one close call that makes it harder to sleep than usual. Those things make me afraid.

And I've spent my relationship with Chip walking on glass, worried that too heavy or careless a step would shatter everything I built. I wasn't anxious and oversensitive, like Chip always said. I was afraid of him.

But I've never feared stepping out onto a stage. I've never been scared to put my truth into my music, because being vulnerable is the only way I know to connect with people. And I'm not afraid now.

Maybe I should be. Maybe I've ignored my instincts so long that they no longer work the way they're supposed to, but right or wrong, Finn makes me feel safe. It was like this last year when he was my bodyguard on tour. He walked into the room and my world shifted, and I never wanted him to walk out again. It's a relief to discover his energy is exactly as I remembered. I don't want to think about what I might have done if I'd driven all this way only to find out Finn isn't the man I needed him to be. Would I have returned to Chip? I don't have the strength to give that any thought.

"You want me to undress you?" he asks flatly, and I meet his cognac stare.

Don't get me wrong. Everything about Finn gives me butterflies. His size. His determination. His attitude. He's hard and immovable, but that also makes him steady and dependable. Being near him makes me feel warm and alive, like falling asleep in the sunshine or writing a song without having to stretch for the melody. He feels *right*.

I spin around and sweep my hair over one shoulder. "You need to undo the row of buttons down my back. They're small and delicate, so go slow."

Finn is still for so long that I wonder if he's going to refuse, but then a floorboard creaks. He gets close enough for me to feel the heat radiating from his body, and then his warm exhalation hits the exposed nape of my neck. I close my eyes and wish away the goose bumps.

He's surprisingly gentle and his movements are slow, but with the release of only the first few pearl buttons, the pressure around my ribs eases. I inhale deeply for the first time in hours and hold my hands to the front of the dress to keep the bodice in place as the fastenings pull free. The rise and fall of my chest are shallow and measured, patient and composed—until the first brush of Finn's fingertips against my back. After that, I barely breathe at all.

I close my eyes as his touch ghosts over me and my imagination runs wild. Is he *really* tracing the contours of my shoulder blades, the dip of my lower back, the curve of my hip, or do I only wish he would? The contact between us is there and gone so fast I can't be sure I feel it, so I keep my eyes closed and pay attention, anticipating the places he might explore next.

Minutes pass, and afternoon is edging into early evening by the time my dress is completely undone. I clutch the corset tighter against my chest, a warm flush creeping up my neck and a shiver cascading to my toes as the fabric parts and bares my back completely. Finn gently tugs on the corset to loosen it the last inch. When he's done, a single finger traces an unmistakable line along my spine, and my breath shakes.

He moves closer, enough that I feel his quiet rumble in my chest. "That's all of them."

His hand falls and he steps back, and although I'm disappointed at the distance he puts between us, I'm relieved to finally fill my lungs.

"Thank you," I say over my shoulder.

Finn clears his throat. "No problem. I'll be out on the porch—"

"Wait. We're not done." I turn to face him, bodice clutched to my front. "I need help with the sleeves."

The way he nods is too patient and too accommodating, like he's determined to suffer whatever torment I inflict, but at his side, his right hand opens and closes, fingers flexing once before he relaxes.

"All right," he says. "What do you need?"

I glance around for the shirt he offered me earlier, swipe it from the back of the sofa, and clumsily hang it from my shoulders so it covers my breasts. Then I extend one arm and awkwardly shift the hand still holding my dress to stop it from slipping.

"Take a firm but gentle hold of the lace at my wrists," I direct, "and kind of pull? Go slow or you might tear the fabric."

Finn does as I ask, peeling one sleeve and then the other from my arms and letting them fall at my sides. One deep, heaving inhale later, the dress slips from my body and pools in a cloud around my feet.

With my hands clasping Finn's shirt to my chest, and otherwise naked but for a simple cotton thong, I step out of the dress in one long stride. I almost lose my balance, but

Finn's hand shoots out to cup my elbow with a confident grip so unlike his uncertain touch.

"Oh my God," I sigh. "It feels so good to be free."

I'm talking about the dress, but as soon as the words are out of my mouth, I know they mean more than that. *I'm free.*

Finn clears his throat again, then drops his eyes as his hand comes up to rub the back of his neck. "You want to put that shirt on?"

Is that irritation edging his tone? I tilt my head with an insolent grin and twist a hip to give him a better look at my ass. "You don't think you deserve a little payback for taking off *your* clothes earlier?"

Finn is stoic, even when I pretend to fumble the shirt and nearly flash a boob.

"Oops." I readjust the fabric over my shoulders, casting him a sideways glance to see if *that* broke him. "Misjudged the juggle there."

He crosses his arms like he's about to tell me off, but then he just shakes his head and walks across the open-concept space to the small kitchen.

"Go ahead," he says mildly before he sticks his head in the refrigerator. "Get dressed. I promise not to look."

I believe him, but I still turn around as I shrug into his shirt. The hem brushes my knees, there's loads of room around the middle, and the sleeves flop over my hands, so I roll them up. Once I've carefully arranged my wedding dress over the back of an armchair, I join Finn in the kitchen, sliding onto one of the two dining chairs at the little round table. Dakota lurches from the sofa, pads over, and curls herself around my feet. I wiggle my toes in thanks for the warmth.

"I'm decent," I say. "It's safe to come out now."

Finn raises a thick eyebrow at me as he straightens from the refrigerator and swings the door closed. "Define *safe*."

I hold up my palms in surrender. "No more nakedness. I promise."

He grunts quietly. "About dinner. I don't have much that isn't gluten or dairy or meat, but I could whip up an acceptable omelet in less than ten minutes."

My stomach rumbles, and I remember I haven't eaten anything since breakfast. I also haven't eaten anything not pre-approved by a nutritionist in the last six years.

"You know what?" I reply. "I could really go for a cheeseburger."

His jaw actually drops. It's cute. "Are you serious?"

My stomach growls again and my mouth starts to water. "Oh yeah. A big one. And I don't suppose you've got the fixings for a strawberry shake?"

He gives me a curious half-smile as he retrieves a carton of milk from the fridge and a tub of strawberry ice cream from the freezer. "Thought I was the only person over the age of twelve who still liked these things."

There's nothing halved about the grin I give him in return. "Looks like there's at least two of us."

I offer to help him cook, but Finn insists on doing

everything himself, so while I sit there and sip on a frothy pink milkshake that may just be the best I've had in my entire life, I try to carry the conversation.

"Your place is nice," I say. "Comfortable. Kind of... small? I don't mean that as a judgment. More of an observation. Like it was only ever intended for one person."

"Two," Finn says as he flips the burgers, and then transfers two golden buns from the toaster to plates.

"Excuse me?"

"It's small because it was built for two people. It belonged to my mom and dad."

I wait for him to elaborate while he assembles the burgers and carries them to the table, but when he takes a seat and then a bite, and it's obvious he's not going to volunteer more, I risk a little nudge.

"So... your parents," I begin as I pick up my burger. Oh Lord. It smells so good. "What are they like?"

I almost abandon any care I ever had about Finn's personal life as the first mouthful of beef and cheese hits my tongue. And the bread. Oh my God. *Bread.* The second, third, and fourth bites follow in quick succession, and I think I might have actually moaned by the entertained look Finn's sending my way. He hands me a napkin, and I wipe the grease from my fingers.

"They were the best," he says, and I have to think back through my food-induced ecstasy to remember my question. "But they passed a long time ago. Mom eleven years. Dad nearly two years after that."

"Oh, Finn." I set what's left of my burger back on its plate. "I'm sorry."

"Thank you."

"And this place? It was theirs?"

"You're full of questions, aren't you?"

"Honestly?" I pick at the last mouthful of my dinner, first sneaking the remains of the burger to the drooling Labrador under the table, then popping the last scrap of bread into my mouth. "I'm tired of talking about myself. I'll have to do a lot of it over the next few weeks, if not for the rest of my life. I could do with a night off."

Finn watches me for a long moment, long enough that I lift my chin self-consciously, but then he drags a napkin over his mouth, leans back in his chair, and folds his large arms across his broad chest.

"Yeah. This place belonged to them," he says. "Silver Leaf Ranch & Vineyard, but also this bungalow. They ran the entire operation here while raising five kids, so Dad built the cabin as a hideaway for him and my mom. Somewhere to go where he could fish and she could read. It was supposed to be a guest rental, but they never actually rented it out." He scans the cabin with thoughtful lines around his eyes. "I think it was too special to them to share with anyone else."

"That's beautiful," I reply softly. It's sad Finn lost his parents, but he's so lucky to have had them at all, and I get the sense he knows it. And for as long as they were alive, Finn was surrounded by love. I can't count the nights I prayed for that as a little girl. "And five kids? That's a big family. Are you still close?"

Finn snorts quietly, but the tug of affection on his lips makes me want to smile too.

"Yeah, I suppose you could say that," he says. "My eldest brother is Chord Davenport—the pro-hockey player?" He waits for me to acknowledge the name, and I do because I've met him twice when he's stopped by Violet's studio. "He and Violet are based in San Francisco now, but he has a house on the property. My older sister, Charles, and younger siblings, Dylan and Daisy, all live up at the main house. Dylan's daughter is there, too, and his new wife, Poppy. It's a little crowded, but everyone's happy."

"So, you're the middle child," I tease. "That explains a lot."

Finn responds with mock offense, eyebrows high and amusement tugging at the side of his mouth. "And what does that mean?"

"The brooding, independent man of mystery living on his own in a bungalow in the woods?" Finn gives me that look of eternal forbearance, and I laugh lightly. "I have no idea if those are the hallmarks of a middle child, but you handed me that one on a platter."

Finn shakes his head and stands, a hand coasting through blond hair neatly trimmed on the side and long enough on top for a single lock to fall forward and catch on his lashes.

"You must be tired," he says as he clears the table. "Why don't you get ready for bed? There's soap and a spare toothbrush in the bathroom if you want to freshen up, and while you're in there, I'll change the sheets. Then tomorrow…"

I sigh as the temporary high of a cheeseburger and conversation is crushed under the weight of what lies ahead. "Tomorrow, I take back my life."

"Yep. Get some sleep and we'll start making plans in the morning."

"Okay. And Finn?" He turns away from the sink to look at me, a plate still in either hand. "Thank you."

His measured blinks could mean anything, but all he says is "You're welcome."

After I've brushed my teeth and washed my face with a bar of plain white soap that leaves my skin dry and makes me wonder how men as a species have made it this far, I find the cabin dark but for the light of Finn's phone. The man himself is stretched out on the sofa. His feet and ankles dangle off the end and he's going to wake up with a crick in his neck if he tries sleeping with his pillow wedged at that angle, but I'm too grateful to point it out.

I pause on my way to the loft ladder, eyeing Dakota, who's curled up in her bed at the foot. "Good night," I whisper.

Finn shifts his phone, but the glow from the screen still lights up his face. "Good night, Rosalie."

In Finn's bedroom, I slip between the sheets and take a moment to inhale the scent of soap and safety and something else that's all Finn. I'm tired, so I hope sleep comes quickly, but that's never been my luck. With the sound of the shower running downstairs, I stare up at the timber-beamed ceiling, exhausted but unable to rest. I still haven't turned on my phone, and I toy with it on the blanket beside me. As soon as I press that button, everything changes, and I want to stay in this ignorant bubble a while longer. It's nice here. I like it. I feel stronger than I usually do, like I really might be the kind of woman to do what she says she's going to do and create a life that doesn't include Chip.

The water downstairs cuts off with the thud of old pipes, and as I listen as Finn exits the bathroom and settles himself on that too-small couch, I burrow deeper into the blankets. Finn's willingness to let me stay might be the only thing keeping me on track right now, and here in the quiet and the dark, the fear I didn't let myself feel earlier creeps in. This isn't a childish adventure. This is my life and my livelihood, and I've never done anything so selfish or so rash as what I did today. The adrenaline is pumping. I'm nervous. I'm scared. Underneath all that, I'm also giddy with hope and possibility.

But if it wasn't for stumbling across that photo of Finn earlier today, I might not have ever been given the catalyst to run. And if he'd been harsh enough to send me away when I begged for help, I might have lost the courage to keep running. And those are truths I have to think about. Especially now. I can't rely on a man to help me rebuild what I've lost, even if that man is as decent as Finn. I need to do this by myself and be smarter and more focused than ever. My head is what's going to guide me to a confident and independent life, not my soft, unreliable heart.

FIVE

Finn

THE CREAK OF THE LOFT ladder would have woken me at one a.m. if I weren't already lying here with my eyes open.

Rosalie went to bed hours ago and I've been on my phone in the dark. I've sent an email to Jack's brother, Drew, and asked him for background checks on both Chip Daniels and Rosalie. A lot will have changed in the year since I took the bodyguard job, and now that Jack's gone, his brother runs his security firm. I'm confident he'll come through, but not until morning, which leaves me with a list of unanswered questions and only the internet to answer them. For all the good it does.

I'm not sure I know any more than I did twelve hours ago. Rosalie Thorne is still one of the most popular recording artists in the world. Chip Daniels is still a music executive with a truckload of industry clout. The two of them together may be the most photogenic couple to ever look down the lens of a camera, and neither has made it known that one just jilted the other for being an emotionally abusive narcissist.

So when I hear Rosalie on the ladder, I'm already rethinking my decision to put myself in the middle of what's shaping up to be the biggest celebrity scandal in years. She descends slowly, one rung at a time, and I say nothing. Tomorrow's soon enough to dive back into the drama. But as she eases her way to the floor and creeps on tiptoes into the kitchen, I feel like an asshole—again—because I know what she needs. I just don't know if it's in the bounds of our new arrangement to give it to her.

Things are different now that I'm not getting paid to be at her beck and call.

I sit up and throw an arm over the back of the couch, then freeze. The way she looks fresh out of bed wearing my shirt... Rosalie Thorne in a rumpled oversized red flannel should be laughable, but it's not. It's really not.

The fabric swamps her, but her pale thighs play peekaboo where the buttons are undone near the hem, and the soft glow of her legs in the light of the open refrigerator makes it hard to swallow. Her champagne-blonde curls are softer now that the day's styling has been brushed out of them, and the natural fall of her hair creates the illusion that Rosalie Thorne is a woman just like any other. Real. Attainable. Not beyond reach.

When I do find my tongue, my voice cracks. "Hey."

Rosalie jumps as she spins around. She smacks a hand to her chest as she takes a deep breath. "You scared me."

"Sorry."

"No, I'm sorry. I didn't mean to wake you."

"I wasn't asleep."

"Oh." She glances around the kitchen, searching for a way to explain why she's out of bed. "I was thirsty."

I push off the sofa and join her in the kitchen, only realizing I'm half naked when her gaze sweeps down my chest and torso, falls to my boxer briefs and thighs, then moves north again.

"You're the one who promised no more nakedness," I mutter with unfamiliar self-consciousness as a blush creeps up my neck.

She lifts her palms and bites her lip to stop a smile, but her blue eyes dance in the refrigerator light. "I didn't say a word."

With a wry eyebrow and flat look to go with it, I reach into the fridge and hand her a bottle of water, then wait as she holds it without drinking.

"You didn't really come looking for something to drink, did you?"

Dakota appears from the shadows under the loft ladder and rubs her head against Rosalie's legs until she's rewarded with a pat.

Rosalie's shoulders drop as she sighs. "No."

"It's late."

"I know."

"And you really should try to sleep."

She wraps her arms around herself and nods. "I know."

The quiet between us stretches, and it's the way she shifts on her feet, fingers plucking at my shirt, that breaks me. And besides, she's not the only one who has trouble sleeping at night. Playing cards is better than pacing for hours or staring at a flickering television without seeing it.

"Fine." I close the fridge, snap on a lamp, then collect my shirt from the floor and pull it on, followed by my discarded jeans. "There's a notepad and pencil in that kitchen drawer over there. You get those and I'll find the cards."

"No need." She crosses the room and swipes up her purse where she left it on the couch. "I have my own."

Her relieved smile shouldn't hit me as hard as it does, and I work hard to keep my expression neutral as I join her at the table. This woman has more money than God and she carries an old deck of cards in case someone's around to play midnight gin rummy.

"Best of five?" I say without preamble.

She replies because she doesn't need it. "Sounds good."

We play for two hours in the kind of silence that can only be comfortable when you've done the same thing dozens of times before. Unfortunately, there's not enough thinking to do to stop my mind from wandering, and when it does, I find myself questioning if having Rosalie stay for a couple days is really so bad. I'd probably enjoy her company if it wasn't for all the baggage, and I'm not even talking about Chip and the whole runaway bride thing. It's the celebrity and the money and the drama. From where I stand, none of it looks worth the shit she has to go through to keep it, but Rosalie without fame is like a combat soldier without military camouflage. The former needs the latter if they expect to survive.

The longer we play, the more often my thoughts aren't the only things that wander. My eyes do too, in a way they couldn't when I was her bodyguard. She's so fucking pretty. Prettier without the makeup she was wearing when she got here and with her hair half mussed from *my* pillow. Her mouth looks sweeter in its naturally pale pink instead of the intense coral color she usually wears, and when she catches her bottom lip between her teeth while deciding how to play her cards, I wonder how quickly she'd melt if I kissed her. How warm and sweet she'd be on my tongue.

Rosalie watches me expectantly for a couple seconds before I realize it's my turn, and I refocus on my cards. It doesn't matter what she tastes like, because I'll never know. I'm smart enough to separate thought from action, fantasy from reality. Kissing Rosalie Thorne is never going to happen.

By the time Rosalie wins three games to two, I've forgotten she's supposed to be an inconvenience, and I'm dealing again when she raises a hand to hide a yawn.

"Time for bed?" I ask.

"I can hardly keep my eyes open," she mumbles. "And that's my cue."

I slide the cards into their ancient cardboard case and push them across the table toward her. "Good. I'll see you in the morning."

But when a heartbeat passes and she hasn't touched the cards, hands tucked out of sight under the table, I know she's got something to say. I lean back in my chair and wait.

"I do appreciate this, Finn," she says in a voice weary for more reasons than not enough sleep. She sets her hands flat on the tabletop like it's a task to keep them still. "I know I'm high maintenance, and I know nothing about this situation is easy. I wouldn't have blamed you if you put me back in Violet's car and sent me straight back to the city, but I don't know what I would have done if you did. Thank you for letting me stay."

She risks a look at me from underneath her lashes, and she's so small curled in on herself that the urge to protect her swells larger behind my ribs, making it hard to breathe.

"I don't know what asshole told you that you're high maintenance," I tell her, "although I can take a good guess. You're the female force behind a billion-dollar brand, Rosalie, and the most celebrated music artist of an entire generation. *That's* hard work. Not you. Don't believe the bullshit people say when they only say it to drag you down."

Rosalie's next breath is a quivering exhale. Her shoulders relax, and she meets my eyes. "I think I've lost the talent of recognizing truth among the lies, if I ever had it in the first place."

"Well, I haven't."

I push to my feet sand rub my eyes as exhaustion crashes over me. I had an early start this morning running the trail rides with Daisy, then did all that work in the yard, so I've been awake for nearly twenty-four hours. If I keep talking like this, I'm going to say something I'll regret.

"So if you ever need the truth from someone who isn't afraid to tell it, you know who to call."

Like that.

Her lips tremble with a grateful smile, and I jerk my head in the direction of the loft.

"Bed," I order. "For both of us."

"Okay." She pads lightly across the room and sets one foot on the ladder, then pauses and watches me closely. "Finn? I want to tell you something. My name's not really Rosalie. It's the name they gave me when they signed me because my real name wasn't pretty enough." She scrunches her nose to show what she thinks of that decision. "My real name is Rosanna."

I could pretend I didn't already know that, but I just promised her to always be honest. "Actually, I already knew. It was in your file when I took the job as your bodyguard."

Her face falls. "Oh."

Her disappointment is an itch in the middle of my back, and the only way to scratch it is to find another way to share something honest.

"Just because the world calls you Rosalie doesn't mean I have to," I say. "Tell me what name you want to use while you're here, and that's what I'll call you."

Her eyes drop to where her fingers tweak the hem of my shirt, and her smile turns wistful. "My grandmother used to call me Rosie, and that's the only name that's ever really felt like mine, but it's been a long time since anyone called me that."

"Would it be okay if I called you Rosie?"

She tilts her head, and the quiet is loud enough that I can hear my pulse in my ears.

"It would be more than okay," she says.

"Then that's what I'll do."

"Okay." The shape of her name passes silently across her lips before they tug up with satisfaction. "Thank you."

"You're welcome."

She climbs the ladder, and when she's safe at the top, I switch off the lamp downstairs. Once I'm stretched out on the couch in the dark, her light, lilting voice floats down from the loft. "Good night, Finn."

I heave in a breath and close my eyes, and with the type of fatigue that feels a lot like a reason to get up in the morning, I wonder what the hell I've gotten myself into.

"Good night, Rosie."

SIX

Finn

THE SOUND OF MY PHONE ringing wakes me the next morning. I reach for it blindly as it skitters across the coffee table and put it to my ear without checking the caller ID.

"Yeah?"

Too late I remember to keep my voice low, and I glance up to the loft to see if I've woken Rosalie. *Rosie.*

"Finn?" says a man's voice on the other end of the line. "It's Drew. I'm calling about your email. I didn't wake you, did I?"

I sit up, rubbing my eyes, suddenly wide awake. "No," I reply in a hushed voice. "I'm up. Just, uh... give me a minute?"

"Sure. No problem."

With another fast look at the loft and no way to tell if Rosie is still sleeping, I wrap a blanket around my hips and

63

take my phone outside to the porch. Dakota follows and waits at the top of the steps for me to carry her down, and I heave all sixty pounds of her to the yard.

"Drew?" I say into the phone, shadowing Dakota as she sniffs at the ground. "Sorry. I'm here. You got my email?"

"I did." Drew's voice is a lot like Jack's used to be. The timbre is the same, and the way he pronounces certain syllables. It's heartbreaking and comforting at the same time. "Your timing is... interesting."

My muscles tense. "How do you mean?"

"Have you been online recently?"

I check the time on my phone, notice that it's already midmorning, then count back the hours. "About six or seven hours ago. Why?"

"Because a lot can happen in six or seven hours—and a lot did. I was already running the checks on both the client and Chip Daniels when the reports started to filter through."

A pit opens in my stomach. "What reports?"

"Well, if I were a cynical man—"

"You *are* a cynical man."

He snorts. "Right. It's a smear campaign. Early stages and no leads yet on the source, but major sites are reporting that Rosalie Thorne has got herself a lover—and that lover isn't the man she's marrying in three days."

The hollow in my gut hardens. "I'll tell you the source," I grind out. "Chip."

"Want to tell me why?"

"Off the record?"

"Of course."

"She's left him. He's an abusive narcissist, and I need to know how safe it is for her to be out in the world with that guy as her enemy."

A little way ahead, Dakota trots out from behind a shrub with a massive stick in her mouth, flops to the ground, and destroys it with hacking bites. I need to get the girl some breakfast.

"It's unlikely Chip poses a risk to Rosalie's physical safety," Drew says, giving me a fleeting moment of relief. "With his history and profile, he'll take out his aggressions on her bottom line, and look, if it was just about this smear campaign, I might tell you to stand down." Drew clicks his tongue, and I get the sense he's shaking his head. "But there's more."

My teeth crack with the tension in my jaw. "Yeah?"

"I've only spent a few hours on this so far, but given what happened last year in New Orleans, the first thing I did was try to locate the guy who nearly got to her."

My hackles rise. "And?"

"We can't find him."

"Fuck." I slam the side of my fist against the nearest tree trunk. "*Fuck*."

"Yeah. Pretty much sums it up. Didn't her previous security team know about this?"

"Good question," I reply. "And one I wish I could answer for you."

Drew mirrors my judgmental tone with a frustrated grunt. "I'll keep looking and get back to you as soon as I can. In the meantime, I'll get a remote team set up to monitor digital activity and assess the client's social media platforms for threats and patterns."

"Call me as soon as you know more. Day or night. Anytime."

"Will do."

"Thanks. And, uh…" Even with anxiety sharp like ice in my veins, my shoulders drop with a sudden surge of regret. "How are you doing? I'm sorry I haven't been in touch before now. Not since the funeral." I close my eyes. "I'm a jerk."

"Nah. You're not a jerk. I should have called to check in on you, too, and ask how Dakota's doing there with you."

I glance over at the Labrador that used to belong to Jack. When Jack died, Drew asked if I'd adopt Dakota and give her a home. It was enough that Drew had to take over Jack's executive security firm and care for his parents after they lost their son. Providing for Jack's dog was the least I could do. It also gave me purpose at a tough time. And a year ago, I'd hoped it would lighten the guilt I felt about letting Jack down when he needed me. I suppose it does. A little.

"She likes it here," I tell him. "Lots to explore. Eat. Destroy. You know."

"Good. I'm glad. Jack would be too."

"Yeah."

Silence follows, and I know Drew's thinking about Jack the same way I am, but he's the first to clear his throat.

"I'll have something to you in a few hours. Eight tops."

"Thanks, buddy. I really appreciate it."

I end the call with a frown at the screen, then hitch the blanket higher on my waist as I return to the porch and take a long look out at the gently flowing river. Twenty-four hours ago, my life was simple. Easy. Complication free. Now my body is on the kind of alert I haven't felt in nearly a year. It's not uncomfortable and I don't hate it, but it's not how I want to live anymore. After ten years as a SEAL and two months as Rosie's bodyguard, I returned to Aster Springs for a different kind of life. One that was quiet and calm with zero stakes. No new attachments and nothing to lose. Has it been easy to adjust to the country life? No. It's fucking boring. But I was getting closer to figuring it out.

And now all that reconditioning has been undone, and all it took was a single phone call.

Behind me, the front door squeaks on its hinges, and when I turn around, Rosie's blonde head pops through the doorway. Her hair is thrown up in a ponytail and her cheeks are pink and pillow creased. I bet that soft place just beneath her jaw is sweet and warm right about now.

She steps all the way out onto the porch, eyes sweeping down my body, and the corner of her lips curves upward at the blanket hanging off my hips. "Good morning."

"Morning. How'd you sleep?"

"Good. Fine." She clasps her hands in front of her, those long fingers made for an instrument. Guitar. Piano. Flute.

Fiddle. I read an article once that said she can play eight, like her idol Dolly Parton. "And you?"

"About the same."

Rosie smiles and her eyes fall to the phone in my hands. "I thought I heard you talking. Is everything okay?"

I promised her honesty, but until I know more about the whereabouts of her attacker and Chip's toxic media campaign, I refuse to give her half-truths that will only scare her.

"How about we go inside, and I'll make you breakfast?" I suggest. "I'm starved and we can talk while we eat."

"No," she says, and at my lifted brow, she rolls her eyes. "I mean, yes, but let me make breakfast as a way to pay you back."

"You don't have—"

"I know." Her hands twist together, back and forth. "But I want to."

"Okay. Thanks. Help yourself to anything in the kitchen. I'll throw on some clothes and collect Dakota so I can feed her first, and then we'll meet you inside."

Twenty minutes later, I'm regretting life.

"How is it?" Rosie piles more underdone eggs onto my plate and tops up my mug of bitter-tasting coffee, then grimaces as she hands me a piece of cold buttered toast. "I've never cooked anything before. I didn't know it would be so difficult."

"It's... great." I choke back another bite of charred bacon and chase it with a mouthful of coffee I do my best not to taste. "It's... It's..."

"Awful." Rosie sags in her chair, then perks up again. "But I'm sure it just takes practice. I'll do better next time."

I thud my fist against my chest as I fight down a mouthful of toast and glance at the scraps of burnt bacon on the floor next to Dakota. She's curled up with the meat scattered right under her nose, and you know food's bad if you can't get a Labrador to eat it. "Next time. Sure. Just takes practice."

"So... that phone call you took outside. It was about me, wasn't it?"

Grateful for the excuse to stop eating, I push away my plate and turn to Rosie where she's perched on the edge of her chair with her hands splayed on the tabletop.

"Yeah. I reached out to the firm that hired me as your bodyguard last year and asked them to do a little research about your situation. You said you don't trust your current security team and I don't want you returning home without a few basic protections in place. This firm is the best I know to provide it."

"That's kind of you, Finn. Thank you."

"You're welcome, but I didn't do it to be kind, Rosie. I did it to be practical, and to keep you safe. Once you leave here, I won't be around to protect you, so if you're serious about ending your relationship with Chip, you need to start rebuilding your teams. Security comes first."

"Of course." Her throat works as she nods her understanding. "And I *am* serious about breaking up with Chip. I wouldn't be here if I wasn't."

"Have you switched on your phone yet? Turned on the television?"

Rosie drops her eyes. "No. I couldn't face it last night and my phone battery was dead when I tried to turn it on this morning. Why? What's going on?"

I haven't seen the evidence for myself yet, so I set my phone on the table so we can both view the screen, then pull up my internet browser and type her name into the search bar.

The results page populates with a dozen headlines saying the same thing in different ways.

Music mogul Chip Daniels dumps pop star Rosalie Thorne three days before their fairy-tale wedding.

The wedding is off! Princess of Pop Rosalie Thorne busted cheating on Chip Daniels.

Where is she? Rosalie Thorne flees her wedding dress fitting after the truth about her affair comes out.

Rosie scans the headlines and scrolls to see more, her eyes flying over the screen and her nostrils flaring with short, overwhelmed breaths.

"I'm sorry," I say. "But it's—"

"A smear campaign. To set me up as a liar, a cheater, and a coward to save his reputation and destroy mine in the process. And the best part? If I try to defend myself, there'll always be people who won't believe me because he's gone and undermined my credibility."

Damn. This woman is smart. I'm ashamed to say I didn't know how smart.

"Yeah."

"Ugh!" She shoves the phone away, folds her arms on the dining table, and drops her head. "How did I ever fall for such an asshole?"

"You're in love with him?"

I don't know why I asked it, and when Rosie lifts her head to reveal blues eyes wide with surprise, I wish I hadn't. I'm saved from taking it back, and Rosie's saved from answering, when somebody knocks on my door.

Rosie startles, and her surprise turns to panic. I set a calming hand on her shoulder and Dakota perks up before she wiggles her butt backward to press against Rosie's ankles.

"Stay here," I say. "Stay quiet. Don't move from this chair unless I tell you to move. Got it?"

I wait until she nods before I cross the room with a kind of stealth I haven't needed in nearly a year. Flexing my fingers in case I need to use my fists, I open the door just enough to see who's outside. When a face comes into focus, my defenses immediately drop.

"Violet. Uh... hey. What are you doing here?"

She lifts her arms to draw my attention to the half dozen shopping bags she's carrying, then tips her head back toward her car still sitting on the gravel drive. A shiny red sports car is parked behind it.

"My car has a GPS tracker," she explains.

"Ah. Right. And the bags?"

"Rosalie made an order for underwe—" Violet's cheeks bloom with spots of embarrassment for the almost-mention of Rosie's personal items. "I mean, she made an order when she was at my studio yesterday. When my car didn't move last night, and she didn't answer my texts, I started to worry." Violet's blush deepens. "I'm using her order as an excuse to check on her. I hope you don't mind."

"Check on her?" I say, acting clueless to play for time.

"I saw what's happening online," Violet says. "I don't have anywhere near Rosalie's public profile, but there was a lot of hate when I started dating Chord. Social media and tabloid gossip can be harsh—and, in my experience, usually untrue. Rosalie never gave me the impression of a woman with secrets, and even if she did, that's her business and not mine. I still want to help."

The door is still barely ajar, the two of us talking through a space no wider than six inches, and I'm not sure what to say next. I hadn't planned for Rosie to be found by someone I trust. "I—"

"Violet?" Rosie sneaks up behind me and swings the door wide open. "I thought I heard your voice."

Violet's eyebrows shoot up as she takes in the petite pop star with bare feet and no makeup wearing my oversized shirt, and I close my eyes briefly to resist a sigh. "And I thought I told you to stay in the kitchen."

Violet gasps, and I realize how that statement must sound to someone unaware of our history.

"No. I didn't mean... It's not like that. I'm not some big, stupid, misogynistic pig. It's like... The thing is..."

Violet looks shocked and yeah, a little judgmental, but I keep struggling for words. I don't know what Rosie wants to share and what she wants to keep secret. I might be cut out to beat the shit out of a psychopath who wants to kidnap her, but I'm not up for concocting stories out of thin air. And this is why I hate bullshit.

Rosie saves me with a condescending pat on my upper arm. "Finn used to be my bodyguard. He's happiest when I do what I'm told."

"You're *safest* when you do what you're told," I grumble.

"Your *bodyguard*?" Violet considers me with new appreciation. "I didn't know that."

"It was a while ago, and only for two months," I explain. "Rosie's here because... because..."

"Because I needed a place to hide out while I figure out my life," Rosie says over my fumbling. "Do you want to come in? I just made coffee."

"Uh, sure. Thanks."

I relieve Violet of the shopping bags as we move inside, accidentally on purpose getting a look at something red and lacy in one of the bags, and Violet gives me a curious glance as I warn her off the coffee with a tight shake of my head. Violet accepts a cup anyway, takes a sip, and does a pretty good job of hiding her disgust as she takes a spot on the sofa next to Rosie.

Violet sets her mug on the coffee table and nods toward the armchair where Rosie's dress is carefully arranged over the back. "I can take your dress back to the studio, if you like. Have it cleaned and stored correctly to preserve the fabric."

Rosie glances at the dress with a regretful sigh. "That's a good idea. I'm sorry I won't be wearing it this weekend. It really is beautiful."

"Please don't apologize. You have enough to worry about without adding a dress to the list."

Rosie responds with a small smile of thanks, then cranes her neck to look around the room. "Did I hear you say something about my lingerie order?"

Violet casts a shy look my way. "Yes. I also brought some shampoo and body lotion. A few T-shirts. Jean shorts. Sweatpants. Sneakers. I had your measurements, and considering the way you ran out of my studio yesterday..." Violet winces apologetically. "I didn't know enough about your situation and wanted to be prepared. Where are those bags?"

I lift them up to prove I have them, then deposit it all on the floor at the girls' feet just as my phone vibrates silently in my pocket. I swipe it out and Rosie looks up with expectation.

Drew's name flashes on the screen, and nervous anticipation hits.

"I've got to take this," I say, already halfway to the door. "Don't leave the cabin by any way other than the front porch."

I take their agreement as given as I close the door behind me and set my phone to my ear.

"Drew," I say. "That was fast. What have you got for me?"

"Nothing you're going to like," he replies. "We can't find Rosalie's stalker via our usual ways. I'm sorry, Finn. The guy could be anywhere."

SEVEN

Rosie

"THANK YOU FOR LETTING ME borrow your car," I say to Violet as Finn strides from the cabin. His urgency can only mean that his phone call is about me, but I'm in no rush to know more. Reading the headlines this morning was a reminder I don't need about how difficult it is to live in the spotlight and how desperately I need a break. "I'm sorry my exit was so dramatic."

"It's fine," Violet says kindly. "I wasn't worried about the car. I was worried about you."

My relationship with Violet has always been more professional than personal, but I've also never been alone with her because Lauren came to all my fittings. Now that it's only the two of us somewhere other than her studio, the dynamic between us vibes more toward friendly.

I consider for a moment that I'm so starved of genuine human attachment that I've read this all wrong, but when Violet offers me an encouraging smile, the tightness in my chest eases.

"I hope things weren't too difficult when Lauren came back and found me missing," I say. "I didn't mean to put you in the middle."

"You didn't," Violet assures me. "She returned and asked me where you were. I handed her the ring along with your message, then told her honestly that you left through the rear exit and I had no idea why. She didn't waste time with more questions. Your bodyguard did a quick check of the parking lot, but Lauren was on her phone and out the door again almost instantly."

I nod with understanding. "She would have called Chip as soon as she realized I was missing. Those two deserve each other."

Violet's face softens and she rests her hand on mine. "I don't know what's happening, Rosalie, but I'm sorry that it was bad enough for you to have to run like that."

"I didn't cheat on him," I blurt out.

Violet's voice falls to a soothing whisper. "I believe you."

I set my other hand on Violet's and grip it tightly. "Can I trust you, Violet?"

Her brows draw in and I explain in a rush. "I know that sounds horrible and I don't mean it to be. I'm not accusing you of anything, but I've been betrayed by the most important person in my life and I'm not sure I trust my own judgment." I glance at Violet's hand between mine. "When it comes to human connection, I'm a little bruised."

Violet squeezes my fingers. "I understand. I wasn't great at friendships until I met Chord's sisters, but I'm trying to be better. You don't have to tell me anything if you don't want to, but if it would make you more comfortable, I can share a little about me first."

"Yes," I say. "I'd love to know more about you, Violet. You can trust me."

She smiles and gives my hand a final squeeze before she draws hers back so she can tuck them between her knees.

"My mom left when I was two years old, and to this day I don't know where she is." The way Violet says it, like it's just a fact of life, mirrors the way I feel about my own abandonment and sparks an instant sense of kinship. "My dad has depression and I worry about him every day. Last year, when word got out that I was dating Chord, people on social media called me a gold-digging opportunist with no talent. And when I decided to build a career on my own and design for a fashion house in Milan, it was the worst mistake I ever made. I was alone and heartbroken in a foreign country. I thought I'd lost it all."

"But you hadn't," I guess.

Violet's smile reaches warm brown eyes lit up with memories. "No. I had friends who saw through my brave face and a man who loved me enough to fly halfway around the world just to bring me back. And I did have talent—talent that allowed me to make my dreams come true on my own terms." She squirms a little before she adds, "Just as soon as I could admit to myself that those terms had evolved along with the rest of me."

"I think I know what you mean," I reply. "I've been in this business since I was eighteen years old and the things that were important then aren't so important anymore. I met Chip when I was twenty-one, and I've always relied on him for everything. He told me what I wanted and made all the plans for how to get it. It's come to the point where I can't tell the difference between his desires and my own. It's like I lost myself."

"How did you meet Chip?" Violet asks.

I roll my eyes at how cliché it sounds. "He introduced himself at an industry party. My record label had dropped me the year before, and I was trying to reestablish myself as a viable artist, but in reality, I was alone and adrift. Chip was smart and suave and sexy, older than me, and an important name. I thought he knew it all, so when he offered to be my manager, it seemed like all my problems were solved." I fidget with the hem of my shirt. "Our relationship didn't turn romantic for another six months, and when it did, I felt lucky. I lost count of the women who threw themselves at him, and there he was, choosing *me*."

"I can imagine that would be intoxicating, especially in your line of work."

"That's a good way to describe it," I agree. "I had no family and no real friends, and I was almost drugged by his attention. I never had to beg him to take an interest in my life. Chip *was* my life. He managed everything. From my career to my money to my body to my wardrobe to my security team to my publicist. My personal assistant." I shake my head and wrap my arms around my middle to stop a shiver. "I interpreted his behavior as acts of love. It took me too long to realize it was about control."

I close my eyes to dispel the shame and open them again, determined to finally say out loud the things I've been too scared to even think. "There are two sides to Chip. He's charming and charismatic and generous, but he's also intolerant and short-tempered, impatient and unforgiving, and he hates being challenged. I learned quickly to go along with whatever he wanted. It was easier than enduring days of the silent treatment or apologizing for things I did wrong. He wanted what was best for me, right? He was smarter than me, wasn't he? He loved me, so of course I should trust him. If I had any sense, I'd let him do the thinking and save my energy for what I did best. Songwriting. Singing. Performing." I shrug and try to pretend the shame doesn't hollow me out. "Eventually I stopped questioning him, even in my own head. I didn't want to fight that battle with my heart anymore."

"When did you start to see things differently?" Violet asks gently.

I scrub my face and laugh quietly. I have to or else I'll fall apart. "About a year ago. Chip booked an entire world tour for my latest album, and it sold out in arenas everywhere.

I'd been working for years to get to that moment. It was supposed to be the highlight of my career... and Chip wasn't going to be there. I know that sounds spoiled. He had a career and a life, and he couldn't be on the road with me every night and for every show, but he had no plans to be there *at all*. We were going to be separated for six months and he didn't care. He handed me a schedule and told me that everyone on the tour—*everyone*—would be his eyes and ears while I was gone, and for the first time, I didn't hear that as love. I heard it as control. As a threat. The message was clear: if I stepped out of line, Chip would find out about it. Never in my life have I felt more like a commodity, or less like a human, or so lonely and insignificant."

"I'm sorry, Rosalie. That sounds incredibly difficult."

"It was, but it also fired me up." I feel the warmth of that old courage, and I fight to hold on to it. "I thought *screw him. I'm a grown woman. I can take charge of my life.* Everything he built was all because of *me*. My voice. My music. My name. I decided he needed me more than I needed him, and that's when I hired Finn as my bodyguard. Chip was fuming when he found out, and I don't know where I found the will to defy him. Maybe it was because he was on the other side of the country instead of in the same room. I told him I wanted an ex-military man on my team and unless he could find someone more qualified, the person I hired wasn't going anywhere."

"Good for you." Violet shakes her head with wonder. "That must have taken a lot of courage."

"Or naivety," I say, still disappointed by how short-lived my rebellion turned out to be. "I realized while I was away that I didn't love Chip anymore, if I ever really had. I'd just made the decision to leave him altogether, break all ties personally and professionally, but then..."

Violet drops her head to the side. "But then... what?"

"There was an... incident." I stumble over the word, and when the memory passes, I carry on like it didn't almost drag me under. "Chip flew out to meet me in Louisiana and decided Finn was to blame for everything. He fired him on the spot, and after what happened, I was too fragile to stop him. All my energy went into my shows, and life offstage passed by in a fog." I recall that time with sadness, regret, and not a small amount of rage. "I didn't see it at the time, but when I look back now, I think Chip liked me that way. Weak and dependent. He grew strong on my weakness."

Violet shakes her head sadly. "You didn't deserve that type of treatment."

I shrug to say I'm not sure that's true. If I were a more confident woman, Chip would never have gained that kind of power in the first place.

"After that, all the reasons Chip couldn't tour with me miraculously disappeared," I go on. "He followed me around the world for the next four months, and I let him. It was all I could do to finish the tour, and by the time it was done, I had a diamond on my finger and a wedding date on the books. If I'm being perfectly honest, I don't remember saying yes to either of those things, but I also don't remember saying no. My therapist called it disassociation."

"Oh, Rosalie. I'm so proud of you for finding a way out of that situation, but... how?" Violet narrows her eyes as she studies my face. "Something changed yesterday, didn't it? At my studio."

Movement at the window catches our attention, and we look over to see Finn staring in through the glass. His eyes are on me and me alone. Steady. Certain. Determined.

"The picture of Finn on my wall," Violet guesses with sudden understanding. "That's what changed. You saw Finn in that photograph, and you ran straight to him."

Through the window looking out onto the porch, I meet Finn's unwavering gaze. His lips move in conversation with whoever's on the other end of the phone. "I saw him and remembered how I felt for those two months he was in my life."

Violet glances at Finn again. "And how was that?" she asks quietly.

"In control," I reflect quietly. "Strong. Safe. Like I knew myself again."

On the porch, Finn ends his call and heads straight for the door. Violet is on her feet before the timber swings open, and I jump up beside her, nerves making my stomach pitch in a queasy swoop.

"I should go," Violet says, lifting my wedding dress from the armchair and arranging it carefully over her arms. "Do you have any instructions for what I should do with your gown?"

I reach over and brush the fabric with the tips of my fingers. "Archive it. I'll never be able to look at it without seeing Chip." I drop my hand with a sigh. "And if that wasn't bad enough, do you know what's worse?"

Violet tilts her head, her expression empathetic, as an invitation to continue. Even Finn seems invested in my answer.

"You made me the perfect dress," I say. "What happens if one day I meet a man I *do* want to marry? Nothing will ever be as exquisite as this, and it breaks my heart."

"I wouldn't worry about that." Violet hikes the dress in her arms, adjusting the bulk and weight for better balance, and gives me a comforting wink. "It's beautiful, yes, but when the time comes, I'll make you something so divine you'll wonder how you ever believed this was the dress of your dreams."

I laugh a little at her confidence, hope flickering at the idea of falling in love again—with a better man *and* a better dress. "You promise?"

"Absolutely."

"I appreciate that," I say. "As much as the clothes and you taking the time to check up on me. Thank you."

While Finn walks Violet out onto the porch and they exchange a few quiet words, I drop onto the sofa again, apprehension a corkscrew in my stomach, and wait.

"It's bad, isn't it?" I ask when he returns. "Whatever you found out on the phone just now. It's bad."

Finn takes a seat opposite me and sets his elbows on his knees. He means business, and I swallow hard.

"How much do you want to know?" he asks.

"What do you mean?"

"I mean do you want to know everything, or do you want to know only as much as you need to know?"

I think about what he's asking and what he's not, and the implication that whatever he's going to share has the potential to rattle me. It's tempting to keep my head in the sand, but I never want to be in the position of letting a man make my decisions again. If I want to take back my life, I have to take back all of it. The good and the bad. The beautiful and the terrifying.

"I want to know it all," I tell him with conviction.

His nod has an air of approval about it, and I don't know why that makes me feel good, but it does, even when he delays our conversation long enough to pour me a glass of water. I accept the drink when he offers it, then focus on the sensation of smooth glass between my palms. Bracing myself.

"Stanley Lowe. The man who almost got to you last year in New Orleans. We can't find him."

My body stiffens and I set the glass on the coffee table before it slips from my hand. From the far side of the room, like she has some kind of sixth sense, Dakota trots over, launches herself up onto the sofa beside me, and wriggles her head into position on my lap. Her warmth and weight ground me, and I gratefully thread my fingers into her coat.

"He..." I take a moment to remember that I'm safe. "He's supposed to be in jail."

Finn grimaces. "He got released, and by your reaction, I assume your security team wasn't aware of it."

I shake my head. "No, or if they were, they didn't think it necessary to tell me."

Finn's nostrils flare with disapproval. "I'm sorry, Rosie, but without reliable protection in place, I'm not comfortable sending you back to LA. You're safest here, where nobody can find you, while I put together a new team, but I don't know how long that will take. A few days, at least. Maybe a week."

There's that word again. *Safe*. Somehow, it's easier to believe when Finn says it than when it comes from the stricken voice inside my head, and my heart rate slows. I glance around the tiny bungalow, at the Labrador beside me, at the great big man within arm's reach who watches me with eyes that have witnessed much worse than a young woman terrorized by a psychotic stalker.

I know why he's doing this. It's the same reason he didn't send me home last night. Finn has an acute sense of right and wrong, and if it's wrong to send me out into the world under these conditions, then he simply won't do it. He might care about me, he might not, but emotional investment is irrelevant to a man like Finn. Duty and honor come first, and I bet he's been torn between his head and his heart.

"A week is a long time," I say quietly, wanting so badly to stay where I feel protected but compelled to give Finn a chance to change his mind. "Are you sure I won't be in the way? You must have work to do. Plans. Commitments."

Finn runs a hand through his hair and the tilt to his mouth is self-mocking. "Nothing I can't delay for a few days."

I wonder what it is Finn does all day and add it to the long list of things I'll never know about him. "Okay," I agree. "If that's what you recommend, then I'll stay."

Finn's nod is short, but the hint of approval passes his brow. "Good. In that case, I've got work to do."

Finn retrieves a laptop from atop a stack of books in the living room, then sets it up on the dining table. I let myself be soothed by his presence, watching him for a while as he taps at the keyboard. He does a good impression of pretending he doesn't have an audience, and soon I let my gaze wander to the window instead.

Outside, the sky is clear and blue beyond the redwoods, and something occurs to me with sudden clarity. For the first time since I was child, I'm not only invisible, but someone I trust is willing to carry my worries so I don't have to. Something precious breaks open in my chest, and I'm flooded with emotion. Relief. Release. Peace. My fingers twitch to strum a note on my six-string or spend a night with my piano, but they're both out of reach for now. Instead, I pick up the notepad Finn used for our gin rummy last night, settle a pencil between my fingers, and write.

EIGHT

Finn

IT'S NEARLY NOON THE NEXT day, and I'm sprawled on the sofa, feet on the coffee table and my computer on my lap, when Rosie climbs down from the loft. She's been writing in bed all morning after not moving from the couch all yesterday afternoon, scribbling away on the notepad we used to play gin rummy again last night. She's been almost constantly distracted for the last twenty-four hours, and we've been co-existing in the kind of companionable silence I could get used to.

Rosie takes the sofa opposite mine and tucks her feet up underneath her. She's wearing another of my old flannels despite the shopping bags I carried up to the bedroom for her, and though today's shirt is just as long on her as the first, she's missed the final few buttons again, creating a thigh-high split that reveals more than the soft fabric hides.

Should I be bothered that she's helping herself to clothes from my closet? Maybe. Am I? Not even close.

"Hey," she says.

I flick her a glance over the top of my computer screen. "Hey."

"Watcha doing?"

"Sorting out your security team."

"That sounds like something I should know about, don't you think?"

"I do think that. Yes."

She sits up straight, clasps her hands on her knees, and hits me with a serious frown. "What's the situation?"

I sit up, put my feet on the floor, and set the laptop on the coffee table. "I'm using my friend's executive security firm because I trust him," I begin, and she immediately interjects.

"How do you know this friend?"

I'm equally pleased that she's taking this seriously and uncomfortable that her line of questioning could move us into territory I don't want to explore.

"His brother was a military buddy of mine," I explain. "My best friend, in fact. Drew, the brother that runs this firm, is a good guy. I trust him or I wouldn't involve him in this."

Thankfully, my brief rationalization is enough for Rosie. "And what does Drew recommend?"

"He's already got a remote surveillance team up and running. They're monitoring your social media accounts and associated online activity as well as searching for your attacker's location. It might take time, but they won't stop until they find him."

Rosie's nod is contemplative as she absorbs this new information. "That sounds reasonable."

"His other task is putting together a ground team to be with you in Los Angeles. Drew is sending through options via email. If any of the candidates pass my quality check, I'll share them with you for review."

Rosie lifts one perfect brow, a few shades darker than her blonde hair. "*If* any pass your quality check?"

"I'm not taking chances. If I'm going to do a job, then I'm going to do it right."

Her quirked eyebrow is amused, but she tilts her head apologetically. "I didn't mean to tease you, Finn. I appreciate how seriously you're taking all this."

I shrug off the compliment. "And what about your next steps? I noticed you still haven't switched on your phone."

We both glance at the small black device on the table between us.

"I don't want to see his name," she admits. "I don't want to deal with the missed calls and unanswered texts. I don't want to face him right now, even if it's only via a screen." Rosie curls her hands up inside the baggy sleeves of my flannel. "I know that makes me a coward but—"

"It means you know your limits," I say. "Trauma isn't weakness, Rosie, and you don't owe him anything. Not a phone call or a text message or an explanation until or unless you're ready to give it to him, and only then because it's something you need to do for you."

"Thanks, Finn." She crosses her arms and lifts her chin a little. "I hope I'll have it in me to confront him one day."

Rosie's mouth is grim, her blue eyes determined, and just when I think I can't hate the asshole more than I already do, I imagine how I'd do things differently if we were in the same room again, and blood rushes in my ears.

"Hey," Rosie says, like an idea just occurred to her. "Can I borrow your computer?"

"Sure."

Her eyes brighten, and she's already reaching for the machine as I close the browser and spin the screen to face her. Her fingers fly over the track pad and then the keys, and when she offers no more information, I decide she's entitled to some privacy.

I stand and click my tongue to get Dakota's attention. "Come on, girl. Time for some fresh air."

The *tap-tap-tap* of Rosie's typing abruptly halts, replaced by the *click-clack* of Dakota's nails on the floorboards.

"You're not going far?" Rosie asks.

"Just off the porch. And not for long."

Her slender shoulders fall, and her exhale is almost a sigh. "Okay. Thanks."

Staying true to my word, I heft Dakota down the porch stairs and stroll along behind her as she sniffs her way around the perimeter of the bungalow. I take some time to think more about the applicants Drew suggested for Rosie's new security team. Of the four so far, none are good enough. They're either too young or too old. Too inexperienced or too cocky. Even revisiting their profiles now in my head, I can't convince myself to give any a second look. And it's not because I don't want to, but because Rosie's too vulnerable for me to risk rushing this. Nowhere is safer for her right now than here with me, and I won't let her out of my sight until that's no longer true.

The afternoon is warm, even for mid-April, and the air is still and silent. I stay within earshot of the cabin, but I'm outside long enough that Rosie eventually comes looking for me. I hear the squeak of the front door, her feet landing on the soft dirt behind me, and then the gentle sigh of her deep exhale as she stops at my side and stares out over the river.

"It's so pretty here," she murmurs.

"Yeah. It is."

"The water's so calm and clear."

"We're lucky," I agree. "This part of the river system is clean and deep. My dad even built the dock long enough for diving. We loved it as kids."

Rosie hums and falls quiet for a moment. I watch her from the corner of my eye.

"I just fired my publicist," she announces with her focus on the horizon and a jump of emotion in her voice.

I glance at her from the corner of my eye to try and get a read on what that emotion might be. Excitement. Nerves. Fear. Confidence. All of the above.

"I also fired my talent agent, my legal representation, and my security team." She huffs out a grim chuckle. "Lauren too."

I grunt with approval.

"I made a list of anyone Chip personally hired and sent emails cutting off every single one of them. If I'm going to make a fresh start, I need to be brave about it, right?"

I risk another quick look at the woman beside me and my mouth tips up at the way she stands taller. All five foot nothing of her. "Right."

"I emailed my accountant and revoked Chip's access to my money," she adds and this time there's no misreading the fierceness in her tone. "And I canceled the lease on the house in Los Angeles. I've got thirty days to work out what to do with my stuff, and he's got thirty days to find a new place to live."

I smirk and imagine the look on the jerk's face when he finds out Rosie is taking back her life.

"You approve?" Rosie asks with a curious smile.

I cross my arms over my chest and try not to grin as I glance at the water. "Not my place to have an opinion."

"You approve," she decides, and a flush of pleasure brightens her high cheekbones. "I can't tell you what this feels like, Finn. I cut every string tying me to him so I can start all over again on my own and it feels... It feels..."

"Good?" I suggest.

"Better than good. Better than *great*. It feels..."

She looks down at the dark phone clutched in one hand, then back up at the river.

"It feels like this!"

Rosie runs on bare feet, red flannel fluttering around her thighs, down to the dock, right to its edge, and flings her phone into the water.

Dakota trots after her, and I shake my head with amusement as I follow at an easy pace.

"I'm happy for you, Rosie," I say, then cut off with a frown as she starts to unbutton her—my—shirt. "What are you doing?"

"I feel free, Finn. For the first time since I was a kid, I'm free!"

Another button passes through her fingers, and another, until the shirt opens all the way, and she lets the fabric fall to her feet. She's wearing the red lace panties I accidentally on purpose spotted in her shopping bags.

"Jesus fucking—" I shove a hand through my hair and drop my eyes, but not before she turns around and I notice the sexy little dimples at the base of Rosie's back. "Put your clothes back on."

"No."

I swipe the shirt from the dock and thrust it at her, the whole time hiding how much I love seeing this side of her. The nudity's nice, sure, and you can damn well bet I'll be thinking about it again later tonight, but her confidence and exuberance and the way her laugh bubbles up like she's been fighting it for too long are what make her so beautiful right now.

"No more nakedness," I remind her. "You promised."

She glances over her shoulder at the shirt, then pointedly ignores it. "I guess I lied."

Dakota barks and wriggles back, tail wagging madly as Rosie drags her underwear down her legs, steps out of it, and faces the water. I should look away. Turn around. Stare at anything but Rosie's bare form but I can't. I fucking can't.

Her body is smooth and pale and perfect. Slender with gentle curves—the soft flesh of her thighs, the contour of her hips, the tempting crease just below her ass. The heavy swell of her breasts and tight pink nipples gone hard in the open air. Skin so smooth I can't help but imagine my hands, my lips, my tongue gliding over every inch of it.

Stunned too stupid to string two words together, I watch in mesmerized awe as Rosie positions her toes on the edge of the dock, flexes her muscled legs, and launches into a shallow dive. She breaks the surface of the water with grace, then pops her head back up with a rapturous smile.

"Are you serious?" I cross my arms and try to look stern, but I'm too captivated by this version of her. "Anyone could see you. You know that, right?"

She laughs and lies back until the slopes of her breasts lift out of the water, moving her arms in wide arcs and kicking her toes to make little surface splashes.

"I'm not in public," she says. "But even if I were, nobody knows I'm here. Do you know what a miracle that is? Do you not understand what that means?"

Dakota barks again and spins in an excited circle, her tail whipping back and forth.

I do know what Rosie means and I also know she's right. I can't imagine a time she's ever felt safe enough to swim naked in a river, and as her protector, it's my job to worry while she lets go of her fears. I need to measure these moments clinically. Professionally. Neutrally. I've done it before, I can do it again, and part of me is fine with it.

The other part of me is, well... hard.

"Come on, girl!" Rosie sends light sprays of water toward Dakota. "Come swimming with Rosie!"

My heavy Lab hurls herself off the dock with a lot less finesse and a lot more impact than the global superstar waiting in the water. Rosie laughs again, a musical sound that ricochets off the river and the trees and even the sky.

"How about you?" she asks.

"Me?" I shake my head with a chuckle. "No."

She splashes me, harder than she did Dakota, and I step back with water soaking my shirt and dripping from my hair.

"Oh, come on." She slaps her hand over her eyes. "If you're shy, I won't look." Her fingers part so she can peek out between them. "I promise."

I snort. "You'd look," I argue, and at her impish grin, I know I'm right.

"The water's wonderful," she says in a singsong voice meant to lure me in. "You don't know what you're missing."

I peel off my wet T-shirt and drop it onto the pile of flannel, then remove my jeans. I laugh low and husky at the devilish glint in her eyes, but there's no way I'm getting in that water. Self-control is one thing. Self-destruction is another altogether. The trick is to find the middle ground.

When I lower myself to the edge of the dock and dangle my feet in the water instead of diving in after her, Rosie pouts and splashes me again. "Spoil sport."

I reach down and splash her back. "You'll get over it."

The next half an hour spans a hundred years.

Dakota lasts no more than half that time before she paddles up to the shore, then circles back to drop her sopping-wet hulk onto the dock beside me. She watches the water with a lolling tongue, and I pretend to be fascinated by the tree line on the far bank as I wait for Rosie to finish her swim. In reality, I'm in knots every time her magnificent ass pops out of the water or when she bounces high enough to reveal the wet, furled peaks of her incredible tits. I cool my jets by listing all the reasons I'm on the dock and not in the water with my hands tangled in her hair and her legs wrapped around my waist.

She's practically a client. She just broke up with someone and she's vulnerable. She belongs in a Los Angeles mansion, not a shack in Sonoma Valley, and she's way too special for a simple guy like me. So many reasons to keep my hands to myself.

When the show is finally over, Rosie swims toward the ladder at the side of the dock and pulls herself out of the water with a gratified sigh. I'm waiting with the flannel held out to wrap her up and my eyes focused on a ribbon of white clouds just over her head.

"That was fantastic," she says as she slips her arms into the sleeves.

"Glad you enjoyed yourself." I frown at her chattering teeth. "Now how about a hot shower before you catch a cold?"

Rosie fastens the final button on her shirt and plants her hands on her hips, then hits me with a grin that takes my breath away.

She's always been radiant—there's a reason Rosie's so successful; she's got *it*, whatever *it* is—but I've never seen her more beautiful than she is now. Soaked in river water. Wearing my old shirt. Happy. Untroubled. And smiling prettily enough to make my heart race.

"Fine," she says, and just when I think I've scored an easy win, she drops her head to one side. "And after I shower, how about I make us an early dinner?"

I clear the groan from my throat. "Sounds... like a plan."

"Great!"

Rosie spins on her heel and heads up to the cabin, and Dakota trails after her without a backward glance. As I lament the fact that my best friend has dropped me for a prettier prospect, a puddle of red lace catches my eye. This time I don't try to mask my moan.

I consider leaving Rosie's panties on the wooden planks, but then swipe them up and ball them in my fist as I follow her to the cabin. I'll figure out a way to sneak them back into her belongings. Drop them in one of those shopping bags or something. It'll be like this never happened. Because she might be brilliant, she might be beautiful, but Rosalie Thorne's also fucking complicated. And I don't do complicated.

NINE

Rosie

I FALL ASLEEP QUICKLY THAT night, but I wake some hours later with anxiety gnawing my stomach. The high of making so many cutthroat moves earlier is gone, replaced with a little voice that says if I wasn't alone before, I certainly am now. And what's it all worth?

All I've ever wanted is to make music. I never set out to be a pop icon or—what did Finn call me? The female force behind a billion-dollar brand? I don't know if I'll be any good at it without an industry baron like Chip in my corner. So what the hell am I fighting for?

I pick up Finn's watch from the nightstand and sigh. It's nearly one a.m. I can't remember the last time I slept through the night.

Staring up at the beamed ceiling, I slip my hand beneath my pillow to touch the notebook tucked underneath. The song I wrote today is different from the tracks on my last two records. Less pop and more country, and although I'm happy with the lyrics, my fingers itch to play it on an instrument. Switch up the bridge. Experiment with the key. See if I can give it a little more... *something*. I hum the melody to myself in the darkness, but I still can't figure out what's missing.

The loft is dimly lit by moonlight filtering through the windows, and as the song's final refrain leaves my throat, I pull the covers up to my chin and tally my years of sleeplessness. It began the week my grandmother died, and I don't need a therapist to explain why. I'd never lived alone before, and even though it's silly to think an eighty-year-old could protect me, I felt her absence so deeply that the night became an empty place without her in my life.

I should have slept better when I moved in with Chip, but that didn't happen, and at the time I didn't understand why. Once we were sleeping together, I'd wait until he was dead to the world, then creep out from beneath the covers and spend hours in the kitchen sipping cocoa and playing solitaire with my grandmother's cards, flipping them the way she taught me until I was exhausted enough to pass out when my head hit the pillow.

I struggled even worse on tour. Abandoned by Chip. Moving constantly between hotels. Physically worn out by my relentless schedule. I should have slept like a baby, but I was overworked and overtired. Too wound up to ever wind down.

I think back to the first night with Finn on my personal protection team. It was the second week of my six-month tour, and I was staying in the best hotel in Chicago. I ordered room service, wrapped myself in a terry robe, and curled up at the suite's dining table with Gram's cards. Finn hovered in a corner while I played, a silent guardian like all the others except that *I* hired him. And I remember thinking how that made things different. In the dark, all alone, I wanted to talk to him when I never wanted to talk to the others.

"Are you thirsty?" I asked with a gesture at the pitcher of cocoa. "There's plenty."

"No," he replied, deep and smooth. After a shadow of a pause, he added, "Thank you."

It was the genuine tone of his *thank you* that nudged me to ask, "Do you know how to play gin rummy?"

His hesitation was obvious this time, like he didn't want to tell the truth but couldn't bring himself to lie. "Yes."

I scooped up the cards and shuffled, then dealt them to the empty seat across from me.

"Those are yours," I told him as I got up to fetch a notepad and pencil. "Let's go."

After a short debate about whether playing cards with a client could be considered *professional*, Finn sat down and picked up his hand, and we played in silence for an hour. We played for another hour the next night. When I had a show, we played as soon as we got back to my hotel room. When I didn't, he was always waiting when I tiptoed out of bed in the dark. He put up a fight every time, and persuading him to play became a game I loved to win.

Finn played every night for as long as I needed until the night my stalker found a way to sneak into my hotel. Made it past security to my room. Knocked on my door. Screamed and lunged and swung his knife when he couldn't pass Finn to get to me.

After that night, Finn was gone.

I blink to stop my tears from falling and flex my feet under the sheets, focusing on my calf muscles tightening and releasing. I can't close my eyes because it'll make the memories bigger, so I stare at the ceiling and count my breaths. In for four. Hold for seven. Out for eight. Over and over, waiting for my heart rate to ease, my throat to open, and the panic to recede. Only tonight, it doesn't.

I curl into my pillow, letting the tears fall silently at first. There's something cathartic about the feel of them on my cheeks, trailing along my nose, dripping onto the sheets, and soon I can't help the small sobs that catch in my throat or the trembling in my body. It's been years since I've cried like this, and now I've done it twice in three days. I was never comfortable being vulnerable around Chip. I knew on some level I was safest when I was small and silent, not falling apart and practically begging for someone to help put me back together. He got off on my fragility, and that scared me.

"Hey," Finn says, his voice soft and careful in the darkness. "Are you all right?"

I didn't even hear him climb the ladder over my weeping, which means I must have been louder than I realized. I sit up, sniffling into the baggy sleeve of Finn's flannel shirt. I borrowed another one from his closet even though there are pajamas among the things Violet brought me. It's soft and big and smells like him, and he hasn't asked me not to wear it, so I have to believe he's okay with it.

The *I'm fine* is on the tip of my tongue, but then I lift my head and see his formidable frame at the end of the bed, moonlight limning his beautiful body in a silver glow and my grandmother's deck of cards almost hidden in his hand. All I want is for him to take me in his arms the way he did my first day here. I want to be held while I cry and not worry that the person comforting me will hold my weakness against me someday.

I shake my head as a fresh wave of tears breaks over me. "No," I blubber. "I'm not."

He hesitates, his body weight shifting toward me almost imperceptibly, and I move the pillows to make it clear there's a space for him beside me. Still, he hesitates, brow creasing as his hand coasts through his hair.

"Just hold me for a few minutes," I say between disjointed inhales. "The way you did before. Please?"

Finn's shoulders rise and fall with a deep, defeated breath before he crawls onto the mattress beside me and pulls me down against his chest. The warmth of his skin and the protection of his arms are everything, and I come apart against him, crying until I've got no tears left to cry.

Soon my wails fade into whimpers, and then silence. I don't remember how we got here, but Finn is stroking my hair away from my hot, damp face, and I've wriggled so close that the covers are twisted between us. My legs are looped around his, and every inch of my body is pressed hard against him. My hands are tucked under my chin, Finn rests his head atop mine, and I focus on the steady rhythm of his heart beneath my cheek to restore my own breathing to something more regular. Gram's cards are on the nightstand.

Neither of us moves, even when I'm no longer crying, and I don't want this to end.

"Can we talk?" I ask.

"Talk?" he echoes.

One of us has to point out it's hardly professional for the two of us to be in bed together, but it's not going to be me. I prepare for him to say no, but to my relief, Finn relaxes beneath me and then sticks his other hand behind his head. His pose is effortlessly sexy, displaying the hard lines of his upper arms and chest and abdomen, body art flexing with his every breath. I glance down to where his legs are crossed at the ankle, his body a shaded figure of sexy ridges and valleys and ink. I try not to stare at the bulge in his underwear, but my eyes return to it over and over.

"Yeah," I say, breathless for reasons other than my recent breakdown. "Talk."

"Sure."

He waits for me to go on, but it takes me a moment to find the right place to start. Finally, I settle on a question that's always interested me. "Did you always want to join the military?"

His fingers grow still in my hair before he begins stroking again. "No."

It's not what I'm expecting, and the little glimpse into his head makes me want more. "So what did you want to be when you grew up?"

"I don't know."

"Really?" I ask. "You don't know?"

I shift my feet to try and cover them with the tangled covers, and Finn sits up a little to rearrange them over the lower half of our bodies before he returns to his position, scooping me close to him again.

"I..." Finn's tone drops, like he's thinking about the answer. "I didn't know at the time."

"What were you like as a kid? What were your favorite subjects at school?"

I glance up in time to see Finn's amused smile, small and subtle to match the guarded warmth in his eyes. "Rosie. I don't want to talk about me."

"Why not?"

"Because my life isn't very interesting."

I sigh and settle back against his chest. How can a man be so hard and distant but feel so warm and safe?

"I don't need you to be interesting," I tell him. "I need you to be real and honest. I need to talk about *life*." I stretch my toes beneath the sheets, comforted by the warmth generated by his body. "I made some choices today—big choices that are going to have even bigger consequences—but I'm wondering if I've forgotten why I got into this business in the first place. Why am I here? What am I doing?" I risk sliding a hand onto his stomach, noting the tension in his abs when I do. "I need a reminder of why music is my reason for existing."

The air between us fills with silence, and I'm about to give up on getting an answer when Finn's husky baritone rolls from his chest.

"I was an average kid," he says. "Average height. Average size. Average student. Average football player. I had interests, I suppose, but I was never good enough at anything to devote my life to it."

My disbelieving snort takes us both by surprise. "You're not average, Finn." I sweep my gaze over his half-naked form, painted and perfect. "I mean, *look* at you."

He chuckles lightly and his arm tightens around me. "I'm not fishing for compliments, Rosie. It is what it is, and I am who I am."

I give him a disapproving glare. "You're the last person I'd ever expect to have low self-esteem."

He huffs out another laugh. This one's dry. Maybe even a little sad.

"I've got a brother who's a professional hockey legend," he says. "Another who's been cooking five-star food since he was tall enough to look over a kitchen counter. My older sister has a brain big enough for both of us, and my baby sister spends more time riding horses than she does on her own two feet. I grew up surrounded by talent and passion and determination, so I know what purpose looks like when I see it. They all have it, and so do you. You're going through a rough patch right now. That's all. It'll pass."

It would be so easy to let him divert me, but he's starting to show a little of the man he is underneath the armor, and I don't want him to stop.

"Maybe you just haven't found your thing yet," I say. "We don't always know what lights us up when we're young. Sometimes we need to spend some time looking for it."

"Maybe you're right." Finn's voice drops. "And maybe there isn't a grand plan for everyone. No big purpose. Maybe some of us need to be satisfied with small wins when we can find them and be grateful for any old reason to get out of bed in the morning."

The soberness of his tone makes me want to wrap my arm around his waist the way his is looped around me. "I think that's true for all of us at one point or another. Purpose doesn't have to be large and sweeping. It can be quiet and slow and have the same impact or even greater. Take music, for instance. Sometimes a ballad I write in an afternoon and perform with a single instrument means more to me than a pop track I spend weeks, even months, trying to make perfect but somehow never sounds right."

Downstairs, Dakota snuffles and steps out of her bed, claws tapping on the hardwood before we hear her lapping from her water bowl.

"Or what about Dakota?" I add. "There's purpose in giving her a home and keeping her safe and nourished. Loved. She'd be lost without you."

Finn answers with an affectionate smile. "Yeah. She's a special girl."

A companionable hush falls as we listen to Dakota return to her bed. It reminds me that it's late, and I'm suddenly sleepy. I snuggle up against Finn, letting my dry eyes close a little.

"Maybe that's your answer," Finn murmurs.

I lift my lashes to look at him. "Hm?"

"The answer to your questions. Why are you here? What are you doing? Is music the thing that lights you up?" Finn turns his cognac gaze on me, and his attention is intense enough to stop my breath. "Maybe the answer is more of those ballads you write in an afternoon and perform with a single instrument and less of the songs that take weeks or months and never sound the way you want them to. Maybe your answer isn't to be bigger and louder and faster. Perhaps it's to go softer. Easier. Slower."

A warm curl of wishful thinking winds its way up from my stomach and takes root inside my chest, and I smile a dreamy kind of smile. "Softer. Slower. Easier."

"There you go," he whispers. "All lit up."

Finn studies me, and something tight and charged crackles between us. I'm too afraid to move because I know it'll be gone if I do, but I can't stop him from looking away. When he does, the tension snaps, leaving residue all around us in the unlit room.

"Maybe you're right," I say. "Do you know that I've spent the last ten years on the fast track to…? Gosh. I don't even know what the end point was supposed to be. I've been running as fast as I can to make more records, more sales, more money. I never considered it might be possible to put on the brakes. Chip never would have allowed it."

Finn grunts. "If doing what you want pisses off your asshole ex, then that's just icing on the cake."

I chuckle quietly and let my eyes drift closed again. "That's true."

"I should go before you fall asleep," he murmurs, but he doesn't move.

"Not yet," I reply. "Just a few more minutes. Please?"

"Okay," he whispers. "But just a few."

"Good night, Finn," I say, feeling easier and more hopeful than I have since I arrived. It's miraculous what a good cry and good man can do.

"Good night, Songbird," he says, or at least I think he does. I might already be dreaming.

TEN

Finn

I WAKE THE NEXT MORNING from the best sleep I've had in years, the familiar feel of my mattress beneath me, my pillow under my cheek, and the fragrance of Rosie's shampoo a sweet cloud around my head. I don't know how we got here, but we're spooning. She's curled up against my chest, tucked underneath my arm, and clutching my hand against her breasts even in sleep. She fits the shape of my body perfectly, as if sharing body heat for eight hours molded us into flawlessly fitted puzzle pieces.

I inhale deeply, committing the smell of her hair to memory.

I really should sneak out before she wakes up and realizes we unintentionally slept together, but I don't want to disturb her. She was a mess last night, and that kind of emotional processing is exhausting. Rosie needs to rest, and if the gentle pace of her pulse is anything to go by, she's still sound asleep.

I can stay a few minutes more if that's what she needs.

I let my eyes float closed, dozing and almost out again myself when Rosie stirs. Her grip on my hand tightens and her sigh is dreamy and disconnected. I smile softly to myself. But then she rolls her hips against me, and my eyes shoot open.

Fuck. *Fuck*.

Rosie's fingers twist in mine as she arches her back, lifting her ass and pressing against my thickening dick. I clench my jaw and try to shift my pelvis back, but she follows me, moaning softly as she seeks contact. This time, I remain still as stone as she rocks her pelvis, her hand gripping mine even harder, like she's trying to keep me close. I breathe through a groan, trying not to picture in too much detail how this would feel without all these clothes and covers between us.

Jesus Christ. I need to stop this before it goes too far.

I extricate my hand from her and gently slide my arm off her body, and the action is enough to jostle her out of sleep. She gasps, breath catching in her throat as she tenses beside me. Her ass is still soft and insistent against my dick, and she slowly shifts forward, like perhaps if she's subtle enough, I'll forget all about the recent grinding.

I put a little more space between us as she rolls to face me, her cheekbones alight with embarrassment and her bottom lip caught between her teeth.

"Sorry," she mumbles, her eyes dropping to the erection currently trying to bust out of my boxer briefs.

I quickly rearrange the covers to hide my boner. She's got nothing to be sorry about, but I don't want to make her more uncomfortable.

"Did you sleep okay?" I ask, thinking that she might prefer it if we pretend this never happened.

After an awkward silence, she sinks into her pillow with a soft smile, and the morning sun hits her hair to make it glow. "Better than okay. I don't think I've slept that well since... well, a long time. How about you?"

"Same," I admit. "I'm sorry. I should have sneaked away as soon as you were out, but I think I might have fallen asleep before you did."

"That's okay," she says. "No harm done. Right?"

The expectation in her eyes hints at her need for reassurance. "Right."

The room falls quiet, and I'm unable to look away from the openness in her gaze. My heart thuds at how beautiful it is, and when she rearranges herself under the covers, I'm reminded of the heat of her skin against mine, the way her fingers twisted in my hand like she was having a sex dream about me, and the agonizing temptation of her ass searching for my dick.

I clear my throat and stand in a hurry, collecting a sheet as I move and wrapping it around my waist to hide my rock-hard cock.

"I'm going to shower," I announce.

"Okay." Rosie's confusion lasts only a moment before she declares, "I'll make us breakfast."

Even that isn't enough to take the edge off my arousal, and I'm barely under the hot spray before my dick is in my hand. A dozen quick, rough pumps later, and I'm leaning against the wet wall, choking back a tortured groan as my orgasm paints the shower tiles. I can't breathe. I can't fucking *breathe*. Rosie has become the oxygen in my lungs, and she's got the power to take it away.

A little while later, after I've cleaned up and gotten dressed, and we're sharing another burned breakfast, I wonder how badly I've fucked up. Up until now, I've resisted the urge to think of Rosie when I come because I knew if I did it once, I'd want to do it again. And damn it if I didn't know how right I was.

ELEVEN

Finn

A FEW DAYS LATER, I'M STARTING to question whether there's a single competent security team available anywhere on the planet. At the dining table with my laptop open and the remains of another inedible breakfast on a plate beside the keyboard, I delete the most recent candidate profiles for Rosie's new personal bodyguard, hit "reply" to Drew's email, and tap out a frustrated message.

None of these are up to scratch. Put the last three together and we might have a half-decent option, and half decent isn't good enough. Sorry. We need to keep looking.

Drew's return email pops up almost instantly.

Noted, but I've exhausted my network and need to do more research. Give me a couple more days?

A couple more days with Rosie living in my shirts and sleeping in my bed. Can I do it? I grimace at the charred toast and bitter coffee, then glance at where she's curled around Dakota on the sofa, notebook and pencil in hand, soft blonde curls escaping the messy knot on her head and her forehead lined with concentration.

Take as long as you need.

"Hey, Rosie?"

She looks up from the notebook on her knees. "Yeah?"

I turn the laptop to face her, the screen opened to a new browser. "Did you want to use the computer today?"

She hasn't touched the thing for days, not since the afternoon she fired most of her team, then jumped naked into the lake. I keep waiting for her to snap into business mode and get on with taking back her career from Chip McFuckface Daniels. Instead, she spends every hour with her head over that notebook or strolling with Dakota around the perimeter of the cabin humming to herself or trying to earn her keep as a cook.

My groceries ran out this morning. Thank God.

"No, thanks," she says before returning to her writing.

Right.

I spin the computer back my way, open a new browser, and wade into the muck that is social media. Chip released a statement about the canceled wedding and there's a lot of online conversation about Rosie now. Articles about the cheating rumors. Headlines labeling her a runaway bride. Media statements from her former publicist, talent agent, and legal team. Even her former security company. Anyone bumped from Rosie's books has made some kind of comment about cutting ties with the pop princess, and most of them have thrown shade. It pisses me off until the comment sections make me sick.

Forcing myself to read the online vitriol makes me want to follow Rosie's lead and throw my computer in the lake. Why anyone would choose to put themselves in the public eye makes zero sense to me, but I grit my teeth and scroll through the results of my sixth keyword search, looking for suspicious patterns in the content and names on my watch list. For the first fifteen minutes it's more of the same, so when something new does pop up, I almost miss it. I scroll back up the page and screenshot the offensive comment wedged between a stream of opinions under an article about Rosie's alleged admission to a celebrity rehabilitation center. It's a statement from a user who in the last five days has more than earned his place as the reddest of red flags.

Mistr_ess_el.

Or as I read it: Mr. S. L. Stanley Lowe. Rosie's stalker. The guy we can't find. The loose cannon who adds creepy comments to posts about Rosie, and today there's more of the same.

Mistr_ess_el: You're so beautiful, Rosalie. So perfect. I love you and hate you at the same time. Why do you make it so hard for me to decide?

Mistr_ess_el: When will you be home, Rosalie? Where are you now?

Mistr_ess_el: I love you with those coral-colored lips, Rosalie. It's so powerful. So sexy. I think about your lips all the time.

I do this at least three times a day and I hate it. I add his latest efforts to a folder on my desktop and snap the laptop closed with a shudder.

I'm starting to think of how best to tackle the no-more-groceries problem when there's a tap on the cabin's door. Rosie pins me with a look that's more cautiously curious than panicked, and I like that the last few days of quiet and safety appear to have calmed her nerves a little. I set a finger to my lips to indicate she should be quiet, then cross the room and open the door.

"Good," says the person on the other side. "You're alive."

My sister Charles—Charlotte by birth, Charlie to everyone, and Charles to me—stands on the porch with a mildly amused, mildly frustrated expression. She's wearing blue jeans, tan boots, and a black collared shirt with the Silver Leaf Ranch & Vineyard logo embroidered on one side. It's what she always wears. Wouldn't be surprised if this one outfit was all the clothes in her closet.

"Yeah. Sorry. I've been... occupied."

"You've bailed on work every day for nearly a week, but can't give me a reason?"

"I texted you."

"Twice." She pulls her phone out of her back pocket and

waves it in my face. "Two vague texts and no replies to mine. I had to hire help to cover your share of the farm labor."

I grimace apologetically. Charles is CEO of the family business and runs its operations. I help with farm laboring, grape harvests, leading trail rides, general maintenance, and whatever needs doing. I love the place because it's home. Charles loves it because it's her life.

"You know this whole recluse-in-the-woods thing doesn't bother me so much when you're up at the main house every other day," she adds.

"Doesn't make me much of a recluse, then, does it?"

I step out onto the porch and close the door behind me, which makes Charles's eyebrows climb to her dark hairline. After ten years of military service and intense high-risk ops training to beat the weakness out of me, there's only one person who can read me these days, and that's my big sister. She always could.

"You're hiding something," she guesses. "Does it have anything to do with the silver Mercedes parked on the other side of the cabin?"

I glare her down, but she catches a twitch at the corner of my eye, and I'm not at all surprised when she gasps and weaves around me to peer through a curtained window.

"Finn Samuel Davenport," she gasps. "You've got a girl in there!"

I shake my head with a quiet groan, then pick her up by the waist and deposit her on the other side of me to put my body between her and the front door. "It's not what you think."

She crosses her arms and looks up at me with a twinkle in her bright blue eyes. "How do you know what I think?"

I pull her ponytail free to distract her—irritating her is just a bonus—and when she goes to retie it, I give the tip of her nose a flick. She drops her hair to swat at me, then scowls and starts again.

"Stay out of it," I tell her.

She stretches onto her tiptoes to try and peek around my shoulders. "Who is she?"

"She's nobody."

A warm flush burns across the back of my neck. Charles, being Charles, is waiting for it and it makes her grin like a loon. "Sure she is."

The front door squeaks as it swings on its hinges. I close my eyes and drop my head back with exhaustion. Why can't Rosie just do what she's told?

Rosie walks out onto the porch, Dakota close on her heels. Today, at least, she's wearing a pair of sweatpants and a simple tank from one of the bags Violet brought over, but she keeps wearing my flannel shirts over the top anyway, which is a bit of a mindfuck, to be honest. A man can't help but feel primal, even a little territorial, when a beautiful woman wears his shirt. My lizard brain hasn't caught on to the fact that this beautiful woman isn't actually mine.

Rosie extends a hand as she approaches. "Hi. I'm—"

"Rosalie Thorne." Charles accepts Rosie's hand with the kind of cheek-splitting smile that makes her look years younger. "I know. Nice to meet you."

"Nice to meet you too." There's an awkward pause before Rosie nudges me with a gentle elbow. "Aren't you going to introduce us?"

"I was hoping to avoid it."

Rosie and Charles hit the exact same pitch of indignation at the exact same time. "Finn!"

I roll my eyes. "Rosie—this is my sister, Charlotte."

Charles scowls at me. She hates being called Charlotte. I return her rage with a shit-eating grin.

"Charlie," she corrects. "You can call me Charlie."

Rosie's face lights up. "I will. Thank you. Do you want to come in?"

"No," I say at the same time Charles says, "Yes."

And then, of course, I follow them into the cabin.

Charles takes a seat on one sofa, Rosie on the other, and I protest the whole situation by returning to the dining table, forgetting myself long enough to take a swallow of bad coffee.

Hiding Rosie was supposed to last a few days and not involve anyone else or raise any questions I didn't want to answer. Violet finding out about us was one thing. My older sister is another, and all I can think is thank fuck it wasn't Daisy at the door.

Charles looks at me, notes my discomfort, and rolls her lips to stop a laugh. "So how do you two know each other?"

My flat stare only makes this more entertaining, apparently, and she gives up the fight altogether with a wide smile breaking across her face.

"I used to be Rosie's bodyguard," I say before Rosie has a chance. Might as well try to regain some control.

"*Bodyguard*?" Charles throws me a stunned look that makes me feel bad about keeping a secret from her. "When? How?"

"It was a favor to a military friend," I explain. "For two months when Rosie was on tour last year. Before I came home in June."

"Okay." Charles nods and then mutters like she's processing the information, "My brother is Rosalie Thorne's bodyguard."

The rest of it isn't my story to tell, and I exchange a look with Rosie that says *if you want me to shut this down, I will.* She replies with a slight shake of her head.

"Kind of." Rosie slides her hands under her thighs and curls in on herself. "I'm dealing with some stuff and needed a place to stay while I figured it out."

"And you came *here*?"

Charles's surprise is borderline offensive, and Rosie clears her throat to disguise her amusement. "I needed somewhere nobody would look for me," she explains. "Somewhere safe while I sorted out my life. It was only supposed to be for a day or two, but it's been nearly a week..."

"Things got a little complicated," I jump in. "Figuring it out is taking some time."

Charles crosses her legs one way, then the other. I rarely see her this fidgety. "I read about the wedding and all that," she admits.

Her confession surprises me. My sister isn't one for celebrity gossip, and she's usually too busy to see much anyway. "You did?"

"I didn't go looking for it," she says defensively before her voice falls apologetically. "But it's kind of hard to avoid."

Rosie mutters under her breath, but I'm pretty sure her words are "I bet."

"So you can understand why we need to keep this under wraps," I say. "Nobody knows Rosie's here, and it needs to stay that way."

"I spend all my time working and I've got nobody in my life to tell, but for what it's worth"—Charles mimes zipping her lips—"your secret is safe with me."

"Thank you." Rosie's voice is soft with genuine warmth. "I appreciate that."

It's hard to believe that after all she's been through, Rosie is willing to share so much with a new person so quickly. It was the same with Violet, though I chalked that up to them having already established a professional relationship. I wonder if this might be part of the reason for Rosie's heartache. She believes too easily and opens up too readily. Charles might have won Rosie's trust because she's my sister, but Rosie is vulnerable for reasons other than her stature and her money and public profile. She's got no walls. She holds nothing back.

She assumes the best in others because there's only good in her, and that's not how the world works. Rosie's vulnerability is a bullseye on her back, and nothing tempts bad guys like an easy target. She needs a protector, but why the hell am I suddenly so sure that protector needs to be me?

I've tuned out the quiet hum of the girls' conversation, but it starts playing in high definition when Charles says, "Why don't you borrow one of Finn's? He's got three of them. He plays all the time."

Rosie straightens in her seat, eyes blinking with disbelief. "He does?"

Uh... *what?*

Both women turn their heads in unison so perfect they might have rehearsed it. Charles hits me with a look of exasperation, like there's any sane reason I would tell a global music icon I can hold a guitar, and Rosie with pleasant surprise.

"Is it true, Finn?" Rosie asks. "Do you play the guitar?"

I scowl at my sister. "I don't play *all the time*, but yes, I do play."

Charles hums with satisfaction before she smacks her hands on her thighs and pushes to her feet. "On that note— I'm going to go. It was nice to meet you, Rosalie."

"You too. And thanks, Charlie."

Charles crosses the room, smirking at how clever she thinks she is, and I retaliate by pulling out her ponytail again as I see her out the door.

"Will you stop that?" she hisses as she swats at my hand.

"Will you mind your own business?" I retort, pushing her out onto the porch.

"I always do." Charles pauses with one foot on the top porch step as she reties her ponytail. "But if Rosalie Thorne wants to talk music with you, then you should talk music. If I can't convince you that it's something worth pursuing, maybe Rosalie can."

I snort. "You've got a funny way of minding your own business."

"Fine. Fine!" She raises her palms in surrender. "I won't say another word about music or Rosalie or any of it, but just so you know, Daisy's got some busy days on the trails lined up later this week. She's going to need your help with the horses."

I rub the back of my neck, thinking about my baby sister and her big, fat mouth. "Think you can cover for me for a few more days? Keep her out of my hair?"

Charles shakes her head as she skips down the steps. "Fine, but you owe me, Finn."

"Thanks. Oh, and hey," I call before she gets too far. "Can you organize some groceries for us? I can't leave Rosie alone and she can't go out in public right now."

"What do you need?"

I wince at the thought of Rosie trying to make anything more complicated than cereal. Maybe I can convince her to let me take care of dinners at least. "I'll text you a list."

I hesitate before heading back inside, preparing myself to dodge whatever questions Rosie's going to ask about my collection of guitars and the revelation that I can play them, but it turns out I don't need to worry. She's in the middle of the room bouncing on her bare toes and the first question out of her mouth has nothing to do with me or my secrets.

"Where are they?" she asks. "Can I see them? Can I borrow one? Please? I'd appreciate it so much, Finn. I'm desperate to play."

None of her gentle curiosity? Good. It's better this way.

"Yeah, of course. I didn't mention them earlier because—"

Because *why*? I didn't want to deal with the hail of questions that I thought they'd set off. I was too busy avoiding difficult conversations. I didn't think about what these instruments might mean to Rosie, so I kept my stupid mouth shut.

Pissed at myself for being a self-centered moron, I jerk my head toward the loft. "Never mind. They're up there."

Rosie follows me up to the bedroom, and I open the long walk-in closet. It doubles as storage, and I go to the freestanding cupboard on the back wall. Inside are three acoustic guitars stored in hard leather cases leaning upright, side by side.

She makes a strangled sound of excitement as she claps her hands, and I can't help my smile. I pass her the first case, then pick up the other two. "Come on. I'll show you what I've got."

I set my cases on the floor by my bed, then relieve Rosie of hers and lay it on top of the covers. Inside is a 1970s Gibson Hummingbird in excellent condition.

Rosie reaches out to caress the gleaming wood. "It's beautiful, Finn. It must be—what? Fifty years old?"

"About that," I agree. "I don't play it much other than to tune it occasionally. It belonged to my mom."

Her head turns sharply. "Your mother was a musician?"

With a sentimental expression, I recall a memory of my mom in our old living room with this guitar on her lap, ink on her fingers, and a rainbow of dried acrylic staining her clothes. "A musician. A poet. A painter. A sculptor. Jacqueline Davenport tried just about everything. She had what my dad called a creative spirit."

Rosie brushes her fingers over the guitar again as she shares my wistful smile. "She sounds wonderful."

I close the case and secure the clasps. "She was."

Setting aside the first guitar, I lift the second one onto the bed and open its case. A vintage Martin lies cushioned inside.

Rosie's hand darts out to reverently stroke the strings. "This is a serious instrument."

"I saved for months to buy this in high school. I visited the store every other day to check that nobody had bought it while I was waiting to get the money together, and I was fourteen when I finally had enough to bring it home."

I heave it out of its case and hand it to her, looping the strap around her neck, and Rosie spares me a speculative head tilt as she accepts the guitar with the familiarity of someone who lives with an instrument in her hands. She immediately strums a smooth note. Then another. She plays eight bars of an unrecognizable melody before she unloops the strap and hands the guitar back to me as she nods toward the final case.

"What about that one?"

"Best for last?" I tease as I stow the Martin and exchange it for the final guitar. I open it and grin at Rosie's excited inhale at the deep, dark wood of the near-new Taylor GS Mini.

"I can't believe you have this," she says as she helps herself. "I play mine all the time." I stand back and watch the delight dance across her features. "It's not really your style," she adds as she tests the strings.

"It was a gift," I explain, "from a friend who thought it might be good to play on the road, but I struggled with the narrow fingerboard and never used it much."

Rosie plays the same eight bars as before, though they sound a little different on the smaller instrument. Higher. Prettier. A little more country. The difference appears to please her, because as the final note fades, she turns her eager eyes on me. "Do you mind if I borrow it? I can sit out on the porch and play for a while. It'll hardly bother you at all."

I nudge aside a hint of disappointment and remind myself it's better if Rosie isn't full of questions about my mom and my teenage years and the person who gifted me the guitar in her hands. There's nothing in my past worth dragging into my future. Especially music.

"It's no bother," I tell her as I reach for the instrument.

She hands it over, then climbs down the ladder, and I pass it down to her once she's at the bottom. Rosie scoops up her notepad and pen on the way to the front door, and Dakota throws me an almost apologetic look as she follows our guest out to the porch swing.

Less than sixty seconds after the screen door swings closed behind her, the uplifting notes of Rosie's playing float toward me on a breeze of warm air. Her voice dances above the music—a strong soprano that vibrates with vulnerability but also hope and determination and relief that she's finally doing what she was born to do.

She sounds like a songbird at sunrise and damn it if it doesn't make me feel things.

I return the other guitars to the closet, and while I'm in there, I dig around in my overstuffed dresser for the fat notebook buried in the bottom drawer. With one ear on the music playing in stop-starts on the porch, I sink onto the edge of the bed, flip open the tattered book, and thumb through the pages.

Music. Lyrics. Poems. Ideas. Things to remember. Things I don't want to forget. Page after page of nothing special. Nothing important. Nothing worthwhile. Page after page of everything that's ever meant anything to me.

When I reach the end, I close the book and return it to its hiding place. Then I go and sit at the dining table and pretend to work while I listen to Rosie strumming her guitar and singing on the porch.

TWELVE

Rosie

I'VE TRIED HARD NOT TO become a caricature of celebrity or a stereotypical pop diva. I never wanted a reputation for being selfish and self-absorbed, or unapproachable and ungrateful, or out of touch with the people who made it possible to do what I do and have what I have.

I grew up with next to nothing. My grandmother raised me on love and a veteran's pension in a two-bedroom trailer just outside of Nashville. We didn't have a lot, but I remember being happy, and I like to think I'm still her little girl on the inside, even when the outside looks very different. I have a driver and security, and I always get the best table at restaurants. I have no privacy, and I can't walk down the street without being mobbed, but designers throw clothes at me, and I've got a five-figure monthly budget for skincare alone. My nails are

"

always polished. My hair is always colored and styled. I have a personal trainer and a private chef, a stylist and a beauty team. A yoga instructor who comes by five times a week to run classes in my own studio at home. Gram's old trailer would be dwarfed by the master suite in my LA house, but looking the way I do and living how I live are part of my brand. They're things I've had to come to terms with.

But money does funny things to people, both those who have it and those who want it, and I've spent nearly a decade having everyday obstacles removed from my path before I'm forced to overcome them myself. I'm used to getting what I want, and in lots of ways my life is easy, which means it's easy to get lost in it. Not the money so much, but what the money enables me to do.

It makes it possible for me to not have to think about anything else while I'm writing or recording or performing. I can tune out the world, be absorbed in my art, and forget that anything else exists outside my own imagination. When my head is filled with poetry and chord progressions and arrangements instead of worries and fears and memories that make me ache, I actually *want* to be there. When I'm creating, every other noise cuts out like someone flipped a switch. I've heard some people call it flow, but to me it's like a vortex or a parallel universe. Some undefinable magic that makes it possible to leave all the bad stuff behind and just be *me*.

So when I raise my head from Finn's guitar and let my eyes pan up from its glossy body and steel strings, over the worn whitewashed boards of the rear porch and past Dakota's sleeping form, to the river sparkling in the distance and the sun almost touching the horizon, I've got no idea what day it is, or what time, or how long I've been sitting outside writing and playing. There's a plate of half-eaten toast and a mug of half-finished honey-lemon tea on the table beside me, but I don't remember consuming either, let alone making them. There's a light cotton blanket over my knees and a bottle of water close at hand, next to a stack of sharpened pencils, a brand-new notebook, and a pile of pale pink picks, and I've got no idea where any of it came from. I've lost my bearings completely.

I push the blanket to one side, and taking care not to wake Dakota, I move into the house. It's quiet and shows no sign of Finn, but the sight of the kitchen makes my stomach rumble, and I realize I'm hungry.

The fridge, which was all but empty the last time I opened it, is stuffed with groceries. I check the pantry and it's the same there, almost overflowing with food. The living room, where Finn has been sleeping every night since I humiliated myself by behaving like a cat in heat, is neat as a pin, with Finn's pillows and blankets folded and stacked at the end of the sofa and Gram's playing cards set atop those. The windows are thrown open and a gentle breeze ruffles the patch-covered curtains. There are even fresh-cut flowers in a glass jar on the coffee table. It feels so homey and complete that I wrap my arms around myself and let the gratitude roll over me in a wave.

Good fortune comes in lots of different packages, and the best of them don't cost a single dime.

I'm checking the date on Finn's open laptop—it's been two days since he gave me his guitar, even though it's impossible that so much time has passed—when a tough grunt floats in through a window. I cross the space to peek outside, then duck behind the curtain before Finn notices me.

My stomach tightens as I nudge the curtain aside and watch with a careful eye. Finn is in the front yard with a shovel, cutting into the ground along a path he's mapped out with stakes and pieces of string, tossing loads of dirt onto a growing mound of earth behind him. He's sweaty and shirtless, his tattoos dusted with dirt, the tops of his shoulders pink from an afternoon in the sun, the muscles in his arms flexed and quivering.

Finn is the kind of beautiful that makes you look twice. He turns and slams the shovel into the soil, his slick back undulating and his ass tensing under his jeans as he sets his boot and heaves his body weight to slice into the ground. His blond hair falls across his forehead, and he sweeps it back with a rough hand that leaves behind a line of dirt on his cheek.

I've been writing about Finn today, lyrics and compositions that practically pen themselves, and it's been confronting to see the degree to which he manifests in my music. I didn't start out with Finn as my muse. My first few tracks were introspective, angry and cathartic, pop-rock female rage anthems spilling onto the page in an exorcism of the pain and frustration I've kept bottled up for years. And while I'm nowhere near done unpacking all the ways Chip has hurt me, the baggage I *have* unpacked has somehow made space for other sensations, emotions, and desires.

I watch Finn work and marvel at how he manages to pull off the right amount of arrogance, like he knows what he's got and what he's worth and has nothing to prove, and while he'd never go looking for trouble, he can take care of it if he needs to. There's something about him that feels dangerous. It was there when I met him a year ago and even here at home, where he should be more relaxed, it exudes from him in waves.

I don't even notice my breath coming faster until a throb between my legs makes my underwear damp, and I jump back from the window like I've been caught doing something bad. What kicked off in bed with Finn the other morning has grown more intense after a few days with my guitar, and having a place to feel safe and emotionally unfettered has freed something else that's been repressed for too long. My need for sex.

It's been a long time since I was this turned on by a man, and I'd eventually decided I wasn't wired that way. I'd only ever been with one man, and any attraction I used to feel for Chip was long gone, waning as the anxiety of being with him increased until sex became a task I performed only when he wanted it. He hadn't made a move in the bedroom in at least three months, and in our six years together, he never bothered to make me come. Ever.

Unable to resist one last peep around the curtain, I bite my lip at the sweat dripping from his chiseled chest and remember my dream about sinking my nails into his inked biceps. There's no doubt in my mind that Finn's cockiness works just as well in the bedroom as it does out. He would never leave a woman unsatisfied.

After a quick change into yoga pants and a black tank, then a visit to the bathroom to brush my teeth and comb my hair, I spot a second mason jar of flowers, this one a spray of pink and purple wildflowers. They're so simple and thoughtful, and I'm suddenly awash with shame. I wanted to be a good house guest, and instead I've behaved like a spoiled child who expects to be waited on hand and foot.

With a renewed determination to do something to repay Finn's generosity, I raid the kitchen for what I need to make my grandmother's baked rice pudding. I haven't eaten it in years—all that milk and sugar placed it in the *practically poison* column of Chip's nutrition plan—but I always watched when Gram made it and I'll never forget the recipe. It was her favorite dessert, and nothing says *home* to me like a bowl of her pudding with peaches and cream.

Once the dish is in the oven and I've set the timer, I dig out my sneakers and head outside. Finn's so engrossed in his work that I'm standing there for three whole minutes, admiring him close up and feeling all warm and tingly, before he notices me.

"Oh, hey." He plants the shovel in the ground and leans on the handle. "Did you need something?"

I cross my arms under my breasts. "I'm sorry I've been checked out the last few days. I haven't cooked or cleaned up after myself or done any of the things good guests are supposed to do. It happens sometimes when I'm writing. I zone out completely and forget anyone else exists. But that's no excuse, and I apologize."

Finn drops his head to one side and squints at me. "Why are you sorry for doing your job?"

"I…" I frown and think about his question. "I don't know."

"You don't need to explain yourself to me—or to anyone. You know that, right?"

I lick my lips and look around the yard to disguise my disorientation. Why *do* I feel guilty for writing? "I feel bad about the way I've behaved. I didn't mean to ignore you."

Finn's smile is small, a little crooked, and a lot sexy. "I appreciate it, Rosie, but I don't need it. My ego isn't so fragile that I can't handle a couple days of distracted silence or a few extra dirty dishes. And even if it were, you're not responsible for managing my emotions. That's up to me, and I guarantee you, I can handle it."

His words float in the air like dandelion fluff, ethereal until they stick to my skin with the sharp pangs of understanding.

"Chip liked it when I said sorry," I say. "He was always pointing out my selfish behaviors and making me feel guilty for things I didn't mean to do. I apologized to keep him happy and so I could feel safe. You know… emotionally."

Finn's jaw hardens and his fingers tighten around the

handle of his shovel, heaving it out of the ground before he closes the distance between us.

"You don't need to worry about being safe with me," he says, towering over me with eyes that burn with ferocity. "Emotionally or otherwise. Okay?"

I hold my head back to meet his stare, breathing deeply at his proximity. He smells real, like earth and hard work, and his eyes are fevered as they trace the lines of my face. He's so big and so close, and it sets heat thrumming everywhere.

"Okay," I whisper.

He holds my gaze a heartbeat longer, hand flexing on the shovel handle like he wants to toss it away, before he breaks the tension with a sharp nod and a step backward. "Good."

My heart flutters unevenly, and I attempt to regain a little control with a casual thumb toward the house. "So... I just put some food in the oven and wanted to offer you my help with the, um..." I gesture at the mud. "Gardening."

He cocks an eyebrow, caramel eyes glinting with amusement. "You want to help me dig?"

As soon as he says it, I hear how ridiculous it sounds, but the suggestion that I can't do something only makes me more determined to try. It's digging. How hard can it be?

Finn swipes at his eyes, apparently to wipe away dust and sweat, but his large hand hides a smile, and what I catch of it makes my pulse flicker. It also makes me lift my chin.

"Where do I start?"

Finn shakes his head as if to say *you're the boss* as he hands me his shovel. "We're excavating to a depth of around five inches," he says. "You shovel out the loose dirt here, and I'll cut the last few feet of this section."

"No problem."

I accept the shovel and pretend to know what I'm doing while Finn retrieves another shovel from a collection of supplies stacked neatly against the cabin.

Turns out scooping dirt and transferring it from one spot to another isn't exactly easy.

The first load is too heavy, and I struggle to balance it. The next is lighter than I realize, so when I misjudge the strength needed to throw it back, my toss sends clods of earth careening through the air. I dart a few sheepish looks at Finn to see if he notices, but he's concentrating on his own stretch of the path.

Even though I get the hang of things after a dozen or so practices and I'm no weakling—I do forty-five minutes of weight training four times a week—within twenty minutes I feel the strain in my shoulders and thighs, my hands sting with the threat of blisters, and I'm covered in a light sheen of perspiration. Okay, so digging is hard.

I'm hefting up another loaded shovel when Dakota pads around from the rear of the wraparound porch and plants her butt at the top of the steps. After she calls to him with a series of woeful little whines, Finn tosses aside his shovel and strides over to meet her.

He stops at the bottom of the steps and sets his fists on his hips. "You can come down on one condition," he tells her.

Dakota wags her tail, tongue lolling.

"Stay out of the mud." Finn points to the pile of dirt, then shakes his finger under her nose. "No. Mud. You got that?"

Dakota barks once, her head jerking in what strikes me as an agreeable nod, and I decide in an instant that I love her.

"I mean it," he warns again, like he doesn't believe her. "No dirt diving."

Dakota barks again, squirming and wiggling with excitement.

"All right, then." Finn climbs the steps and lifts her heavy body into his arms. "As long as we understand each other."

The second Finn sets the dog on her paws, she takes off at full speed, throws her ungainly bulk into the air, and plows into the mound of dirt. I don't know what's funnier: Dakota deliberately disobeying orders or Finn's fatigued moan, like he knew this was going to happen. Either way, I laugh. Loudly.

"You think this is funny, do you?" Finn asks, his eyes flitting once to me and away again as he stalks Dakota, his steps low and stealthy.

"I think it's hilarious," I correct with another delighted chuckle.

Dakota zooms around the far side of the pile and leaps into it again, and Finn scowls. "I knew she was going to do this," he mutters.

"So why did you let her off the porch?"

He rolls his eyes and rounds the dirt pile, trying to get to Dakota from a better angle. "Because I'm a weak-ass dog-dad, that's why."

Oh my God. I rest my fingers on my throat, checking that I'm still alive as my body swoons.

Dakota's filthy now and totally loving life. She rolls one way, then the other, bathing in the dirt, twisting and tossing and burying herself deeper. She's got one eye on Finn, luring him in with apparent defeat before dodging his grasp at the very last moment over and over. Finally, Finn makes a frustrated leap for her, but she's too fast, and he lands face down in the dirt just as Dakota bolts into the trees.

"I'll get her!" I cry before I take off at a run.

"Damn it," Finn curses, and a moment later I hear his foot falls behind me as he follows me into the woods. "Rosie?" he shouts. "Come back!"

His voice triggers my instinct to run, and maybe I should slow down but I don't. I can still see Dakota's coat flashing between the trees in the distance, and I don't want to lose her, plus the sound of Finn gaining on me only makes me move faster. I want to test him. Tease him. See what will happen when he catches me.

My heart hammers in my chest. I've never felt alive like this. Free, flying, and safe to chase the high of a little danger without being afraid for my life. I don't realize I'm laughing until I hear the echo of it in the air, and the sound pushes my soul even higher.

Dakota makes a sharp right turn and I follow her, weaving between the trees as we round our way in an arc back toward the cabin. I can sense Finn gaining on me and I know no matter how hard I pump my legs, his are longer. It's only a matter of time before he gets me.

I'm still taken by surprise when his hard arm wraps around my waist, and he lifts me clear off the ground. I shriek and squeeze my eyes closed as he spins me around once, then twice. Dirt and leaves crunch under his feet and my back presses against his hard, hot chest until we've slowed enough that he can set me down without both of us tumbling to the ground.

When he does release me, it's against a tree trunk, and he cages me in with his hands set above my head and his heaving, sweaty body crowding me against the rough bark.

I'm laughing, trying to catch my breath, when an amused smirk lifts his mouth, and I become extra aware of the way my heart speeds up. He's filthy, covered in dirt and sweat, and it's so damn sexy.

"You think you can fly from me, Songbird?" he asks quietly before he slips a hand behind my head and presses me harder against the tree. His entire body is up against mine with a hard kind of heat that makes it impossible to think. His thumb sweeps up over the pulse in my neck, across my jaw, and over my cheekbone, leaving a silty trail of dirt on my skin.

I tip my head back to meet his eyes, my heart fluttering in the hollow of my throat. "I think it's fun to try."

His full mouth twitches into a crooked smile and he dips his head closer—close enough that I can see all the individual flecks of gold in his caramel-colored eyes.

"You're so fucking beautiful," he murmurs, brow furrowing as if my face tortures him.

I swallow and watch his mouth as it inches toward my upturned lips. *Kiss me*, I beg silently. *Please, Finn. Put your mouth on me.*

I don't know where his breath ends and mine begins when an urgent, high-pitched screeching of an alarm pierces the air. We both startle, and Dakota bolts back through the trees, barking and tossing her head. Finn jerks away from me like the warning is meant for him.

I run a nervous hand over my hair and try to regain my balance with a glance in the direction of the screeching. "What is that noise?"

"It sounds like the smoke alarm," Finn says, "but—"

"Oh no!" I catch his eyes with a horrified look. "The pudding!"

It takes him less than a heartbeat to understand the danger. Then hhe grabs my hand and takes off at a run. He shortens his stride so I can keep up with him, but I run as fast as I can, terrified that I've burned down Finn's home. The cabin his parents built. My refuge. The place I'm starting to wish I never had to leave.

Finn's hand is large and warm, his skin worn and rough, and I wish I could enjoy feeling it wrapped around mine, but

I'm too anxious to get back to the cabin. Chasing Dakota didn't lead us too far in the other direction, and all my weaving around trees hasn't messed with Finn's bearings, so the way he leads me back only takes a minute or two. When we burst into the clearing with Dakota yapping at our heels, I'm relieved to see there's no smoke in the air, but the sound of the alarm is louder and more insistent, so I don't assume we're out of danger just yet.

Finn rushes up the porch steps, dragging me behind him, and throws open the front door. The cabin is hazy and smoke seeps from the oven in thin, gray vines. I blink at the sting in my eyes and cover my mouth to filter the smell, but Finn bolts to the kitchen, flings open the oven door, and grabs a nearby dish towel to pull the baking pan off the metal rack.

I hang back, embarrassed and guilty, as he drops the dish into the sink and then pushes open the nearest windows. Taking the hint, I hurry to the opposite side of the cabin and open the windows there too, while Finn flips on the ceiling fan. When every door and window in the cabin is opened and the smoke starts to drift away, Finn climbs up onto a dining chair and switches off the blinking smoke alarm. The silence afterward is loud in comparison.

"I'm so sorry, Finn," I say. "I wanted to do something nice for you. It's my grandmother's favorite and the only thing I know how to make." I rub my eyes and hope he assumes my tears are due to the smoke. "I guess it's not as foolproof as I thought."

"Hey." Finn's big hands land on my shoulders and he pulls me against his bare chest so he can envelop me in his arms. "It's okay. It could have happened to anyone."

"I doubt it."

He gives me a small smile. "Okay. Maybe not *anyone.*"

I laugh through my tears, but both cut out completely when Finn drops a casual kiss on my forehead.

"And I'm as much to blame as you are," he says, like he doesn't even realize he's done it. "I shouldn't have let Dakota near all that dirt. Rolling in mud always gets her riled up. We'd have been here to take your dessert out of the oven if we weren't playing games in the trees."

"Right," I agree absently, resisting the urge to brush my fingers over the spot where his mouth landed on my head. "Thanks, Finn."

He releases me and glances out the front door, where the instigator waits for her ride at the base of the porch steps. Finn goes out to get her, but when she pads inside, nose wriggling, she gives us a single disapproving sneeze, turns, and heads straight out again.

Finn lets her go with a weary sigh. "Troublemaker," he mutters with affection before he turns to me. "I'm going to head out and finish digging out that path. Did you want to join me or go back to your writing?"

"I can help a little while longer," I say. "If you want me to?"

He sweeps his arm toward the open door. "After you."

Dakota is sprawled on the porch swing, her paws and

muzzle caked with dirt, and she watches us pass her with a disinterested gaze. Back at the scene of her crime, Finn passes me a shovel with a murmured warning and the hint of a teasing gleam in his eyes.

"Just try and get the dirt *on* the pile this time, all right?"

That secretive little smile, like the world entertains him in ways nobody else bothers to notice, plays on his lips. My cheeks heat with embarrassment, but I don't care. How is it possible that I've spent two days lost in my music and when I reemerge, feeling stronger and more myself than I ever have, I discover Finn's experienced a transformation too?

We work together until the sun goes down. Well, Finn works. I'm so preoccupied by the shape of his muscles and the lightness in my chest that by the time we go inside, I haven't helped at all. But I do have the inspiration I need to write another song.

THIRTEEN

Finn

AS TEMPTING AS IT IS to imagine Rosie not having anything to wear beneath my shirts at night, eventually we need to do laundry. I usually take a bagful up to the main house once a week, but there's no way I can leave Rosie at the cabin to do that, and the house is never empty, so I can't sneak her in with me, but there is an alternative.

Rosie's on my laptop when I step out of the bathroom, two bags of dirty laundry clutched in one fist. It's the first time she's opened the computer in days, and I wonder if she's reviewing the bodyguard applications I shared last night. There are three of them, and if she approves any, I'll be out of a job. Again. But maybe that's best.

My thoughts and feelings about Rosie are more complicated today than they were yesterday, and if things continue between us the way they have been, tomorrow's only going to be worse. She's beautiful. She's smart and so incredibly strong. She's funny, and she's got a kind of tenacity I find attractive, like she'll try anything once and isn't too proud to try again to get it right. Her voice—fuck me, her *voice*. It's this bewitching mix of vulnerable and powerful that reaches into my heart and picks at its carefully stitched seams. And every space is starting to smell like her. The blankets on the couch, the towels in the bathroom. The air itself is laced with the fragrance of her soap and her body lotion and *her*. I'm not thinking clearly, and if there's one thing a bodyguard needs, it's a straight head.

I almost kissed her. That's how close I am to losing control. I need Rosie to leave while I still have the strength to let her go, and before I mess up badly enough that it puts her safety at risk.

"Hey." I stand on the other side of the kitchen table and lift the bags into the air. "Feel like a field trip?"

It takes Rosie a moment to pull her eyes from the laptop screen, and when she does, she snaps it closed like she's relieved to be free of it.

"A field trip?" She sits up straighter and anticipation makes her eyes gleam. "Where?"

"You need clean clothes. I need clean clothes. It's time to do laundry."

"Laundry," she echoes, and I get the impression she's just given herself a one-word pep talk because she bounds to her feet with more enthusiasm than anyone has ever felt for washing clothes. It's cute. "Let's do it."

While she laces up her sneakers, I find an old baseball cap to cover her hair. It's too big, and I adjust the strap at the back while she waits patiently with her back to me. When she passes me at the open front door, I land a little love tap on her ass, high and tight underneath her yoga pants. It just happens, like I've got a right to do it. Like I've done it a thousand times before. Like Rosie is my girlfriend.

"Sorry," I mutter, hoping she doesn't notice the heat in my neck as I heft the bags down to the bed of my truck. "I didn't mean to... I mean... Shit. Can we forget I did that?"

She laughs as I open her door, and she hops up into the passenger seat. "I don't know. Can we?"

By the way she sneaks glances at me under the brim of her cap, lush lips pressed together like she's fighting a smile, I can guarantee she's not going to forget it anytime soon, and all I can think is *good*. I don't want her to forget it. Wherever she is, whatever she's doing, I hope Rosie thinks about my palm landing on her ass all the damn time.

I guide my old truck over the interior off-road trails that crisscross Silver Leaf, passing acres of vineyards and avoiding the stables in case Daisy is around, toward Chord's house. It's empty most of the year, but definitely now while my brother preps for Cup playoffs. I've got the entry code because I sometimes use his home gym, and he won't mind my using his other facilities just this once.

I pull the truck up to his place, an impressive architecturally designed two-story building with a wraparound porch all clad in white and natural stone. Rosie gapes out the windshield, craning her neck to get a better look at the house's façade as I round the hood and open her door.

"It's gorgeous," she says as she exits the vehicle with a delicate hop. "Who lives here?"

"Chord and Violet, but don't worry. They're not here, so we have the place to ourselves. Let me show you around first, then we'll come back and get the laundry."

I don't have to hold her hand—in fact I probably shouldn't—but after how natural it felt when we ran through the trees yesterday, I want her fingers entwined with mine. And with the way this woman tangles my thoughts, it's too easy to justify handholding as another form of protection. It keeps her close, therefore holding her hand is doing my job. But when I slip my palm against hers to lead her up to the double front doors, Rosie hisses quietly.

"What's wrong?" I ask with concern.

"Nothing." She pulls away from my grasp, but at the wince of pain around her eyes, I turn over her hand to see what she's hiding.

"Blister," she confesses as soon as I spot the tender pink circle on her skin. "I used to get them occasionally playing the guitar, but it's been a while. I guess I'm not accustomed to manual labor."

My chuckle mingles with a sympathetic sigh, and I take her other hand in mine instead. "Yeah. That looks like it hurts. Let's go inside and I'll take care of it."

I punch the access code into the security panel and at the green-lit click-and-beep, I push open the door and lead Rosie into the expansive hardwood foyer with its oversized winding staircase. There's a study to one side and a living area off the other, where sunlight streams through floor-to-ceiling windows and bounces off warm white walls. I have every intention of giving her the grand tour, but first we go to the enormous kitchen where Chord keeps a first aid kit. I locate it in the sixth cupboard I open, then set it on the counter next to the sink.

Rosie's in the adjoining dining area admiring the furniture, and I give her a minute to complete a circuit of the space before calling, "Hey. Come here a sec."

When she reaches me, I wrap my hands around her waist and hoist her up onto the counter. Nudging her knees wide so I can get in close, I hold her wound under a gentle stream of cold water from the faucet.

"Does that hurt?" I ask.

"No." Her eyes flit from her hand to my face. "It feels good."

I wash the wound with a little soap, using the pad of my thumb in light circles on the spot of delicate skin. The motion makes me think of other ways I'd like to use my thumb, and with her thighs opened to me on the counter like this, I swallow hard as my dick swells. Rosie is very still and very quiet as I rinse her hand, then dry it with a clean towel.

The energy between us thickens, the air quiet and crackling, and I pretend not to notice the gentle lean of her face toward mine. Fuck, I want to kiss her so badly, but I'm scared to cross that line. It's stupid, I know, because I'm already walking it like a tightrope, but there's still space to take a step back. If I kissed her? Retreat would be impossible—if it didn't kill me.

I apply a little antiseptic to her wound, and when it's covered in a small Band-Aid, I lift Rosie onto the floor and put a respectful distance between us.

"Thank you," she says.

"You're welcome." I clear the husky arousal from my voice with a quiet cough. "Let me show you around."

I take her hand again, loosely catching my fingers in hers so her palm is clear, and it's not until we finish a circuit of the ground floor and enter the master bedroom upstairs that her hand falls from mine.

She floats across the soft white carpet toward the glass wall in wonder. "This whole house is gorgeous," she says, "but *this* is unbelievable."

I open the doors and we step onto Chord's balcony, complete with deep outdoor sofas around a sunken fire pit, a hot tub in the corner, and the most spectacular view over Silver Leaf and Sonoma Valley beyond. Rosie's expression is one of wonder as she trails her fingertips along the balustrade and absorbs the never-ending horizon. Lush vineyards turn to patchwork fields that bleed into indigo mountains and a cornflower sky, and all I can look at is her.

"Yeah," I agree. "I can't quite believe it either."

Her gaze moves to mine before her lashes drop, and my stomach falls with them. This is why the line needs to exist. Rosalie Thorne is too beautiful, too talented, and too important to involve herself with someone as insignificant as me. She belongs in a house like this with a man like my brother who can give her everything she deserves. She's too big to live small and she knows it, because when all this is over, and she doesn't need me anymore—and that moment will come sooner than I want it to—she'll return to her world, and I'll remain in mine. Rosie will fly away and forget me, and I'll grow old remembering the handful of days I almost had it all.

"Let's get those clothes in the machine," I say gruffly. "And then I'll show you the pool."

Rosie follows me back out to the front drive, this time taking my hand before I get a chance to hold hers, and guilt thickens my throat at how much I like it. She doesn't let go when I haul the bags out of the truck, and she's still hanging on when we take the stairs down to the basement, passing through Chord's impressive home gym to the white marble laundry room on the other side. She finally relinquishes my fingers when I hand her the bag of laundry that belongs to her, and then I do the gentlemanly thing and turn my back to give her privacy to sort her lingerie.

"Hey, Finn?" she asks as I'm stuffing everything I have into one of four machines. Why my brother owns four washers is beyond me. Because he can, I suppose, and he needed something to fill this ridiculous room, which is at least half as big as my entire cabin.

"Yeah?"

"I don't have a lot of experience with this sort of thing, and I don't want to embarrass myself by making something out of nothing, but if I'm going to be more in control of my life, then I should try to be confident in all respects, don't you think?"

I glance over my shoulder at Rosie nervously twisting a shirt in her hands with her chin lifted in some kind of challenge. She's nervous and determined, and I know a trap when I see one. Unfortunately, I've got no idea what she's angling at, so I do the only thing I can do. I give her my honest answer.

"Yeah," I agree. "I think that's smart."

"Good." She tosses the shirt aside and stands taller. "You're attracted to me, aren't you?"

I swear, my heart stops beating and time stands still. I relive the other morning in my bed, waking up with my cock hard and her ass against my hips. I think about yesterday, chasing her through the trees and fighting the primal urge to catch her and make her mine. I imagine what might have happened less than an hour ago if I'd kissed her in the kitchen when I had the chance. It's moment after moment of temptation and torture.

I'm about to deflect, brush off the question or change the subject, but the words won't come. I think about how she's been manipulated, gaslit, and lied to by the people who were supposed to protect her, and how that has compromised the belief she has in herself. I can't be part of that, not when she's so brave and so vulnerable and so right.

Fuck it.

"No, Songbird," I say as I turn around. "I'm not attracted to you."

I pause, closing my eyes and taking a breath before I step over the line and into the deep end. When I open them, Rosie's watching me with baby blues filled with so much hurt and hope that I couldn't stop now if I tried.

"I'm a fucking mess for you."

Her eyes widen, and the world glitches into slow motion as Rosie heaves in a breath of her own and springs forward. I catch her as she flies at me, lifting her up so she can wrap her legs around my waist and greeting her hungry mouth with my own. Her lips are frantic, her tongue desperate and needy. She tastes like sugar and she smells like sunlight, and my shaky grasp on my self-control snaps. I kiss her like a man denied water for far too long. Lips and tongue and teeth collide as the tension between us explodes like fireworks.

"I've wanted you since the moment I saw you," I confess between kisses in words that come out choked and rough. "You deserve better than me, Songbird, but if you want this, I'll give it to you." I delve into her mouth, our tongues lashing as I grab her ass and hold her hard against my dick. "I'll give you everything I have to give."

Her kiss is as desperate as mine. A moan escapes her throat, and the vibration meets my tongue in a wave of temptation. I stumble toward the laundry room counter, setting her down so I can use my hands for other things, but the distance it puts between her thighs and my cock is unacceptable, so I pick her up, spin us around, and pin her against a wall.

"Give it to me, Finn," she pants between short, sharp breaths. "I need this."

My groan is pained, and as Rosie tips her head back, inviting me to explore her jaw and her collarbone, I drag her shirt down to bare her shoulder and run my tongue and lips down her smooth neck.

"I want to taste you," I tell her. "I want my tongue to know every sweet inch of you."

Rosie whimpers between kisses. "Yes. Yes."

My dick is hard and throbbing, trapped painfully inside my jeans. I shift a little for some relief, but when Rosie feels the press of my erection against the warm, wet fabric between her legs, she rolls her hips against me, seeking friction on her clit. I push harder against her, giving her something to ride, and she gasps between thrusts of her pelvis, fingers weaving their way into my hair and growing tighter as the arousal inside her builds.

"I want to touch you," I murmur against her ear before nipping her earlobe. "Tell me it's okay to touch you. It's been hell keeping my hands off you all this time."

"Touch me, Finn," she replies breathlessly. "Oh, God. Please. Touch me."

I tug harder on her shirt, tearing the fabric in my frenzy to free her tits, losing my mind as she rubs herself against me. She's wearing a lacy bra underneath her T-shirt, pale blue and pretty, the pattern swirling over her peaked pink nipples. I can't reach them with my mouth without moving her off my cock, so I cover one breast with my palm, squeezing and then tugging, brushing and then circling, until I find the technique that makes her writhe. She likes it rough, short sharp tugs that make her body jolt and her yoga pants damp. I keep it up, fighting the climax building at the base of my spine.

Rosie's face is flushed, her hairline is matted with sweat, and her pussy is grinding hard on my lap when she closes her eyes and draws that lush bottom lip between her teeth.

"I want you to come," I say, low and husky. "Hard. On my dick. On my hand. On my mouth. I want you to come while I watch you touch yourself. I want your orgasm to be the reason I exist."

"Finn?" Her voice is low and confused, her eyes closed tight, her long throat exposed as she arches her spine away from the wall. Rosie digs her nails into my shoulders and swivels her hips on the hard ridge of my jeans. "I think... I think..."

"You think what, Songbird?" I pinch her nipple again, then soothe it with my palm, sweat edging down my temple as I watch her skin flush and her breath quicken as her body tightens toward release. "You're such a good girl grinding your greedy wet pussy on me, and *fuck*, look at you. You're so beautiful. Now tell me what my beautiful Songbird thinks."

"I think I'm going to come!"

"Yes, baby," I say, canting my hips to give her the angle she needs. "Come so fucking hard just for me."

I slide my hands underneath her ass and lick the moisture from her collarbone as she cries out with a wordless scream of release. I set my forehead against the wall beside her, breathing through my own arousal until the threat of blowing in my pants eases. Her body slows, her grinding shifts from frenzied to lazy, and her muscles soften until her thighs release me and the only thing keeping her up are my hands under her ass. Slowly, she snakes her arms around my neck and lays her cheek on my shoulder, and I push off the wall to carry her to the counter.

"Well," she says as I set her down. "That was unexpected."

I rest my hands on her thighs, only letting them go when I brush a damp curl from her forehead. My fingertips sweep across her flushed cheekbone, then attempt to fix the ripped fabric of her T-shirt before giving up. She's disheveled and flushed and gorgeous.

"Unexpected," I agree, "but fucking amazing."

Rosie ducks her head with a shy smile, then peeks up at me through her thick lashes. "I've never done that before."

"What?" My hands have a mind of their own, because one minute I'm tenderly squeezing her thighs, and the next I'm cradling her jaw, then stroking her back. I'd stop, but I don't want to. "Made out with your bodyguard in his brother's million-dollar laundry room?"

"No." The pink in her cheeks burns brighter. "I've never... you know."

I smile at her discomfort, which seems silly after what we just did, but also because I've got no idea what she means. Then, at the self-conscious fall of her eyes again and the rising flush in her cheeks, the answer hits me like a smack across the head. My grin melts away.

"You've never come before?" I ask.

She shakes her head and avoids my eyes. "No."

"But... you've been in a relationship for six years."

Her nod is small and embarrassed. "Uh-huh."

"He never... And you didn't...?"

"Nope. It was never high on his list of priorities."

My jaw clenches and I glare at the white wall over the top of Rosie's head. That selfish asshole. That piece of shit who had the most wonderful woman in his bed and he couldn't even fuck her worth a damn.

"But you liked it?" I ask her, lifting her chin so she has to look me in the eye.

"Yes," she admits quickly, and I smirk at the feverish thirst in her bright blue eyes.

"And you'd like to do it again?"

She nods, small and quick, which makes me wonder if she thinks I mean right now. My dick's hard enough that I wouldn't need much persuading.

"So do I." I lean in until our lips are a hairsbreadth apart. "And guess what, Songbird?"

"What?" she replies.

"As long as you're safe, there is no higher priority for me than your pleasure. So, for as long as you're here, and for as long as you want me to, I'm going to make you come... and come... and come... to make up for all the orgasms you've been denied." Her body trembles in a full-body shiver that makes me smile. "What do you say to that?"

"Okay," she whispers, her lips close enough for her breath to tickle.

I cover her mouth with mine and kiss her slowly. It's nothing like what we just did. This one is slow and deliberate. We both know what we're doing this time, and we both know that this kiss is real.

I might have made Rosie come, but she's given me a gift today without knowing it. She's made it possible to believe there might be something I can give her after all. Nothing that will last and nothing worth leaving her life for, but something she might take with her when she goes. I can teach her what she's worth and what she should expect to get from the man who loves her.

FOURTEEN

Rosie

I'M TRYING TO CONCENTRATE ON the email from my record label, I really am, but the words on the screen swim like tiny black fish in a sea of white, and no sooner do I bring a sentence into focus than the letters fuzz into oblivion again.

I can't stop thinking about what happened yesterday in the laundry room. Part of me is mortified I could be so brazen, the other part is desperate to do it again, and I can't help but wonder... if it was that good grinding on Finn's lap, what would it feel like to have his hands between my legs? His tongue on my clit? His cock deep inside me?

"You almost done there, Songbird?"

I startle at the question and the sudden appearance of Finn who's leaning on the back of the opposite dining chair. His gentle rumble is edged with amusement, and his tiny smirk is insolent in a way that makes my stomach twist. He knows what I'm thinking about. I know he knows what I'm thinking about. What I don't know is when he's going to make good on his promise, and I can't very well ask when he's going to make me come again.

I'm a *lady*.

I glance at the screen and click through to the email about applicants for my new security team. Finn was insistent I look at it this morning, saying he needed to respond to his military contact, and I begrudgingly agreed. There are three résumés attached and they all look fine to me. To be honest, if they've passed Finn's check, I'm happy enough to hire them, but that would mean leaving here and going back to my life in LA. Finalizing my separation from Chip. Rebuilding my life with me at the helm and not him. Rebranding myself as an independent businesswoman in this industry, one who is creative and capable and a force to be reckoned with. When I ran from Violet's studio, those goals were pushing me forward, but not anymore. Now I'm searching for reasons to delay.

I minimize Finn's email and close the laptop with a snap. "I'm done."

Finn raises his right eyebrow. "And?"

"And none of them are right for the job." I shrug. "Sorry."

His mouth pulls into a knowing smile that warms me in unusual places. "You don't sound very sorry."

I lift my chin and stare down my nose at him across the dining table. "You don't know my mind."

Finn chuckles. "You might be surprised." He straightens and rolls his head toward the loft. "Upstairs," he orders, tone firm and eyes hot. "Now."

I stand slowly, balling the hem of his flannel into my fists as butterflies the size of swallows spin and dive in my stomach. With all the poise I can muster and all the calmness I can feign, I walk to the ladder, sparing a pat for Dakota who's dozing in her bed, and climb my stairway to sex heaven.

But when I get to the top, I'm not sure what to do. Finn's bed is neat and the covers are smooth. There's a mirrored dresser opposite the bed and an armchair in the corner. The guitar I've been playing leans against the far wall, my notepad and pencil are stacked on the nightstand. Do I stand here? Sit? Lie down? Stay dressed? Get naked?

When Finn promised to make up for all the orgasms Chip neglected to give me these last six years, I didn't stop to wonder about the logistics.

I'm fussing with the buttons on my shirt when Finn appears at the top of the ladder. He looks completely in control of his nerves, if he has any, and his confidence relaxes me. If Finn thinks there's nothing to worry about, then there's nothing to worry about. He slides his hand around the back of my neck and drags my mouth to his in a soft but demanding open-mouth kiss, and the butterflies spiral lower, teasing and tightening my core.

He releases my mouth much too soon and, with his eyes closed, presses his forehead against mine. "This is how it could go. I make you come."

My exhale quivers at the word alone, and Finn's mouth tips up on one side.

"I make you come," he repeats, "and it'll be the kind of orgasm you think about later when you're touching yourself. But that's no good to you if you don't know *how* to touch yourself. Right?"

"Right," I agree absently, craning my neck for another kiss, which he bestows with a grin against my lips.

"So that's what I want you to do," he says. "Before I touch you, I want you to touch yourself."

His words and his hands and his kiss—oh my God, he's such a good kisser—have fogged my brain past the point of coherent thought, so I replay his words to understand what he's saying.

Heat rises in my cheeks as I pull his hand from my face. "I can't do that!"

"Why not?"

"Because I... Because you..." My cheeks burn like fire. "Because it's embarrassing."

Finn shakes his head, mouth tipped up on one side. "There's nothing embarrassing about a gorgeous woman who knows how to get herself off. Believe me."

The intensity of his tone, matched by his caramel eyes, makes my breath come fast. I drop my gaze down his hard body, and I'm met with an erection tenting the front of his gray sweats. Is it possible that the idea of my own hand between my legs is making him hard? The thought is enough to make me want to stroke myself, and suddenly I'm considering it.

"You don't have to," Finn says. He collects my hands in his, twining our fingers between us. "I'd never ask you to do anything that makes you uncomfortable, but you need to know your own body and understand what brings you pleasure before you're able to tell a man what you need in the bedroom. I can help you, if you want, or I can give you some time alone. This isn't about me. I want you to do this for you and only you."

I bite my lip and look down at what I'm wearing, then glance at my reflection in the mirror behind Finn. Flannel shirt. Hair in a ponytail. No makeup. I'm not what anyone would call a sex kitten... except for one small detail. I'm wearing a white lace thong from Violet's collection, and I recall what she said about her designs when we were in her studio. She created her lingerie line to make women feel confident, comfortable, and beautiful. Sexy. Empowered. In control. I bite my lip and cast a shy look up at Finn.

His expression, bright and burning and so ready to shut this down if I say the word, makes me want to do this. I want to take back my life, and that includes owning my body. If I'm not going to let myself be treated like a commodity anymore, I need to take control of my own pleasure as much as anything else.

I unbutton my shirt and let it pool on the floor around my feet. Finn's throat bobs in a swallow as his eyes fall, sweeping over my bare breasts and belly, past my lacy thong to my thighs, and up again with a tension so tight I feel its touch.

Goose bumps flare and my nipples furl into hard, aching tips.

Finn's hand flinches at his side, and I silently beg him to touch me, but he balls it into a fist with a heaving breath of self-discipline.

"I'm ready," I murmur. "Will you stay?"

"Mm-hmm." His quiet hum cracks with desire. "I can do that."

"Where should I go?"

"On the bed," he whispers.

As I lay myself down on the covers, Finn takes a seat in the armchair by the foot of the bed. He leans back, knees wide and sweatpants clinging to his hard-on, and from here I have a full view of myself in the mirror above his dresser. I study my near-naked body and pull out my hair so it splays over the pillows, and when I run a hesitant hand down my neck and toward my breast, Finn responds with a choked groan.

"That's it," he murmurs. "Touch yourself, Songbird."

I cup my breast and tweak a nipple between my thumb and forefinger, pulling it just enough to cause a twinge of pain, then gasp at the unexpected wet pulse in my pussy.

"What next?" I ask.

"Grab both tits," he orders. "Squeeze them a little. Harder. Push them together. Just like that."

It's not like I haven't touched myself before. I've played a little, tried to do what Chip never could, but it didn't feel erotic and I couldn't ever *get there*. But now, my body buzzes with arousal, and the reason is Finn. Not only how attractive I find him or how safe he makes me feel, but the press of his eyes on me. Finn watching me is turning me on.

I do what he says, massaging my breasts, lifting them and squeezing them, exploring the way my body responds, but I don't get the zingy zips of lust I felt when I pinched my nipple. I try it again, then both at the same time, and... Oh! There it is. A pang of pain followed by a warm flood of pulsing need.

"I like it like this," I tell him, pulling on the erect tips until they're hard and aching. "So the next time you touch me, do it like this."

"Okay," Finn says, voice low and husky, fists tight on the arms of the chair. "What else do you like?"

"I'm not sure yet. Maybe if I..."

I trail a light fingertip over my ribcage, moving slowly—but certainly—south, and at the sound of Finn's quiet moan, the desire in me jumps, alongside another kind of high that I'm all too familiar with. The high of standing on a stage with all the attention on me. The rush of the spotlight. The thrill of holding vulnerability in one hand and power in the other. The ultimate paradox of being an artist: baring my soul just to hold a person captive with it.

This is a performance and Finn is my audience. And I'm nothing if not a world-class act.

I try a harder pinch on my nipple, then close my eyes with a moan as my pussy drips. Finn shifts in his chair. I imagine his cock getting thicker at the picture of me on the bed, and the ache between my legs intensifies with a heavy throb.

I open my eyes again and see myself in the mirror. Flushed skin. Glassy eyes. A wild mane of untamed hair and a hesitant hand on my breast. Knees that have fallen open without meaning to, and a thin strip of white lace wet and clinging to my pussy. Watching myself in the reflection and wondering who this woman is, I follow the path of my hand down over my sternum and across my stomach, then spread my thighs to get a better view of my fingers slipping into my panties.

In the corner, Finn groans and drops his head back, nostrils flaring with a strained inhale, and I release my own breath with a trembling whimper. This power I have over him right now? Without touching him? Without trying? It's everything.

"Is this what you had in mind?" I ask.

Finn keeps his head thrown back, the long line of his throat struggling to swallow and his eyes closed tight.

"You're going to have to look at me, Finn, if you want to know how to touch me. Isn't that what you said?"

The growl in his chest is broken and tortured, but he lifts his head and pins me with eyes that are more out of control than I've ever seen them. Feral and frustrated.

And I'm not scared. I'm satisfied.

"Like this," I murmur as I pull the lace to one side and spread my legs a little wider. I brush the tips of my fingers across my folds, coating them with my wetness, and I don't know where to look—at myself in the mirror or Finn as still as carved stone in the corner—because both images are driving this moment from incredible to unbearable.

I drop my head back onto the pillows and close my eyes as I circle my clit, varying the pressure of my fingers. The small, tormented grunts from Finn make me smile to myself, and I press harder, move more quickly, tilt my hips up to meet my hand. It feels good, but not as good as riding Finn's hard-on. No matter how I tweak my nipple or rub my clit, the tease of my climax rises like a wave that won't ever break, taking me closer to the edge without pushing me over.

I clench my jaw and try to focus, but I'm in my head and I can't get out of it. My orgasm, so close just a moment ago, moves out of reach.

I glance at Finn, about to ask him what I should do next, but my eyes catch on the hard ridge in his pants, a dark spot of precum staining the cotton, and desire flares all over again. The veins on his forearms pop with the strength it takes to keep his hands on the arms of the chair, and the hard set of his jaw, the furrow in his brow make my core clench.

I slip a finger inside myself and release a heavy, relieved breath. "Finn?"

"Yeah?" he answers, or I think he does. His response is barely more than a moan.

"Can I see you?" I ask him, and when his head tilts with puzzlement, I nod at the hard length straining against his pants. "There. Can I see it?"

Finn rakes a hand through his hair, then grips the arms of the chair with even more force than before.

"This is about you, Songbird, and what you need. It's not about me or what I want."

"But what *do* you want?"

His nostrils flare. "I think you know what I want."

"Oh, God." My finger makes wet sucking sounds as I pump it in and out. "Please, Finn. I want to see you." My breath comes faster at the idea of touching myself while Finn watches with his dick in his hand. "I can't get there on my own. I need to see what I do to you."

His groan is deep and pained, but he drags his thin cotton T-shirt up over his hard, inked abs, and then tucks a thumb into the waistband of his sweats. With a turn of his wrist, he drags the fabric over his swollen length, and I groan at the first sight of his thick and throbbing cock.

For the first time in my life, I want to get on my knees for a man. I want to wrap my lips around his dick, feel his fingers twist in my hair, and have my throat fucked by a god who can't control himself around me.

I wonder if Finn would be rough with me. I wonder what he'd say if I asked.

"Stroke it," I whisper as I slide another finger inside. "Show me how *I* should touch *you*."

He hesitates, and I frown as he dips a hand into the pocket of his sweats. It reappears with a scrap of red lace, and it takes me a moment to recognize the panties I thought I'd lost on the dock. When I finally understand, I whimper and slip another finger inside.

"Have you been carrying those in your pocket this whole time?" I ask breathily.

Finn wraps the fabric around his hand, then lifts it to spit in his palm. He wraps his fingers around his cock and gives it a featherlight pull. I match his rhythm with a thrust of my fingers.

"What do you think?" he says, voice strained and neck tensed.

"Oh, God," I moan, driven mad by the thought of him getting off by rubbing my panties along his cock. "Do it again," I command, watching him between glances at the mirror where some wanton woman who can't be me is fucking herself with her fingers.

Finn tugs again, harder and more than once, and when I match my pumps to his pace, he scrambles to push his sweatpants farther down his heavy thighs, giving him space to thrust into his fist. His thighs are hard and thick as he fucks his hand, and my body rocks and writhes as I curl my fingers inside my core and coax myself to the edge again.

But this time, with my eyes on Finn as he pumps himself to climax, thick ropes of cum shooting up over his rock-hard stomach, I topple with him, core muscles fluttering and pulsing around my fingers, wet heat exploding and dripping down my thighs, sparks of light dancing over my skin. I come hard, eyes closed tight, pleasure racking my body until the waves recede and I'm back on the shore. My eyes flutter open and land on Finn in the corner of the room, breathing hard and staring at me with unleashed lust.

"I think I've got the hang of it," I say, sinking into the pillows with soft-muscled exhaustion.

"Understatement." Finn shakes his head at the mess on his torso, then looks back at me with suspicion glinting in his caramel gaze. "You like being watched, don't you, Songbird?"

"I like being watched by you," I say.

He growls and stuffs my panties back in his pocket before dragging off his shirt and using it to wipe himself clean. He crosses the room and cups my face before brushing my lips with his.

"You put on one hell of a show," he says.

"Thank you." I lift my head to return his kiss. "You did pretty well yourself."

His mouth tips up. "Yeah?"

"Oh yeah." I look pointedly at his pocket. "Are you going to give those back?"

He smirks and kisses me again. "Fuck no."

I throw my arms around his neck and drag him down to the bed. He falls onto the covers beside me, and I roll against him. "That was so hot," I say. "Now I want to know what else you can do."

I say it lightly, but I want to know everything. Every inch of his body, every thought in his head, every dream in his heart. The music in his soul.

He chuckles quietly sand kisses me again. "That's good information to have, Songbird, because I can't wait to show you."

FIFTEEN

Finn

I USE THE BATHROOM AFTER Rosie, pulling myself together under the hard spray of a cold shower. When I said I was a mess for this woman, I wasn't lying, and now that the line between us has been obliterated, I've got a feeling I'll be spending a lot of time putting the shattered parts of me back in their places, only to go back and be destroyed all over again.

I swing past the kitchen on my way to the loft, dropping a cupful of kibble in Dakota's bowl before collecting a couple bottles of water, the basket of strawberries in the fridge, and a bag of dark chocolate chips from the pantry. I pluck a pink wildflower from the mason jar on the dining table, stick it behind my ear, and then precariously balance my bounty as I climb the ladder.

Rosie's sitting on the bed wrapped up in one of my shirts, which makes the fact that she's not still naked a little more tolerable.

She stretches out her arms with grabby hands as I proffer her snack. "I'm starving."

I pluck the flower from behind my ear and tuck it behind hers, then arrange the food on the covers before stretching out beside her. "Thought you might be after that performance."

Her skin, still glowing from her orgasm, flushes a pretty pink hue. "You were right. Thank you."

She lifts a strawberry to her mouth, and I'm so mesmerized by her soft lips closing around the tip, then the shape of them as she speaks, that I don't register her question until she gently pokes my shoulder.

"Finn? Are you listening?"

"Hm?"

"Can I ask you something?"

"You can ask me anything."

"But will you answer?"

"Rosie." I hold another berry to her lips and wait until she sinks her teeth into it. "After what we just did, there's not a shot in hell I'll deny you anything."

It's terrifying how much I mean those words. How they twist like roots and embed themselves deep in my chest. But by the bright excitement that lights up Rosie's face, she's got no idea I just promised to give her everything.

"Why didn't you tell me you could play the guitar?" she asks.

I'm relieved that of all the pieces of me she could choose to hold up to the light, she starts with the one with the simplest pattern. "Why doesn't an art student tell Monet he knows how to hold a brush?"

Rosie drops her head, and her eyes soften. "You think I'm Monet?"

"Yes, and in case the analogy wasn't obvious, I'm the preschooler with his fingers in the paint."

She shakes her head like I've made a bad joke, but I'm serious.

"Can you read music?" she asks.

"Yes."

"And can you play any other instruments?"

"Nope."

She hums. "Have you tried?"

"Haven't had the chance."

Rosie takes another strawberry from the basket, but she plucks at the leafy green stalk instead of eating the fruit. "Have you ever performed for anyone?"

I take a slug of water, then lie back on the pillows, one hand under my head as I look up at the vaulted ceiling. "I've never been on a stage, if that's what you mean," I say. "My six-year-old niece, Izzy, is learning trumpet and we've had some jam sessions."

I smile to myself at the idea that our lessons could be called jams, but she loves them and so do I. Rosie catches the curve on my lips, and her mouth mirrors mine with a curious smile.

"We played together at one of our family nights a few months ago," I add. "And I've played with people nearby to listen. In high school, in the military, at home, on the road, but I never cared if people paid attention. I played for me."

Rosie returns her berry to the others, moves the basket and chocolate to the end of the bed, and then lies down beside me, hands tucked under her cheek as she studies my profile. I'd turn to look at her, too, but it's easier to be honest with the faded drywall than her eager eyes.

"I love that," she says. "I didn't realize how much I missed playing for myself until I started writing here. I mean, I get time alone to be creative at home, but there are always people waiting and watching—figuratively if not literally. Fans. Producers. Label execs. Chip." She sighs. "It's been wonderful working on material without any of that outside noise. It's like accessing all this untapped inspiration I never even knew was there."

Now I turn my head. "I'm glad something positive has come out of this situation."

Her lips curve up in a gentle smile. "That's not the only thing."

The energy between us feels easy and natural, and I reach over to tuck a lock of hair behind her ear.

"Finn?" she says.

"Yeah?"

"Would you play something for me?"

My muscles tense. A reflex action, but the near memory of Rosie on my bed, head tossed back, breasts bare, legs open and her hands everywhere, softens me again within seconds. Rosie performed for me. She was vulnerable when I asked her to be, and as uncomfortable as I am at the idea of Rosie being disappointed in my musical aptitude, I can't ask her to trust me with the things that scare her if I don't trust her in return.

"Sure," I say. "Let me get my guitar."

I disappear into the closet and go first for the Martin, but on second thought choose Mom's Hummingbird. If Rosie is surprised by my choice, she gives no sign of it as I settle into the armchair in the corner and set the instrument on my thighs. I test the strings and tweak them until I'm satisfied with the tuning.

On the bed, Rosie rolls over to watch me but remains lying against the pillows, and I'm grateful she's at least pretending to have low expectations about what comes next.

I play the first song that comes to mind. It's an acoustic track that was all over the radio in the nineties and one of the first songs my mom taught me. She loved it, so I loved it. I play the introduction, the chords coming to me with the benefit of fifteen years of muscle memory, and at the first verse, I start to sing. I don't mean to. I don't even realize I'm doing it until the chorus, and by then there's no point in stopping. I play the song through to the end, eyes closed the way they always are even though my mom constantly reminded me to open them. I play and I sing, and I almost forget Rosie's watching. That's how good it feels to be wrapped in music. Playing. Singing. *Being*.

As the last notes fade into silence, I open my eyes, a little dismayed that the song passed so quickly, but then I notice Rosie's expression. It's soft and sweet and... sad? Yeah, sad. There's a single tear rolling down her cheek.

"I'm sorry." I set the guitar against the wall. "That wasn't what you're used to. You don't have to pretend—"

"Finn?"

She rises to her knees, scoots to the end of the bed, and reaches out her hand. I get up and take it, looking down into her eyes, and she squeezes my fingers tight enough to almost hurt.

"You're good," she says. "You're *really* good."

My smile is self-conscious and a little disbelieving. "That's generous of you but—"

"Shut up," she says, and my brows climb high. "I wouldn't insult you with empty praise, so don't insult me by assuming I'd lie to you about your talent. And you do have talent. You're good, Finn. Better than good, and I loved it."

I glance at the guitar against the wall. "Thank you."

"So you read music," she says slowly, almost thinking out loud. "And you play it. Do you write it?"

I narrow my eyes at the sparkle in hers. It feels like wearing too tight a sweater to be so open about this part of my life, but the delight in Rosie's smile makes it impossible to be closed off. It's odd. Almost everyone in my life takes my quiet solitude as given. A personality quirk. They let it go and I'm grateful for that, but Rosie won't let it go, and I never thought I'd be grateful for that too.

"I write," I confess. "Or I used to. I haven't written anything in a long time."

Rosie opens her mouth, then closes it again with a snap. I can see the question hovering there still, in the twitch of her cupid's bow and the fidgeting in her fingers under mine.

"You want to read something?" I guess with apprehension. I won't say no, but sharing my own music is nowhere near the same as covering a tune already validated with decades of radio play. And I've never shared that part of myself with anyone before. Vulnerability does not fit me well, but I'd be a creep and a hypocrite if I didn't give as much of myself to Rosie as she's already given to me.

Rosie drops her head to one side and increases the pressure in her grip. "No, Finn. That'd be like asking to read your diary, and I'd never do that. I was wondering if there's anything you're ready to share. It could be a melody or a chorus or an idea... It's okay if the answer is no, but I'd be honored to hear it."

I dart a look at my mom's guitar again and ask myself if there's anything I want to lift from that notebook hidden in my dresser and finally give wings. My head says *no* but a persistent kind of expectation makes my stomach tighten. There *is* something that deserves to be more than black inky scribbles on a lined white page. There's *someone* who deserves to be more.

With a small nod, I drop Rosie's hands and collect the guitar, but this time I sit on the edge of the bed, predicting that once I get started, I'll need her close by to get through it. With a hesitant strum and a second thought that flits through my head so fast that it barely registers, I set my fingers on the fret, play the strings with a light-as-air plucking motion, and sing.

The music is supposed to feel stirring and ethereal, delicate and hushed to encourage a listener to lean in and *hear* it. And when they do, the words follow, full of heartbreak and desolation, frustration and guilt. Surrender and acceptance that some of us will always be haunted by regret.

I wrote this song the night that Jack died and I was feeling all those things. I still feel them most days—or, rather, most nights. I lie awake thinking back on what he did and what I didn't do. How I couldn't be what my best friend needed, and the reason why I wouldn't change anything even if I had the chance. Jack asked me for help, and I gave it. I took the job he asked me to take, and I left him behind. It's why Rosie is here in my bed now and not the victim of a psychotic fan, injured or disfigured—or worse. But maybe it's also why Jack's gone.

I didn't know he was suffering as much as he was. He never told me, and I didn't see it. Would he still be here if I'd been a better friend? Paid closer attention? Recognized the signs? I don't know, and I never will.

The song echoes what happened when my parents died and I couldn't be here when they passed. It's seasoned with the guilt I carry that Charles and Dylan had to run Silver Leaf Ranch on their own for years and it nearly broke our family and ruined the business. The feelings are so big and so powerful, and they're the reason I don't feel comfortable in gray spaces. I need clear lines and consequences so I can do what needs to be done. I can't live with another person I care about getting lost in the in-betweens.

The final notes of my song float from the strings and drift into stillness. Rosie slips a cool hand over my shoulder, then around the back of my neck, and her thumb brushes my hairline in soft, soothing strokes. The room is quiet, and it's only when she tries to hide a sniffle that I realize she's trying not to cry. I set my guitar beside me and wrap an arm around her to pull her against my side. When that doesn't feel close enough, I lift her onto my lap.

"Hey." I press my lips against the top of her head. Her hair smells like she sleeps in rose petals. "That's two songs and two times I've made you sad. Keep this up and I won't play for you anymore."

"That was so layered." Rosie nuzzles the curve of my neck. "The melody, the tone, the lyrics." She pauses, for the second time today thinking before she asks a question, and it's that kind of consideration that makes it easier to open up.

"You can ask," I tell her. "Though I think I know what you're going to say."

"Is that song written from experience?" she asks. "Maybe... about your mom and dad?"

"No, not my parents, or not only them." I tighten my arms around her frame and rest my cheek on her hair. "Jack. The friend I served with in the military."

Rosie lifts her head with sharp understanding. "The same one who owned the security firm that hired you for me?"

"That's right," I confirm, and the story falls into the space between us like it's been waiting for its moment to be free. "He was discharged from service years before I was, but we stayed in touch. He never tried to hide the fact he got out for mental health reasons. Jack was good like that, or so I thought. Always upfront about what it took to stay grounded and balanced. Purpose, he'd say. A reason to exist. I thought things were getting better for him in civilian life. He moved to the East Coast to be closer to his parents. He built a successful business from nothing. When he needed more, he found Dakota at a local rescue shelter. He never told me that it wasn't enough."

"Oh, Finn." Rosie snuggles closer, and her warm lips pressed against my collarbone help me stay in the light when my thoughts try to pull me into the darkness. "I'm so sorry."

"He died not long after New Orleans," I murmur. Regret surges alongside the memories before receding to its baseline again. "I was on my way back to see him after I left you, but it was too late."

Rosie slides her arms around my body and hugs me tightly. It helps.

"So, I came home," I finish.

"With Dakota," Rosie adds, not quite a question.

"Yep," I agree. "And that Baby Taylor you're so fond of."

Rosie raises her chin, eyes wide with understanding. "Jack gave you that guitar? He knew about your music?"

"Yeah. We talked about it sometimes when we wondered what our lives were going to look like outside the SEALs. What would we do? How would we fill our time? What would our reason for living be if we weren't serving anymore?"

"And Jack thought your purpose was music?"

I drop my voice. "I don't know."

"You're such a riddle," she muses. "So strong and tough on the outside. You've been to war and seen awful things."

"Done awful things," I add at a volume barely above a whisper.

Rosie brushes the hair from my forehead with a tender touch. "You're a good man, Finn, and an artist. Inside, where it matters, you're softness and beauty and light."

I snort at how unlikely it is that I was ever put on this earth to make art. My contribution to that world, if you could even call it that, is too small. A single grain of sand on an endless beach, and for the kind of purpose I need to feel good about myself, I'll have to leave more in the world than a speck of sand.

"What?" Rosie pulls back, and I can tell she's a little hurt. "You think music isn't meaningful?"

"No! God, no. I think music is magic, but I'm not magic, Songbird." I gesture at the guitar. "This music is just for me. It's not a legacy. It's not going to save anybody."

Her brow creases and I can tell she wants to argue, so I cover her mouth with a kiss to stop it before it starts. I don't want to waste time wondering if it's possible to have what she has—something in my life to be passionate about and throw myself into with everything I have. Something that will make a difference and give me what I need most. Something to live for.

SIXTEEN

Rosie

I LOSE MYSELF FOR ANOTHER two days. With a guitar in my hands, Dakota at my feet, and what feels like a bottomless well of inspiration to draw from, lyrics and melodies pour out of me, coalescing into songs that feel complete even without a studio or production team around me. Perhaps because I don't have those things. The music is raw and real in a way it hasn't been in years. Not since before I was signed to a label and the world was watching to see what I'd do next.

Kind of like the way I'm watching Finn right now.

He's at the dining table again and frowning in the glow of his computer screen. I'm outside on the porch swing, writing and playing with one eye on the window. In a moment, he'll stand and start to pace. I can almost count down the seconds until he gets to his feet. Five, four, three, two...

And there he goes. Back and forth with a look of contemplation as he wears a path in the hardwood floors. My heart breaks for him. After he played for me and he shared more of himself than I ever thought he would, I was inspired to write, and I think he was too. The only difference is, I gave into it. Finn's fighting it. I can understand why even if I don't agree with it.

This man was born to make music, but that's a calling he has to answer for himself. He has to want it badly enough to do the work required to mold it into his own vision. He can't fight it, and he can't force it to be something it's not, which is ironic, because I'm starting to wonder how long he's been doing the opposite. Pushing himself to be hard, closed off, and straight-talking when in reality he's a composition of color, compassion, and complexities. And why? *Why* would he fight that so hard? Why won't he embrace it? Life isn't lived in black and white. The real stuff—the good and the bad—happens in the spaces between, but Finn seems determined to ignore it all in favor of a monotone middle ground.

I dip my head again and watch my fingers dance across the guitar strings. Two days and two songs... almost. The first came together quickly, a track that relives the high of a first kiss, a first touch, the first time you sink into the skin of a man and reemerge more of a woman, not less. The second is richer, more complex and layered. A meditation on intimacy in all its forms. Physical. Emotional. Spiritual. The first chord I played gave me goose bumps, but I can't complete it.

It already feels special in a way that's going to change my career, but something is missing, and I don't know what.

I'm staring into the blue distance, humming to experiment with the melody, when Finn clears his throat loud enough to make me jump.

"Sorry," he says. "Didn't mean to startle you."

"It's my fault," I reply as he scratches Dakota's head and sits on the other end of the porch swing. "I was lost in thought."

"How's the writing going?"

"It's…" I pick up the notebook at my side, glance at the scrawls on the page, and hand it to him. "I was going to say it's going well, and it was, but I'm stuck on this song. Something about it just doesn't feel right."

"What's the problem with it?"

"That's the thing. I don't know. The chorus is smooth and the bridge is strong. I keep trying to imagine how it would sound with more layers to the music, but I'm not sure what it needs. Maybe it's me. Maybe my voice isn't powerful enough to carry it."

"Can I hear it?"

"Of course, but it's nowhere near ready. Remember that so you're not disappointed."

He settles back on the porch swing, making it rock a little. "You could never disappoint me."

His gentle smile and easy confidence make my heart race, and his eyes on me make me nervous. I've played in front of thousands of people at a time. I've played in small rooms for pitiless execs. I put on an entirely different show for Finn forty-eight hours ago, so sharing an unfinished song with him now should be a walk in the park. But that's not the reason I'm nervous. This song, like the others, is about him, and I think he's going to know it.

Finn's mouth twitches in a smoldering kind of curve that dries my throat, so I take a sip of water, then shift the guitar to make myself more comfortable. Lowering my eyes for no other reason than because watching Finn watch me makes it hard to concentrate, I set my fingers on the fretboard and strum the first chord. By the time I play the fourth bar, I've relaxed into the music. My fingers move instinctively, my gaze turns inward as I reach for a deeper key, and I lose myself in the music. I stay lost until the last note drifts away on the breeze.

My eyes float into focus and meet Finn's straightaway. His brow is furrowed, his fingers tucked into fists.

I shrug self-consciously "I love the song," I tell him. "But something about it feels incomplete, and I can't figure out what."

"What would you normally do in a situation like this?" he asks. "Maybe work with another songwriter or find a producer who can help you?"

"Sometimes," I reply. "But even if I wrote this back in LA, I'm not sure there's anyone out there who could help." I finger the notepad again, hoping Finn reads between the lines. "This material is too personal to share with anyone yet... except you."

He's still for a moment, blinking at me like he's struggling with something. "Hang on a minute," he says before he stands and disappears inside the cabin.

I turn my head to watch him go and through the window see him scale the loft ladder, then return with his vintage Martin slung across his body. He lowers himself onto the swing and spins my notebook to face him, eyes scanning the page like I've seen so many other musicians do. Reading my song like he can hear the notes on the page.

"Play it again," he says as his fingers move expertly over his strings, extracting the first bar of chords from his own guitar. "But give me a few chances to get it right. I'm nowhere near as good as you."

I clear my throat and try to get a handle on my eagerness. "No problem. Let's take it from the top."

He doesn't need a few chances to get it right, and my respect for his talent grows. He follows the music perfectly the first time, and when he plays off-page, it's intuitively and with intention. I almost lose my place, distracted by the soft competency of his hands, so I drop the lyrics as we play together, each following our instincts to add a little something here or take away something there, flirting with the sounds to see what works and what doesn't. When he hums, his voice is a smooth and husky baritone that drops deep enough in some places that I feel its reverberation in my chest, then in my stomach. And then a little lower.

I lean into it, pouring the chemicals in my veins into the music coming from my fingers and the poetry falling from my lips. When I stumble, Finn picks up the next note. His eyes close, the way they did when he played for me in his room, and it means I can watch him without having to pretend I'm not. The shift of his brow as he sings so low. The careful movements of his fingers on the strings. I play along so he doesn't stop, but I'm not playing to write anymore. I'm playing to listen.

And that's when the answer clicks into place. This song is a duet. It'll never be finished if I sing it alone.

We reach the final bar, and our instruments grow quiet. Finn opens his eyes and reaches for my notebook, picking up the pencil and scratching a few changes to the chords. I study them, fascinated by how naturally this comes to him, until he scribbles out a suggestion that sparks a new idea in me.

"How about this?" I take the pencil from his grip and rearrange a few things on the page, then turn it back to face him.

Finn answers by playing those chords on his guitar. "Looks good. Should we try it?"

We play the song again, and it already sounds better, but another round of polishing uplifts it even more. We reorganize some of the lyrics, Finn swapping a word here and there, and when he opens the song with a line that makes my throat catch with emotion, I furiously write it down before it's lost forever. My skin pebbles with chills of fever and fascination. This song is everything I've ever wanted to feel about a man and what I dreamed he would feel about me. It's all I've ever wanted to feel about *life*, and Finn's the one here putting it all into words.

When we're between renditions, I make notations on the page for us to follow. "Can you sing only these parts on your own?" I point to the first verse and chorus, and then the first bridge. "I'll sing these other sections solo, and then we can both try these parts here. But you should play around with it. Try whatever feels good."

"Yeah." Finn frowns at the page and makes one last amendment to the lyrics, then assigns himself the outro. "Do you mind?" he asks. "I've got an idea."

I play down the joy I feel at how completely he's giving himself to this process. There's no hesitation or self-consciousness, and I'd give him anything now if he asked for it.

"I don't mind at all," I reply. "Let's take it from the top."

It comes together like no song I've ever written. Each word and chord and note and harmony weaves into place like it was waiting for Finn this whole time. Our guitars and our voices spin into perfection, one climbing and chasing the other until we reach the summit. And when we slow into stillness, settling in the real world on a gentle waterfall of lighter notes, the residues of whatever alchemy we just created together are thick in the air between us. It cocoons us and tethers us and forges the kind of connection I've got no will to break and will never experience again. I'm outside time, in animated suspension, silently hoping the world outside the two of us no longer exists.

My chest rises and falls with shallow breaths. Finn's cognac gaze is still and steady but searing enough to consume me, and maybe my yearning is as obvious, because he sets his guitar aside and reaches across the space between us, curling his hand around the back of my neck.

"That song is about you, you know," he says, eyes searching mine for acknowledgment. When he finds it, because of course it's about us, he drags my mouth to his.

Finn's mouth is hot and his tongue is soft. I moan into him. His kisses are heaven, and I don't know how I'll ever live without them. I shift my guitar onto the timber decking and move to his lap, his thighs tensing beneath me to balance the rocking of the porch swing as I straddle his hips. His cock is thick and hard between us, and I grow wet at the feel of it. I press my chest against his, thread my fingers into his hair, and stroke deeper into his mouth, like I can close the smallest distance between us, but even then, I'm still not close enough.

Finn's arms envelop me, clutching me against his body to tell me he feels the urgency too, and his kiss grows more demanding. I peel off his shirt, frustrated at the thin layer covering his skin, and he does the same to mine before unclasping my bra and tossing it aside.

I flatten my body against him, responding to his kisses and his hands and the gentle thrust of his hips with encouraging but wordless sounds. The rock of the swing heightens the sensation of our skin finally making contact. The scorching heat of his muscled chest crushed against my aching nipples and the drag of my nails over his carved shoulders, make my panties wet and my heart race. I could sink into him, burrow underneath his skin, and I still wouldn't feel complete. Nothing but the feel of him inside me will soothe this ache.

But when I slip my hand between us and dip two fingers into the waistband of his jeans, Finn pulls away and, with a pained groan, wraps his hand around my wrist.

"Are you sure?" he asks breathlessly.

I kiss him deeply and roll my center against him. "I've never been more sure of anything in my life."

Finn kisses me back, his free hand finding its way to the back of my neck and a fistful of hair, but he doesn't release my wrist.

"You promised to make me come... and come... and come... remember?" I whisper against his ear, circling my hips against his hard-on to emphasize each word.

Finn moans, then turns his face into the curve of my neck. "That isn't what this is," he replies, and the movement of his lips, the warmth of his breath, the gravity of his words make me shiver. "And you know it."

"Finn—"

"I'll make you come," he says roughly. "I'll make you scream. I'll make you beg me to stop before you beg me for more."

I whimper and curl myself around him, sinking my teeth into his shoulder as I tug the waistband of his jeans, but his fingers only tighten around my wrist.

"But I never want to be the reason you cry," he says quietly. "You're coming out of a serious relationship. You might regret this one day."

"I won't," I tell him, and when he opens his mouth to argue, I cover it with my free hand. "Can't you feel how right this is?"

When I'm certain he's not going to disagree, I let my hand fall, and he drops his mouth to run his lips over the length of my neck, over my shoulder and back again. His clasp on my wrist loosens a little and his other hand traces the dip of my spine. "Yeah, I can."

"And if you're worried about my vulnerability, how's this for honesty?" I set my forehead against his and whisper, "I want to erase all traces of *him*. I need to reject the final claim he has on me—that he's the only one to have been with me like that. I hate that of all the ways I can remove him from my life, this is the thing I can't undo. If I have any regrets in life, it's him. Not you."

Finn's body tenses, and I ghost my lips over the hard lines of his shoulder. His physique is overwhelming in its perfection and a testament to his self-discipline and commitment. He does what needs to be done and works hard for the things he values, and nothing moves Finn unless he wants to be moved. Nobody could convince him to do a thing he didn't want to do.

"I want to be free," I murmur. "Fuck me. Please."

With a pained moan, Finn lifts me off his lap and sets me on my feet between his open knees. Then he slides his fingers into the band of my yoga pants. He hesitates, eyes falling to Dakota, who watches us with canine disinterest.

"Dakota," Finn snaps. "Inside and on your bed."

She pushes to her feet with a yawn and disappears into the house without a backward glance.

With a look to make sure I'm still okay with the placement of his hands and a fast squeeze of his ropey forearms to let him know that I am, Finn drags my pants down my legs. He steadies me with his palms on my hips as I step out of them and then tucks his thumbs into the fine lace of my panties. He skims the edge of the fabric around to my inner thighs and curses under his breath when he finds them damp, then peels off my underwear too.

When I'm naked on the porch, warm rays of spring sunshine falling against my back, desire pooling at my core and my inner muscles rhythmically clenching with need, Finn grips my waist and rests his forehead on my stomach, eyes closed as if in prayer.

I weave my fingers into his soft blond hair. "Finn?"

He drops a gentle kiss on my skin, then ducks his head to leave another on my pussy, just above my clit, holding his hot lips against me and inhaling deeply. I close my eyes with a shiver.

I've never had a man go down on me, and if that one kiss is a preview of what it would be like to feel Finn's mouth on me, I might not survive it.

"I've fantasized about this a thousand times," Finn confesses. "I've spent hours—days, weeks, eternity—thinking about how it'd feel to sink inside you. To feel this tight pussy wrapped around me, my dick filling you up till you couldn't take any more, then giving you one more inch. So if this is what you want, I'm too weak a man to say no."

His declaration stuns me. Has he really been so distracted by me? My coiling desire twists alongside a growing sense of confidence and control. Finn sees a woman when he looks at me. Not a paycheck. Not a chess piece. Just me. And that's a powerful aphrodisiac.

"I need this, Finn," I say breathily. "I need you."

Too soon he pulls away, and I palm a breast as I watch him unbutton his jeans and push them down his legs. His underwear follows, his cock springing free, and I whimper. Long and thick, rock hard and velvety smooth, strained and throbbing, head tight and slit beaded with precum.

Up close, he's bigger than I first realized. Much bigger than I'm used to. My heart pounds with want and worry, and the swoop in my belly is ninety percent lust and ten percent apprehension, like a pulsing bass under a soul-changing melody. I want him, but can I handle him?

I lick my lips as Finn gives himself a gentle stroke and rolls his thumb over the hint of moisture. "I have condoms inside."

I shake my head and widen my legs so that my thighs brace his knees. "I'm on birth control, and when I discovered *he* was unfaithful, I got tested for everything. If you tell me it's safe to do this with nothing between us, I believe you."

Finn groans and kneads his fingers into my hips. "It's safe," he says hoarsely. "You're always safe with me."

I gasp as he lifts me up and settles my knees on either side of his hips, then leans back and holds me over the head of his cock. The muscles in his abs and thighs cord with the effort of keeping the swing still, and his forearms rope with strength as he balances me over his length.

The first brush of him against my pussy almost tips me over the edge, and I gasp at the zip of arousal that sparks in my clit.

"You like that, Songbird?" Finn's smirk is smug, his eyes intense on mine, but tiny beads of perspiration on his brow give away how hard it is for him to go slow.

I drive my fingertips into his shoulder and give him an assenting nod, and he eases me down farther. I maintain eye contact, needing to read what this does to him as much as I want him to know how this moment is changing me, and I hiss at the feel of him finally inside me. Finn grunts as my pussy stretches for him, pupils dilating and the line between his brows growing deeper.

He moves one hand off my hip so he can set the pad of his thumb on my clit, massaging it with slow circles that make me breathe deep and lean into him.

"That's it. Good girl." Finn slips his fingers through my slickness, swirling the wetness all over me and then down the shaft of his erection. "You've only got the tip, beautiful, so if you want more, you're going to have to relax."

Only the tip? Oh, God. Finn's dick is going to end me, but I'm ready for my rebirth.

"I want it all," I say as I ease down, moaning at the fullness. Saying what I want out loud turns me on even more, and my core relaxes enough to accept another inch. "Give it to me, Finn."

"Fuck, yeah." His fingers work between my legs while his other hand digs almost painfully into my hip and his voice drops to a growl of restraint. "Deep breath, Songbird. The deeper you breathe, the deeper I get."

I sigh out a little more tension and slide again, already sensing the first hints of my orgasm coiling behind my navel and fluttering around Finn's impressive girth.

He breathes heavily as he clenches his jaw. "Fuck," he grunts. "*Fuck.* We're going slow this time, beautiful, because I want you to remember every second of the first time my cock sank inside you, but I'm never going to manage this again. Remember that. Next time I'm fucking this pretty cunt, you'll be doing some of that begging we talked about earlier."

His words trigger a flood between my thighs because yes, *yes*, I want him to ruin me. I fold myself over him with a shaky moan, my pussy stretching to accommodate more, and I can't stop the way my hips roll.

"Such a greedy pussy," Finn murmurs, turning his head to nip at the curve of my neck, answering the rhythm of my pelvis with a thrust of his own. His hands travel up my body, one to cup a breast and tweak the nipple, the other to tangle in my hair and pull back my head to expose my throat to his hot tongue. "Already taking more than she thought she could handle, and you want to know why?"

I grind against him, closing in on the base of his dick,

and the revelation that I'm about to be fully seated on Finn's magnificent cock infuses every cell of my being with uncontrollable lust.

"Why?" I demand.

The undulation of the porch swing, rocking with our movements, amplifies the friction between our bodies, and Finn groans, wrapping a large, hard arm around my waist as he anchors me to the last inch of heaven. I cry out as my clit hits his pubic bone, then gyrate like an unhinged person. My climax is so close, his words driving me higher and wilder.

"Because she was waiting for me. Waiting for a cock that would fill her up." Finn grunts, arm tightening around me, our damp bodies sliding against each other, his hips rocking to meet mine. "Waiting for a man that would stretch her the way she needs to be stretched. Waiting for the moment she was treated the way she deserved to be treated. The day she'd be fucked"—he pumps upside me, hard and feral, and I respond with a wordless cry—"by a man—another thrust, and I'm almost there—"who knows"—Finn's cock throbs and twitches inside me, and I can feel his orgasm bearing down alongside mine—"what the fuck"—another pump of his hips, hard and nearly violent, that pushes me over the edge—"he's doing."

Finn's final words are delivered with a primal moan. My inner muscles clench around his cock and I'm racked with an orgasm so intense I don't know if my eyes are closed or if I've slipped into semi-consciousness. I tremble through it, waves of pleasure dragging me under, Finn's cock pulsing inside me.

He softens as we cling to each other, catching our breaths and our thoughts. Finn's mouth finds mine first, but I'm waiting for it, and our kiss is deeper and more connected than ever. I wrap my arms around his neck and open my mouth, inviting him in again. How can a kiss feel this intimate after what we just did?

Maybe because Finn and I made more than music together this afternoon. We made magic.

SEVENTEEN

Finn

THERE WAS THE WORLD BEFORE that afternoon with Rosie and there is the world after. The first was compartmentalized with all the moving parts and priorities ordered and packed away in little boxes. I knew where everything went, where to find what I needed, and what I had to do to get through a day. No chance that anything or anyone would slip through the cracks.

The second world is a spilled drawer with questions and passion scattered all over the floor, and I'm standing in the middle, surrounded by it all. The strange part is I don't have the vaguest desire to tidy up. When it's time to make my life neat again, it'll be time to say goodbye, and I'm not ready to do that.

After what happened on the porch, Rosie dug another flannel from my closet and curled up on the sofa where she watched me cook dinner. Following her near-fire, not to mention almost constant distractedness the last few days, she's given up her claim on the kitchen. I prefer it this way because, yes, it means the food on our plates is actually edible, but more than that, I like taking care of her.

Rosie's eyes never leave me unless it's to scribble something on the notepad at her side. When that happens, I throw her knowing smiles and affectionate winks. She's thinking about sex. She's thinking about the song we wrote. I wonder if her moans and dirty talk have imposed themselves on the notes and lyrics we wrote together, creating a song nobody will ever know but us, and if it's on repeat in her mind the way it is in mine.

I might be onto something, because she rests her head on the back of the sofa and replies to my smiles with looks so soft they could be caresses. There's a peacefulness about her that wasn't there before. An energy of acceptance or surrender, like everything is right in her world and there's nothing left to fight. That's what I'm focused on. Not the mind-blanking rage of knowing that jackass ever got to touch her—and when he did, he didn't do it right.

Her asshole ex better hope we never cross paths again because the list of reasons I have to knock that fucker on his ass gets longer every day. It makes no sense to be jealous of a man Rosie was with before she ever knew me, but I hate that guy for fucking up the privilege of being Rosie's guy. She put her body, her spirit, and her soul in his hands, and he desecrated them.

Rosie honored me with that holy trinity today. Making

music with her. Sinking into her. Understanding her. She stripped me down and made me hers, and I'll never be the same.

"Food's ready," I say, and when she gives me a lazy smile, like she's still recovering from what we did on the porch swing, I collect our bowls and cozy up beside her on the couch. She shares a light blanket we really don't need, throwing it across my knees, then accepts her macaroni and cheese and hums with delight.

"Pasta ai quattro formaggi," she says, scooping up a forkful and blowing over the hot sauce to cool it.

I'm temporarily distracted by the tight O of her mouth, picturing her plump pink lips wrapped around my cock, but finally manage to say, "It's mac and cheese with toasted breadcrumbs on top."

She volleys back one of the winks I've been throwing her way. "I know, but my version sounds better."

Fuck, I love her like this. At ease in her own skin.

"So." I swallow a mouthful of pasta that's too hot because I don't have the patience to wait until it cools. "Today was…"

"Magical?"

Rosie turns her body to mine and snuggles closer, and when Dakota notices the lovefest happening without her, she launches herself onto Rosie's other side and cuddles against her hip.

I kiss Rosie's forehead. "It was," I agree. "How soon until we can do it again?"

A pretty blush warms her cheeks as she turns her glittering baby blues on me. "You're thinking about next time already?"

I chuckle and bury my nose in her curls. They're tighter and fluffier than the style she wears for the cameras, and in my opinion, much prettier. "Ah, Songbird. You've got no idea."

She seems to like my answer because she burrows in against my side. I'm not liking even the hint of space between us, so I wedge my bowl between my thighs, wrap my arm around her, and tuck her in close.

I down another forkful of pasta and think about our afternoon. Not the sex—or not only the sex because the bounce of Rosie's tits isn't a picture I'll ever get out of my head—but what led to it. Writing and playing and singing. I've never created music with another person before, and I'm curious if it's like that for everyone. The way we fed off each other, finished each other's lyrics, read each other's minds. Is that what making art is like? Because I could do what we did today for the rest of my life.

Rosie squints up at me like she knows what I'm thinking. "You want to talk to me about something," she guesses.

"Yeah," I admit, deciding not to ask *is it always like that for you?* I'm not prepared to hear her say that what the two of us shared is something she's experienced with a dozen other musicians. Instead, I go for something with lower stakes. "Isn't the music enough?"

Her brow creases, and she drops her head to one side. "What do you mean?"

I set my half-eaten dinner on the coffee table, out of reach of Dakota's quivering snout, so I can circle Rosie with both arms.

"I suppose what I'm trying to say is there are things about your world I don't understand. When your calling in life is your music, how can you stand all the shit that goes with it, like people centering you in their lives and wanting things from you that you shouldn't have to give? How do you live with people looking at you all the time? How do you prioritize the important stuff? When you're so freaking good at the art, why isn't the music enough?"

"Well..." Rosie gazes up at the vaulted ceiling beams like the answers are hidden in their shadows. "I think if I had to choose, the music would be enough. I mean, even if all the other things went away, I couldn't *not* be a songwriter. It's who I am."

There's a pause, and I prompt her with a gentle "but?"

She drops her head onto my shoulder. "But what would that look like? Yes, fame comes with drawbacks, and money makes things complicated, but they allow me to do things that other artists can't. For instance, I don't need to divide my time or my focus. I don't need to spend my days waiting tables and my nights writing songs. Music *is* my job, and I'm lucky to do what I love for a living. How many other people can say as much?"

I frown to myself and brush my thumb along her flannel-clad shoulder. "That makes sense."

"And money isn't necessarily evil. It makes it possible for me to help people." She pokes at her dinner, stirring the cooling macaroni around the base of the bowl, then sets it on the table beside mine. "I give away a lot of it. I want to set up my own foundation one day, but the plans aren't there yet."

Pride and admiration and a fuck-ton of respect almost drown me, and I tip up her chin so I can kiss her full on the mouth. "You're something special, do you know that?"

Rosie darts in for another kiss, a smile on her mouth when she does it, and for the first time I can see an upside to her situation. It'd be awesome to have the power to change the world. It might even make a complicated life worthwhile.

"Those sorts of things turn fame into a trade-off I'm willing to make." She wriggles closer against me, and Dakota follows, resting her heavy head in Rosie's lap. "I know lots of talented songwriters and producers who make plenty of money, but nobody would recognize them if they walked down the street."

I perk up at this, thinking it doesn't sound so bad, but then Rosie rolls her head back to grin up at me.

"But Finn? That's not me. I love the rush of performing. Maybe that makes me shallow, and yes, it's a fickle measure of validation, but nothing compares." Her eyes grow bright and her back straightens, like she's reliving a moment on stage. "The lights and the energy. Thousands of people screaming my name. Those same people singing along to songs that started as a tiny spark in my soul and now burn bright in the hearts of so many others. The humanity of it. The connection. Reaching people and validating *them*. Changing *them*. Yes, I'll always make music, but I also want to share it. What use is art if we don't give it to the people who need it most?"

Rosie makes sense, and even the uplift in her tone tells me

that she'll never walk away from the stage. Not that she should, and not that I'd ask her to, but it makes her life and mine that much more incompatible. I live in a one-bedroom bungalow on a property I share with four brothers and sisters. Charles pays me a salary, but I barely touch it because my costs are covered by the family business. Ten days ago, my sole purpose in life was digging up twenty feet of old flagstone. Today it's making this beautiful woman come.

Empty hands. That's all I have to offer.

I slip my fingers into hers and lift her knuckles to my lips. "You're stunning on stage," I tell her. "You belong up there."

She shoots me a puzzled smile before understanding falls across her features. "You mean the shows you saw on the tour."

I tilt my head side to side. "Those and every clip I could find on YouTube and social media of you performing on the tour. Before the tour. After it. In bars and in stadiums. On television. I think I've seen everything there is to see and you're unforgettable in every single one."

Rosie feigns a gasp and then pokes me playfully in the ribs. "Have you been stalking me, sir?"

I snatch her hand and hold it against my chest, hoping she can feel how steady my heart beats beneath our palms. Always the truth.

"I couldn't stop caring even after *he* kicked me off your security team. I watched it all. Your performances. Your social media. Interviews. News reports. I kept an eye on you as best I could. I promise."

Tears fill her eyes as Rosie glides her hand around my neck and pulls me down for a kiss. It's deep and soft and slow. A taste of what's to come the next time I get her naked.

She pulls away just enough to press her forehead to mine. "Thank you."

I slip my hand under the hem of Rosie's shirt, palm skating the smooth length of her thigh. She moans and shifts to give me greater access, and I glance at Dakota over her shoulder, who's watching with liquid eyes that are more curious than I'm comfortable with.

"Hey, Songbird," I murmur before kissing her again. "Why don't we—"

My phone chooses that moment to light up with a call from my brother, and the vibration makes it scoot sideways along the coffee table.

"He won't give up," I grumble as I reach over to reject the call, but Rosie stops me with a hand on my forearm.

"Has he been trying to reach you?"

"Yeah." I pick up the phone and let it vibrate in my palm. "A couple texts the last few days. There's a thing happening up at the main house tomorrow evening and he wants to make sure I'll be there, but—"

"What kind of *thing*?"

"Izzy, my niece, puts on family nights where we get together for dinner and games or whatever she wants to do. Dylan's trying to pin me down, but I can't go and I can't tell him why, so I've been an asshole and avoided him. He'll get the hint."

Rosie twists her fingers in my hair. The phone grows still in my hand, and my dick takes both as positive encouragement. I set the device aside and resume exploring Rosie's upper thighs.

"You should go," she says even as she offers me the hollow of her throat to kiss.

"To the house?" I mumble against her sweet skin. "No. I'm not leaving you here."

"I'm not suggesting you do."

I nip at her earlobe then kiss the soft skin at the juncture of her jaw, and Rosie sighs, pretty and needy enough to send blood bolting for my crotch.

"I'll go with you."

"You'll..." It takes a second for her suggestion to pierce the sex-fog, and when it does, I sit back. "You want to go with me? To family night? At the Davenport house?"

"Yes?" Rosie narrows her eyes cautiously. "Why? You say it like it's a bad thing."

"Not at all. I mean, they'll give me shit for bringing a girl, but that's to be expected. You've already met Chord and Violet and Charles, so that's a third of the family already done. It's just..."

She picks up my free hand and gives it a supportive squeeze. "Just what?"

"It's a little exposed," I explain. "We all know how to keep our mouths shut—even Daisy, thanks to growing up with a famous hockey player for a big brother—but I can't promise that Izzy won't let something slip at school or her extracurricular activities. She's only six, and I don't feel comfortable asking her to keep secrets. And it won't be just my brothers and sisters. Violet's dad will be there too. Possibly Poppy's mom. They're good people, but even good people can unintentionally do the wrong thing."

Rosie draws her bottom lip between her teeth, nibbling the pink pillow as she contemplates her next steps, completely unaware that one little action has my dick fighting for freedom. I try not to squirm.

"Finn." She adds her other hand to mine, trapping my fingers between her palms. "I've been off the grid for three weeks, and as much as I love it here, I can't stay forever. We've been avoiding the obvious, but..." Her shoulders drop, and she gives me a regretful half-smile. "I can't hide out much longer. The last lot of security personnel you sent me were good enough to hire, and my record label is connecting me with a new publicist and legal team." She studies my hand in hers, tracing the veins underneath my skin as her voice grows quiet. "It's probably time for me to go back to LA."

EIGHTEEN

Finn

MY THROAT IS DRY AND my stomach is in knots, but I don't know what I expected. Rosie was always going to return to her world and leave me behind, and I'm proud that she's gathered enough strength to do it, but beneath that is panic. How do I know she'll be safe on her own? How am I supposed to live without her?

I clear my throat, but keeping my voice even takes effort. "There's still the problem of the guy from New Orleans. We don't know where he is or if he's planning something."

Rosie drops her head to one side. "And we may never know," she says gently.

"Yeah." I look at our hands, noting the smooth softness of hers against the rough texture of mine. She doesn't belong here. We both know it even if neither of us wants to say it. "Maybe."

Rosie lifts her chin, shaking off the gloom of our conversation. "But we don't need to talk about that now, and I can delay long enough to meet your family. Game nights for me growing up were only ever playing gin rummy with my grandmother. Yours sound a lot more, uh... energetic?"

I snort. "They're pretty low-key, but yeah, they're kind of fun."

"So... can we go?"

She bounces with enthusiasm, which means it's impossible to disappoint her. I shake my head, adoration tugging at my mouth, as I swipe to open my phone and return Dylan's call.

"Put it on speaker," she whispers as she squirms against me, and I can't quite believe she's this invested in a night with my siblings.

I hit the microphone icon, and the sound of an outgoing call reverberates around the cabin.

"Bro," Dylan says on the other end of the line. "I was twelve hours away from doing a welfare check. Everything all right?"

I cast a look toward Rosie to make sure she knows Dylan's joking, but her brow creases. In the background of the call, the noises of a commercial kitchen fade as Dylan moves to a quieter location at our family restaurant, The Hill at Silver Leaf Ranch.

"Sorry about that," I reply. "I've, uh... I've been busy."

"Oh, yeah? What's going on?"

"I relaid Dad's flagstone path down to the river dock," I tell him.

"It took two weeks? Man. You should have said something. I'd have come down there to help out."

"Nah. I had it under control."

"Charlie mentioned you've been focused on your own projects and made us promise to give you a few days to yourself, but Izzy's planning another family night. Are you up for it?"

I throw a cautious look at Rosie, a warning that this is her final chance to back out. She digs her fingers into my bicep, nodding as she tries to shake a reply out of me.

"Yeah. Of course, bro. Wouldn't miss it, but..."

"But?"

"But I'm going to bring someone. You think Izzy will be all right with that?"

There's a beat of silence that lasts a little too long, and I share a puzzled look with Rosie.

"You still there?" I ask.

Dylan laughs. "Fuck, yeah. You got yourself a girl? About time."

The back of my neck grows hot as, beside me, Rosie covers her mouth to stifle a giggle.

"How old are you, little brother?" I ask dryly.

Dylan hoots again. "Young enough to know our sisters are going to flip out over this. Does your date know she's the first girl you've ever brought home?"

Rosie grows still at my side.

"Just set an extra place at the table, okay?" I say into the phone.

"Sure, sure." The grin on Dylan's face is obvious in his voice. "Can't wait to meet the first woman who finally made it through your front door."

"Great," I say. "That's awesome."

My voice is flat, a knee-jerk defense to my brother's good-natured ribbing, but there's more to it than that. He's right. I've never been serious with anyone. Not as a teenager. Not when I was home between deployments. Not in the year and more since I've been discharged. Sex is simple. I'm good at sex. Relationships are complicated and I don't do complicated.

But the thought of Rosie sitting at my family's table, the one where my mom and dad served their kids breakfast every morning and dinner every night, fills me with a rising kind of satisfaction and joy, but also grief and sorrow. I swallow down a confused swirl of emotions for all the things I can't share with my parents. The things I don't have and will never have. The things I want but can't keep.

I can't look at Rosie in case she reads the torment in my eyes, and from his restaurant all the way on the other side of Silver Leaf, Dylan's got no idea what he's just stirred up.

"Oh, and the theme for this month is tacos and tunes," Dylan tosses out as an afterthought. "So let me know if your girlfriend has any dietary restrictions. Poppy rented a karaoke machine, and Izzy asked if you could bring your guitar. She's been practicing that damn trumpet morning and night so she can perform with you. Heads up: her tune of choice is 'Mary Had A Little Lamb.'" He pauses, then adds, "I think."

"Noted," I reply. "And not a problem. See you tomorrow."

As soon as I end the call, I spin to Rosie to offer her an out. "I'll tell them you're sick. We're sick. We got food poisoning or something."

She laughs lightly. "That's so not necessary. Let's do karaoke. It'll be fun."

I pinch the bridge of my nose and take a deep breath, imagining Rosie with a ratty rented microphone in my parents' old house singing along to a static "Total Eclipse of the Heart" backing track while my siblings play it *really* uncool.

"You do not have to sing in my family's old living room," I say.

Rosie takes my hand and gently pulls it from my face. "I'm the first girl you've brought home, huh?"

I play dumb. "You heard that?"

She drops her head to the side. "Yes, I heard it, but if you don't want to talk about it, we don't have to."

Rosie brushes my lips with a quick kiss, then collects our bowls and takes them to the kitchen sink. I watch her walk away, flannel shirt fluttering around her thighs, smooth calves lithe and lean, and her hair a natural tangle of curls.

I'm still watching when she gets to the foot of the ladder, ready to ascend for bed, and pauses with her hand on a rung. I drag my eyes up her body and she's watching me with a smile that confirms she can read my mind.

"About our sleeping arrangements, Mr. Morals. I'm wondering, after what we did this afternoon, if we can forget this whole sleeping-on-the-couch thing?"

I launch myself over the back of the couch, smooth enough to barely disturb my sleeping Labrador, and I'm across the room in half a dozen strides.

I loop my arms around her waist. "Hell, yeah, we can do that."

After a kiss that makes her moan, I follow her up the ladder. My bedroom is cloaked in shadow and tinted with the moon glow seeping through the windows, and soon we're naked under the covers, Rosie with her head on my chest. She cranes her neck to kiss me, breasts pressed against my side, hips nudging mine, our legs tangled beneath the sheets. I'm hard and ready to go when she whispers against my chest.

"Can we stay like this for a while?" She reaches down to stroke my rock-hard dick, and I drop my head back with a groan. "I know that probably isn't what you had in mind for tonight, but I feel so happy and so safe right now. In my whole life, I've never gone to sleep feeling like this."

She slips her hand up my stomach, tucks it between her cheek and my pec, and watches me closely for an answer. I tighten my arm around her body and kiss her again. Softly. A silent promise to be the man she needs tonight, whoever and whatever that might be.

"We can do that," I tell her, and we do. We sleep twisted around each other without waking once. All night long.

I wake up with a soft, slender hand on my abs, temptingly close to my morning hard-on. I turn my head toward the blonde, rose-petal scented locks fanned out over my shoulder and inhale deeply, moaning and flexing my thighs as that same hand flutters lower.

I push the covers down over my hips, exposing Rosie's naked form beside me and her hand edging closer to my dick.

"You have the most perfect..." She sighs and kisses my chest, then looks up at me. "Can I touch it?"

I lift my hips and nudge her hovering fingers with the crown. "You can do whatever you want with me, Songbird."

Her fingers are cool as she wraps them around my shaft, and my breath hisses between my teeth.

"You're so hard." Rosie strokes me from root to tip with a featherlight touch that's too much and not enough all at the same time. "And... big."

I grunt and resist the instinct to thrust up into her hand. There's a divine torture in lying perfectly still and letting her explore me. Her admiration does things to me, and my dick swells as my arousal heightens.

Rosie responds with a light squeeze that makes me close my eyes, and when her thumb glides over my slit, it takes a bead of precum with it. She spreads the moisture over the head of my dick in soft swirls, and I watch as she lifts her wet thumb to her lips. Her pleased hum when the taste of me hits her tongue pulls at my fraying self-control, and her mouth curves up with satisfaction.

"The other day, when you made yourself come in that chair over there?" She waits for my pained nod of understanding. "That was the first time in my life I wanted to kneel for a man."

I moan and shift my hips in a silent plea for her to put her hand on me again. She obliges, keeping her touch light and gentle as she drags her palm to the base of my dick then slips her fingers underneath to cup my balls. Her fingers dance over me before she gives them an almost rough tug.

"Fuck, Songbird." My words come out through gritted teeth, and the hand I slide into her pillow-mussed hair grips the strands with more force than I intended. Her eyes grow bright at the brief tension on her scalp. "You're going to kill me."

Her mouth quirks again, like she enjoys having power over me. "I've never fantasized about a... a cock before," she says.

The way she hesitates before she says *cock* only makes her dirty talk hotter. My fingers twist in her hair again, and my pelvis jerks in a frustrated thrust.

"What happens in your fantasy?" I ask, voice low and aroused.

Color paints her sharp cheekbones and she lowers her lashes. "How about I show you?"

I die the first time Rosie wraps her lips around my dick. I swear my soul leaves my body and makes a brief appearance in heaven, and the only thing powerful enough to bring me back is the hot, wet curl of her tongue across the sensitive skin at the tip.

Fuck. *Fuck.* Her lips clamp around me with toe-curling suction, and I realize with desperation that I'm not man enough to take this. Another minute and I'm going to blow down the back of her throat.

I clench my jaw, recite the phonetic alphabet in my head, and try my best to be a damn gentleman. I do not thrust. I do not push her head down. I do not fuck her mouth the way I want to. I sweat and moan, I claw the sheets, and I remind myself how lucky I am to have this woman worship my dick. The least I can do is treat her with respect.

I stuff another pillow under my head to better watch her slide down my length, head bobbing as the wet heat of her mouth envelops more and more of me. When she gags and pulls back, a trail of saliva dripping from her lips, I assume it's all over, but she descends again, this time working me with hand and tongue. Licking me from root to tip like a popsicle. Toying with my balls. Lapping at the crown.

"You taste better than I imagined," she murmurs, laving the slit again, humming with pleasure.

I dig my heels into the mattress. *I* taste good? I'd laugh if I wasn't too turned on to make more than strangled grunts. I'm going to be a fucking madman when I get my head between her legs.

I'm slick now, wet with her spit, and Rosie pumps me harder and harder with a slippery grip. Her mouth roams over my stomach, across my thighs, tongue skating over my balls. Hands, lips, tongue. Heat. Moisture. Pressure. I'm overloaded with sensation, rock hard and desperate to buck, and hanging on by my fingernails. And just when I think it can't get any better, Rosie gazes up at me with puffed-up lips, breath coming fast, and a glint in her innocent blue eyes.

"Finn?" she says with surprising aggression. "I don't know how to phrase this right, so I'm just going to say it. I don't want you to be gentle with me. I don't want you to fight whatever it is that I do to you. If you're crazy for me, then show me. Pull my hair. Fuck my mouth. Lose control. Show me I own you by how desperately you want me."

Jesus fucking Christ. Is Rosie really this unhinged for my dick? I can't string two words together to ask, so I nod pathetically and tighten my grip on her curls. Tighter, until she winces, licks her lips, and dips her head.

"Good boy," she whispers before she dives.

Rosie slips the tip of my dick into her mouth again, and I slide against her hot tongue. When she pulls back too soon, I thread my other hand into her hair and encourage her to go deeper with a thrust of my hips and a gentle push on her head. She groans, the sound vibrating against my dick, and I pump again, harder this time, straining for the hard back of her throat. Rosie chokes and rallies, then sucks and licks and pulls on me with a kind of frantic enthusiasm that has my hips lifting off the mattress, sweat lining my spine, and my balls tightening in the first hints of my orgasm.

I give her hair an insistent tug, and she releases me with a wet pop.

"What's wrong?"

I laugh and it comes out choked. "Absolutely nothing, but I'm going to come and—"

"Good." She wraps her hand around the base of my dick and gives it a firm pull. "Maybe now I can stop dreaming about what it would be like to swallow you down."

I moan and arch my back against the inferno that belts through my body, and Rosie falls on me again, sucking with a renewed determination, taking me deep enough that she gags, saliva leaking between her lips. I jerk my hips and am rewarded with a moan, so I do it again. Harder. Feral. Delirious.

My climax hits hard. Every muscle in my body seizes up and I curl around Rosie's head, cradling her jaw as she fights hard to swallow it all. Her throat works and her lips clamp down, and I unload in wave after pulsing wave until slowly, slowly, it's over.

Rosie lifts her head, swiping her mouth with the back of her wrist, and I slump onto the pillows with a depleted sigh. She curls up beside me, and I scoop her up in the circle of my arms.

"That was nice," she says as she wriggles closer.

"Nice?" I close my eyes and grin at the image of Rosie's lips wrapped around my dick, a picture now permanently burned into my retinas. "That was fucking earth shattering."

"Yeah?"

Her voice is delighted, and I chuckle. "Yeah." I plant a kiss on her forehead. "I hope you're happy, Songbird. I thought I was a mess for you before, but you've just gone and fucking ruined me for life."

NINETEEN

Rosie

WE STEP ONTO THE BACK porch of Finn's family home, Finn with his guitar case, and I latch on to his forearm a split second before he opens the door.

"Are you sure I look okay?"

I glance down at my outfit, uncharacteristically nervous about what I'm wearing. It's dinner at Finn's house, not the GRAMMYs, but I usually have a stylist for these sorts of things. God help me if I'm snapped looking less than the Rosalie Thorne sky-high standard. I've seen the headlines.

Pop Princess braves the crowds with no makeup.

Sexy celebrity dresses down for drinks with friends.

Look at that frizz! Forget the blow-out—she's just like us!

The press takes criticism and ridicule, dresses it up as girl power, and thinks we're all too stupid to notice. It's gross, but it makes money, and it's the world I live in.

Finn scans me from head to toe, examining the tight white tank under the smallest flannel shirt I could find—rolled to my elbows and tied at the waist—my short denim cut-offs, and my white sneakers. The lust in his gaze sends a rush of heat to my cheeks and other inconvenient places.

"Stop it!" I admonish, and he stops my heart with that secretive smirk.

"You look good enough to eat," he says, then dips his head to press his lips to the soft spot between my jaw and my ear that he likes so much. "And don't think I won't be doing that later."

The flush in my face burns hotter, and I turn into his neck. "Nobody's ever done that to me before."

Finn straightens, the arousal in his eyes flaring into animalistic desire. "You really shouldn't have told me that."

My blood catches fire, sparking and rushing like liquid flames down my back and into my fingertips, warming my inner thighs and melting my core. "I—"

The door swings open and I jump away from Finn, a reflex response that makes me feel like a teenager caught kissing after curfew. Charlie is on the other side, and she greets us with a knowing grin.

"I thought I heard someone out here." She swings the door open wider. "Come on in."

"Hi, Charlie," I say. "It's nice to see you again. Thanks for having me."

Finn takes my hand, and his eyes tighten ever so slightly, but Charlie reads his irritation easily enough.

Her smile widens and a sparkle shines in her blue eyes.

"Thanks," he says gruffly, but as he passes by his sister, he still drops an affectionate peck on her cheek.

Once we're inside, the butterflies in my stomach start to spin a little differently, no longer fluttering with desire but anxiety. Finn's brother may have accidentally revealed that Finn had never brought a girl home before, but I've never been the girl brought home either. Not like this. Chip's parents are quintessential blue bloods from old money. Meeting them felt like having dinner with overzealous investors, their approval predetermined by Chip's good business sense and my status as rich and famous. Those were circumstances that proved, once again, that being a global icon gave me an easier path.

I don't think those conditions apply here. At least, I hope they don't. I want Finn's family to like *me*. The person not the pop star. It's a micro kind of pressure I don't face often anymore.

I let Finn lead me into the kitchen of his childhood home, and I'm embraced by the mouthwatering aroma of dinner in the oven and on the stove. Plates, bowls, and napkins are stacked on a serving sideboard, along with a pitcher of something pink next to frosted margarita glasses. The hardwood floors are worn, the kitchen lived-in but tidy, and the enormous timber dining table polished but scarred with years of history. Through the far doorway, I spy a living room with mismatched sofas and an oversized armchair, and a cold fireplace below a mantel littered with family photographs. The walls are cream, the windows clean and furnished with faded plaid drapes, and a staircase on the far side disappears into the top floor.

Soft plush rugs line the floors in there. It's hard to miss how new those look compared to the aged decor everywhere else, but it all fits. It's giving off cozy and comfortable, not dated and drab, and I immediately want to be like one of those rugs. A new addition, sure, and at first glance maybe a little out of place, but when you take a moment to measure one thing in relation to the others, you realize the new things just need time to become part of the final picture. Even now, on a second look at the space, I'm not so tripped up by the color of the rugs, and I wonder if maybe they weren't here all along.

"This is it." Finn gestures around the kitchen, then through the doorway to the adjoining living space. "Eat-in kitchen. Dining table—the location of choice for family dinners, family meetings, family fallouts. You know, the usual. Living room is through there. There's a bathroom and a den on the other side of the hallway, and the porch wraps around... Oh, Jesus." His fingers tighten around mine and I shift a little closer, instinctively seeking his protection. "I apologize in advance for whatever happens next."

He must have already heard the footsteps overhead, and I swallow deeply at his warning as an attractive redheaded woman skips down the stairs, her long hair in a braid, her denim shorts and T-shirt not so different from mine. She's alone, her steps light and breezy as she crosses the living room and heads straight for the kitchen.

"Everyone else will be down in a minute," she announces. "Slight issue with sticky trumpet valves."

She reaches up on her toes to give Finn a warm hug, then extends her hand to me.

"Hi, I'm Poppy," she says before a lightning strike of puzzlement hits her brows. "Holy shit. Has anyone ever told you how much you look like—"

"I'm Rosalie." I accept her hand and give it a friendly shake. "It's nice to meet you."

"You're...?"

Poppy flits a look toward Charlie, and even though she's behind me, I can read the moment she confirms my identity by the momentary shock on Poppy's face. I've seen it before, so I take it in stride, and Poppy recovers pretty well.

She spares an exasperated look for Finn, and he shrugs one shoulder before she shines her smile on me. "Right, well. Hi, Rosalie. It's nice to meet you too."

More traffic descends the stairs, this time a good-looking guy with a neat five-o'clock shadow and his long hair tied back, and a little girl with her dark hair in a braid that mimics Poppy's style almost to the last strand. She's got a brass trumpet in her hands, and they're moving carefully to make sure she doesn't trip.

"Dylan!" Poppy calls, eager impatience making her voice shake a little. "*Finn* is here."

Dylan's grin is the kind you'd expect to find on a little brother who's about to give his big brother shit, and as he approaches the kitchen, I roll my lips to stop a smile.

"About time." Dylan approaches with his daughter's hand clasped in his.

"Dylan?" Finn sets his wide hand on the small of my back, and it's ridiculous how good it makes me feel. "This is Rosalie—"

"Thorne." My name falls out of Dylan's mouth like it was a thought he didn't mean to say, and once it's out, his eyes widen with mortification.

I can feel Finn roll his eyes. Beside Dylan, Poppy snorts and slips an arm through his, a silent kind of reassurance that tells the world these two are a team. I like them both instantly.

I offer Finn's brother my hand. "That's right. It's lovely to meet you, Dylan."

"Rosalie Thorne?" the little girl asks, and we all drop our gazes to look at her. "The *real* Rosalie Thorne?"

I try not to smile because the look on her little face is so serious. "Yes, the real Rosalie Thorne."

"If that's true," she says, "then you should be happy to answer a few questions."

"Izzy." Finn crouches to look his niece in the eye, voice softer than I've ever heard it. "This pretty lady right here really is Rosalie Thorne. You know I'd never lie to you."

Someone find a mop because I'm melting into a puddle.

"Uncle Finn!" Izzy gives him a scolding look. "You're *embarrassing* me."

I laugh. "It's fine, Finn. Truly. What are your questions, Izzy?"

Finn stands again and thanks me with a pulse of his hand around mine.

"How many GRAMMY Awards do you have?" Izzy demands.

I grin when her dad groans quietly. "Seven," I confirm.

Izzy drops her head to one side. "What's your middle name?"

"Betty," I reply, and when her mouth pops open again, I preempt her next query. "After my grandmother."

"What's your favorite color?"

"I have two. Blue, like the ocean when it laps around your ankles, and pink, like cold watermelon in summertime."

Izzy pushes her lips into a contemplative pout, weighing up the chances that this is all some elaborate hoax before her eyebrows shoot up, her brown eyes brighten, and she bounces excitedly on her toes.

"Mommy got a karaoke machine for tonight. Uncle Finn and I are going to play 'Mary Had A Little Lamb.' You can do the singing, if you like?"

"Oh, honey. Rosalie is here as a friend, not a... not a..." Poppy says, trying to save me, but the look she gives me is a little helpless.

"It's fine," I reassure her before I follow Finn's example and stoop to match Izzy's eye level. "I'd love to sing with you tonight. What's your name?"

"Izzy," she confirms, and even though Finn already told me as much, I extend my hand the way I did with everyone else.

"It's wonderful to finally meet you, Izzy. Uncle Finn has told me all about your music lessons and I can't wait to hear you play."

Izzy's flabbergasted face makes me grin, and when I straighten, Poppy and Dylan both mouth *thank you*, which I accept with a small shake of my head and equally silent *no problem*.

"Where's everyone else?" Finn asks, but before anyone can answer the question, there's noise at the front door. Chord and Violet quickly follow, accompanied by a fit guy somewhere in his late forties or early fifties. He looks so much like Violet that even if Finn hadn't already warned me he might be here, I'd assume he was Violet's father.

"Rosalie," Violet says as soon as she notices me, and I'm the first she takes into her arms to say hello. It feels nice, both the hug and her recognition.

Behind her, Chord throws a raised eyebrow at Finn before he schools his face to stillness. "Good to see you again, Rosalie."

"Same to you," I reply.

"This is my dad, Luke," Violet says with a motion toward the other man. "Dad, this is Rosalie."

"It's a pleasure to meet you," he says with a polite nod of his head.

"Likewise," I respond.

An awkward, expectant lull falls over the room as we wait for Luke to place my name, if not my face, but all he does is glance around in confusion.

Poppy covers her mouth to hide a smile, and Charlie steps in to break the tension. "So, where's Daisy?"

"She's—" Poppy begins, before she cuts off with a horrified expression. "Oh, shit."

"Bad word!" Izzy exclaims.

"Here I am!"

It's a tight squeeze with us all crowded into the kitchen, but I don't realize it until we collectively spin in the direction of the new voice. I can't make out the newcomer yet, but someone gasps—I think it's Charlie—and Finn drops his head back with a groan.

"Holy hell," he mutters. "I'm so, so sorry, Rosie. I have no excuse."

"Ta-da!"

Chord snort-laughs, then covers it up with a cough, and everyone shifts enough for me to see Finn's sister, Daisy, spinning in a slow circle to show off her Rosalie Thorne costume from all its various angles. She's wearing a replica of the indigo boned and beaded bodysuit I wore on my recent tour. Her blonde hair is blown out in my trademark curls, her lips are painted intense coral pink, and her white knee-high boots are stacked with a platform heel. She's clutching a bedazzled microphone in one hand, and she sets the other on her hip to strike my signature pose.

"I thought it would be fun to dress up," she says, "because you know I'm singing nothing but sweet Rosalie Tee tonight. I look good, don't you think?"

She really does, and if I weren't here, I bet Izzy would love that her aunt dressed up for the party. Daisy lifts her chin and her hand as she waits for applause, but the vibe is quiet and discomfited, and I hope it's not on my account. I think this is funny. I cross my fingers and hope Daisy will too.

"Ah, Daze?" Poppy slips from our little knot, closes the short distance to Daisy, and takes her hand to put it back by her side. "Finn's here with his date, and... well." Poppy sighs and her posture sags. "Daisy? Meet Rosalie."

Daisy's expression, all bright and excited, searches the group for the only face she shouldn't recognize. I raise my hand to wave awkwardly, then wince at how fast her face falls.

Daisy's throat bobs and she straightens out of her pose, arms dangling dejectedly. "Well, fu—"

"Fancy that!" Dylan shouts. "It's time to eat!"

Everyone takes the hint, turning toward the dining table, and I slip out of the way so I can say a proper hello to Daisy. Finn is with me, but Daisy hangs back, cheeks aflame, and when I reach her, she drops her face into her hands.

"It's a great dupe," I comment, touching the sequins sewn into the fabric cinching Daisy's waist. "Where'd you find it?"

"A costume store I found online," Daisy admits. "Where'd you get yours?"

"Dior."

"Ah." Daisy shifts her feet. "Of course."

I pick up her hand to admire the delicate charm bracelet

on her wrist. "This is gorgeous. You'll have to tell me where I can get one just like it."

She smoothly removes her hand from mine and shifts her weight to one foot, then the other. "I'm not sure. Sorry. It was a gift."

"I don't think I've ever seen you this flustered," Finn says, his tone a mix of amusement and disbelief. "Think you can pull yourself together enough to enjoy your night?"

Daisy suddenly stands taller, rolls her shoulders back, and glares at her brother. "If you'd given me a little warning that you were bringing *Rosalie Thorne* to dinner, maybe I wouldn't have made a complete ass of myself."

Finn chuckles but has the good sense to rub his neck with chagrin. "Maybe you're right, but this moment will go down as a highlight of Davenport family night."

I warm to the idea that I've somehow made it into Finn's family history, but Daisy smacks his chest, hard enough that Finn at least pretends to flinch. Satisfied, Daisy turns to me.

"I'm going to change," she says, "but before I do, let me complete my humiliation by confessing that I am, most probably, your biggest fan. I know every word to every song you've ever released. I went to three of your shows last year, and I paid way too much for a piece of trash that you may or may not have dropped coming out of a hair salon in 2022." She finishes with a flourish and a bow. "Make of that what you will. I'm off to find an open window."

I laugh and stop her from leaving with a hand on her

shoulder. "Don't change your clothes on my account. You look fantastic."

"Thanks, but I can't possibly share air and food and karaoke with you dressed as you. It's too shameful."

Even though Daisy is the one that's made our introduction one of the most unusual I've experienced, I'm the person anxious to rescue it. I want Finn's siblings to like me. "I'll save you a seat at the table?"

"Okay. Thanks."

With a final scowl for Finn that only makes him laugh, Daisy disappears upstairs. I watch her retreat until Finn scoops me up in his arms and kisses me tenderly enough to make my knees weak. I have to grip his upper arms to keep myself from swooning.

"I hope she's okay," I say.

"Who? Daisy?" Finn grins. "She's fine. Trust me. My baby sister's tough enough to get over a little unexpected embarrassment, and as soon as she is, she'll be telling this story for the rest of her life."

"You think so?"

"I know so." He kisses the frown from my mouth with a series of soft kisses, and I take a relaxing breath. "I promise you there's no need to worry. Tonight might already be the best family night ever."

TWENTY

Finn

THERE'S A SHORT GAME OF musical chairs when it's time for us to sit at the table. Izzy begs for a seat beside Rosie, and Rosie stands by her promise to save the chair on her other side for Daisy. I'm bumped to the seat directly opposite, and while at first I'm disappointed that I'm not close enough to slip a sneaky palm on Rosie's thigh or wipe the spot of sauce from the corner of her mouth before she gets it with her napkin, there's the small consolation that from this vantage point, I can keep my eyes on her for the hour we're sitting down to dinner.

It's a lesson in all the ways Rosie shines.

I've thought before that even stripped of professional makeup, designer clothes, and a celebrity spotlight, Rosie is the brightest star in any room. If I had any doubt about how right I was, this dinner with my family puts it to rest. She's dazzling, yes, and it takes me a little study to figure out why. Finally, in a moment that hits me like a blow to the stomach, I realize she's a reflection of people lighting up around her. Rosie steers the discussion away from herself by asking the people I love about *their* lives, *their* passions, *their* dreams. You'd think they'd be too starstruck to respond with anything real, but there's no mistaking how curious Rosie is or her genuine interest in other people's stories. In a surprisingly short span of time, everyone's opening up and relaxing and sharing stories that make her laugh and cry and reach across the table to clink her glass, exchange a tortilla chip, or offer a hug.

Rosie is perfect in a way I didn't know a person could be perfect, and it makes me forget all the reasons she shouldn't belong here.

Sometime after the last round of tacos, while Dylan's dishing up slices of caramel flan, I catch Rosie's eye across the table. Her face is framed with wild tendrils of curls that have escaped her ponytail, and her creamy cheeks are flushed from one and a half margaritas and the rush of laughter and conversation. When she notices me staring, her smile falters, and she drops her head to one side. I can read her unspoken question.

What's that you're hiding behind your eyes?

And the answer. *I don't know how to let you go.*

When our plates are stacked in the sink and Poppy has washed Izzy's face to remove the last traces of caramel, my buzzing six-year-old niece herds us into the living room.

"Boys?" Izzy points to the sofas. "Move these back a little so there's more room for the stage. Oh! And the coffee table too."

"Bossy little thing, isn't she?" I mutter as Dylan and Chord lift the larger couch while I carry Dad's old armchair to the far corner.

Dylan snorts and shakes his head, but he doesn't disagree.

While my brothers and I clear an open space in the middle of the room, Poppy and Charles hook up the karaoke system, which includes a display screen, a sound system, and some kind of strobe light. Next to them, Daisy sets up two microphone stands, and in the kitchen, Violet and her dad make coffee. Rosie's helping Izzy set a book of sheet music on her music stand, and I'm about to cross the room to steal a moment with her when a strong hand lands on my shoulder and yanks me into the hallway.

I stumble as Chord drags me farther from the living room, only spotting Dylan loitering down the corridor once I've got my feet underneath me again. He's got a goofy grin on his face, which, come to think of it, isn't so unusual these days. Ever since he hooked up with our sister's best friend, and worse, since he married her, my younger brother has been happier than I've seen him since we were kids.

"When you said you were bringing a girl, you didn't tell me she was *the* girl." Dylan lands a playful punch on my shoulder. "How the hell did you meet Rosalie Thorne?"

I glance back down the hallway to make sure we're alone. "Long story short: I was her bodyguard for a couple months last year before I came home. I got the job through a friend. It didn't work out, but things with Rosie... Well..." I'm too ashamed to confess that I fucked up the single most important rule of protecting a client. Don't get involved.

But I don't have to say it. The implication is clear enough that Chord nods, amusement on his lips. "Things got complicated."

"You could say that."

Chord gets it. Violet was his personal assistant before they started dating, and when news of their relationship went public, there was viral backlash accusing Violet of being a gold digger. It nearly destroyed their relationship, and it occurs to me now that if word got out about me and Rosie, criticism would fly the other way. I'd be the one taking advantage of her, and while that's garbage, even I can admit that from the outside, I don't add anything of value to our relationship.

"She's cool," Dylan says. "And I say that in spite of the celebrity factor, you know? Not because of it. It's easy to forget she is who she is to the rest of the world."

"Yeah." I tip my head toward our high-profile and higher-paid hockey player brother. "Living with this asshole for a big brother kind of desensitizes a guy to all that fame and fortune. You learn quick that it's total bullshit."

Chord rolls his eyes. "Insults aside, I agree with you. The status and the money are all smoke and mirrors, but that woman in there? She's the real deal."

I didn't know I cared about my brothers' approval until they gave it so easily, and the weirdness I feel having it takes me off guard. I love that they like her, but it carves a pit in my stomach that I don't quite understand. All I know is it's got something to do with her leaving.

"You've got no idea," I say with a reflective sigh. "She's smart and feisty, funny and determined. She's been through a lot and hasn't given up. And she's talented. You wouldn't believe how talented. The music she's been writing while she's been here? Like nothing you've heard before. Rosie is a force of nature."

My brothers stare at me with near identical amusement dancing in their eyes.

"What?" I demand.

"Never knew you could put that many words together at one time," Chord deadpans.

I give him an elbow in the ribs. "Shut up."

"You like her," Dylan says.

"What's your point?"

Chord and Dylan exchange a glance, the kind that says they know more than I do but whatever the secret is, I'm going to learn it soon.

"His point," Chord says, "is if you've found someone who has the power to get through to *you*, you might want to find a way to hang on to her."

I huff out a laugh. The irony of my brothers saying the exact thing I've been thinking all night. "If only it were that easy."

By the time we return to the living room, Izzy and Poppy are ready to kick things off with their rendition of "Bye Bye Bye" by *NSYNC. I slip around the edge of the room to capture Rosie's hand, pulling her with me as I find us a seat, and she curls up against me on the end of one sofa. She's warm, soft, and close, just the way I need her.

Thanks to an extra-large pitcher of Poppy's margarita mix, prepared using a recipe made infamous at her mom's local dive bar, the girls have loosened up enough to give the karaoke machine a real go. Once Izzy and Poppy graciously accept their round of applause, Daisy drags Violet to the microphones, and they bless us with an off-key cover of "This Is Me" from *The Greatest Showman*. Well, Daisy does. Violet sways in the background as backup, and when the song's finished, she returns to her place beside Chord on the opposite sofa, her cheeks pink and a shy smile on her mouth.

Dylan and Luke do a decent version of "Livin' on a Prayer," followed by Daisy, Charles, and Izzy with a take on "Shotgun" that involves a coordinated dance they've obviously rehearsed.

Next to me, Rosie laughs and cheers and demands encores. It takes my family time to work up enough nerve to ask her to perform, but thirty minutes in, Izzy takes her hand and tugs her up onto the makeshift stage. Rosie graciously obliges, giving me a swift kiss before she rises.

It's that one small gesture that tips me past the point of rationality. One passing kiss after dozens and dozens before it. She did it so naturally. I responded so easily. It's like there's never been a time in my life or a place in my world where Rosie *wasn't* kissing me, reaching in and dragging out the parts of me I've always kept to myself. After tonight, there isn't a reason I want my world to be any different.

Izzy and Rosie step behind the microphones, and from her position as unofficial emcee, Poppy cues up the next song. From the first few bars, we recognize it as one of Rosie's most popular tracks, and probably the one that catapulted her stratospheric rise to success. It's an upbeat dance number, popular with kids, about self-love and self-esteem, friendships and freedom, and Izzy's a frantic mess at the idea that she's about to sing her favorite song with the real-life Rosalie.

I catch Rosie's eye and mouth a question. *Is this okay?* She gives me a wink and removes the microphone from its stand, and it takes less than three and half minutes for her to wrap us around her little finger.

Rosie keeps her voice controlled and low, giving Izzy space to belt out her share of the lyrics, but there's no question that Rosie is a natural performer. Her voice is as strong as it is soft. Her charisma is magnetic. You can't help but look at her, and with a quick scan of the room, I can see her effect isn't limited to me. Every person in the room is enthralled.

The song ends and Izzy throws her arms around Rosie, her laughter large and infectious. I share a grin with Rosie, who wraps her arms around the little girl hanging off her waist until Izzy gives her shirt a tug and asks Rosie to lean down to hear a whisper.

I know that whisper is about me when they both turn their eyes on me.

"Uncle Finn!" Izzy says. "Where's your guitar? It's time for 'Mary Had A Little Lamb.'"

Izzy dashes to the side of the room to collect her trumpet, and while Dylan helps her set up, Rosie shoots me a satisfied look as I retrieve my guitar. I also pick up two counter stools from the kitchen and set them behind the mics. If I'm going to play, I'm going to need something to sit on, and Rosie might want somewhere to perch too.

I settle myself on the stool and strum to check the tension in the strings. Something that isn't quite nerves yet isn't exactly impatience makes my chest tighten. I've played a few times for my family, and although Charles is the only one who knows how much music means to me, it's unspoken knowledge that of the five of us, I'm the one who inherited Mom's affinity for music and art. Unspoken because I don't like to talk about it. I never thought it mattered. Now, with "Mary Had A Little Lamb" on the horizon, I feel like I've got something to prove.

I risk a glance at Rosie, sitting on the opposite stool, and catch her watching me with blue eyes so deep I could fall into them and never meet the bottom. That's when I get it. I do have something to prove. To me and to her.

Izzy counts us in with the tap of her toes, and the three of us manage a recognizable performance of the classic nursery rhyme. It's next to impossible to make out the gentle accompaniment of my guitar or Rosie's voice underneath the ear-piercing blast of Izzy's trumpet, but when we've rounded out the final note, Izzy beams at me, then Rosie, and I'm grateful I could make a dream come true for her today.

Poppy jumps up to help Izzy with her instrument, and Rosie stands, too, but I stop her with the first chords of the song we wrote together. With a flash of surprise followed by a smile only for me, she settles back on her stool, shifting until she's found a position that's comfortable.

I raise my eyebrows slightly in question, she answers me with the drop of her chin, and I start to play.

I remember every note and word of the song we wrote on my porch because I've replayed every layer of it a thousand times in my head. I'm peripherally aware of the hush that falls over the room and the energetic thrum that tells me that, one by one, my family is catching on that we're playing a Rosalie Thorne original. Her voice dances with the music from my guitar, balancing every inflection and note with expert control and instinct. Rosie gives an understated and emotional delivery of the first chorus, and as I fill the next space with my fingers, I don't think anyone expects me to open my mouth and sing. Least of all me.

I almost chicken out, but I want Rosie to know how much this song changed me. Writing it with her and for her. I want her to know I take her art seriously and that whatever is happening between us means something. And I have to believe, by the way she watches me croon the words she wrote, she understands what I'm trying to say. She watches me like she always knew I could do this.

The song draws to a close and we transition into silence with my fingers light on my strings. There's a sense of a collective held breath as I set my guitar down against my chair and Rosie slowly comes to a stand. She closes the few steps between us and stops between my open knees. In front of everyone, she loops her arms around my neck, pulls my mouth to hers, and kisses me.

There may be applause. There may be cheers. There might even be a few sniffles. I don't know and I don't care. I'm too busy kissing the woman I love.

TWENTY-ONE

Finn

I HOLD ROSIE'S HAND ON the drive home, and she cuddles against me on the bench seat of my old pickup truck. When the warmth of her skin and the twist of her fingers aren't enough, I scoop her bare legs over mine until she's all but sitting in my lap. She rests her head against my chest, and I release her hand so I can loop an arm around her. The need to be closer than my truck allows is palpable.

I pull up to the cabin and when the headlights cut out, we're plunged into the kind of blackness that only exists in the middle of nowhere. Moonlight dapples the river with shimmering silver, the porch light illuminates the front door and not much else, and Rosie has never looked more beautiful. I slip out of the cab and turn around, slide her toward me, and set her on the ground, then take her hand again to lead her up the porch steps. The silence between us feels sacred, like one word might snap tonight's enchantment and so before we speak, we need to *do something* to transform the fragile possibility between us into something nobody can break.

Now, I think when we're standing by the door. *Now. Before it's too late.*

I freeze with my hand on the door handle and kiss her. She kisses me back, and the entire universe contracts into the infinitesimal space between our lips.

I kiss her as I scoop her into my arms. I kiss her while I carry her inside. At the bottom of the ladder, when she tightens her arms around my neck and refuses to relinquish my mouth, I shift the way I hold her, wrapping her legs around my waist and kissing her while I take us up to the loft.

I kiss her until we're in my room and my legs hit the mattress. I kiss her and she won't let go, so I fall with her, stretching over her as she clings to me. She smells like *her*, and when I attempt to pull away, just long enough to get her clothes off, she twists her fingers in my hair to keep my lips where they are. I give her what we both need, long, luxurious strokes of my tongue and hands that caress her sides. My cock thickens and I roll it against her center, but when Rosie slips her fingertips inside the waist of my jeans, I tilt away and finally release her mouth.

She's pretty as a picture beneath me, and I kneel so I can peel the clothes from her body, starting with my flannel shirt and following with the white tank underneath. Her bra goes next, full breasts bouncing free, nipples tight and hard enough that I drop my head to suck one, then the other.

"Oh," she moans as her soft, cool hands glide round the back of my neck.

She skims the skin at the opening of my shirt, and I drag it off. She approves with a contented sigh, and those inquisitive fingers tickle a path over my shoulders, down my arms, across my throat and chest, until the tease of her touch becomes too much for me to bear. I kiss her again, slowly and softly, inviting her to open her mouth with the tentative brush of my tongue, and when she obliges, I stroke a little deeper. Her welcoming mewl makes me groan, and I kiss her harder and rougher, with nips and tugs that will leave her lips swollen and bruised.

Rosie's arms tighten around me, and I can tell by the shift of her hips, the way her fingernails cut into my skin, the hard stroke of her tongue, that she needs more. But fuck, I want this to last forever. I want to kiss this girl until the sun comes up. I want to go slow before we go fast. I want to be the first man to put his mouth on her pussy and make her come with my tongue.

I want to sink into this dream and not surface until... maybe ever.

Rosie seeks the button on my jeans, and I catch her hand with my own. When she tries to yank free, I tighten my grip and pull her hand from my waist, pinning it to the mattress above her head. I transfer my weight to my knees so I can catch her other hand too, lifting it higher and crossing her wrists to trap them there.

"What is it?" she asks, tossing her head. "Why can't I touch you? What do you want?"

I lift my mouth from her neck, trailing the tip of my nose over the hollow of her collarbones and up to her jaw, inhaling deeply when I reach that delicious soft spot below her ear. I snake my free hand up her sternum before wrapping it lightly around her throat.

"I've got what I want," I growl. "Now let me play with it."

A sound escapes her throat. A whimper. A moan. A wordless surrender, and my dick throbs at the sound.

I kiss her again, pushing her into submission with the pressure of my mouth, and she writhes beneath me. I twirl and spiral the tip of my tongue over the swell of her tits and with a rough hand, I cup one breast, squeezing it, bringing her to my mouth. I graze the sensitive nipple with my teeth, and the slight pain is chased with a shot of pure pleasure as Rosie arches against me, begging for more. Her knees fall open, and I take that as my cue to unzip her shorts.

So much for patience and taking it slow. I let her wrists go so I can remove her shorts and panties, and the minute she's naked, I fall between her knees, desperate to be the man to discover the way she tastes when she's turned on. The way she tastes when she comes.

"Fuck, Songbird," I moan as I open her thighs wider and shift to get my head between them and closer to her glistening perfection. "You're soaked for me."

Rosie braids her fingers into my hair as I glide a finger

along her slick center, gathering her arousal and massaging her clit until she squirms.

"Don't tease me, Finn," she begs. "I need to feel you. I need to come so bad."

"I don't mean to tease you, beautiful." I kiss her sticky inner thighs, licking at the hint of her taste with a groan. "And you're going to get what you need, but I'm having the best fucking night of my life down here. I wish you understood how pretty you are. How good you smell. How delicious you taste."

I reach up to touch her face, and Rosie's eyes widen as I paint her famous lips with the wetness on my fingers. She waits, pillowy mouth parted, as I lean in to kiss her. The taste of her arousal mingles between us, the flavor of her pussy hitting both our tongues, and I swallow it along with her moan.

"You like that?" I ask.

Rosie replies with a stunned nod, eyes hazy with lust, and the corner of my mouth lifts. I'm so fucking hard for her, and there'll never be a more overwhelming high than having the power to open this woman's eyes to mind-blowing sex and her own sensuality.

I slide a finger into her, recalling the way she touched herself and mimicking the pumping motion she liked. The wet suck of her cunt makes me close my eyes, and as her hips roll, I apply my thumb to her clit, massaging those swollen nerves in a tight, firm circle.

Her pussy clenches around me, fluttering in rhythm with her needy moans, and I thrust again. When she tries to touch herself, I hold back her hand and increase the pressure of my thumb on her clit, stimulating her until she bucks. As her core clenches and she edges close to her first orgasm, I push another finger inside her, pumping slow and then fast, crooking my fingers, finding that spot on the wall of her core that'll push her into release.

She comes hard and fast, tightening around my fingers and dripping over my hand, and I slow my plunges as her body relaxes into satisfaction.

"Remember how you said you've never had a man's mouth on your pussy?" I ask.

Rosie looks at me with a languid toss of her head, a contended curve to her lips. "Yes?"

"And remember how I said you really shouldn't have told me that?"

She shivers. "I remember."

I grin and swipe my knuckles through her arousal, and she flinches when I sweep past her extra sensitive clit. She closes her eyes and cups a breast, fingers tweaking the nipple, and her exposed throat bobs in a deep swallow as I drop my head between her legs.

The first touch of my tongue on her pussy is a tentative tickle, a test of how responsive she is as well as an attempt to condition myself to her flavor so that her first experience being eaten out isn't a desperate mess made by a man who behaves like a fucking animal.

Unfortunately, she tastes incredible, and at just the brush

of my tongue, she's lifting her hips and hunting for more, hands seeking my head and fingers twisting in my hair. My dick pulses against my jeans, and I shove at my pants to get naked before I drop back onto the mattress. Rosie grips my hair again, hanging on for dear life, and I chuckle under my breath.

If that's the way it has to be, then that's the way it has to be.

She squeaks when I flip our positions, putting me underneath her open knees, then again when I lift her off my waist and settle her on my face.

"What...?" She looks down at me. "I can't sit on your mouth. You won't be able to breathe. I'll kill you."

I laugh and drag my tongue over her soaked folds. "And what a way to die."

Rosie's eyes flutter closed, and she falls forward, one hand gripping the headboard, hips already grinding down, so I dig my fingers into her soft hips, encouraging her to rest her weight on me.

"Sit, Songbird. Ride my mouth and fuck my tongue. Don't stop until you're coming and I'm drowning. You got it?"

"I got it," she agrees between heavy breaths.

She learns fast, and soon I don't need to clutch her against me because she's using me the way I need her to, and I spend the entire time trying not to blow all over my stomach. I eat her hard, tongue and lips and teeth thrusting and sucking and licking and grazing, working to keep up with the pounding pace of her pelvis. Her taste, her scent, her power are intoxicating, and when I sense she's ready to come again, her moans growing louder, her circling hips getting wilder, her ass slicked with sweat, I reach up to pinch her nipple, tweaking and stroking until it's hard and aching.

"Oh, God," she cries, voice climbing with the sharpening motion of her hips. Her pussy is soaked and my face is drenched, and I find myself silently begging for the flood of her climax to take me down. "I'm going—to—come! *Finn*."

I grab her ass, shoulders and arms burning as I hold her while she comes hard on my face. She tastes different after her orgasm, better if that's possible, and when her body moves from tension to release and she shimmies down my body, watching me with a look of wonder mixed with a little bashfulness, I slip a hand around the nape of her neck.

"You're a fast learner," I tell her, and when she drops her eyes shyly, her cheeks flushed and blonde curls sticking to the frame of her face, I grin. "Or maybe I'm a fucking good teacher."

She laughs lightly, and I swipe my face clean with a fistful of the sheets as she collapses onto the mattress, naked and spent.

"Definitely option B," she says, her voice low and sleepy. "Maybe a little of the other too."

I chuckle and get to my knees, covering her sticky body with kisses, following her curves with my tongue and owning every inch of her from her neck to her ankles.

"You've got one more in you," I tell her.

Her smile is radiant as she tosses her head on the pillow. "There is absolutely no way."

I rise to my knees, take her wrist, and wrap her hand around my straining cock. She groans and flexes her fingers, making me moan in return.

"Just one more," I say as I stretch out above her and line up the tip of my dick with her soaked, swollen entrance. "You can do it."

She lifts her knees, then her hips, in invitation, and I slip in the tip. My head drops and I breathe through the resistance, then push a little more. "You're so fucking tight," I grunt with another rock of my hips. "So—fucking—*tight*."

"I can take it," Rosie says as she claws at my ass.

"I know you can, baby." I give her another inch, a fresh line of sweat popping up on my brow. "You're doing so good, but let me play a little, okay? Let me... fucking... play."

I thrust a little deeper, relishing the exquisite torture of sinking in so slowly, but it's not going to last. I can feel the urgency building in the base of my spine, and I almost lose it instantly when I glance down at the place our bodies are connected, the sight of my dick sinking into her.

"You've got no idea how pretty you look stretched around my cock," I tell her, dropping to my elbows so I can whisper in her ear, sweat dripping from my face onto her skin and the sheets. Her fingers claw at my shoulders and sexy little sounds escape her throat. "But you should know that I'm hanging on to control by the tips of my fingers. I can wait till you're soft and ready to take everything I'm going to give you, but as soon as that happens, I'm going to fuck you the way I need to."

She loops her legs around my waist and arches her back, tits flattening against my chest. "And how is that?"

"Messy and wild and desperate, because that's what you do to me, Songbird. You make me all those things. Messy. Wild. And so fucking desperate."

Rosie whimpers as she tucks her face into my neck, and I sink deeper inside her. Deeper and deeper, the slide made easier thanks to her two earlier orgasms, her pussy slippery and supple, and soon I'm buried to the hilt.

"Ready?" I murmur, slipping a hand between us and teasing her sensitive clit, opening her lower lips so I feel the place where she ends and I begin. But there's nothing—no space, no air, no breath—between us.

"I'm ready," she says, and then, "Fuck me, Finn. Please."

I kiss her—hard—and then I fuck her.

I slide out and then in again with a single, almost brutal thrust, and Rosie cries out in reply. She turns her mouth, seeking mine again, and I give it to her, our tongues tangling messily as I piston in and out of her throbbing core. Our bodies slip against each other, sweat and arousal coating our skin, as Rosie meets my frantic thrusts with urgent jerks of her hips.

When the shallow fit of her pussy is no longer enough, I throw her legs over my shoulders. The angle shifts and I hit something deep inside her, and Rosie responds with staccato cries that drive me wild. I grind against her, filling her pussy and stimulating her clit, holding off my own climax until I feel the telltale contractions of her muscles around my dick.

I lean in, bottoming out, and circle my hips. Rosie clamps down on me, her orgasm shuddering through her body, gasping and moaning with her head thrown back in ecstasy. With a few final pumps, I unload inside her, my release pulsing in waves of cum and burning in bright sparks in every cell of my being. I drop my mouth to Rosie's, needing that connection between us as we come together. I keep kissing her until the final throes of our climaxes have receded.

Eventually, our kiss slows and softens just like our muscles, until I'm peppering her mouth and cheekbones, her eyelids and jaw, the tip of her nose and the length of her throat, with adoration and gratitude. Rosie loops her arms around my neck and presses me against her, and I collapse alongside her, scooping her against me, unable to tolerate for even a second the distance between us now that I'm not inside her. Messy and wild and desperate is right. That's exactly the way I feel. How am I supposed to live now that anything short of constant contact feels like too much distance to stand?

"Finn?" Rosie's voice is soft, her back hot and slippery against my chest, and I tuck her in tighter between my heavy arm and my body.

"Yeah, Songbird?"

"I had a really great time tonight," she says.

I kiss her head and curl myself around her body. "Me too."

"I mean all of it. Every moment from the very start. Meeting your family. Sharing a meal. Singing with your sisters." Her voice drops lower. "Singing with you. Making love to you."

I drop my head onto her damp hair, close my eyes, and surrender to the inevitable. I've lost the fight against my head because my heart can't live without her. Not now and not ever. If it means giving up the easy nothing of my life for the chaotic everything of hers, I'll do it. I'll make that choice over and over again.

I pull her tighter against me. "Rosie, I—"

"Don't say it," she interrupts. "Whatever it is, it can't improve on perfect. We can deal with reality tomorrow as long as this dream lasts a little bit longer."

I hold her against me, feeling her breath move in and out, and burrow closer. Whatever changed between us tonight, Rosie feels it too. She might be scared that what we've created won't be the same outside Silver Leaf, but I can't imagine a universe where things are any other way.

"Sure, Songbird," I agree with every intention of making this moment last the rest of our lives. "We can stay like this for as long as you want."

TWENTY-TWO

Rosie

STRETCHED OUT ON MY TOWEL, timber dock at my back and afternoon sunshine wicking river water from my skin, I close my eyes so I can focus on the way this place smells and sounds and *feels*. I never want to forget what these weeks at Silver Leaf have given me, even if the thought of leaving makes me want to cry.

I roll my head to the side so I can examine Finn's profile next to me. My throat, already sharp with the idea of saying goodbye, tightens even more, and my stomach twists into bleaker knots. For the thousandth time since we made love last night, I swallow the plea that hovers on my lips. *Come with me.*

I'm too afraid to say it, even after all my talk of taking back my power and being more confident and in control. Maybe it was only ever bravado, or maybe I'm only strong with

Finn by my side. After spending six years expecting a man to supply my self-esteem, the idea that I might be doing the same with Finn makes it impossible to ask him for this. After all, if he wanted to, he would.

He's been quiet all day, stoic and focused while he finalized security plans for my return to LA, and I'm trying to follow his example. I know he's hurting as much as I am, and after the last three weeks, I know he deals with difficult emotions by staying busy and getting things done. It's selfish to want him to break down to prove he loves me the way I love him, but it would make it easier to take his hand and not let go until we reached Los Angeles.

But that's not going to happen, and I'm choosing to be distracted by everything waiting for me in LA. When I told my record label I had new music, they were understandably ecstatic. My creative juices haven't exactly been flowing in the last year, and I was on tour before that, so they were already impatient to get me back in the studio. They've offered me a private house until I find my feet and a new manager, and they recommended a fantastic new publicist with loads of experience. She's meeting me at the airport at ten a.m. tomorrow so we can talk strategy on the flight to LA, and my new security team will be in place when we get there.

Everything's coming together. Almost everything. After I leave Finn, I wonder if the world will ever feel complete again.

I turn to my side, prop my head above my elbow, and ignoring the pang of anticipated loss behind my ribs,

I try to memorize the shape of the man before me. Finn's strong, hard body is a masterpiece of flesh and ink. His tattoos are a thick maze of intricate shapes and patterns, some faded and others still rich and dark. I reach over to trace a labyrinthine collection of clouds. Delicate line work in swirls and swoops beckon my finger to trace them over the gentle dips and ridges of his ribs and muscles.

Finn cracks one eye and turns his head to look at me. "Thought the swim and the sun might have put you to sleep."

"No. Well, maybe. Just for a minute."

I glide my fingertip through the wetness on his skin and wonder how light or firm I'd need to press to make him flinch. He's hard as stone and about as responsive too.

"I like this one," I tell him, following the lines of sunlight streaming through the cloud bank. "The shading is incredible."

"Thanks. I like that one too."

I track the shapes in his art, circling details as they make themselves known. An angel here. A constellation of stars there. Roses. Thorns. Birds. Angels. Sheet music. Guitar strings. Geographical coordinates. Song lyrics. Poetry.

"*Invisible and idle,*" I read as I brush my thumb over a line of script. "*Waiting.*"

Finn hums, eyes closed again, face to the sun.

"Did you write that?"

His mouth pulls up at one corner. "It was the first thing I ever wrote. Thought it was profound at the time, so I did what any idiot kid would do—I got it in ink."

My eyes sting and I blink to stop the tears from falling. I can still recall the first song I ever wrote, and I can't imagine being so enamored with it that I'd permanently etch it on my body. That Finn felt so certain about his art from such a young age breaks me. What happened that he gave up on it so completely?

"I love it," I whisper, and I dip my head to kiss the lettering across his heart.

Finn strokes my damp hair, and a deep breath expands his chest. In and out.

"I like the birds," I add, outlining the shape of two little flying birds on Finn's stomach. "What are they? Sparrows?"

"Song sparrows," Finn confirms.

"Pretty."

I dance my fingers over his skin, experimenting with the pressure until I find the featherlight touch that leaves goose bumps in its wake. Victory.

"These roses are gorgeous," I murmur, admiring the line work on a piece close to his hip. "I wish I could see them in color. Red, maybe. No. Pink. And green."

Finn's mouth quirks in that secretive smile he has. "I can do that for you."

I straighten, weight leveraged on my arm, for a better look at his face. "You *drew* that?"

"I drew them all."

My breath catches, and I release it with his name riding my exhale. "Finn. They're beautiful."

His grin widens, which is the only warning I have before he flips his body over mine, carefully rolling me onto my back, cradling my head as he flattens me against the timber.

"I've been thinking," he says before he applies his mouth to mine.

I kiss him back and savor the play of cool and warmth between us. The sun, the water, our skin, his tongue. Oh, God. I'm going to miss this.

"Mm?"

Finn moves along my jaw and down over my neck, lips grazing me as his head moves lower. With a gentle pull, he drags the fabric triangle of my river-ruined bra down over my breast, revealing a nipple already peaked from the water and my arousal, and laves at the tip.

"I thought that maybe... It might be a smart idea..."

He yanks at the rest of my bra, rougher this time, desperate to get to me, perhaps hearing a clock ticking the same way I do. When I'm exposed, he teases me with tongue and lips and teeth, tugs and twists with nimble fingers until I'm wet and aching and lifting my hips to search for more.

"What?" I can barely get the words out, too distracted by the path Finn's mouth is moving down toward my navel. "What's your idea?"

My hands are tangled in his hair, and they grow tighter when he lifts his head and turns his intense caramel-colored eyes on me.

"I want to go with you."

I gasp, and my heart rockets into my throat, but I'm too scared to believe what I think I'm hearing. "Go with me where?"

Finn rolls off me again, falling to the timber and resting his head on his hand so he can trace my face the way I memorized his earlier. I slip a hand around his neck to stroke his hair, dissatisfied with being so close without touching him. This is the part where he's supposed to smile a little, my uncertainty giving him one of those secret moments of entertainment that light up his eyes. Instead, his brow furrows, and he mirrors my gesture by cradling my face in his palm.

"I want to go with you to LA."

I yank him to me, lips crashing together as warmth flushes me all over and my chest fills to bursting. Finn kisses me, licking up the salty tears that fall down my face, until he smiles against my mouth.

"You like the idea?" he asks, and when he pulls away a little, I drag him back so I can bury my face in his neck.

"No, I love it. I *love* it."

I breathe in the smell of his skin, savor the safety of his hard arms around me, and I'm tempted to take his gift and run all the way to Los Angeles with it. But once the dizzying high of his offer passes, an irritating voice of reason turns my head. I look out over the river, over the redwoods and the blue sky above, the rolling hills of Sonoma and the ranch that is Finn's legacy. He's going to give all this up, and the question I don't want to ask tumbles out anyway.

"Are you sure, Finn?" I extract myself from his arms so I can read his face. "My schedule will be overwhelming and there won't be many chances to come back to Silver Leaf. I want you with me, but have you thought about what it means? What you'll be giving up?"

"I don't need to think about it." His jaw clenches and his cognac eyes are bright, and I tell myself it's his confidence and not willful blindness that makes my heart pound. "You need me, and I need you. I can't let you go, Songbird, and you can't stay here. The only option is for me to follow where you lead, and that's what I'm going to do."

Finn hooks his big arm around my waist and rolls us to the side, trapping me against his chest with his embrace. The pounding of his heart is deep and measured against mine, which flutters like a bird in comparison.

"Thank you for giving us a chance," I tell him.

"I'm the one who needs to thank you," he says. "For trusting me enough to come here when you needed help and for giving me purpose. I'll do anything to make sure you're safe and protected." His voice drops and his throat bobs in a nervous swallow before he adds, "And loved."

My chest isn't large enough to contain the hurricane of emotions swirling inside me, and they bubble up in my throat.

"I love you, Finn," I whisper, tucking my head against his chest.

I'm the luckiest woman in the world because he kisses my hair, holds me tighter, and says, "I'm sure I love you more."

TWENTY-THREE

Finn

THE MOMENT I STEP ONTO Rosie's private jet is the moment I realize I've underestimated the differences between her world and mine. I'm not talking the miles it takes to move between Silver Leaf and Los Angeles. I'm talking her forty-million-dollar personal aircraft with cream-colored leather seats and timber-topped work desks, fluffy white carpets and fully equipped kitchen, comfortable bedroom and full bathroom. It's bigger than my entire bungalow, and someone has filled the white ceramic vases with meticulously designed floral arrangements. I think about the handfuls of wildflowers I picked to brighten up Rosie's time with me, stuffing them in old mason jars and plonking them wherever I found a bare shelf or windowsill. The comparison is laughable, so it's a good thing I believe money is a joke. It's impressive, sure, but I don't see this kind of wealth and want it for myself. All I'm thinking is how damn proud I am of the woman who built this from nothing. How the hell did I get lucky enough that she looked at me twice?

The flight from San Francisco to Los Angeles takes over an hour and we're not alone. Two pilots and two cabin attendants make up the flight crew, and Rosie's new publicist is with us as well. With half the flight still to go, Rosie has her head together with Pia, a thirty-something woman with deep auburn hair worn in a slick bun at the nape of her neck. I'm at the other end of the jet, laptop on my knees, filing away the latest social media comments from *mistr_ess_el*. He's as active as ever, popping up on every post, liking every comment, making creepy promises that he'll be with Rosie soon. It makes my reason for being here defendable, giving me a clear and compelling purpose to underpin the fact that Rosie and I belong together. That motherfucker should be behind bars, and I'm not going to rest until he is.

I add his most recent social media activity to the folder on my desktop before I send the links through to Drew via email.

Any luck on tracking this guy's location?

Not expecting an answer straightaway, I snap my laptop closed and glance toward Rosie. She's reading something from Pia's lit-up tablet, and without my own device to distract me, my mind strays to Silver Leaf and what Rosie and I left behind.

Mom and Dad's old cabin, locked up and empty again after I spent a year trying to restore it. The new flagstone path to the river that'll be worn by weather before it feels the fall of new feet. My family, farewelled with hurried goodbyes and well wishes yesterday afternoon. And Dakota, temporarily fostered by Charles at the main house, until Rosie and I are settled and can bring her back to live with us.

A sharp pang of guilt grabs me beneath the ribs, and I reach for my phone to send a text to Charles.

Me: How is she?

My phone pings almost immediately. My sister knows who I mean without having to ask, and she responds with a picture of Dakota asleep in Charles's office, her old bed set up in one corner and her bowls filled with water and kibble.

Charles: She's good. How are you?

I tap out my reply.

Me: Call you later.

I lock my phone screen and set it face down next to my untouched flute of champagne. I can't lie to my sister. I want to say everything's fine, because it *is* fine. It's fucking unbelievable. I'm with Rosie, which is everything I want in the world, and who cares where we are as long as we're together, but there's tension in my stomach that won't budge. The problem is going back to LA when there's an active threat to her safety. I can't relax until it's neutralized.

"Finn?" Rosie calls from the other side of the plane, but by the time I've raised my head off the leather recliner, she's already padding over on her bare feet and leaning in to drop a sweet kiss on my mouth. "Are you busy?"

"Nope." I bound to my feet, thankful for something to do. "What do you need?"

Rosie's smile is amused, and she takes my hand as she rolls her head toward her workstation. "Pia wants to talk to you."

"Ah." I rub the back of my neck. "Sure."

I drop into the chair next to Rosie's, Pia opposite and giving me a look I can only describe as professionally wary. Rosie doesn't let go of my hand, and I pull our twisted fingers onto my lap.

"So." Pia sets her clasped hands on the desk and gives me a perfunctory kind of smile. "Rosalie tells me you two are in a relationship?"

Rosie and I haven't had a conversation that would make it official, but we don't need to. We know what we are. I meet Pia's inquisitive look with the kind that lets her know I might not be interested in all the bullshit trappings of celebrity life, but I *am* interested in Rosie. She could declare that the ocean was made of lemonade, and I'd fight anyone who said differently.

"We are," I confirm.

Pia nods, not easily ruffled, and that's got to be a good thing for a woman in her line of work. "We need to talk about how to handle this in the press. The most recent public statement made about the status of Rosalie's personal life was released by Chip Daniels, and it didn't paint her in a particularly positive light."

"He accused her of cheating," I say. "And implied that he left her after discovering her infidelity."

Rosie shifts on her chair, and I brush my thumb over the back of her hand to soothe her.

"Correct." Pia's focus switches from me to Rosie, then back again. "The challenge we face is timing. If you go public with your relationship now, so soon after the last-minute cancelation of the wedding, the optics won't work in our favor. The speed of your attachment will appear to confirm the cheating rumors, and that'll fly in the face of the statement we'll make denying any of it was true."

I turn to Rosie. "You're putting out a statement?"

"It's one option," Rosie says. "And releasing an official statement makes it easier to refuse further questioning from the press and the public."

"Will it expose Chip and the way he treated you?"

Rosie meets my stare with blankness, and I know the answer before she says it. "No."

Ignoring the weight of Pia's analytical gaze, I speak directly to Rosie. "Are you sure that's the right way to manage this? It'll mean Chip gets out of it easier than he deserves. He lied about you. He's an asshole and everyone should know it."

Rosie cups my face with one soft hand. "You're right, and he is, but there's no use fighting him in the court of public opinion. There'll always be people who don't believe my version of events, and he'll always have another trick up his sleeve. I've got no desire to waste time down in the mud beside him, and I won't give him an ounce more of me than he's already taken."

The injustice of Rosie's situation infuriates me, but I'm so impressed by her strength that I moderate my tone and nod like I understand why it has to be this way. "I get it."

Pia clears her throat. "It might help you to know that inside the business, most people know Chip's a..."

She grimaces, her public relations training perhaps clashing with an honest assessment, and I offer a word to help her out. "Dick?"

Her mouth twitches. "His reputation undermined his smear campaign against Rosalie, at least among industry players, but the fact is he makes a lot of people a lot of money, and that's all that a lot of people care about. Plus, you know. He's a rich and powerful man, and that makes those same people willfully ignorant of a wide variety of bad behavior. It's not right but here and now, even with the resources I have at my fingertips, there's not a lot I can do to change it. What I *can* do—and what I care about most—is protecting Rosalie. Her reputation. Her brand. Her business. And, if I can help it, her sanity."

I consider Pia again, seeing her in a new light. She's getting paid to care, I get that, but something about the rising ferocity in her voice makes me think Rosie made the right choice adding this woman to her team.

"Pia wants us to wait to make any announcements about us," Rosie adds. She leans against me, arm pressing on mine, fingers curling tighter in my hand. "Just until the dust settles on the breakup. Once the celebrity news cycle has something more scandalous to talk about, it'll be easier for us to make our public debut."

"I'm not interested in staying locked up inside while Rosie's moving about in the world," I say to Pia. "I don't need to be in the spotlight—in fact, I'd prefer not to be—but I do need to be close by."

"Pia has an idea," Rosie says, but her hesitancy puts me on guard. Pia might know her stuff, but at the end of the day, I'll do what Rosie wants me to do, not her publicist.

"What is it?"

"Continue to operate as Rosie's personal bodyguard," Pia says. "We'll hide you in plain sight. It'll give you a valid reason to be by Rosalie's side, and nobody will blink twice when they see you in pictures, if they notice you at all. If anyone, Chip included, accuses you of being anything more, we've got the receipts to back up our story. You're ex-military. You've been on Rosie's security team before, and you've got no other employment, skills, or commitments that might catch us in a lie."

"Finn's family owns a ranch and vineyard in Sonoma Valley," Rosie protests. "He has a beautiful fur baby and he's a gifted artist. I explained all this already."

I appreciate Rosie coming to my defense, but I don't need it, and I press on her fingers to let her know it's okay. Pia is right. Rosie's world isn't made for a man like me unless he's providing the muscle. I don't want to be at the center of any celebrity storm, and anyway, this is her life and not mine. Rosie's spotlight would shine right through me, and I'm comfortable in the background, preferably in camouflage, because that's where I belong.

"Pia says that when we're ready, we can tell everyone we fell for each other while working together," Rosie adds. "It's not a lie, and it might not take long. But if you're not on board with any of this, we can come up with another—"

"I'm on board," I interrupt, determined not to make Rosie's life harder than it already is. "Let's do it."

"Are you sure?"

I ignore Pia as I slip my hand around the nape of Rosie's neck and press my forehead against hers. People watching us is something I need to get used to, and there's no way I'm censoring the way I love Rosie when we're behind closed doors.

"I don't care what people on the outside think," I say. "We know the truth, don't we?"

Rosie answers with a relieved smile. "We do."

"Excellent." Pia's voice is take-charge and impatient now that she's been given the green light. "Finn. I don't think I need to brief you on the correct behavior and protocol for the person acting as Rosalie's personal bodyguard, but just so we're clear, you will need to keep your hands off each other."

"In public," I mutter, Rosie's lips too close to resist, and she smiles against my mouth as I kiss her.

"In public," Pia agrees. "Keep up the charade for as long as you can and let me do some work in the background to build the best launching pad for you both, then we'll revisit the plan when the time is right."

"Sounds good," Rosie replies, or that's what it sounds like, mashed up and murmured between my lips.

Pia clears her throat. "There's one more agenda item before I can leave you two alone," she says, and I begrudgingly let Rosie pull away. "A personal assistant."

Rosie slumps a little but nods her agreement. "I suppose I'll need one of those eventually."

"You will." Pia hands over a thin stack of stapled documents. "I've got three recommendations here, all vetted and with excellent references. I'll leave them with you, but..." Pia pauses, like she's considering her words, then sighs. "I thought you might also want to know that I've heard from your previous assistant."

"Lauren?" Rosie asks with surprise. "She contacted you too?"

I frown at this exchange of information. "What do you mean *too*? Has she been in touch with you as well?"

"Only about a dozen times." Rosie sighs and rolls her eyes. "Emails begging for my forgiveness. I deleted them all."

I glance at Rosie's laptop. "Mind if I take a look?"

She pushes the device across the table toward me. "*Ugh*. I can't believe she had the nerve to contact my publicist.

What did she want from you?"

"Her job back, apparently," Pia says. "According to my sources, her affair with Chip is over and she's only now realizing that being fired by you for undisclosed reasons essentially blacklists her in all other areas of the business. People talk. She can't find employment and is desperate to repair her reputation. I told her absolutely not, of course, and she won't bother you any further, but I did want you to be aware that she and Chip are no longer involved and she's suffering for it... if that's any consolation."

I retrieve the deleted emails and scan their contents as Rosie shakes her head.

"What a mess. I wouldn't wish Chip on anyone, even Lauren, and if she hadn't been so deceitful and manipulative and willing to walk over my limp body to get her own recording deal, I might even feel sorry for her, but I just never want to hear her name again."

I'm taken by a cold chill at the picture Rosie paints before she adds, "Does that make me a bad person?"

"No," I say at the same time as Pia, and we share a brief look of agreement while Rosie sighs and leans into me for support.

Pia slides a printed piece of paper across the table toward us, followed by an unopened box containing a new smartphone, and I set aside my email analysis to read what she's offering.

"This is yours," Pia says to Rosie. "I've sent you electronic information for your diary, but here's a hard copy too. I've packed a lot in to fast-track your return with the most important players. It includes getting you in front of your fans and reminding them why they love you plus catching up on the commitments you missed while you were away, including a dress fitting for your guest appearance on *The Night Show* next week. Marco is waiting for us at the house in Beverly Hills."

"Marco?" I ask.

"A designer," Rosie says distractedly. "I wear his dresses to lots of high-profile events."

She narrows her eyes at the paper as she scans the first page then flips to the second, then the third, and I read over her shoulder. Sessions with stylists. A meeting with her recording label. Private performances. Public appearances. She doesn't have a spare minute for the next fourteen days.

I glance at Rosie's expression to gauge her reaction. Her teeth worry at her bottom lip, the only indication she might share my unease, otherwise she nods like it's all to be expected, asking insightful questions about locations and logistics. She's competent and in control. Smart and sophisticated. Gorgeous and capable and a force of nature, but a different version of the woman who spent the last three weeks on my ranch.

TWENTY-FOUR

Rosalie

WHEN WE LAND IN LA, I step into the plane's bedroom to change into the designer ensemble Pia brought with her. It's a midday interpretation of the quintessential revenge dress. A mint green mini and matching spaghetti-strap tank. Melon-hued platform stilettos with six-inch heels. Creamy leather bag, oversized sunglasses, wide-brimmed hat. Fresh tube of coral lipstick and powder for my nose. All laid out like I'm a four-year-old.

I peel away Finn's flannel shirt with a fleeting twinge of regret. Goodbye Rosie. Welcome back Rosalie.

Finn finds me in front of the mirror swiping on a second coat of lip color, sneaking up behind me to wrap his arms around my waist and cover my shoulder with slow, soft kisses that make me shiver.

"You look incredible," he says.

"Thank you." I tilt my head to coax his mouth up my neck, then reluctantly turn away from his lips when they search for mine. "I'm sorry. I can't mess up my makeup."

Finn's mouth ticks up, like he thinks I'm joking. I turn to look up at him, the apology in my eyes, and I wince as his face falls. He drops a final kiss on the top of my head and steps back.

"Guess we need to think about those kinds of things now," he says before his attention lands on the faded flannel folded neatly at the end of the bed.

I scoop it up, tuck it into my expensive handbag. "I'll be wearing that to bed tonight," I tell him as I throw my arms around his neck. "And every night from now on."

His smile is small but real and his eyes grow hot. "Will you wear this lipstick for me too?"

Finn's eyes drop to my mouth, and I fantasize about all the places on his beautiful body I could leave my bright mouth-shaped marks. "If you want me to."

His eyes sparkle as if to say *is there any question?* and a hint of his hardness nudges my stomach, but what he says is, "Is there a reason you need to dress up for the drive home? We're going straight from here to the house. Nobody's going to be taking your picture, and even if they were, I say you're even hotter in shorts and sneakers."

"There's always somebody taking my picture," I say with a sigh. "We're in LA, which means I can't swan around in torn denim and men's flannel shirts, as much as I wish I could."

A frown passes his brow, there and gone so fast I might have imagined it, and I press my glossy lips to his cheek. "Wearing designer clothes is part of my job," I murmur, "and I like to look nice. I know you think it's silly—"

He stops me with a kiss, and after a split second of panic that my lipstick will never survive it, I sink into him. I'll fix it later.

"You're a hell of a lot smarter than me, Songbird," he says when we're done, holding me close, gaze fierce and thick thumb coasting underneath my lip to wipe away the smeared color. "I might not always understand your decisions, but I'll never doubt them. Nothing you do is silly."

My throat tightens, and I swallow with difficulty. "Thank you."

Finn grins and takes another swipe at my chin. "You might want to look at yourself in the mirror before you say that."

I chuckle at the coral lipstick smeared all over his mouth. "Same goes for you."

A tap sounds on the other side of the curtained cabin wall, and Pia pokes her head in. "The car is on the tarmac," she says. "Ready when you are."

"Thanks, Pia. We'll be there in a minute."

She retreats quietly, and I absently rub the color from Finn's skin as I ask, "Are you sure you're happy with Pia's plan? I don't want you to feel objectified or sidelined or—"

"Keep this up and I'll ruin your hair as well as your lipstick."

I roll my lips to stop a smile and coyly flutter my lashes. "But *seriously*—"

"I warned you, Songbird."

I squeal as he tosses me on the bed, then again as he cages me against the mattress with his enormous frame, dusting the tip of my nose with his.

"I'm not the kind of man who does things he doesn't want to do," he says quietly. "I want *you*, Rosie, and I'll do whatever it takes to be the man you deserve. Promise me you'll stop second-guessing my choices. I need you to trust my judgment as much as I respect yours."

"You're right." My chest sinks into hollowness as I recognize my old thought processes. "Old habits die hard, and maybe returning to LA has triggered some old patterns."

"It sounds to me like it's time to write new ones."

I stare into his eyes, earnest and sincere above me, and brush his lips with mine. "We already are."

Finn smiles and pushes away from the mattress, then takes my hand and helps me up. As he fixes himself in the reflection above me and I reapply my makeup in the mirror, warmth sparks in my middle and suffuses me with contentment. It's a weird kind of domesticity, sharing a mirror with the man I love in a private jet I bought with my own money, but it's a reassuring picture of how we're going to balance our different lives. All we need is love.

My label has given me access to a temporary residence in LA. I've been house-hunting for a permanent address for years, but the right property hasn't come up, and I'm grateful for that now. If just being in the city can reignite my old insecurities, I can't imagine what it would feel like to return to a place filled with memories.

Finn's been briefed on the duration and route from the airport to the house, and until I meet my new security team—three men and a woman who are already at the property—Finn is my only protector. I can tell by the set of his shoulders as we disembark that he takes his responsibility seriously, and although life might be easier with Finn playing this role for now, I hate that we have to pretend to be something other than what we are. I want his hand in mine, his body heat warming my skin, and the world to know what an incredible man he is.

Instead, he leads the way down the plane's stairs and across the tarmac, a looming force that exudes don't-mess-with-me energy. God, he's sexy, and it reminds me of the months we spent together on tour, when all I knew about Finn Davenport was that he was a skilled bodyguard who smiled like he had secrets. Both are still true, only now those secrets are mine too.

The car ride is uneventful. Pia sits in front with the driver, a middle-aged man named Robert who gains Finn's approval when he lists his defensive driving qualifications. Finn sits in back with me and stares out the windows, assessing for danger as my publicist and I pass ideas and devices back and forth. Her brain works fast, and so far, I've kept up fine, but the pace she wants us to move over the next two weeks is daunting. Not unusual by any stretch, and my schedule has been even busier at times in the past, but after three weeks relearning to feel comfortable on my own, I can't tell if returning to LA and a house full of people is knotting up my stomach with nerves or excitement. Am I happy to be back, or anxious, or both?

I hope the answer doesn't matter and the tension will ease once I'm back in the swing of things, but as the car turns onto a leafy Beverly Hills street and we approach the staging ground for this new phase in my career, my middle pulls tighter. This is it. This is what the scared woman who flew out of Violet's studio was running toward, and there's no turning back now.

My eyes are closed so I can focus on my breath when Finn growls next to me. I glance at him, then out the window, and my heart sinks. The entrance to our gated property is thick with paparazzi, shouting and shoving and lifting their cameras to get a money shot through the dark car windows. It's a familiar sight, and out of necessity and a desire to live something resembling a normal life, I've developed a tolerance for photographers tailing my every move. Still, it's a shock to find them here when I thought I was safe, and after weeks without having to worry about who's out there watching me, this reintroduction to life in a fishbowl is especially jarring.

"How did they know she'd be here?" Finn demands, scowling at Pia as she twists around in her seat.

"The leak could have come from anywhere," she says calmly, which earns my respect. She's got a spine of steel to sit up straight under Finn's glare. "Rosalie's label knows she's here, as do her stylists and couture team. The house has staff, of course—housekeeping, gardeners, a chef—and her flight would have been logged the minute we left the ground. Anyone could have followed us here."

The driver opens his mouth, but Finn gets in first. "We weren't followed," he grumbles, and the driver agrees with a short nod.

I lift a hand to set on Finn's thigh, then remember what our relationship is supposed to look like and set it back in my lap. The flashes on those cameras will light me up through the tinted glass, and one shot of me groping my bodyguard would make headlines within the hour.

"It's fine," I say, paying no attention to the subtle flutter of my pulse. "I'm used to it. Let's just get inside where we're safe."

"Can you get through them?" Finn asks the gentleman behind the wheel.

"Yes. Hang in there, Miss Thorne. It'll take a few minutes."

Finn's hands ball into fists on his knees as we edge through the throng, rolling forward at a snail's pace. He scans the bodies pressed up against the car, eyes darting back and forth and visibly impatient to get to safety, but he doesn't tell the driver how to do his job, and as disgusting as I find their profession, I don't want to be responsible for accidentally injuring anyone. Paps throw themselves at the car, waving lenses at the back seat windows, and I lean on years of practice to keep my face impassive and my body unflinching. I've got my glasses on, but I still dip my chin. When I reach for my hat for added protection, Pia stops me.

"No," she says, phone to her ear as she calls inside for one of my security team to open the gate. There's a protection officer already there, speaking into his earpiece as he accesses a security panel and scowls at the throng. "You've got no reason to hide and nothing to be ashamed of. They know you're in here. Hold your head up high."

I glance at Finn to check what he thinks, but he's understandably distracted. Plus, he's already made it clear that he trusts my instincts. So as the gates to the compound swing open and the car presses through the swarm, I lift my chin, remove my sunglasses, and turn my head toward the incessant flashing. Cameras explode with enthusiasm when the photographers realize I'm offering them a money shot.

The first images of Rosalie Thorne since she was publicly dumped and disgraced by her industry heavyweight fiancé. Why is she looking so hot and composed? Where are the red-rimmed eyes? The tearstained cheeks? The muted wardrobe and the drive of shame?

Not here, I tell them silently. I've got nothing to be sad about and no reason to feel humiliated. *See me now, Chip?* I think with an unintentional smile. *You're never holding me down again.*

I should have known that smile would be the one seen around the world, plastered all over social media almost before we finally reach the front door.

TWENTY-FIVE

Finn

I BREATHE A BIG FUCKING sigh of relief when we clear the gates to Rosie's new home and another when they swing shut behind us. I was comfortable acting as her only bodyguard between here and the airport because nobody was supposed to know where she was. The risk was small, and I was prepared to manage it alone, but the image of two dozen paparazzi lying in wait at the place she's supposed to be safest kicked my heart into my throat.

I'm pissed I wasn't prepared. An NDA only goes so far, and I should have expected leaks. I tell myself it's only for now and not forever, but I'm incapable of bullshit, even in my own head. This is it. This is Rosie's life, which means it's also mine.

At least soon I won't have to ignore the urge to wrap her in my arms. It was hell keeping my hands to myself in that car when all I wanted was to hold her close. None of this is new to her, I know, and she handled it like a pro, but I can't stand the fact that she had to. And I don't want to be the one to remind her that her stalker could have been hiding in that crowd. If it didn't occur to Rosie at the time, there's no point scaring her after the fact.

As we make our way along the crushed gravel driveway, a restored 1950s behemoth of a house, if you can call it that, complete with manicured gardens and a round driveway with a fountain in the middle, comes into view. The entire property is unnaturally beautiful, wilderness tamed into something palatable for the suburbs, and when the car sweeps around to the front door, I'm the first to step out. The driver is almost as quick, but I still reach Rosie's door before he does. He nods once before rounding the hood to open the passenger side for Pia.

Stationed outside the open double front doors is the senior member of Rosie's new security team, a burly guy with ten years on me who I recognize from his application profile picture as John. I spoke to Drew when we landed to let him in on Pia's plan and he called ahead to tell the team. That means of the nine staff with access to the house over any twenty-four period, Drew's protection personnel are the only ones aware of my personal relationship with their client, and they've been instructed to keep that information confidential.

John and I exchange professional nods as I lead Rosie inside. "Miss Thorne," he says with an outstretched hand. "I'm John, your new lead security officer."

Rosie gives his hand a strong shake. "It's nice to meet you."

"Likewise. The property is secure, and you should feel comfortable moving about," he reports. "Would you like a full briefing now or after you've settled in?"

Rosie glances at me, but I want her to make the call. She considers it for a moment, then says, "Finn can tell me what I need to know later. I'll let you two get acquainted while I finalize a few things with Pia."

John inclines his head, and we follow him deeper into the house. Inside, the place is hard to believe, a display of extreme wealth and refined tastes. Lush carpets and layered rugs, open fireplaces and libraries of books, large windows and crystal chandeliers. At first impression, the only thing I like about it is the art, but when Rosie's eyes light up at the grand piano in one of the living spaces, I decide I like that too.

"The residence is secure," John says when we reach the kitchen, Rosie and Pia on the other side of the opulent adjoining dining room. "We arrived yesterday to evaluate surveillance capabilities and assess potential risks. As far as private security systems go, we can't ask for better. The property is fitted with CCTV at all entry points to the house as well as external perimeters."

"Is there a control room?" At John's nod, I add, "I'll need to see that later today. What else?"

If John's confused about seniority here or my assuming the lead, he doesn't show it. "Marissa, Jarrod, Tareq, and I are operating in four shifts: screen monitoring, property patrol, personal client security, and rest. Drew says you're retaining the role of bodyguard?"

"That's right, so whoever's working personal security can help with property patrol unless they're required for travel. Next?"

"There's a fashion designer and his assistant in the guest wing," he says. "They had an appointment, and we confirmed IDs against the approved list. Bags also checked. No red flags."

"Noted. Thank you." I glance toward Rosie and Pia, oblivious to this conversation, but drop my voice anyway. "I don't need to remind you that Rosalie's stalker could be anywhere, including LA, so I'll accept nothing less than meticulous attention to detail. Bring any unusual activity to me immediately, no matter how small or seemingly insignificant. Understood?"

He defers with a swift nod, and the fist around my heart loosens slightly. I appreciate that Drew has already driven home the gravity of Rosie's situation, and with a full team in place, I take the first full breath since Rosie told me she was ready to leave Silver Leaf.

John and I make our way over to Rosie, and I mirror his professionalism. As long as I'm responsible for Rosie's personal safety, I'm going to do the job right, no matter how hard it is. One wrong choice when it doesn't matter could easily be one wrong choice when it does.

"Your afternoon appointment is waiting in the guest wing," I tell them. "John can take us there when you're ready."

Rosie casts me a kittenish look, glancing up underneath her lashes. "Thank you, Finn."

I'm good at not smiling when I don't want to, but it's never been this hard to keep a straight face—or my hands to myself. "You're welcome, Miss Thorne."

We follow John along wide halls and across a covered courtyard to a self-contained part of the house with three enormous bedrooms and two full baths. On the other side of a white-painted door is a king-size suite with a four-poster bed, extra-wide stand mirror, and a man dressed top to toe in well-fitted black, his long hair slicked back and gray at the temples, his forehead smooth and lashes dark.

He's fussing with fabrics flung over the bed, a younger guy at his side shifting and rearranging things as directed, but he glances up at our arrival, and his eyes grow bright.

"Mio passerotto," he exclaims with his arms flung open. "It is so good to see you."

Rosie takes two steps in his direction, but mine are longer.

"Finn," she says, setting a gentle hand on my arm when I block her way. "Marco and I are old friends."

She darts around me and into the old guy's embrace, and he hugs her with an amused look for me over her blonde head.

"New bodyguard?" he asks dryly.

"Not exactly," Rosie replies lightly as she moves back a few steps. "Finn worked for me on tour. He's recently returned."

"Ah." Marco presses a finger to the side of his nose. "Part of the spring clean?"

"The spring clean?" she asks, then grimaces. "You mean the breakup with Chip. What have you heard?"

He waves a hand at Rosie's clothes with eccentric flair. "Strip, darling, and let me see you. We'll talk while I measure that gorgeous little figure of yours."

I scowl as Rosie peels off her skirt and tank, sending a little extra heat in the direction of the designer's beady-eyed assistant who drops his eyes and scurries for the measuring tape. I keep scowling as Rosie, wearing nothing but a thin lace bra and panties, steps onto a small dais arranged in front of the mirrors. I know it's ridiculous and she's only doing her job, but nobody's ever more vulnerable than when they're naked around strangers, and I'm uncomfortable with any hint of Rosie's fragility right now.

"You are *glowing*, darling," Marco gushes as he circles Rosie with a discerning eye. "I have never seen your skin so fresh. Where have you been these last three weeks? I couldn't get hold of your team when you missed your fitting for the benefit concert next month, but you must have been having lots of fun to forget all about me and then show up today with a face as pretty as this." He gasps and smacks his cheek. "Have you had one of those ponytail face lifts? Is *that* why you've been missing for weeks? Oh, that's so smart. Get in while you're young before all that skin has a chance to sag."

The guy's a tool, and I grit my teeth so I don't accidentally say so.

Rosie meets my eye in the mirror, then dips her chin with a blush. "I'm sorry to disappoint you, Marco, but any glow you think you see is thanks to three weeks of rest, lots of spring sunshine, and loads of water."

I smirk to myself. *And multiple orgasms.*

Marco snorts as he clicks his fingers for the measuring tape, which his assistant places in his open palm. "Three weeks off? I can hardly afford that now, can I?" He winks at Rosie. "So, you're no longer engaged, my love?"

Rosie lifts her chin while Marco loops the tape around her thighs, snapping numbers to the assistant who scribbles them down. "No, I'm not."

"Good. I can stop holding a grudge that you chose a nobody to design your wedding gown instead of me."

I growl, then turn it into a cough when all eyes in the room turn on me.

"Give it a rest, Marco," Rosie says. "You know I love you."

"Hm. Maybe, but not Chip, eh?"

I'm *this close* to telling this guy to back off when Rosie plants her fists on her hips. "What have you heard?"

"Everything, darling. You know that." At Rosie's exasperated sigh, he rolls his eyes, but by the smile on his face, I'd bet he's loving every minute of this. The tape goes around Rosie's waist. "Okay, fine. But you didn't learn this from me."

He leans in, pretending to whisper, but his voice reaches all corners of the room. "I was at an industry party three nights ago, and an associate at Chip's firm swears that you've already begged him to take you back. It was all a mistake, so says this associate, and the boytoy you were banging behind Chip's back dropped you the minute things got serious. Now you're *desperate* to reconcile because you're *nothing* without him."

I cross my arms, in control on the outside, fucking fuming underneath the cool façade.

"You know that's a lie, right?" Rosie says. "I'm happier now than I have been in years."

"Of course! You're too good for that horrible man, but..."

"But what?"

Marco makes a show of hesitating, like he might actually rein it in when we all know he's living for the gossip.

"A little bird I slept with at *Celebrity* magazine told me that Chip's parents were quoted as saying they've reached out to you to mend bridges, and you've told them it's just a matter of time before the wedding is back on." He wraps the measuring tape around Rosie's bust. "That kind of thing carries some weight."

"I did not talk to Chip's parents! We are *not* getting back together."

"Oh, I know, darling. It's nonsense. Nobody will believe it." Marco holds out his hand for the notebook of measurements, then frowns at the numbers noted on the paper. "Speaking of weight... What were you eating while you were away? Cheeseburgers and milkshakes? Darling, you know dairy is the devil."

Rosie glances at the paper, and a pink flush stains her cheeks.

"You've gained an inch everywhere and two in the chest." Marco clicks his tongue. "If you're not careful—"

"If *you're* not careful, you're going to be eating your next meal through a fucking straw."

The look Marco gives me is startled. His assistant looks terrified, and from her chair at the dresser in the corner, Pia raises her head with a withering look. But all I care about is Rosie, her blue eyes glassy even as she gives me a tremulous smile.

"Right." Marco clears his throat. "It's not a problem. We can work with curves, and I've got half a dozen silhouettes that'll accentuate this gorgeous bust. Adam! Fetch the second rack and we'll look at our options."

I loom as Marco and Adam zip around the room, assisting Rosie as she steps in and out of gowns that turn her into a Hollywood goddess right before my eyes. Perhaps my growly quip has ruined the mood, because Rosie and Marco's conversation moves from pointed jabs and vague digs for juicy tidbits to chatter about fabrics and necklines and colors and vibes. It takes three hours to arrive at any real decisions, but eventually Rosie has a dress for her television guest spot, and Pia has instructions on where to pick up the shoes and jewelry to match.

Rosie steps down from the dais, and as Pia wraps her up in a flowing silk robe, she turns to me with a sparkle in her blue eyes. "Okay, Finn. Your turn."

My eyebrows draw in. "*My* turn?"

"As my personal bodyguard, you need at least two or three well-fitting suits in your closet. You never know when I'll need you on a red carpet." Rosie bites her lip to stop a smile, but it's there in her cheeks, lighting her up. "You don't mind, do you?"

Ah, yeah, I mind. Suits have never been my thing. They're hot and uncomfortable, and the fabric makes it hard to move fast if I need to. I'm a jeans and flannel and muddy boots man, not a guy who struts his stuff down red carpets. But Rosie's the boss, and she's enjoying this. Stuffing myself into a suit is not only in my job description—and, ironically, a way to blend in when I need to—but it's also an easy way to make her happy, and that's reason enough for me.

I move toward the mirror, ignoring the dais because I'm already head and shoulders taller than Marco.

"Strip, please," he says distractedly, phone to his ear as he calls through to his studio with instructions for Rosie's dress. "Adam will measure and fit you today."

With a twitch in my eyelid, I peel off my boots, jeans, and shirt and stand still as stone. The room is already quiet, but it grows silent with a weirdly intense hush, a glitchy kind of lull that makes me feel like a backwoods idiot with no right to be here.

But then I notice Rosie standing behind me in the mirror, her fingers resting against her throat and her gaze hot on my nearly naked form. I swallow with difficulty, glancing away before my dick gets any wild ideas, and Rosie smirks over my shoulder like she read my mind.

Marco clicks his fingers and Adam jumps to pick up his measuring tape, running it around my chest, waist and thighs, up my inseam, across my shoulders, and down my arms. He makes sounds under his breath, quiet whistles and mumbles accompanied by raised eyebrows as he jots down my size, then pulls a single suit from a rack of readymade menswear. He's smart enough to let me get into the pants myself but insists on buttoning the crisp white shirt and helping me into the dark suit jacket. I grit my teeth and tolerate it for Rosie.

It's at least half a size too small, too tight to roll my shoulders, and stretched thin around my thighs, and I'm grumbling like a toddler in my head. I tug at the fabric, pulling at the sleeves and running my thumbs around the waist, trying to settle the clothes better on my body as I shift from foot to foot. I look ridiculous, the mirror reflecting a man who obviously does not belong in a five-thousand-dollar suit, and if there were only me and Rosie here, I'd say so.

I cast a look her way, expecting her reaction to be the outward expression of my inner frustration and discomfort, but instead she's staring with open admiration. Her eyelashes flutter and her hands are pressed in the prayer position against her mouth, and it's enough to stop my fidgeting.

Today's metamorphosis of Rosie from the girl who swam in my river and sang in my living room to global icon is impossible to ignore. She's goddamn beautiful no matter what she wears, and her eyes are the same whether she's in flannel or silk, but here in LA, she deserves to walk with a certain kind of man by her side.

Rosie's gaze meets mine in the mirror and she winks. She shouldn't, but she knows that, and I give her a secretive smile in return. And with a small nod that from the outside stays within the bounds of our celebrity-bodyguard pretense, I let her know I'm here for her. In denim and dirt or satin sheets and suits, I'll always be what she needs.

TWENTY-SIX

Rosalie

I STAND AT THE VANITY mirror, Finn's old flannel hanging from my shoulders, massaging expensive lotion into my hands and analyzing the reflection of my makeup-free face. It shines with a thin layer of organic oil, its herbal scent strong enough to make my stomach twist with a queasy roll. I can't believe how much work and money it takes to replicate the kind of glow I captured without even trying at Silver Leaf. As soon as Marco pointed it out, it became hard to miss, and I don't know that artificial radiance can ever compare to bathing in sunshine, swimming in rivers, running through the woods, and washing with a plain bar of white soap. *That* should be the prescription for beautiful skin. Not twelve different serums and oils and creams and sprays applied morning and night under harsh overhead lighting in a white-tiled bathroom.

My gaze drifts down my reflection, searching for the hints of softness in my stomach and hips that had Marco so scandalized. They're also hard to ignore now I know they're there, and I suppose some women might choose cosmetics and potions over homemade cheeseburgers and shakes, but I don't want to be one of them. And besides, it's kind of nice to have a little more to show off in the bust.

The shower cuts off behind me and Finn opens the glass door, steam tumbling out around his naked, dripping body as he steps out and reaches for a towel. I watch him in the mirror, admiration and desire coiling in my middle. The way his muscles flex as he dries his hair. His thick thighs and tight ass. The inked lines and ridges of his shoulders and arms. The undulation of his tattooed back. He's breathtakingly beautiful and so damn sexy.

Eventually, he catches my eye in the mirror, and a knowing smirk steals across his lips. He throws the damp towel to the floor and stands behind me, his frame towering over mine, skin hot and damp and smelling like soap, his cock thickening against my lower back.

He reaches around me, his skin barely brushing mine yet making me shiver, and picks up my hand lotion, then the face oil. "What's all this for?"

"To make me pretty," I reply matter-of-factly.

He scoffs as he opens the bottle and releases a few drops into his palm. He rubs his hands together, warming the oil, and I wait with amusement for him to apply it to his own skin.

Instead, he reaches inside my open shirt and cups my breast, massaging the oil into me, tugging at my nipples until they're peaked and tingling.

"Found a better use for it," he murmurs, studying the play of his hands on my body in our reflection. "I don't care how much it costs. There's no way this stuff can improve on perfect."

I drop my head back onto his chest, fighting the rising lust even as I reach behind me and wrap my fingers around his length. Finn sucks in a breath and closes his eyes, the roped muscles in his shoulders tensing, and I drag my lip through my teeth.

"Before we get too carried away," I say, "I want to tell you how handsome you looked in that suit today."

He hums. "Felt like a fucking idiot."

"What?" I swallow and try to concentrate as his hands play over my breasts, my fingers brushing up and down his cock. "Why?"

"I'm not comfortable in suits," he says.

"But you could be."

Finn's eyes narrow, his focus on what we're doing in the mirror, but some other thought passes over his brow. "Maybe. If they make them a little looser."

I smile and tighten my fist around him. "You're a big man, Finn. There's no hiding that, no matter what you wear."

He growls and drops his head to my neck, sucking lightly as his hands move down my torso. His palms are slick with oil, slipping past my navel and over my hips, fingertips digging into the bones like handles. He shifts his pelvis until his cock nudges my ass, and I instinctively widen my legs to make room for him.

"It's been a long day," I say, breath coming faster.

"It has."

"And we haven't had much time to talk."

"Talk about what?" He rolls his hips against me, and I moan. "Because right now I'm debating whether I'm going to drop to my knees and eat you from behind or fold you over this vanity and fuck you until you see stars. But that can wait, Songbird. Just say the word."

Oh, God. I release him so I can grip the edge of the counter, giving in to the wet ache between my legs and the weakness that buckles my knees. Finn smirks again as he snakes his hand around to my pussy, and we both watch as his fingers skate closer to my thighs.

I moan at the same time I stretch up on my toes, back arching and ass lifting as invitation. Finn's large hand retreats, only to find a place at the base of my spine. He rests it there, but the fire in his gaze makes me desperate for a little pressure, pushing me down and opening me wide. I spread my legs a little more, and Finn runs his thumb down the top of my ass.

"I love you, Finn," I tell him, letting my eyes drift almost closed as my thoughts float away then reassemble in my mind. "I wanted to say those words a thousand times today. I love you and seeing you in that suit made me realize how hard and fast the world is going to fall for you too. I know it's not what you're used to, or even where you're most comfortable, but I'm so grateful you're here, and I can't wait for everyone to know I'm yours."

Finn blinks, his jaw feathers, and his fingers dig harder into my hips. His gaze remains firmly on my ass, eyes burning at the view of me arching toward him, and I'm not sure if the intensity in his expression is desperation to be inside me or because I said something wrong.

"I love you more, Rosie. You have no idea how much." He runs his hot palm up my spine, curling his fingers over the curve of my neck and then turning my chin so he can kiss me deeply. "And that's all I need. I don't care about suits or spotlights when I have you."

He means it as a throwaway, I'm sure, and my brain is too fogged with lust to pick it apart right now, but the idea of Finn existing in my shadow forever is a stone in my stomach. I don't want that. I want to stand on stages and red carpets and river docks and living room rugs with him by my side. Me on his arm. The whole world aware of how wonderful and talented this man is and how important he is in my life. How important he is period.

But now is not the time to have that argument.

"Can I prove how much I love you, Songbird?" he asks. "Can I show you how hard it's been for me to keep my mouth off you today?"

At my whimpering nod, he falls to the tiles behind me.

I gasp as he wraps his hands around my ankles and repositions them, spreading me open and burying his face between my thighs. The shock of his hot tongue licking at my pussy, the delicious friction of his finger on my clit, his tongue and his fingers fucking me with rough, desperate thrusts, has my legs shaking and my core contracting in just a few minutes. When my orgasm subsides, Finn stands with a satisfied grunt, and I tilt my hips as, with that big, strong hand against my back, he does what he promised and bends me over the counter.

I'm wet and swollen and ready, and he slides inside with no resistance. We both moan, me at the sensation of being so fully filled by him.

Finn looks down at where our bodies are joined, moving in and out of me with torturously slow thrusts that make me wiggle my hips and him sweat with the need to control himself.

"I wish you could see the way your pussy takes my dick, beautiful," he whispers, and I stare at the mirror with aroused fascination as he spits on his cock then uses his hand to swirl it into the juices already coating us both. "It's such a pretty sight to watch you sucking me in and letting me go over and over again. This pussy's so fucking greedy for me, isn't she?"

I moan quietly, unable to speak and entirely mesmerized by the man in the mirror with the filthy mouth and the feverish eyes that can't look away from where our bodies are joined.

My core aches for more as Finn pistons into me, hard and fast, finding those extra hidden inches that a moment ago I would have sworn did not exist. I grip the stone countertop, arch my back, and brace myself against the hard smack of Finn's hips, whimpering as his cock reaches nerve endings no finger or tongue or any other man could find. His hand tightens on my shoulder and the other latches on to my hip, anchoring my body against his so he can fuck me with restless, ruthless, *glorious* pumps.

"Oh my God. *Finn*. Finn!"

My words come out choked, my impending climax making it hard to stand let alone think. Finn understands, and he loops his arm around my waist to keep me against him and upright. His thrusts turn short, sharp and shallow, and with a gentle brush on my clit, I tumble over into light and heat and pleasure so intense it explodes everywhere. All over. It drips down my thighs and leaks from my eyes and slips from my throat in a string of wordless cries.

Finn's cock pulses inside me, his orgasm releasing in hot jets as he bows against my back. His abdominals are tight, his neck is strained, and his eyes are closed as he grunts and ruts to completion. His fingers stroke my pussy, gently guiding me back to the real world, and minutes later he gently pulls out while we're clutching the vanity for support.

Finn kisses my shoulder, light brushes of his lips that travel up toward my neck and back again. Tender and reverent and sweet.

"Oh, Finn," I say, twisting to wrap my arms around him and kiss him full on the mouth. "I'm so happy."

He looks down at me, brown eyes soft and unreadable,

and then he takes my hand in his so he can kiss my palm, which he then flattens on his heart. "That's all I want."

Finn swoops me up in his arms just to deposit me in the shower, then he joins me under the hot spray to lather me up. Under Finn's capable hands, covered in soap and softened by warm water and multiple orgasms, I let myself be soothed by his tender touches, his whispered words, his hulking presence that make me feel safe. Because that's all that matters. I'm safe with Finn. Always.

TWENTY-SEVEN

Finn

MY PHONE RINGS AND I fumble at the nightstand to silence the tone before it wakes Rosie. She stirs, rolling toward me and nuzzling into my chest, and I scoop her closer. After two days in LA, it's safe to say my favorite location is underneath the sheets for the simple fact that it's one of the few places we're guaranteed to be alone.

I flip the phone over to check the caller ID, and Drew's name lights up the screen. My stomach jumps, and I carefully extract myself from Rosie's sleeping form to roll out of bed, drag on a pair of sweats, and move into the master suite living room. Marissa, the protection officer on the morning shift, gives me a nod of acknowledgment from across the room, then steps out into the hallway when she sees I'm about to take a call.

"Drew?" I answer. "What's up?"

"We've got a location for the user posting those social media comments you've been monitoring," he says without preamble. "Sorry it took so long. I didn't want to resort to *other* means while the client was safe and out of sight at your ranch, but now you're back in LA, we've had to be more direct."

The subtext is clear. I'm not stupid enough to use the words "illegal" and "hacker" in this conversation, and right now I really don't care. The fact that Drew took this risk at all means I've had a reason to be worried.

"And?" I ask.

Drew sighs. "He's in Los Angeles."

"Fuck," I curse, then louder again. "*Fuck*."

"Yep. That's all we have now, so be vigilant. Don't take unnecessary risks. I'll brief the team myself, but I'll instruct them to continue to defer to you while they're on the ground. And now that we know our suspect is in the city, we can start combing the place for his physical whereabouts. He won't evade us much longer."

"Thanks, Drew. I appreciate you taking this seriously."

"It's what Jack would have wanted," Drew replies. "I'm only doing what he would have done."

I fall quiet, thinking how this conversation might have gone if it were Jack on the other end of the line instead of his brother. I might have helped him through the darkest moments when we were serving together, but if I'd been there for Jack when he really needed me instead of guarding Rosie in New Orleans, my world would be very different right now. Maybe *she* wouldn't be here, and I wouldn't be having this discussion at all.

I clear my throat, and Drew seems to sense some of my struggle because he falls quiet before he says, "That's all I've got for now. Reach out if you need anything and take care of yourself. I'll be in touch."

I end the call, check the time, and decide against going back to bed. It's tempting to get back under the covers and delay my worry for another hour, especially knowing how warm and sweet Rosie tastes when she's waking up, but it's nearly seven a.m. and I want to review her schedule. My head was already spinning with the commitments she's supposed to keep this week, and after a wild day in LA yesterday, I've got a clearer idea of how messy things can get. And now I know her stalker is out there somewhere waiting for his moment. I can't relax until I've found a way to keep Rosie out of his reach.

Rosie wanders from the bedroom less than an hour later, draped in my red flannel, pale legs bare, blonde curls wild, and cheeks pink. I lift my head from where I'm hunched over her printed schedule at the dining table, pen in hand, and do a double take at how much she looks like the woman who climbed down the ladder of my loft for the first time all those weeks ago. Yesterday she was a smoke show in designer heels and cosmetics. This morning she's making my blood race in a worn cotton shirt and bare feet. How is it possible that one person can fit so perfectly in two entirely different worlds?

"Hey." She comes to stand behind me, draping an arm around my neck and kissing my cheek before she rests her chin on my shoulder. "You're up early."

"Yeah." I clear my throat. "I had a call from Drew."

Rosie goes still at my side, then sits herself across from me. "What's wrong?"

I considered keeping this from her, arguing with myself that there's no point scaring her when there's nothing she can do to help, but I promised Rosie I'd always be honest with her, and this isn't the kind of thing I'd hide well anyway. And she has a right to know.

"The team got a hit on the location of the user making all those hideous comments about you on social media."

"*Mistr_ess_el*?" she asks, her voice too steady to be natural. "Mr. Stanley Lowe?"

"That's right. I'm sorry, Rosie, but he's in Los Angeles."

"Oh, God." Rosie's breath escapes in a quivering exhale. "He's here?"

"It looks that way," I say grimly. "And that changes things."

The color drains from Rosie's cheeks, leaving her ashen, and I get up just so I can lift her off her chair, settle myself onto it, and tuck her onto my lap. Her chest moves in short, shallow rises and falls, and her hands are clamped together in her lap. I pry them free to twist my fingers around hers, hoping my warmth will transfer quickly.

"I can't believe he's here," she whispers. "I'm so... so..."

"Scared?"

"Yes, I'm scared. I'm also angry." She curls against me and turns her face into my bare neck. "I hate this."

"Me too, Songbird. I hate it so fucking much."

I rub her back in soothing circles, waiting for her muscles to loosen, and when her breathing slows into a more natural rhythm, I reach for her schedule and twist it around so she can see the notes I've written in blue ink across the black-and-white printout.

"We need to cancel your appointments for today," I tell her, pointing at the engagements with her hair stylist and her beauty team. "And delay your meeting with the label on Monday morning. We'll stay here, lay low for the next twenty-four hours, and hope Drew has more information in a few days. Even if we don't, your television appearance might still work out. I'll reach out to the studio for more information about their security protocols. If they're not good enough, we'll cancel your guest spot too."

"Hang on a minute." Rosie pushes against my chest, staring at me with confusion in her red-rimmed eyes. "I'm not canceling anything."

"What do you mean? Of course we're canceling."

"No, Finn. We're not. I can't and I won't."

"Rosie," I say, panicked at the determination creasing her forehead. "Think about it. The guy's psychotic, and this comeback tour that Pia's organized puts you right in his hands."

Rosie fidgets with the hem of my shirt. "Not necessarily."

My arms tighten around her, like if I hold her close enough, I can keep her here until she sees reason. "Yes, it does. She wants you to be seen. Isn't that what she said? She's deliberately tipping off the press over the next week or two so there'll be pictures of you looking good and moving on from *him*?"

"It's my job, Finn. One of the more frustrating parts of it, yes, but that's the way it is. And I trust Pia. She knows what she's doing."

I shake my head, unable to hide my distaste for the whole concept. My rage is easier to disguise, but it's there. It may be the way the entertainment business works, and Rosie seems to accept the interest in her personal life as par for the course, but the whole treating-Rosie-like-a-commodity approach makes my blood steam.

"*Mistr_ess_el* already knows where you are, Rosie," I say, desperate to make her consider the risks from my point of view. "All he needs to do is follow the paps to get ahead of your next location. We don't know what he's capable of, and he might have more than a knife this time. It's too dangerous."

Rosie slips off my lap with a sigh, taking the chair beside me and my hands into hers. They're trembling, but I get the impression she's trying to soothe me and not the other way around. "I hear what you're saying, and I understand why you want to handle it the way you do, but we need to come up with a different strategy. I'm not hiding from anyone. Not anymore."

"It's not hiding," I protest. "It's... It's..."

She drops her head to one side and reaches up to brush my cheek. "It's hiding."

"Okay. It's hiding. So what? We were hiding at Silver Leaf for three weeks, and that was pretty great, wasn't it?"

Her mouth tips up at the corner and she leans in to kiss me. "It was wonderful, but it was also temporary, and being back here in LA, making plans with Pia, who really gets me, knowing how keen my label is to hear my new music... I'm excited, Finn. For the first time in a long time, I feel energized about what's next. I'm finally in control of my own life, and I'm not prepared to give that up so soon after I found it again."

My heart drops as my yearning to give her everything—safety as well as confidence, security as well as courage—gains the upper hand over my terror. I brush a thumb across her bottom lip, then her cheekbone, the color starting to come back into both, then lean in and kiss her softly. "I don't want to jeopardize any of that, but I need to keep you safe."

She latches on to my wrist, holding my palm against her jaw, and closes her eyes briefly.

"But, Finn, I need to be the me I want to be, even if some days it's hard. You've shown me it's possible to trust my instincts and not allow myself to be pushed around by a man who scares me. It doesn't matter if that man is Chip or a music exec or a pap on the street or... or a deranged fan who goes too far. I need to be brave enough to say *no*. No, I won't be weak for you. No, I won't run from the hard things. No, I won't let fear win."

She's right. I know she's right. But that doesn't make me wrong.

"Songbird, I get it. I do. And I'm so damn proud of you. You're smart and you're strong and the whole world should know it, but this thing with your stalker is about more than proving what a powerhouse you are. It's about your safety. Possibly even your life. I can't send you into the world knowing there's a very real threat out there."

Rosie blinks, eyes trained on mine, and I appreciate that she's thinking about this, and when she doesn't argue right away, I feel a glimmer of hope that I've persuaded her to see things my way, but then she shakes her head.

"No," she says. "I'm not letting him win. Tell me what we need to do to make you comfortable with sticking to Pia's schedule, because that's what I want to do."

"Rosie..."

My protest stalls on my lips, and I drop my head. I'm not used to saying out loud all the complicated things I think and feel inside. Once the words are out there, there's no taking them back, and then when the worst comes true, there'll always be a record that once upon a time, before my heart broke into a thousand pieces and life once again proved that bad things happen more often than good, I was stupid and naïve and arrogant enough to believe I could have done something to avoid the inevitable.

"What is it?" Rosie shuffles closer and ducks her head to meet my eyes. "You can say it."

"What am I supposed to do here?" I straighten my spine and square my shoulders, needing to feel more in control than I am. "If you were my client, I'd have no choice but to do what I'm told, but I love you. You want me to trust your judgment, and I do, but I don't think you understand what's at risk here. If anything happens to you, I won't survive it."

"Oh, Finn. Nothing is going to happen to me." She crawls back into my lap and balls herself against my chest. "How do we make this work for both of us?"

I hold her tighter against me, inhaling her hair that smells less like rose petals and more like coconut. New shampoo, I suppose, to go with her new soaps and lotions and perfumes.

"Two extra protection officers at all engagements," I say, the words rough with the defeat caught in my throat. "There are to be no other clients at any of your appointments today, and only bare minimum staff. At any confirmed sightings of your stalker, we return home immediately. No arguments or negotiations. You can hate me later, but at least you'll be alive to do it."

Rosie is quiet for a long moment, and when she does speak, her voice is low. "Okay. We'll do it your way, but I really think it'll work out fine. Nothing is going to happen on a busy LA street, and he won't get past security again. We're ready this time."

I stroke her hair and try not to let all the examples of things not working out in my life dim the gentle hope in Rosie's words.

"I can't stop living because the world doesn't look quite the way I want it to," she adds, reading my mind and overcoming my protests with her innocence. "Everything will be okay as long as I have you."

TWENTY-EIGHT

Finn

THE GATES TO THE PROPERTY swing outward and the photographers around them scatter, cameras lifted and ready to shoot as our car rolls toward the street. John is behind the wheel today, Marissa in the front seat, and I'm in the back with Rosie. She's wearing a long, tight top in black with white high-cut shorts, tall patent leather heels, and coral lipstick, and her blonde hair falls in loose waves around her shoulders. She's gorgeous, her spine straight and chin lifted as we pull out onto the road, and I wish I could appreciate her instead of urgently scanning the faces outside and fighting my rising dread.

Our first stop is a Beverly Hills hair salon, and although the street is relatively empty when John pulls the black SUV to the curb, by the time Rosie is done with her appointment, the sidewalk is teeming with paparazzi and fans clamoring to get a snap or a selfie when she walks out the door.

"It's chaos out there," Marissa reports as she joins us at the back of the salon, which is empty but for us. "I've never seen anything like it."

"I have." Rosie flips and fluffs her hair in the lit-up mirror, the perfect curls an inch shorter, a shade brighter, and glinting with unnatural gloss. "Thank you, Richard," she adds, holding out her hand to the gentleman standing behind her chair and admiring his handiwork. "I love it—as always."

"You're welcome, honey," he says. "Try not to leave it so long between visits next time, and I won't have to be as brutal with those ends."

Rosie laughs lightly. "I won't."

The general cacophony of sound rises in pitch as Rosie gets to her feet and people catch a glimpse of her through the curtained glass-paned storefront. My nerves surge along with the screams, and I shift my position to block her from view.

"John will step outside first," I direct, and he nods in agreement. "He will go straight to Rosie's car door. I'll follow with Rosie," I add, staring at the woman I love and will do anything to protect, "who will stick by me like glue."

"Yes, sir," she says with a teasing glint in her eye.

Another time, I'd rise to her challenge, but today, I've got no bandwidth for it. It's a relief to know that she's not feeling intimidated by the crowd outside, but there's a special pressure knowing that the reason for her apparent nonchalance is her unshakable faith in me.

"We go straight to the vehicle with Marissa bringing up the rear," I say. "Do not engage or encourage any interactions, all right? It's too uncontrolled to stop for pictures or autographs, and our goal is to get out of here quickly and without incident. Are we on the same page?"

Rosie looks up at me through her lashes, expression calm as she loops her handbag over one shoulder. The stilted bob of her throat is the only hint that she shares a little of my apprehension, and I give her an encouraging dip of my head.

"Let's do it," she says.

The hollering picks up when people realize we're about to leave, and when the door swings open, the shouting rises to an uncomfortable fever pitch. My senses shift into high alert as John moves out first, Rosie following with me at her arm, and Marissa one step behind.

It's impossible to hear anything above the near-hysterical cheering of Rosie's name, and there's no way to scan the crowd for threats other than pushing back the unwelcome reach of hands from a hundred different directions. Rosie smiles politely, eyes forward like she's not the reason for this demented screaming match, and I scowl at every raised hand that holds a smartphone as I hold out an arm to stop from anyone getting too close. Rosie ignores the phones first thrust in her face then in the direction of the car interior as she ducks through the open door.

I slip in after her, impatient to get her behind the protection and semi-privacy of the bulletproof tinted glass, and I'm not at ease until the car pulls into the street, leaving the uncontrolled throng waving their hands and cameras as we edge into traffic. As soon as it's safe, John hits the gas and cruises at the speed limit, not slowing until we pull up to a set of lights.

"We got company," he mutters a moment before a paparazzo on a motorcycle scoots past us on the inside.

"Stick to the road rules," I remind him, though he knows better than to risk Rosie's safety with reckless driving. "It's a fifteen-minute drive to our next location. We might lose him on the way."

We don't, and the dangerous way the rider weaves in and out of traffic sets my teeth on edge. John is an excellent driver, and my only other consolation is that as long as we're moving, I can at least hold Rosie's hand across the seat.

"Are you okay?" I ask, scanning her face for hints of fear and brushing my thumb along the rise and dips of her knuckles.

"I'm fine," she says tightly enough that I don't believe her. "Let's just get to where we need to go."

Where we need to go is Rodeo Drive for a solo late lunch at a restaurant popular with Hollywood celebs. Like our arrival at Rosie's hair salon, nobody's around when we pull up outside, and Rosie slips past the on-street café seating just as heads start to turn and the stunned whispers grow wings. By the time she's seated at the back of the restaurant with a salad and sparkling water on her table, a line of people has begun to form outside, other diners inside the restaurant won't stop staring, and there are too many variables for me to predict all the ways this could go wrong.

John steps away from his position at the front of the restaurant and leans toward me. "We need to leave before things get too tricky out there."

"Agreed," I reply. "I was about to say that same thing."

I'm close enough to Rosie, standing on guard at her back, that I can dip my head and speak quietly into her ear. "We need to cut this short," I tell her. "Too many people know you're here and the venue isn't secure."

She calmly lifts her napkin to her mouth, then sets it on her plate. "Okay. Let's go."

I take it as a bad sign that she gives in so easily, and she floats out of the restaurant with enough poise and confidence to make me wonder if she's got another reason for wanting to leave. I'm certain of it when John opens the door to the street and she drops her chin to quietly say, "Stay close. I'm going to take a few pictures."

"Rosie—"

She steps out and ignores me completely, and with a curse under my breath, I follow.

The noise on the street is different this time. There's no shouting or shoving, but the minute Rosie walks out into the afternoon sunshine, a teenage girl with her phone held up at arm's length slides up beside her and snaps a selfie. Rosie smiles politely, even though the girl didn't ask first or say thank you afterward. She dashes off squealing as Rosie moves forward another inch, only to be stopped by a middle-aged woman with her phone in the same position, posing and snapping beside Rosie like the woman I love is a tourist attraction and not a real person. I am fuming.

Around us, people take pictures from afar and up close, as one by one, people dart from the crowd to get a picture with Rosalie Thorne. The energy shifts, people desperate for a picture before it's too late. John carves a path toward our car, arms flung up as he pushes people back, and Marissa follows at the back, shielding Rosie from disappointed fans who try to push into her path for their own shot with her.

My stomach churns, head whipping this way and that as I look for potential threats, terrified that I'll never see them coming as the press of people grows thicker and louder. My hackles suddenly rise, intuition telling me that we need to get Rosie out of here. Someone lurches forward, getting too close, and I raise an elbow to drive him away.

"Get back!" I growl, keeping a hand raised to allow Rosie room to breathe.

Another person darts past me on the far side, getting close enough to Rosie that his fingers get close enough to brush her skin. The way he lunges is too similar to the way Rosie's stalker threw himself into her hotel room in New Orleans. I snatch the guy's wrist and twist his arm back, then shove hard enough that he stumbles into the person behind him.

"Keep your fucking hands to yourself," I growl.

"We need to move," Marissa says, sensing that I've lost

some control and knowing that we need cool heads to keep a situation like this from getting dangerous. "No more pictures, Miss Thorne. We're done here."

Rosie bows her head and shifts her body closer to mine, seeking my protection as we follow John's bulky body to the car. I usher Rosie onto the back seat, then follow her in. I buckle her seat belt as John slams the door behind me, and as soon as he's behind the wheel with Marissa beside him, he edges away from the curb.

"Miss Thorne?" John glances at Rosie in his rear-vision mirror. "Are you all right?"

I look at Rosie. She's a little pale, her hands very still in her lap, and I fold them up in mine.

"You're safe, Songbird," I tell her, needing to hear the words myself. "John—take us home."

John nods grimly, but Rosie lifts her face like she's waking from a dream. "But—"

"Please, Rosie. That's enough for today." I swallow and school the emotion from my expression, hoping she can't see my fear simmering so close to the surface. "Let me take you home and we can argue about it there."

Rosie's fingers twist in mine, and she glances up with uneasy eyes. And maybe she reads me too well now, or maybe I'm worse at hiding my emotions and she recognizes the terror I'm trying to keep at bay. Maybe she feels it too because her shoulders fall, and she nods slowly.

"Okay, Finn. Let's go home."

TWENTY-NINE

Finn

IN ROSIE'S BEDROOM THAT NIGHT, under too-soft ivory satin bed sheets, I close my eyes in the darkness and try to imagine us in this exact position back at the cabin at Silver Leaf. The picture is gone before it has a chance to coalesce. It smells too different here, like scented candles and stale air instead of fog and the river and clean, damp earth. There are too many people and too much noise, even now that it's after midnight because on the other side of the closed master suite door, a skeleton staff of people is available to make sure Rosie is safe and comfortable.

With sudden sharpness, I wish I could reach out and feel Dakota's fur underneath my fingers, and how much I miss her is the last straw. I creep out of bed, leaving Rosie sleeping beside me, and go to the adjoining living space. Out in the main hallway, Tareq walks by on night duty, and following a quiet nod of acknowledgment, I close the door to the master suite.

I need the quiet and the privacy.

Rosie's suite is more of a wing, a luxury setup with two bedrooms—the second one belongs to me to keep up appearances—and a living area with a soft sofa and wide-screen television. There's a deep timber desk for a workspace and a dining nook with a long table and bench seat that looks out over a sparkling lap pool and neatly trimmed hedge fences. Flicking on one of the lamps dotted around the space, it takes a few minutes to locate Rosie's old deck of cards atop a stack of papers on a side table. They belonged to her grandmother, she told me, and it's not just the process of playing that comforts her, but the notion that by moving the cards about in her hands, Rosie is closer to the one person in life who always brought her solace.

I could use some of that solace myself, so I seat myself at the dining table and begin to shuffle. Without Rosie there to play, I get started on a game of solitaire.

Today was a fucking shit show and my nervous system still hasn't returned to its baseline. The memory of paparazzi clumped around the car door when I opened it so Rosie could step out keeps flashing in my head, and I can't shake the agitated sounds of fluttering camera lenses and screaming fans from my ears. It was loud and hot and uncontrollable, with too many bodies to get a read on the faces or pick a single threat out of the crowd. And on some level, it doesn't matter that we got her safely in and out of her salon appointment, or that we lost the second guy tailing us through the streets, or that this is our new normal. I keep replaying the afternoon in my head and the ending comes out a little differently each time.

Sometimes it's a cloaked hand that grabs her and drags her so far away that I can't get to her before she's gone. Other times it's a blurry face that launches from the crowd and attacks before I can stop it. More times than I want it to be, Stanley Lowe gets the better of me, darting past my blind spot and sinking his knife into Rosie right in front of my eyes.

I should be stronger than this. I should be tougher, but this isn't the first time my head has felt like a war zone. Sometimes I'm haunted by the friends I lost during active duty, and the ones who were never the same after it. Other times it's not being there for my dad and the ranch when my mom got sick, and then being on deployment when we lost him too. I remember Jack and wonder what signs I missed when they were right in front of my face. The ghosts are why I'm better off keeping busy, and although I'm not a stranger to restless nights, this is the first time I've been unable to sleep with Rosie in my bed.

Fifteen minutes with Rosie's cards and I'm still no closer to calmness, so I set them aside and move to the sofa, collecting one of Rosie's acoustic guitars on the way. I play as low as I can, no real method or melody in mind as my fingers move across the strings, but soon I'm toying with a tune that feels good enough to occupy my thoughts and settle my racing heart.

Half an hour later, still nowhere near sleepy, a gentle hand slips into my hair, and I close my eyes briefly at the sensation, leaning into the touch.

"Hey." Rosie strokes my head gently. "What's going on?"

"Can't sleep," I tell her.

She hums quietly, and I lean my head against her soft breasts, moving aside her open flannel to give me much-needed contact with her skin. She runs her fingers through my hair, and I take comfort in her touch and the quiet thrum of her heart.

"Do you want to talk about what happened today?"

"Not really," I whisper. "Maybe. I don't know."

"I thought I was doing the brave thing," she murmurs. "I should be able to get my hair done at my favorite salon or have lunch at a café without fearing for my life, shouldn't I? Why can't I experience the normality everyone else takes for granted? I didn't want to let the paparazzi or the public win."

I turn my face toward her body, kissing her sternum and letting her warmth soothe me. "In theory, Songbird, I agree with you, but in reality—"

"In reality, it's not practical. I know that now." She sighs. "I love creating and writing and playing for people, but I didn't love feeling scared today."

I swallow deeply and press my forehead against her chest. "Me neither."

"I've been conditioned to believe this kind of exposure is part of my job," she admits. "Nobody cared about Rosalie

Thorne for a long time, and when they did, things escalated so fast I couldn't keep up. I didn't want fame to change me or take over my life, you know? I wanted to do the things I've always done and pretend the noise around me didn't exist. But I can't do that anymore. I need to figure out a new normal."

I close my eyes and exhale with relief. "You don't know how glad I am to hear you say that."

"I talked to Pia tonight," she says as she strokes the back of my neck. "I'm performing at a benefit concert in two weeks, and between now and then life will be a little tricky, but I've told her that's my hard limit for her comeback campaign. If we haven't reset the news cycle by the night of the concert, she'll have to come up with another plan to rehabilitate my image. We can move to my house in Nashville, or we can build something bigger at Silver Leaf and travel back and forth between the two. Dakota will come with us, and we'll stay out of the public eye. Keep our private life quiet. Maybe I'll focus on writing for a while and take a break from performing. I'll never be invisible, but we can disappear as best we can."

Rosie drops her mouth to the top of my head. "I want to make a life with you, Finn. I'll do anything to make that happen."

My chest aches with how badly I want this version of a future with her and what a selfish asshole that makes me, but it's not going to happen. I could never be so self-involved that I'd let Rosie make herself small to fit my idea of an easy life or change what she wants for herself because I've always wanted something else. I need to compromise at least as much, and probably more, than Rosie should ever have to. Whatever the future holds for us, our happily ever after exists somewhere in the middle.

"What are you playing?" she asks, nudging the guitar on my knees with her thigh.

"Nothing in particular," I confess. "I just needed to feel the strings."

"Can I help?"

To answer her, I lift the guitar over my head, and she ducks underneath the circle of my arms, settling herself on the sofa between my knees. I lower the guitar in front of her, and her fingers dance across the fret, brushing along the strings.

We play together, each of us extracting different chords and refrains to coax music from a single instrument. We're in sync, talking with music instead of words, dipping in and out of each other's melodies until all I want to hear is her. I lift my hands from the wood, set them on her shoulders, and gently push the fabric down her arms.

Her playing stumbles when I apply my mouth to her bare neck, her fingertips tripping over a note and then pausing when I let my tongue flicker across her skin.

"Keep going," I tell her. "Play the guitar while I play you."

Rosie moans lightly, but she starts again, this time with a song I know too well. It's the song we wrote together on my cabin porch. As I move my lips over her shoulders, I slip a hand around to squeeze her breast, then pluck at a nipple already hard with arousal. And when our song shifts into its second verse, I hum my part against her skin, setting off chills in her body.

Rosie whimpers as she drops her head back against my chest, but she doesn't stop playing even as she sinks against me and spreads her legs. The lamplight warms her skin with an orange glow, and I skate my palm down her stomach to dip my fingers into her panties, seeking her clit and finding her already wet.

I mimic the press of her fingers on the fretwork with pulses of my fingertips on her clit, then glide through her wetness until the song she's playing falls apart and she's squirming against my hard-on. Still, I play her, my fingers strumming her pussy and my lips swirling notes and lyrics over her shoulders. My dick is rock hard and I'm starting to sweat, but I'm enjoying our shared desperation too much to end it. As long as we're teetering on the edge like this, I can make myself believe that whatever we want in life will come as easy to us as how perfectly we fit together in music and in bed.

"Please, Finn." Rosie sets the guitar aside and digs her nails into the muscle of my thighs. "I need you inside me."

"I don't want this to end," I whisper as I roll her swollen clit between my fingertips. "I'm obsessed with the pain of wanting you."

"And I'm obsessed with the pleasure of having you." Her head tosses and her breath is short as I tease her with the tip of my finger slipped inside her core. "So let me sit on you. Now."

I growl at her bossiness, then wrap my hands around her waist to lift her off the sofa long enough to drag my underwear over my cock. I settle her on me, sliding into her from behind, taking it easy to get the angle right but not stopping till I'm all the way in and she's riding me like a fucking cowgirl.

Rosie's hips swivel and grind down against me, and within moments my thighs are soaked with her arousal. I cup her tits, tugging at her nipples hard enough to make her moan, and meet the frantic bucks of her hips with slapping pumps of my own. I draw in a shuddering breath at the tight, wet heat of her pussy, and my orgasm gathers, tension building and balls tightening while Rosie uses my cock like I'm some kind of sex toy.

"I'm almost there," she says as I swell inside her. "I'm so close."

I reach around and set my fingers to her clit, stroking and strumming until she cries out. Too late, I cover her mouth with my hand, and an urgent knock sounds on the suite door.

"Are you all right in there, Miss Thorne?" Tareq shouts from the other side.

"Fuck," I grunt as my orgasm bears down and Rosie tears my palm from her face.

"Yes!" she screams as her pussy clamps down around my dick and we both tumble into ecstasy. "Yes. Yes. Yes!"

THIRTY

Rosalie

FIRST THING MONDAY MORNING, I have a meeting with reps from my record label. They want to hear my new music, and they're bringing in a hot new producer who recently worked magic with a debut artist who's been labeled as the pop scene's Next Big Thing. A couple of years ago, Chip would have made me feel insecure about a younger, prettier, more talented singer-songwriter snapping at my heels, but now all I feel is compassion. I hope she has a good support system so she isn't broken by the business like I've been.

Finn insisted we move the meeting from a studio downtown to the house, where my protection team has more control over my safety. After the way things spun out of control two days ago, I'm not inclined to argue. We've cleared everyone but security personnel out to prevent any leaks of my new material, and now I'm loving the home field advantage. It means that when three industry players I've never met file into my living room with Pia at their head and the label president bringing up the rear, I hold out my hand and welcome them like they're supplicants instead of the people who own my art via a multi-million-dollar contract.

Finn hovers at my shoulder and Jarrod stands guard out in the empty hallway while Pia makes the introductions, gesturing at the newcomers one by one.

"Rosalie—you know Louis Wilder, the label president," she begins.

"Of course. Good to see you, Lou."

We exchange kisses on the cheek before he holds me at arm's distance. "You doing all right, kid?" he asks.

His frank concern takes me by surprise. Lou's always been a little gruff in the past and usually distant, preferring to let his team manage my business, but today his blue eyes are as soft as they are searching.

"I'm doing better than all right," I reply, and he releases me with a satisfied nod.

"Rosalie—this is Cynthia Graham," Pia says next. "She's your new A&R rep."

One of my requests when I cut Chip out of my business model was booting the Artist & Repertoire rep I'd worked with for years. He and Chip are good friends, having developed a long list of talent together, and I'm uncomfortable with him in my inner circle. Cynthia is a tall, thin blonde woman with cool hands and warm gray eyes, and I get a good vibe from her straightaway.

"This is Nya Young from the marketing and promotion team," Pia goes on, pointing to the gorgeous Black woman barely an inch taller than me. She looks nervous, and I take her hand with a reassuring smile.

Pia waves toward the last person without a name to his face. "And this is Zane Petty. He's the producer I was telling you about."

"I remember." I shake Zane's hand and wonder just how much younger he is than me, since I'm only twenty-seven. "It's great to meet you."

"It's a real thrill to meet you," he replies. "Pia tells us you've got new material to share?"

"Well, yes." Pia and I share a bemused look. Until I hire a new manager, she's agreed to stand in the role, and we're both surprised by Zane's no-nonsense approach. "Shall we get right to it then?"

We're in the room with the grand piano, and there are refreshments set out on the coffee table between the forest-green velvet sofas, but they remain untouched as the group takes their seats and I pick up my acoustic guitar. It's the same one Finn was playing when I woke up and found our bed empty the other night, and I hide a blush with the dip of my head, casting a sidelong look at the man taking up space in the shadows while the secrets we share play on his mouth.

I take a seat on a wide armchair, guitar set on my knees,

and pause with my fingers resting lightly on the instrument. The only person who has heard these songs is Finn, and he's moved behind me where I can't see him. Instead, I'm confronted with a small but overeager audience and a sudden fear that none of them will like what I share. Or worse, they won't get it.

"The music you're going to hear today is a little different to what I've done in the past, and I want you to be prepared for that," I say. "It's more real and more me. My heart and my soul reside in every note, every lyric, and it leans more country than my earlier work. One or two of these tracks I'd love to release as acoustics and another..."

I clear my throat to stop my rambling. "I'm nervous," I confess. "So I'll just play and hope you like it."

As soon as I start, from the very first bar, I'm transported back to Finn's cabin at Silver Leaf and my worries melt away. I have eight songs to share, and I play them in the order I wrote them. First, I relive the fear and rage of leaving Chip, followed by the rediscovery of a desire and a sensuality I thought had long since died inside me. Next is the revelation of Finn and all the ways he reminds me of who I am and what I want to be. The second-to-last song is the duet we wrote together, and although we've never spoken about sharing it, it's the most important part of this story, so I play it on my own, knowing it'll never be what it's supposed to be without him performing it with me.

As the final song ends and the room settles into stillness again, I set aside my guitar and wait for someone to say something. Anything. It seems to me that everyone is trying hard not to look at each other, an odd choice that makes my mouth feel dry, and the longer I wait, the more certain I am that this music means nothing to anyone but me. But I can't regret it, and I'll fight for it until it gets the platform it deserves. This is going to be the album that defines me, and popular opinion isn't the measure of its worth.

Cynthia is the first to speak. Finally. "I'm speechless, Rosalie. That was…" She puffs up her cheeks and blows out an overwhelmed breath. "That was *good*."

"Oh, God." I release a breath and sag in my chair. "Really?"

"It's so much more than good," Nya says. "It's…" She looks for help around the room, breaking whatever hypnotism had everyone in suspended animation a moment ago. "What is it? What's the word I'm looking for? Whatever it is, the market is going to *die* for this record."

"It's a confessional, right?" Zane leans forward with elbows on his knees and passion in his eyes. "It's about pain and self-loathing, falling apart and putting yourself back together, finding hope and claiming love. It's vulnerable and it's powerful. It's transparent and it's mysterious. It answers a hundred questions then asks a hundred more. It's a paradox and it's universal truth. It speaks. I've got so many ideas already for how to lay these down. Damn it, Rosalie. I think you broke my brain."

A laugh falls from my throat, a mix of relief and gratitude for Zane's insightful analysis, and the butterflies in my stomach start to feel less like nerves and more like impatience to get into a studio and make this album the best it can be.

I risk a glance at Finn, who couldn't stand taller if he tried, then turn back to the group feeling warm all over. I reach for my water and try not to worry when Zane, scribbling down notes on a notepad on his knee, shakes his head before lifting his narrowed eyes at me.

"Song number seven," he said. "It's good, but it's missing something."

"You're right," I agree. "I—we—It was written as a duet."

His head bobs with understanding. "Yeah, I can hear that. Did you have any artists in mind to record with you? I can think of two who'd really push the track into country, if that's the way we want to go." He rattles off a list of artists, some at the top of the charts, other smaller acts who he tells us are going to be big someday. "What do you think? I'll make some calls."

This time, I carefully avoid looking Finn's way. I don't want him to see that I'm quietly wishing he'll step into the conversation and insist he play with me. "I already had somebody in mind for that track."

"Oh, yeah?" Cynthia leans forward, too, mirroring Zane's eagerness. "Anyone we know?"

"I don't think so, and I haven't asked him yet," I say. "I'll let you know when I do."

There's a curious murmur but the discussion is diverted easily enough when Pia suggests I play the set through again. My performance is more confident this time, already having received positive reviews, and another hour passes after that as we talk about the music and possible recording schedule, marketing and promotions, and maybe another tour.

My head is spinning in the best possible way when Pia finally escorts the group to the door, leaving me alone with Finn for the first time that morning. I turn to him with a hopefully sheepish smile.

"So, what did you think?"

"I think you blew them away," he says, collecting me in his arms and spinning me around before kissing me hard. "But I knew you would, so I'm not surprised. I'm so proud of you, Songbird."

I land on my feet with a rush of energy and warmth, his arms around me and his cognac eyes warm and wrinkled at the corners with joy. When I'm with him, I'm fearless, which is why I ask without thinking first. "You know who I have in mind for the duet, don't you?"

Finn lifts one eyebrow and shakes his head. "Not going to happen."

"What? Why not?" I settle back on my heels, the impulse to bounce on my toes gone, and I squeeze his biceps. "What better way to tell the world we love each other? And if it proves your talent as an artist, it could launch your career as—"

"I don't want to," he says. "And I don't want to argue about it."

I frown, letting my hands fall, and he takes that as a signal to release my waist and take a step back. The distance between us feels greater than arm's length, possibly because I can't understand why a man with as much potential as Finn doesn't embrace it.

"But why not?" I ask. "You're gifted, Finn, and I don't think I can sing this song with anyone else. It belongs to us."

He runs a hand through his hair and paces three steps away, then three steps back.

"I know, and the idea of another man performing it with you hurts like hell, but I'm not going to be that guy who tells you what to do with your career or your art."

"Our art," I correct him softly. "And if you're not going to record it with me, then I won't record it at all. If it was only ever written to be a song for us, that's okay. I can absolutely live with that because I love you, but can you help me understand it? Please?"

Finn meets my eyes, and for a moment I'm sure he's about to say *no*, but he sinks into the armchair I used to play for everyone, and when he opens his arms to me, I accept the invitation to snuggle up on his lap.

"I'm not sure what the problem is," he confesses. "I just know that something inside me is fighting so hard to remain unseen. Out of the way. Quiet. Simple. Sharing a song I helped write is too much like handing strangers all the best parts of me and inviting them to tear it apart."

I sigh, because I know exactly what he means, and rest my head on his chest. "I think we all feel like that sometimes. That's part of being an artist. You have to find strength in vulnerability and hold tight to your vision even when certain people can't connect with what you create. Someone else will. That's the magic of music."

"That's not it," he says. "I am okay with people not liking it, but putting my thoughts and feelings on the outside is like sitting still while bugs crawl across my skin. Hopes and fears become real, they take on a life of their own, and I can't get them back. I can't pretend like they never happened."

I grow still, sensing there's so much more to Finn's words than fear of being on stage or putting his name to a song we wrote together. "Why would you want to pretend your hopes and fears never happened?"

Finn inhales deeply and breathes out again slowly. "I can't stand the idea of another person looking at me and seeing the pain of not being there when my mom died or the regret of missing my dad's last breath. The horror of witnessing the destruction of war. The guilt of not knowing what Jack needed before it was too late for me to help him."

I burrow closer, tears in my throat, love in my heart, and so much gratitude that Finn has finally found a safe place in me to speak about his silent regrets.

"Life is easier when I know what the goal is, when I'm on a path, when there's something to focus on," he says. "I can keep the mess from spilling out, and I can explain why the world doesn't make sense. I can say: this thing had to fail so I could serve my country... or so I could protect you."

I sniffle against his shirt, and Finn rubs my back as he adds, "I don't want people to know that I dream of making a difference. That I want to make more of myself than I have in the past, or that I'm delusional enough to believe there's a way for me to leave this world a better place. What if I can't? What if I fail?" He sighs. "I don't want to share my hopes and fears with the world because then I'll have to face them, and I'm not ready for that."

I slip my arms around his waist and wish I could hold him together with my love alone. "I'll never make you do anything you don't want to do, but I think you've got this all wrong. Fears and hopes don't make a person weak. They make them *real*. How can we experience the big highs of love and truth and art and music if we don't sometimes open our hearts, even at the risk of getting hurt? I don't know how a person can have one without the other, or how we're supposed to appreciate the sweetness of the good times without enduring the difficulty of the bad. That's how we know when we've got something right."

Finn gathers me closer as he buries his nose in my hair. "How did you get so wise?"

I smile up at him. "Not wise. I've just got a good reason to be brave."

A little moan sounds in his throat but his lips have barely met mine when his phone starts to ring. He shifts to retrieve it from his back pocket, eyes widening at Drew's name on the screen, and he answers the call with a fast swipe.

"Drew?" he says, tapping into speaker mode. "What's going on?"

"I've got good news," Drew replies. "Stanley Lowe has just been arrested for an unrelated assault in Tucson."

Finn's eyes widen on mine, and his heart races under my palm, echoing the galloping relief in my own chest.

"Are you serious?" Finn demands. "When? How?"

"Never been more serious in my life," Drew replies, his tone light and victorious. "Police picked him up about an hour ago and it's serious enough that he's not getting released anytime soon. He's done. It's over."

Finn's head falls backward with a relieved sigh. "Thanks for letting us know. Thank you so fucking much."

I don't realize tears are leaking down my cheeks until Finn brushes them away with his free hand, and then he's ending the call and kissing me. It's deep and real in an entirely new way, the unspoken fear that's been cushioned between us all this time only obvious to me now that it's gone. I melt into him, kissing him and needing him harder than I ever have, knowing that *this* is what I meant by vulnerability being a balance of the bitter and the sweet.

We earned this. I earned *Finn*. It's time to put my pain in the past and step into the kind of love I've been waiting for all my life.

THIRTY-ONE

Finn

ROSIE HAS TO TAPE HER guest appearance on *The Night Show* the next day. We're due at the studio at five p.m., which means we spend part of that morning in Rosie's suite going over the details with Pia and a freelance stylist.

"So you'll wear this," the stylist confirms, pointing at a peach-toned mini dress with beaded detail hanging on a rack next to a dozen other outfits they've already discarded.

"And these pumps," Pia adds, moving a pair of coral shoes to one side before gesturing at a set of simple gold hoops, a matching bangle, and three plain gold rings arranged on Rosie's dressing table. "And those accessories. Hair and makeup will be here early this afternoon, so you'll arrive at the studio ready to go."

"That sounds great," Rosie replies. "I can't stand being holed up in those green rooms longer than I have to be. Let's get in and out as quickly as we can."

Her freshly washed hair hangs in damp curls down her back, her face is scrubbed clean of makeup, and she's swathed in a fluffy white terry robe. I wish we were alone so I could wrap my arms around her waist and bury my face in her neck. I love her like this, natural and relaxed, but there's more to it today. The undercurrent of apprehension that had become so ingrained in both of us this last month is gone, and the brightness in her eyes is less guarded. She's even more at ease than she was at the cabin. Now that we know her stalker is in jail where he belongs, a dark cloud has lifted, and Rosie looks and feels lighter.

I feel it too, but to a lesser degree. It'll take more than a day for me to shake the weight of remembered worry from my shoulders. Yes, it's a relief to know that Stanley Lowe got himself arrested before he could get close enough to Rosie to hurt her, but I'm having trouble forgetting how afraid I was of losing her. Maybe I'll never be free of it, and this sinking pit in my stomach is a side effect of loving Rosie that I just need to get used to. The price I pay for calling her mine.

"I wasn't going to suggest it," Pia says, "but now that the risk to your security is reduced, you have the option of arriving at the studio's street entrance. The upside to that is taking advantage of any fans and paps staking out the place for celebrity sightings. Alternatively, we can use the private underground access point to avoid a public sighting altogether. What would you prefer?"

I shift on the sofa, but when I can't get comfortable, I get to my feet with a scowl. Are we already back to this? Throwing Rosie to the wolves in exchange for a cheap blip on social media? It doesn't even matter that the major threat to Rosie's safety has been neutralized. The world itself is rabid.

I know what I want Rosie to do, but I'm not going to say it. She warned me this period would be tricky. We need to get through the next two weeks, and then these kinds of decisions won't be ones she's forced to make every day. In the meantime, I'm determined to keep her happy and safe.

"We'll take the underground access," Rosie says. "Stalker or no stalker, I'm in too good a mood after my meeting with the label, and I'm not ready to bring it down with a repeat of what happened with the paparazzi the other day."

I exhale with relief, and Rosie tosses me a knowing smile. Our gazes linger as Pia prattles on and the stylist fusses with Rosie's accessories.

"I thought you might say that," Pia says. "And it's fine by me. We've gained more traction than I expected over the last few days, and your spot on *The Night Show* will go a long way in erasing any memory that you briefly disappeared from public view. I've revised a few of our goals for the next twelve days as we lead into the charity benefit. I'll set aside some time tomorrow to go over your updated schedule, which includes a little more time to yourself. How does that sound?"

"Pia. You've made a great day even better." Rosie pulls her publicist in for a hug. "Thank you."

"You're welcome." Pia casts a knowing look my way, then straightens her clothes as she steps out of Rosie's embrace. "I think we've done all we need to do here. I've got people to call and things to arrange, so I'll be in the study downstairs if you need me."

"The woman knows how to take a hint," Rosie says with a laugh as the suite door closes behind Pia and the stylist.

I cross the room and scoop Rosie into my arms, spinning her around and making her laugh again.

"You're cute when you're grumpy," she says as I set her on her feet.

"I'm not grumpy."

Rosie lifts an eyebrow. "When Pia suggested taking the street entrance tonight, I thought you'd burn a hole in her head with those eyes."

My lips twitch. "These eyes aren't hot for Pia." I growl as I lift her up and throw her over my shoulder. Rosie giggles and squirms as I smack her ass. "These eyes are hot for my woman."

I stride toward the bedroom, gently tossing Rosie onto the mattress, and she laughs as she props herself up on her elbows. "You're different today," she says.

"So are you."

Rosie sits up, tucking her legs underneath her, and I balance on the edge of the mattress. We were up all night celebrating the arrest of Stanley Lowe with food and wine and orgasms in bed, and the sheets are still a tangled mess.

"It's this shared sense of relief," Rosie chirps. "It makes me more certain that we can make this life fit the both of us. Don't you feel the same way?"

I brush a stray lock of hair from her face, and she turns her cheek into my palm. "It's definitely easier to tolerate when there isn't a psychopathic stalker out there somewhere."

Rosie's smile falters and I regret being so blunt, but she gathers herself with a quick shake of her shoulders. "My thoughts exactly. So, listen. As much as I'd love to go back to bed, I've got a session with Zane in half an hour."

I blink with surprise. "The producer from yesterday?"

"Mm-hmm. He has some ideas for the next album, and he wants to work on them while his thoughts are fresh and alive." She falters, pink tongue sliding over her lips before she lifts her chin. "You could join us if you—"

"I'll be there," I interrupt. "As your bodyguard. We talked about this, Songbird. I'm not ready. Let's move on, all right?"

"Okay." Rosie lifts her shoulders, then lets them drop with a bashful smile. "Can't blame a girl for trying."

I kiss her softly. "Blame implies my girl did something wrong, and you could never."

The house is cleared again for the three hours Zane is here to jam with Rosie. They set up at the piano, Rosie on the keys while Zane paces and talks through his ideas. After about an hour, the producer takes Rosie's spot on the piano bench, and she moves to the guitar. The songs Rosie wrote at Silver Leaf, already perfect to my ear, unfold over and over again, a little different each time, a new note or a new lyric elevating the music from raw and inspired to refined and electrifying.

It's an education, one that makes my synapses fire with questions and suggestions that I stubbornly keep to myself. Every minute I spend watching Rosie work with someone who matches her and pushes her and takes her art to the next level is another minute of evidence that I could never do what she does. If I'm meant to be in a room with Rosie, here in the corner is exactly where I belong. Cheering her on and out of her way.

John drives past network security and pulls into the underground lot of *The Night Show* studio. Pia's in the front seat, Rosie and me in the back, and he turns around to check that we're still comfortable with the plan to go inside without him.

"I don't want to draw more attention to myself than necessary," Rosie insists. "Nobody knows I'm here, and the more people I have with me, the more eyes I draw. I want to slip in and out under the radar if I can."

"The building has its own security," I add, "and we're going straight from backstage to filming and out again, right?"

Pia nods. "I've timed it so we're not here any longer than we have to be."

John and I exchange a final look, silent agreement passing between us. "I'll be here if you need me," he says. "Just radio in."

We exit the car, I check in my weapon at the studio security office, and a producer greets us at the entry door. Her headset and clipboard giving the impression of speed and efficiency, which is proved by the pace she sets as she walks us through the gray-painted corridors toward the green rooms. She talks fast, sharing the rundown of events and instructions on how to reach her if needed, sweeping past walls of autographed celebrity head shots and preoccupied crew members with staff IDs and bright pink wristbands. She stops when we reach the open door to a small but well-appointed dressing room.

"You can wait in here," she says. "I'll be back to collect you when it's time to go on."

"You know what I love about television producers?" Rosie asks as she and Pia step into the dressing room, our escort already halfway down the corridor in the other direction.

"No," I say, closing the door behind us. "What?"

"They're immune to stardom. Famous people walk in and out of this place every day, and after a while, these crews have seen so much they stop looking. It's nice to feel ordinary for a change."

Rosie opens the bar fridge to retrieve a bottle of water, and I check that the door is locked before moving farther inside. Pia drops onto the two-seat sofa and Rosie perches in the swivel chair in front of the brightly lit mirror, scanning her reflection to make sure her hair and makeup are still in place.

"I know I've already told you this," Pia says, "but I'll say it again in case anything is unclear. I've pre-approved all questions and vetoed anything about Chip. You can hint at what went wrong—perhaps an off-the-cuff comment about his particular interest in *undiscovered talent*—but don't throw mud because we'll have a hard time washing it off. The tour is a safe zone, as is talk about new music. Tell them you're working on new material and you're excited to collaborate with Zane, but no release details for now. Their legal team is well aware that what happened in New Orleans and the recent arrest of your attacker is under a gag order while the case is handled in the courts, so don't worry about them raising that subject on air. I've supplied a couple of cute anecdotes about the baby bird you rescued when it fell out of a tree on your property last year and the signed sheet music you donated to the performing arts high school in Philadelphia last fall."

"Chip bad. Music good. Small talk painful." Rosie nods sharply. "Got it."

Pia shakes her head with a chuckle, then picks up her bag and gets to her feet. "Can I leave you two alone for now? I need to chat to the promotions team about coordinating our social media efforts."

Rosie waves her hand. "Go. We're fine. We'll see you back here after the show?"

"Sounds great. Good luck. I'll be right offstage if you need me."

Pia disappears into the hallway outside, the door clicking shut behind her, and when Rosie and I are alone, I cross the room to be closer to her. I wonder how long it'll be until this anxiety to always be near enough to touch her fades away. Is it the need to protect her or the desire to feel her that pulls me in—or both?

"You cannot mess up my lipstick today," she says, stepping backward with a smile. "So stop looking at me like that!"

"Like what?" I ask innocently. "I was merely admiring your... ah..."

Rosie giggles and plants her hands on her hips. "My what?"

I pull up short, drinking in the woman before me, and answer her from my heart. "Your resilience. Your intelligence. Your determination and your kindness. I'm standing here looking at you and wondering how someone so perfect on the surface could possibly be more beautiful inside where it matters the most."

Her blue eyes well up, and I slip my arms around her waist before brushing my lips against her forehead. "I'm not going to kiss you, Songbird, but I really, really want to."

"Oh, Finn," she says before she's interrupted by a knock on the door. She glances around my shoulder at the mirror, weaving out of my embrace to pluck up a tissue and carefully dry her eyes. Her laugh is watery. "I told you not to ruin my make up!"

"Sorry," I say with a grimace. "Should I tell the producer you need a few more minutes?"

"No. I think I'm okay."

The knock sounds again at the same time my phone rings,

and I pull it out of my back pocket to check the caller ID. It's Drew, and the surprise at seeing his name on my screen rings in my ears like an alarm bell. I answer the call at the same time Rosie calls out, "Come in!"

"Drew," I say. "How are you?"

"I'm not sure. You know those social media comments you've been tracking? We got three more today and they're still coming from LA."

My heart skips a beat. "What?"

"Yep. This *mistr_ess_el* you've been tracking. It's got to be someone else."

My stomach drops at the way he says it. *Mistress L* instead of *Mister S L*, the way it's always sounded in my head. It's like a key slipping into a lock with an audible snap.

Mistress L. Lauren.

I realize my mistake in the split second it takes for someone to slip through the dressing room door, but the person who does isn't the producer who brought us here. It's not Pia, either, and it isn't someone from the television crew. I know who it is, and Rosie does too.

"Lauren?" Rosie's tone, shocked at first, turns to rage. "How did you get in here?"

"Please don't be mad, Rosalie," Lauren begs, clutching nervously at the oversized tote slung across her chest. "I know the talent booker. He sneaked me. I had to see you and you wouldn't answer my emails."

"You need to go," I say firmly, setting my phone face down

on the dresser, keeping the line between me and Drew open. Fuck. *Fuck.* How could I get this so wrong? "Now."

"No, I can't." Lauren shakes her head, her once-dark hair bleached as blonde as straw and her lips coated in coral lipstick. She turns her wide eyes on Rosalie. "I have to explain what happened with Chip so that you forgive me and make me your assistant again."

Rosie scoffs delicately. I try to caution her with a look she doesn't see, and I'm already debating and discarding the different ways to get her out of here.

"You can't be serious," Rosie says. "You slept with the man I was planning to marry."

"He made me do it!" Lauren cries with a petulant stomp of her foot. "He said he loved me and that he'd make me a star, just like you. But then he blamed me when you left, and now he wants nothing to do with me. I told him I could be just like you, and that he wouldn't even notice the difference between us, and he called me... he called me *crazy.*"

"This is wild! You can't possibly believe I'll rehire you. It's ridiculous!" Rosie crosses her arms over her chest as her attention drops to Lauren's feet. "Are you wearing my *shoes*?"

I take a step toward Lauren, and her head whips my way. "Don't come any closer," she barks. "I'm not leaving. You can't make me."

"Yeah," I tell her firmly. "I can."

She's got a gun in her hand before I take another step, pulled out of the handbag she just flung to the floor.

My stomach hits my throat and my thoughts drift to the empty holster at my waistband. Rosie gasps as Lauren lifts the weapon, holding it like she's not used to it.

"Back off," she spits, swinging the gun from Rosie to me and back again. "This is between me and Rosalie. And if you even think of making a sound, I'll kill her. I swear to God I'll shoot."

Terror takes me by the heart, and I beat it back with every skill I've ever learned in all my years in hostile situations. I lift my palms to let Lauren know I see her and I'm listening, and I stop my advance without stepping back, but I'm still not close enough to disarm her without putting Rosie at risk.

"I hear you," I say calmly. "You want to talk to Rosalie. Chip took advantage of both of you, and you both got hurt. You want to talk about it, and that makes sense, but this isn't the way to do it."

"I don't *want* to do it like this," Lauren says, her tone pitchy and manic as she talks to Rosie and not me. Her hands shake as she keeps the gun aloft. Her eyes, burning and filling with tears, are frightening. "But you won't listen any other way. Your phone was off for weeks! You didn't answer my emails. I found your publicist and she rejected me. I commented all the time on social media, but I know you don't check your DMs. What was I supposed to do? You left me no choice!"

As desperate as I am to look at Rosie to make sure she's okay, I don't take my focus off Lauren, and what I say next is as much for Rosie as it is for her.

"I'm sure Rosalie wants to talk to you too," I say evenly, patience dripping from every word. "If you put down the gun, we can have a real chat. What do you think?"

Lauren starts to sob, and she shakes her head. "It's too late for that. I know what will happen next. I'll put down the gun and lose all my power. You'll have me arrested and thrown into prison. I know it."

I swallow and edge sideways, sensing an escalation in her emotional dysregulation, which means I'm losing control of the situation. I need to get between Lauren and Rosie in case... Fuck. In case it's the last thing I do.

"What do you want from me, Lauren?" Rosie says, her voice shaking so badly that I'm taken by a rise of nausea. "You want to talk? Let's talk. I'm here and I'm listening. We can talk about Chip if you want or how I can help get your career back on track. Let's make a plan, okay? Let's figure this out."

Lauren chuckles darkly as her grip on the gun grows steadier, and a chill runs up my spine. "You're just saying that. I knew this would happen. I knew once I had all the power here, I'd finally get what I want, but I wanted it *then*. I wanted you to want it too. It's too late now. It's too late for all of it."

"It's not too late," I tell her, moving across the room with the subtlest of movements. "It's never too late to make the right choice."

"I just wanted to be you." Lauren's sad little laugh turns into a sigh. Her tears stop as suddenly as they started, and her line of sight over my shoulder tells me Rosie's safely behind me now. "You have everything, Rosalie. Fame. Fortune. Talent. Men. And who am I? Nobody. What do I have? Nothing."

She raises the pistol higher, the barrel pointed right at Rosie, finger hovering on the trigger. "So, I guess that means I've got nothing to lose."

I lunge, predicting correctly that she's about to fire, and as the first bullet leaves the gun, Rosie screams behind me. I take Lauren to the ground, bile rising in my throat at the possibility that Rosie's been shot, but then the door flies open, the gun goes off again, fire explodes in my thigh, and the world goes dark.

THIRTY-TWO

Rosie

"WHERE IS HE?" I DEMAND, pacing from one end of the tiny hospital room to the next. It smells like antiseptic and the window won't open, neither of which is helping my state of mind. "What's going on? Why won't anyone tell me anything?"

"He's in surgery," John says, and even though it's for the hundredth time, his gentle reassurance is unwavering. "The doctor will be here as soon as there's news. In the meantime, I'd be more comfortable if you got back into bed."

I open my mouth to argue, and he cuts me off.

"Or at least sit down for more than thirty seconds at a time. Wrap yourself in that blanket over there and please drink something. You've got a head injury and you've lost blood. You need to rest."

I gingerly touch the bump on the back of my head where I fell and hit the wall, then scowl at the dressing on my upper arm, covering the shallow gash where Lauren's bullet grazed me. It's not deep enough to require stitches, so when the emergency room doctor realized who I was and predicted the spectacle I'd create waiting to be treated in a public space, she ushered me into the first empty room she could find. A nurse took my vitals and drew labs while the doctor dressed my wound. Neither one of them would tell me anything about Finn, and now I'm stuck in this room under observation.

"I'm fine," I grumble, but at John's firm look, I drop into the green-plastic covered armchair, throw the hospital blanket over my knees, and pick up my cup of water. "Tell me again how you knew Lauren was in my dressing room."

"Miss Thorne—"

"Please, John." My voice wobbles, and I lift my chin, hoping that if I pretend I've got it together, I'll have a chance of getting through this before I totally fall apart. "Tell me again."

He nods from his position on this side of the closed door. "I didn't feel right waiting for you in the car, so I was already in the studio when I got the call from Drew. He was on the phone with Finn when Lauren entered your dressing room, and Finn left the line open so Drew could hear everything. I don't know how long Drew waited to call me—not long, I'd guess. Less than a minute or two for me to have reached you when I did. I ran, but the first gunshot sounded when I was still out in the corridor. She shot again after I opened the door, and Finn was down by the time I gained control of the weapon."

I shiver and lift the blanket over my shoulders, wishing I'd thought of it sooner when the blood stains on my peach-colored dress disappear beneath the thick cotton.

"Security apprehended the shooter," John continues, "and I applied first aid to Finn's wound. He was unconscious at that point, but I was able to stanch the flow of blood until paramedics arrived. We traveled by ambulance, he went straight to the operating room, and—"

"And I ended up trapped in a confined space with no way of knowing if Finn's alive or... or..."

I curl in on myself, too afraid to cry in case I never stop, too terrified to consider that the man I love might have sacrificed his life to save mine.

"He'll be all right, Miss Thorne," John says gently. "Finn's tough and he's been through worse than this."

"Thanks, John." I lift my head and wipe my nose with the back of my hand. "And you called his family to let them know?"

He nods grimly. "They're on their way."

"Good." I inhale deeply to get on top of the fear and overwhelm. "That's good. Thank you."

There's a tap on the door, and I jump up expectantly as John opens it to see who's there. A glare crosses his face, and he tries to close the door again but is stopped by whoever's on the other side.

"She doesn't want to see you," John says, voice ominous. "I suggest you remove your hand before I remove it for you."

"John? Who is it?" I take a frightened step backward, knowing in my head that he'd be a lot more forceful if the threat was real, but scared that someone knows I'm here and was able to find the room where I'm hidden.

John's face darkens. "It's Chip Daniels."

"It's Chip?"

My head is too foggy to work out why or how he's here, but a fountain of rage suddenly explodes in my blood. Unmanageable fury at Chip and at Lauren and at the world for giving me Finn if all I was ever going to do was lose him. Under the rage is so much fear, but I don't want to be scared now. It's so much easier to be angry.

"Let him in," I order quietly. "I want to see him."

"Miss Thorne, I don't think that's a good idea."

"I don't care. Let him in."

Chip steps through the open door, dressed as always in an expensive suit with his dark hair coiffed to within an inch of its life. He spares John a disdainful look before he crosses the room and takes me in his arms. I accept his embrace, arms stiff by my side, breath stuck in my lungs, and that white-hot anger bubbling higher and higher.

"I came as soon as I got the call," he says, releasing me with a flicker of distaste for the blood on my dress. He surreptitiously checks that none rubbed off on his designer jacket. "Are you all right?"

He talks like we haven't been estranged for a month, like I didn't dump him days before our wedding, like he owns me now the way he owned me then. Chip always treated me like a recalcitrant child, one that needed a firm hand and hard rules instead of love, trust, and respect. One look at him now, in his tailored suit with that shiny hair and the distance in his eyes, and I realize nothing has changed.

"The call?" I ask. "What call?"

"From the hospital. I'm your emergency contact." He lifts his hand to brush my cheek and when I flinch from his touch, his jaw feathers with anger. "They want to keep you overnight because of the knock to your head, but they're chasing down your labs so I can take you home as soon as possible."

"I'm not going anywhere. Not without Finn and certainly not with you."

Chip's nostrils flare, and he glances once at John before he rolls his shoulders back. We have an audience, even if it's a single person who will never breathe a word of what happens here today, but Chip always puts on a show when there's somebody around to watch. Nothing matters more to Chip than appearances.

"You're not thinking straight," Chip says, his voice smooth and soothing. "You're in shock and you've had a head injury. The best place for you is home, in your own bed, where it's safe and I can take care of you."

"Home?" My voice cracks, then rises in pitch. "*Home?* You mean the house I made for us even though you were hardly ever there? You mean the bed you used to fuck my assistant when I wasn't in it?"

Chip blanches but his eyes get hotter. "Keep your voice down."

"Why? Because it suits you to keep your infidelity a secret? Too late, Chippie. The cat's out of the bag."

I'm losing my grip, and maybe I've left my body, because I can *see* myself unraveling in real time. The scary thing is it feels good to let loose.

"Are you going to mention the fact that I practically left you at the altar?" I demand. "Are you going to acknowledge the disgusting lies you fed to the media? Are you going to man up and admit to smearing my brand and my reputation to save your own? Or do you expect me to take the blame for all of it the way I used to do? Are you here so I can *apologize*? Because I'm telling you now, in no uncertain terms, that is never going to happen." Tears well in my eyes as I think about how different my life would be if I hadn't acted on that impulse to run toward Finn. "I'm not sorry. I'm not sorry for any of it."

A vein in Chip's neck pulses with his anger. "Okay. You want me to say it? Fine. We were both wrong. We both made mistakes, but we can fix it. We'll apologize. We'll go to therapy. It's not too late to save this. Save us. We belong together, Rosalie. You know that as well as I do." His calculating eyes slide to my bodyguard again. "Let's talk about this later. At home."

"Are you stupid?" I hiss, and when John takes a concerned step toward me, I stop him with a flung-out hand.

"Do you know who put me here?" I ask Chip. "Do you know who tried to shoot me and did shoot the man I love? A beautiful, brilliant, big-hearted man who is now in surgery fighting for his life because he put his body between me and the next bullet to come out of that gun?"

I'm shrieking now, tears streaming down my cheeks, but I can't believe the gall of this man. I don't know why I'm surprised. Arrogance and narcissism are pages one and two of the Chip Daniels playbook, but for him to come here and think he can treat me like he always has... It's more than I can handle.

Chip swallows. He knows the answer, and when he refuses to say it, I laugh. It comes out wet with tears, yet so, so dry.

"You did this," I say. "You played me, and you played Lauren. The difference is when we found out who you really are, I broke free and she just broke. She wanted what she thought I had and all you wanted was some action on the side." I laugh again and shake my head. "Lauren wanted me dead and it's all because of you."

"You're hysterical," Chip says in a low, taunting voice I know so well. How many times has he used this tone to make me feel small, weak, and helpless? Too many to count. Enough to know I'll never be victim to it again. "And you've bumped your head. This isn't like you, Rosalie. I'm here to help. You love me, I know you do, so let's—"

"Get out," I interrupt, the last of my rage peaking at his words. I'm about to collapse with the fear that's edging closer and closer, and I'll never forgive myself if Chip witnesses my weakness. "Get out now."

He doesn't move, his tall, lean frame taking on a stubborn stance. "Rosalie—"

"Walk out before I ask John to throw you out."

John strides over like he's been waiting for the green light, and his hand lands on Chip's shoulder with a meaty *thwack*. "You heard," he says. "It's time for you to go."

"Get your hand off me," Chip snarls as he violently rolls his shoulder, and John scowls as he shoves him toward the door.

"Never contact me again," I say to Chip as he walks out of the room and out of my life. "If you need to discuss business, do it through my lawyer. Oh, and Chip?"

He turns his head, eyes cold enough to turn my stomach, and I lift my chin because he's not getting any more emotion from me.

"If you ever so much as *look* my way again, I swear to God I will air every dirty secret, every questionable business deal, every private moment we ever spent together, and I won't stop until your career is beyond resuscitation. Do you hear me?"

Chip's gaze finally grows hot as I speak the only kind of language he understands.

"Forget you know me, Chip," I say. "Forget you ever met me. Forget you know my name."

THIRTY-THREE

Finn

I WAKE WOOZY AND DISORIENTED, body aching and throat dry, the air sharp with the scent of disinfectant, and something beeping obnoxiously by my ear. It takes me too long to realize I'm alive, then no time at all to remember what happened.

"Rosie?" I call out, or at least I try to. It's little more than a strangled croak, and I start throwing off my blankets and pulling at the tubes and wires stuck to my chest, arms, and hands. A sharp pain shoots through my thigh, and I groan as an angel flies across the room, gently pushing me back onto my pillows with sweet, shushing sounds.

"I'm here," she whispers. "I'm right here. Don't move, baby. Lay down. I'm not going anywhere."

I'm swept away by relief, and it leaves me weak enough that I can't fight the soft pressure of Rosie's palms on my chest. I don't want to. She's here, and right now, she's doing much better than I am. That's all I need to know.

"Songbird?"

My eyes drift shut on their own accord, so I reach out my hand, and relief swamps me as Rosie twines her fingers around mine. The warmth of her skin and the subtle flutter of her pulse are the most magical things I've ever felt.

"You're all right," I say with a sigh as I force my eyes open.

Her tired smile swims in my vision. "I'm all right," she echoes. "And so are you, or you will be."

I grunt at the discomfort in my left leg, glancing at the dressings wrapped around my thigh. "Is it bad?"

"She got your femoral artery," Rosie says, trying to sound clinical even with her voice shaking. "You're going to be fine, and with rehabilitation you'll make a full recovery, but if John hadn't been there or if he hadn't known what to do…"

Fuck. A close-range gunshot wound to the femoral artery is… not good. I've seen first-hand how it can play out for the worse, and I take a moment to process how close I came to the end.

I'm intimately acquainted with death. I've had wounds that could have killed me and watched enough people die to have long ago come to terms with my own mortality. It's part of the reason why purpose has been essential to me—and so elusive. Nothing in my life has ever felt so significant or so profound it's made me afraid to die. But then again, I've never had a reason like Rosie to keep living.

"Why was John there?" I ask. "How did he know?"

"Drew heard everything over the phone," she says. "He called John for backup."

"Ah." I sag back in the bed with a small sense of triumph. "At least I did one thing right."

"What were you thinking throwing yourself at Lauren like that?" Rosie chokes up as tears leak over her cheeks. "It was rash and reckless and selfish."

Something about the way she says it, like she knows how silly it sounds but sticks with it anyway, makes my eyes well and my mouth tick up. "I'm sorry."

"You should be," she retorts but the words come out thick with emotion.

I try to swallow, but it hurts. Rosie responds to my wince with a cup of water and a straw to my lips, and I struggle to sit upright before I take a sip.

"Are you hurt?" I ask, my focus drifting until it snags on the blood staining Rosie's dress. There's a bandage wrapped around her upper arm, and the machine beside us starts beeping erratically.

Rosie hurries to stroke my hair. "Shh. It's okay. I'm fine. The bullet barely grazed me. It doesn't even need stitches. I've also got a slight bump to the head where I fell against the wall, but I've had every scan and test available. The doctor says it's nothing to be concerned about."

I wonder briefly why nobody has brought her clean clothes to wear, then realize I have no idea how much time has passed. I don't have the energy to ask right now, so I close my eyes, breathing slowly through the easing panic and rising pain. And guilt. So much guilt.

"I'm so sorry, Rosie."

"Oh, baby. What for?"

"For missing the signs. For not realizing before it was too late that Lauren was a threat to you. I was distracted. I was too busy loving you when I should have been protecting you, and I got my priorities all backward. If anything had happened to you..."

I trail off with a broken groan.

"But it didn't," Rosie says as she lowers herself into the plastic-upholstered chair by the bed. She picks up my hand again, taking care not to disturb the tubes wrapped around my wrist, and carefully kisses my fingers. Her tears hit my knuckles in warm, wet splashes.

"Please don't cry," I beg. "Please."

"I've never been so afraid in my entire life," she confesses, head bowed and gasping in breaths between choked-back sobs.

Rage for Lauren and what she put Rosie through fires in my system, barely dulled by the pain medication. "Lauren is going to pay for what she did today," I growl. "I promise I won't rest until—"

"She was arrested," Rosie interrupts. "She's going away for a very long time, but that's not what I meant. I wasn't afraid of Lauren. I was afraid I'd lost you and I—I—couldn't—"

She can't talk through her tears, and my heart breaks

into a thousand pieces, shattered into oblivion by regret for all the things I did wrong this last month. And frustration at all the choices I made that led us here. And devastation that Rosie trusted me to keep her safe and I failed. Worse. She handed me her heart believing I would never break it and I'm watching it fracture before my eyes.

I sweep my fingertips over her cheek as best I can with all the machines and sedatives hindering my coordination. "Marry me," I say.

Rosie's head jerks up and her baby blue eyes, red-rimmed and watery, grow wide. "What?"

That stupid machine starts beeping wildly, and I pretend it's not giving away how fucking terrified I am. This is the stupidest and most impulsive thing I've ever done. It's also the first thing to ever feel this right.

"Marry me," I say again. "I know I haven't done enough to prove that I deserve to put a ring on your finger, but I'm going to spend every day for the rest of my life earning your love, earning your trust, and earning the privilege of being the man who wakes up next to you every morning, falls asleep beside you every night, and watches you fly to greater heights every goddamn day of his life, knowing that the brighter you burn and the more music you make, the better the world will be."

"You can't mean that," she whispers.

The ache in my thigh is nothing compared to the agony of waiting for Rosie to answer my question.

"I mean every word of it," I say.

She shakes her head and I blink away tears, preparing to accept her rejection with as much composure I can manage. And she'd be right. I blame the meds. What the fuck am I thinking proposing to this magnificent woman when she's got blood on her clothes and I'm half wrecked on intravenous pain relief?

Instead, Rosie carefully climbs onto the bed, arranging herself on my right side and tucking her body against mine. She rests her head on my chest.

"How can you say you've done nothing to earn my love or my trust?" she asks. "How can you look at what happened last night and believe that you didn't demonstrate your commitment in a split second that's going to last a lifetime and more? How can you lay here and tell me you need to prove anything when you literally sacrificed your life to save mine?"

The lump in my throat has nothing to do with my physical well-being anymore and everything to do with the vulnerability swelling too quickly in my chest. If she hasn't thought of this herself, I don't know why I'm determined to point it out. Maybe I do have a death wish.

"I'm the reason Lauren was there in the first place," I tell her. "I'm the reason you were ever at risk."

Rosie glances up, fierce enough to murder me with her bare hands, and I've never loved her or been prouder of her than I am in this moment.

"You're the reason I'm alive," she says, fresh tears rolling down her cheeks all over again. "And you're the reason we're going to be..."

Her chin quivers, bottom lip trembling and eyes overflowing with tears.

"What is it?" I ask, tightening my arm around her as best I can. "What are we going to be?"

Rosie shakes her head as a hesitant smile steals across her lips. "We're going to be parents," she says in barely a whisper.

My brow furrows and I'm certain the medication is scrambling my head as well as my hearing because I can't make sense of what she's saying. "Parents? What do you mean?"

She places my other hand on her flat stomach. "The hospital ran routine labs to make sure I was okay after the shooting and a doctor just told me…"

Something in my face must be reading all wrong, because Rosie frowns and swallows deeply.

"I didn't know but it all makes sense now. The extra weight? My cosmetics smelling so strong they made my stomach turn? They're early signs of pregnancy. And it *is* early—just a couple of weeks. My birth control must have failed. I didn't—"

"I'm going to be a dad?"

Rosie replies with a silent nod, and I stare into nothing as my entire future flashes before my eyes. Rosie. Children. A family. The tears I've been so valiantly holding back start to fall. All this time I've been searching for purpose and here it is. Love.

"Finn?" Rosie squeezes my hand where it still rests on her stomach. "Say something. Please."

"I love you," I tell her, hoping she can see the weight of those words shining in my eyes. "I want to give you and our child the life and the love that my parents gave me. Every day of the rest of your life will be filled with joy and laughter and pleasure and fulfillment because it'll be my mission here on this planet to make it so. I love you, Songbird. Marry me. Please."

"Yes."

"Yes? Are you sure?"

Rosie laughs, and when she leans in to kiss me, it's soft and sweet until I tangle my hand in her hair and press her mouth harder against mine.

"Yes," she says again. "I'll marry you."

I can't stop kissing her, and I don't—until the incessant wild beeping of my heart monitor sends the nursing staff running.

THIRTY-FOUR

Rosie

I ACCEPT A SALTY CRACKER from Marissa, take one nibble, then hand it back with a grimace.

"Thank you," I say to my bodyguard as my wave of nausea passes. "But if I never eat another one of those in my life, it'll be too soon."

She grins and steps back as I reposition my in-ear monitor and accept my guitar from a member of the stage crew. He hovers for a minute while I settle the strap across my body, then moves away when I nod to say I'm set and give him a smile of thanks.

Beside me in the darkened wing, Pia slips her phone into her pocket and turns her attention to the host of tonight's charity benefit concert. He's giving a presentation about the importance of therapy dogs on the mental health and well-being of military veterans. The statistics are promising and the case studies heartwarming, and I'm close to tears when Pia gently touches my arm and guides me away from the stage.

"Are you all right?" she asks.

I sniffle and try to laugh. "I'm fine. It's the pregnancy hormones. My emotions are so muddled these days. I can't stop crying."

Pia gives me an empathetic smile and offers me a tissue from her purse. "It's not the hormones, Rosie, or not hormones on their own. You've been through a lot these last couple of months. More than most people experience in a lifetime."

Understatement of the century, and though it might look like I've got my act together, the truth is that my emotions have never felt so out of control. I've gone from the debilitating lows of fear, rage, and helplessness to the heady highs of more love, hope, and happiness than I've ever known. I've embraced the very worst and the very best of life and I'm not going to lie. I could use a nap.

Preferably in bed, where the man I love is recovering from his injury, and not just in a physical sense. I'm worried about Finn. He's been quiet and introspective since they released him from hospital more than a week ago. He's compliant and uncomplaining with the rehab, so he's healing well, and he's more attentive to me than ever. I've never felt more loved, but I can't shake the feeling that he's struggling with something. Too often he becomes lost in his thoughts, like something is bothering him and he won't tell me what. But I've got a good idea.

I'm here to perform tonight because this cause means so much to me, but I'm impatient to return home and tell him he's got nothing to worry about. I know how to make things right.

I accept Pia's tissue and dab at my eyes. "But the show must go on, right?"

She sighs and pulls me deeper backstage, finding an empty nook away from prying ears. The noises from the concert fade into the background.

"It's not always easy to do my job," she says quietly. "I need to balance a client's personal life with her public image, and the choices I make don't always make sense on the outside. I thought I was doing all the right things."

"Pia." I take her hand and give it a reassuring squeeze. "We've talked about this. What happened with Lauren wasn't your fault, and you've been so incredibly supportive ever since. Canceling my appearances. Handling the media. Giving me the time and space I need to rest and be with Finn. You've been wonderful."

Her smile is warm, but I can see she's still struggling with a misplaced sense of responsibility, so I give her an awkward one-armed hug around my guitar.

"We're good," I say as I let her go. "I promise."

"Well, I have some good news on the publicity front," she says. "I would have waited until after your set to tell you, but the production manager just let me know there's a five-minute delay to our slot time, so we've got a little time to fill."

"Good news?" I give her my full attention. "What is it?"

"It looks like Chip will be called as a witness in Lauren's trial. Their affair will be officially exposed, the truth about the breakdown of your relationship will become part of the public record, and the smear campaign he so diligently coordinated against you will be wiped from the collective memory. He's already feeling the ramifications in the industry. Clients and company heads are canceling their meetings left, right, and center. Nobody wants to be associated with him. I predict a disappearance from LA altogether in the not-too-distant future."

My smile is weak. "Thanks, Pia. That *is* good news and I'm glad Chip's going to get what's coming to him, but you know what?" I laugh with a little disbelief. "I don't care. Isn't that strange? I don't care if he's happy or not happy or in the business or out of it. I don't even care all that much about what people think of me. I have everything I could ever want in life and I just... I don't need anything else. You know?"

Pia frowns for a moment, like she's never heard a celebrity declare they aren't invested in their public image, then she tilts her head with a friendly smile. "Keep this up and you might be the easiest client I've ever had."

"Well, if you're looking for easy, stick with me. I've been thinking about my next move, both in music and in life, and I've decided that the best thing for my family is to step away from the spotlight altogether."

"Oh?" Pia frowns. "What do you mean?"

I smile to myself. "Running away to a little cabin in the woods maybe."

Her brows draw in deeper. "And what does Finn think about this?"

I scoop my hair off my shoulder to reset my guitar, and Pia fusses with my curls until they're sitting just right.

"Finn doesn't want this life," I tell her. "He doesn't want to be chased and photographed and splashed all over people's social media feeds, and I can't blame him. Look at what my fame has put us through already. I need to start thinking about more than just me and what I want. I need to think about the people I love—Finn and the baby—and I've never had to do that before. Isn't that wild? For the first time in my life, I have a real reason to be selfless."

Pia rolls her lips, like she's considering her words carefully. "Rosie. You've worked damn hard and sacrificed so much to be where you are today. You're one of the good ones, and I don't say that lightly. Not everyone with your kind of money and influence uses their power to make the world a better place. And I admit I don't know Finn that well, but he doesn't strike me as the kind of man who would expect you to give up everything you've earned just because he's uncomfortable with the spotlight."

"No, he's not." I lift my chin. "He's the kind of man who would give up his *life* for me. The least I can do is love him enough to hear him even when he's not speaking. He's not happy, Pia, and I'm determined to do everything I can to fix that."

My publicist worries her bottom lip and her brown eyes warm with concern. "Even if it means sacrificing everything you've worked for? You've fought so hard to claw back control from Chip. Are you really going to put your fate into another man's hands all over again?"

"Not my fate," I tell her. "My heart. And yes, because I'm safe with Finn in a way I've never been safe before."

A stage manager approaches and ducks his head politely. "We're ready for you now."

"Thank you," I say before turning to Pia. I roll my shoulders back and shake out my hair. "How do I look?"

Pia smiles softly and something like pride lights up her pretty features. "You look perfect."

"Thanks. Let's go."

We follow the stage manager back to the wings, and I'm about to step on stage when I notice someone is already out there. I hesitate, looking toward Pia for instruction, but she's grinning like she knows something I don't, and when she inclines her head back toward the stage, I look again at who's taken my set.

It's a man carefully perched on a chair so that his injured leg is propped and set for comfort. He's wearing a tight white T-shirt over his tattooed arms, hair brushed back like he's just run a hand through it, a familiar vintage Martin on his knee, and a look of anxious anticipation in his tender cognac eyes.

He watches me approach, and I float across the stage toward him like I'm walking on air, the crowd going mad with cheers and whistles. I barely have time to register the earpiece in his ear or the battery pack at his waist before he strums the first notes of a song I don't know. And then he starts to sing.

The hush that falls over the stadium is absolute as Finn's smooth, sexy baritone weaves its way around the enormous room. It trembles a little at first, and I'm stunned that someone who has never performed in any real capacity has chosen this moment to make his debut. The glow of a single spotlight falls on Finn and his guitar, and his voice reaches all the way to the rafters and to the depths of my soul, his lyrics speaking of adoration and devotion and taking chances. He sings to me about warm blankets and cool rivers, running through trees and red flannel shirts. He sings about courage and commitment and wanting a life of adventure more than what might have been. He sings about desire and trust and what's meant to be. He sings about us.

I'm standing right there beside him when the final notes escape from beneath his fingers and the audience erupts in rapturous applause. Finn scans my face with nervous expectation, his brow furrowed and his manner more vulnerable than I've ever seen it.

"You wrote that?" I whisper. "For me?"

He nods as his throat bobs with a swallow. "Did you like it?"

My laugh is choked with emotion. "I loved it. And I love you."

"I love you too," he says, and when the audience breaks into ecstatic applause, he winces and covers his microphone with his large hand.

"How do you turn this thing off?" he asks, loudly enough that a stagehand swoops in to disconnect the mic from the sound system.

"What are you doing?" I ask in wonderment, glancing out at the thousands of people watching us with curious anticipation. "We can talk about this later offstage if you prefer."

Finn shakes his head as he takes my hand. "What I have to say can't wait. I've never been so scared as the moment I thought I was going to lose you, and it made me realize that I didn't want to live another day without letting the world know how much I love you."

"Oh, Finn." I start to cry, and he carefully brushes the tears from my cheeks. Around us, the stadium cheers, and I laugh. "You didn't have to do this."

"I wanted to do it. You've given me so much, Songbird, including your trust. This was the only way I could think of to give you mine in return. To let you know I heard you when you said there's strength in vulnerability, and I believe you. That it's safe to step out of the shadows and be seen. And that no matter what happens next, if I have you, I've already got everything I want. Whether our life is on a stage in LA or a dusty cabin in the middle of nowhere, I'm up for all of it as long as we're together."

I lean in and kiss him, laugh-crying against his mouth as the crowd starts to whoop and whistle. "Will you sing with me, Finn?" I ask.

"Yes," he says. "Anywhere. Anytime."

I release him with a sigh, then wave to a crew member to let him know we're ready to go back on. He switches on Finn's equipment and hands me a mic.

"Hey, Los Angeles!" I call out to the audience. "Have y'all met my man?"

They clap and call out, and I laugh as Finn drops his head with an embarrassed shake.

"If it's all right with you, we're going to give you a brand-new song that we wrote together. How does that sound?"

The crowd roars, and someone rushes out to give me a seat and put my microphone on a stand. When I'm settled, Finn strums the first notes of our song, and I play with him, our voices rising with the lift of my heart as we give our love wings.

EPILOGUE

Finn

SIX MONTHS LATER

"YOU NERVOUS?" DYLAN ASKS AS I adjust my light gray suit in the mirror in his bedroom.

"Nope," I answer honestly.

He grins at me in the reflection, his dark hair cut shorter than I've seen it in years, his scruff neatly trimmed, and his own suit a match for mine. He's been a lifesaver these last six months as I wrapped my head around the idea of becoming a husband and a father, keeping my feet on the ground when I've felt like I'm floating on air, and it was an easy choice to ask him to be my best man.

"It's wild, isn't it?" he asks.

I poke my fingers through my hair until it sits just right. "What is?"

"Knowing that when you go to bed tonight, you'll be married to the woman you're meant to spend the rest of your life with."

I huff out a laugh as I straighten up. My heart beats a little faster with impatient excitement. "Yeah. It's wild."

My little brother pulls me in for a manly hug. "I'm happy for you, bro."

"Thanks." I check the time on my watch. "We should get downstairs."

He follows me into the Davenport family living room where my family is dressed in their finest and waiting for their cue to step outside for the ceremony. Dakota waits at the bottom of the stairs, dressed in a mini coral-pink waistcoat with a white rose pinned to the lapel.

I give her head a rough pat, check that the ring box attached to her collar is securely fastened, then pull the wedding bands from my pocket and tuck them into the box.

"You've got an important job today," I tell her as I crouch to meet her deep, dark eyes. "You get those rings down the aisle to me and Rosie safe and sound, all right? Do not eat them. I mean it."

Dakota shuffles backward and tosses her head, and I give her one last pat before I stand. I'm checking my watch again when Chord approaches, looking like a million bucks in a navy suit and Violet on his arm.

"It's time to head outside," he says. "You ready?"

"Almost," I reply. "Just one more thing."

I glance around for Daisy and Charles, then beckon them over when I catch their attention. Daisy grabs Poppy, and they join the little knot of me, Chord and Violet, and Dylan at the foot of the stairs.

"Are you sure everything's ready at the cabin for after the wedding?" I ask my family. "Everything's all set?"

"We're sure," Daisy says excitedly. "And it's perfect."

I breathe easier. "Thanks for all your support. I couldn't have done this without you."

"That's what family does for family." Chord claps me on the shoulder. "Now let's go get you married."

With Dakota at my heels, I lead the way out of the house and across the wide stretch of lawn out back, my strides getting longer and faster the closer we get to the flower-draped arbor set up underneath the gnarled, widespread branches of a circle of oak trees. Simple white chairs for no more than twenty guests are half filled with familiar faces, and I nod politely to Lou, Nya, Cynthia, and Zane as my family fills the rest of the seats. They're arranged around a white rose-petal strewn aisle, where our officiant stands waiting to perform the ceremony. To one side, a guitarist perches on a stool as he quietly plays. Farther out, a hired photographer discreetly starts snapping pictures.

"I can't believe you're marrying Rosalie Thorne in the backyard of our parents' old place," Dylan murmurs as we take our places at the head of the aisle. "If I were the kind of man to make a bet, my money would have been on a big event with all the bells and whistles. Something at your house in Nashville. You guys have seemed happy there these last six months."

I glance over at John, still head of Rosie's security team and standing on the outskirts of the gathering, and acknowledge him with a brief nod.

"I would have done it if Rosie wanted," I say to Dylan, one hand absently stroking Dakota's fur, my eyes on the driveway up ahead as I wait for Rosie's car to appear. "But she didn't. So much has happened, so much has changed, and with the baby... We wanted today to be small and intimate, and we wanted to do it somewhere that's special to both of us. There'll be time later to deal with all the attention our marriage will bring us. Until then, we both feel most at home here at Silver Leaf."

"Smart," Dylan says, and as I stand straighter at the sight of a white Mercedes pulling into the yard, I can hear the smile in his voice. "Today's about you and Rosie—and nobody else."

Tareq and Marissa step out of the car, and as Marissa opens the passenger door, those nerves I wasn't feeling before hit me like a punch in the stomach. My breath catches and my heart races, and Dylan takes a hold of my forearm, like he senses my impulse to run up the aisle to Rosie instead of waiting for her to come to me.

Pia steps out first, wearing a Violet James original in Rosie's signature coral pink. Our flower girl, Izzy, follows in a complementary shade of pink. Pia clutches a bouquet of simple white roses, Izzy a basket of petals, and they both step aside to give the bride room to exit the car.

My heart stops, and every sense but vision shuts down at the sight of her. I can't hear or feel or taste a single thing. All I can see is Rosie, and she's never looked prettier. When my heart begins beating again, it's at triple time.

The ivory lace of her dress, woven from a pattern of birds and roses I drew by hand and Violet had specially made for today, falls from Rosie's shoulders, leaving them bare. The dress swishes as she moves, showing the shape of her legs between the panels of translucent tulle, and as Pia helps arrange the falls of fabric, I swallow hard at the way they cling to the swell of Rosie's breasts and the elegant curve of her growing stomach. She wears a crown of peach-blushed roses on her head. Her feet, like the day she drove up to my door and asked for my help, are bare. I don't know why I love that so much, but it's perfect.

Rosie lifts her head almost shyly, a peachy glow to her cheeks and a demure drop to her lashes, as if she's not used to everyone turning to look at her. And maybe today is different. This isn't a stage or a public street. Nobody's here for a selfish look at a pop princess. Everyone is here because they know her and love her, and nobody more than me.

The music shifts into a soft interpretation of the song I wrote for Rosie and played at the benefit concert, and Izzy takes her cue to start down the aisle. She tosses her rose petals with the kind of concentration reserved for suturing a wound, and I give her a wink and a whispered "well done" as she arrives at the front of the gathering to take her seat.

Pia paces slowly down the aisle, and I do my best to spare her a grateful nod, but as the music seamlessly changes and the first notes of Rosie and my duet start to play, I don't see anyone but the woman walking toward me.

Rosie glides forward with her back straight, her chin lifted, and her blue eyes bright, and my heart pounds with adoration and amazement. She hands her bouquet of white roses to Pia so she can slip her hands in mine, and I swallow hard as she gazes up at me.

"You look beautiful," I whisper, and because I can't help it, I lean in and kiss her upturned lips.

It lasts long enough that our officiant clears his throat, and our guests respond with quiet laughter. I pull away reluctantly, the fact that I need my mouth to make my vows the only thing keeping me from sweeping Rosie off her feet immediately.

The ceremony is sweet and simple. I spent days agonizing over all the promises I wanted to make today, then settled on the most significant one.

"Rosanna Betty Thorne," I say when the celebrant invites me to speak. "Ever since I can remember, I struggled to figure out where I belonged. How did I fit in my family? Where was my place in the world? What was I supposed to do with this pull I felt to make art and music? I'd lived through too much sadness to believe it was safe to hope that my life would be different. I didn't want to let love in, and I didn't want to let my fears out."

The words I've practiced over and over stick in my throat now that I'm sharing them with Rosie, and as nervous as I was to be this open and honest with people watching, it's nothing compared to the emotion of finally putting all the things I feel for this woman into words she'll understand.

"And then you came along," I say with a smile, sweeping Rosie's tears away with a brush of my thumb. "A bird with a broken wing. You put your life in my hands and more than that. You gave me something to believe in, and it undid me. I fell in love with you so greatly and so fiercely that I had to take a chance or risk losing you, and I was never going to let that happen."

I swallow and blink away the love welling in my eyes. "Thank you for showing me the way. Thank you for teaching me and supporting me and loving me. Thank you for letting me love you in return. I promise to adore you, cherish you, and protect you and our baby girl every minute of every day for the rest of my life."

Rosie gazes up at me with a smile framed by tears, and I kiss them away. It earns me another firm cough from our officiant.

"My turn," Rosie says with a light laugh. "Oh, Finn. I don't think you know how safe I felt with you right from the start. When so much in my life felt superficial, senseless, and scary, you were real, honest, and steady. You were exactly what I needed at exactly the right time."

Rosie tightens her grip on my hands, and I nod to let her know I'm listening.

"You remind me of who I am and who I want to be," she says. "You give me space to fly free and a soft place to land when I fall. When my world had shown me all the ways I had failed, you made me believe in myself again. You gave me back my confidence and my trust in myself. You reignited passions in me—for music and love and life—that I thought would be dulled forever. Without meaning to and without even trying, you showed me that I was right to hope that real love was out there somewhere, waiting for me to find it."

Rosie lifts up on her toes, then settles back on her heels with a grin. "Thank you for being the light in my darkness, guiding me to a new home. Thank you for being brave enough to take a chance on me when I know it hasn't been easy. Thank you for being *you*. I promise to adore you, cherish you, and protect you and our growing family every minute of every day for the rest of my life."

Dakota, having grown anxious with all the crying, moves from her place at my feet and nudges her head against Rosie's thigh. She laughs, and I kneel down to extract our wedding rings from the little box on Dakota's collar.

And then finally, with vows and rings exchanged, the celebrant sanctions our kiss. It lasts forever, the way it's supposed to, and the crowd cheers, the way we knew it would.

Rosie beams at me across the front seat of my truck, and though I'm more accustomed to the tail of John and Jarrod in the car behind us than I might have been six months ago,

I'm glad they've agreed to remain outside while Rosie and I are on our honeymoon.

"Are you sure this is what you want to do?" I ask as I bring the back of her hand to my lips. "We could go anywhere in the world—literally anywhere—and you want to spend the next five days in my old bungalow?"

I don't know where she found it, but somewhere during our wedding reception, Rosie threw my old red flannel over her gown to keep warm, and the way she wears both makes my heart feel too big for my chest.

"I'm sure." Rosie inhales deeply, then releases it like she's letting all her worries go. "I miss this place a little more every day."

I watch the path ahead even though I could drive the dirt trails of Silver Leaf with my eyes closed. I've grown lax keeping my expressions in check around Rosie and I don't want her to read the eagerness in my eyes.

"But it's so small," I say. "Nothing like we're used to in Nashville."

"I wanted to talk to you about that." Rosie fusses with the fabric of her dress, and her distracted expression melts into dreamy admiration as she traces the shapes in the lace. "When Violet told me she'd one day make me the perfect dress, I'll admit I didn't believe her at the time, but *look* at this! It's so stunning and you're so talented. I love it so much."

My mouth lifts at the corner. Rosie's trains of thought are easily derailed these days, and it's just one more thing I love about her pregnancy. "Thanks, Songbird, but what were you going to say about Nashville...?"

She screws up her nose. "It's too big," she says. "We could fill it with a dozen babies—"

I growl eagerly at the idea, and Rosie laughs. "Down, boy. We've got to see how we do with this one first."

"You're going to be a wonderful mother," I reassure her. "No doubt in my mind."

She sighs and strokes my cheek. "And you're going to light up the world when you're a daddy, but my point is, we could fill that house with children, and it would still feel empty. It's too big and too cold, and I'm not sure it'll ever be *home*. I miss the way your cabin felt like a nest. All cozy and warm and intimate. I want to spend more time here, Finn, especially after the baby is born. I want our first weeks of parenthood to feel as cocooned as the early days of us falling in love. Nowhere will ever feel like home the way this place does." She shrugs with a frustrated sigh. "I'd move in tomorrow if it had another bedroom. I'm not sure I can get up and down that ladder with this belly, let alone a newborn baby."

"I'm really glad you said that because I have a confession to make."

"Oh?" Rosie's mouth twitches with curiosity. "What is it?"

I squint through the windshield as the cabin comes into view then slow my truck to a roll. "One of the first things I did after you told me about the baby was call my brothers and sisters for a family meeting."

"What? How?" Her brows pull in. "You were recovering from a gunshot wound and you never left Nashville. How did you organize a family meeting? And, more importantly, why?"

I chuckle. "Chord and I dialed in, and we did it over video conference. You wouldn't know this but when Chord proposed to Violet, he called a meeting and had us vote on building her a studio at Silver Leaf. He wanted to make sure she understood she was now part of the family, and our family *is* Silver Leaf. By giving her a piece of it, we made her one of us. We all voted yes. No question."

"I didn't know that," Rosie says quietly. "That's very sweet."

"At that same meeting, right after Dylan proposed to Poppy, my little brother had us vote to give Poppy her own slice of Silver Leaf. We agreed on the spot to speed up plans to establish a day spa and make it Poppy's to own and run."

"Finn," Rosie says slowly, eyes searching my face for answers. "What did you do?"

I pull the car around to the cabin, coming to a stop in almost the exact place Rosie got stuck in the mud that fateful day she came asking for my protection, and nod out the window.

Rosie turns toward the old bungalow, which is now five times as large as it was when we left it, and gasps.

"I told my brothers and sisters I wanted to give you a home," I tell her. "Expand the cabin to make it fit for our family. Not knock it down and start again, because I didn't want to lose the memories we'd already made inside those walls.

I wanted to preserve everything my parents built and every moment we spent together here, using it as the foundation for a bigger place and a beautiful life. For us. For you. And all of them said yes. No questions asked."

Rosie's chin quivers and a tear rolls over her cheek. "I can't believe you did this."

"You've got a family now," I say. "I'm not saying we need to live here permanently, though I'd be up for it if you are. I just want you to know that no matter where we go, no matter how many houses you own across the country and around the world, this place and these people will always be home."

"But…"

"But nothing." I reach over and settle my hand on her stomach, and Aria Haven Davenport nudges me in response. "This little sliver of Silver Leaf belongs to you and our daughter now. It's what I want, it's what my siblings want, and I know without a shadow of a doubt, it's what my parents would have wanted too."

"Finn." She chokes back a sob and marvels at the property with a disbelieving shake of her head. "People think I've got it all, but I never had anything until I had you. Thank you."

"You're welcome, Songbird."

I get out of the truck and rush around to Rosie's side so I can open the door and lift her out. I carry her in my arms all the way to the porch steps, and then over the threshold the way I did back in the spring, only this time she's my wife, and when we step through the door, I don't have to let her go.

I glance around the space. Charles has been keeping me updated with pictures, but it's the first time I've stepped inside, and it's more perfect than I could have hoped for. Open-concept spaces, warm woods and white walls, loads of natural light and hardwood floors. Most of the original cabin has been preserved, even with the new, larger kitchen and extra bedrooms at the back. At the very rear is a fully equipped recording studio. It's not large, but it's enough that Rosie and I can make music while we're here whenever the mood takes us.

Thanks to Charles and Daisy, bunches of wildflowers in mason jars brighten up nearly every flat surface, a cheery fire dances in the hearth, and white rose petals point the way to the new master bedroom.

"Did you want the grand tour first," I ask, "or...?"

Rosie takes my lapels in her fists and kisses me. Hard.

"I want to make love to my husband," she says. "We have the rest of our lives to make new memories in this house, but tonight, I only want to make memories with you."

And that's what we do. We relive old memories and create new ones, and I spend the entire night proving to my Songbird just how much I love her.

BONUS SCENE

Rosie

TEN YEARS LATER

Finn and Rosie's story doesn't end here!
Visit my website at samanthaleighbooks.com/books/
bonus-content or use the QR code to download
a bonus scene set 10 years in the future...

ACKNOWLEDGMENTS

Thank you

Thank you for reading *Songbird*. Finn and Rosie were a joy to write, and I'm so happy their story is finally out in the world.

Now is the time I say thank you to the amazing people who helped make this book a reality.

Tabitha and Bryanna—my alpha reader dream team. Thank you for your never-ending patience, unbridled enthusiasm, and wildly insightful feedback as this book moved from my head to the page. Thank you for making me laugh and keeping me motivated. I appreciate you so much.

Echo Grayce—thank you again for sharing your creative genius with me. These covers keep getting better.

Emily Leigh—I'm so grateful for your attention to detail, professionalism, kindness, and patience. Thank you for keeping me on track!

Thank you to my editing team, Brandi and Beth. I'm so grateful for your work and support.

Enormous thanks to @dachshundsandbooks for being the creative talent behind my Instagram feed. I'm in awe of your vision, your work ethic, and your warmth.

Gratitude to @boundtoread and Mindy Menotti for the content support!

Eternal thanks goes to my beta readers: Abbey, Kat, Katie, Meka, Sarah, and Yondette. Thank you for the practical help of making the manuscript better, as well as the kind of comments that make the beta reader stage my favorite in the whole writing process! And thank you for loving Finn and Rosie as much as I do.

Thank you to my team of clever and committed content creators—your energy is unmatched, your creativity is inspiring, and I'm so lucky to have your support.

Shout out to @the.apollon.arts, @artbysoniagx, @pro_art_digital and @michillart for creating stunning character art for this book.

Thank you to Stephanie Archer for her advice and humor; Melanie Harlow for her unfailing generosity and kindness; Sharon Woods and Samantha Skye for their support and DMs; Ellie at Love Notes PR for her promo expertise; and every book influencer and reader who couldn't wait to meet Finn and Rosie. I couldn't do this without you.

Thank you to my husband and children—my biggest cheerleaders and my greatest loves.

And thank you to my readers—for picking up *Songbird* and for giving me a reason to keep writing.

xSam.

ABOUT THE AUTHOR

Samantha Leigh

Samantha Leigh is an Australian author of steamy contemporary romance. When she's not playing matchmaker in imaginary worlds, Sam is reading books with all the feels and all the spice. In the tiny slices of time she has between word wrangling, Sam likes to hit her yoga mat, go for walks in the bush or on the beach, continue her search for the perfect poke bowl, drown herself in coffee and hot cacao, and binge-watch nineties television.

samanthaleighbooks.com